Are You In?

Rachel Pluck

ISBN-13: 979-8-218-29525-7

Playlist

"Monday" by The Regrettes
"Whistle (While You Work It)" by Katy Tiz
"I Can See You (Taylor's Version)" by Taylor Swift
"Wish You Were Here" by Incubus
"Ship to Wreck" by Florence + The Machine
"Summer Lightning" by Bad Suns
"Maroon" by Taylor Swift
"Cloud 9" by Beach Bunny
"Stellar" by Incubus
"thoughts i have while lying in bed" by The Maine
"Cruel Summer" by Taylor Swift
"Bad Habit" by The Kooks
"Sports" by Beach Bunny
"All I Need" by Taylor Roche
"Fire Alarm" by Castlecomer
"WISH ME LUCK" by Wallows
"Dancing on Quicksand" by Bad Suns
"Take on the World" by You Me At Six

Chapter 1

Maybe this was a bad idea.

I stared at my reflection in the bathroom mirror and took a deep, steadying breath, then let it out. The puff of air fogged up the glass for a fleeting moment before vanishing. I was alone, and I didn't feel any steadier.

This was definitely a bad idea.

I tucked a strand of strawberry blonde hair behind my ear, then pulled it out again so it framed my face, repeating this motion twice more before finally leaving it jammed behind my ear. I had always wanted to be one of those stylish girls who could rock curtain bangs or a cute face frame.

I wasn't. I was an ear-tucker. When I wore a low ponytail, I was more likely to look like George Washington than Kylie Jenner.

A very feminine George Washington, but still.

I braced my hands against the sink I now shared with my best friend, Olivia. *She* was one of those stylish girls who could rock a cute face frame. She was also the most genuine and loyal person I knew, even when she was being brutally honest and putting me in my place. If she were in this bathroom right now, she'd tell me to pull it together, get dressed, and get to work.

Work. The reason I was frozen in the bathroom in the first place.

I'd quit my stable job at the full-service branding agency I'd worked at for the past two years, left my mom's house in rural Pennsylvania and moved to Brooklyn to live my dream as a digital marketer at Rabbit's Foot Label Group, a mid-sized independent record company with offices around the globe and some major talent on their roster, including a few of my favorite artists in the rock and pop scenes.

My mom had been here just two days ago, helping me carry all my possessions up three flights of narrow stairs to my new apartment. It was one of three units in a converted old townhouse. The building itself had to be at least one hundred years old, but the apartment had been recently renovated and listed for a steal when Olivia found it. It was a miracle we got it.

Fate, if you believed in that sort of thing.

My mom left Olivia and me to our own devices on Friday afternoon, driving the three hours back to our small town with silver lining her eyes. It wasn't like three hours was that far… but when you lived with someone for the better part of twenty-six years, leaving only for temporary university housing, it was kind of a big deal. It had been just me and my mom against the world for as long as I could remember—with my dad out of the picture from the time I was in diapers, my mom had been my rock. My constant in all things.

This time, moving out of her homey, two-bedroom rancher felt final. At least, I hoped it would be. Running back to Lancaster with my tail between my legs was not an option now. The lease was signed. The tribe had spoken.

How had my life changed so drastically in the span of one weekend? Right now, it felt less like I was living my dream and more like I'd stepped into a nightmare.

"Hannah Maxwell, you better not be freaking out in the bathroom right now," Olivia called from somewhere down the hallway. "You're going to be late!"

Ever since we'd met freshman year at Syracuse University, Olivia had possessed a second sense about me. She knew what I was thinking, or what I was going to say before I did.

I groaned quietly so she couldn't hear me through the door and pushed myself away from the two-bowl sink before I could think better of it. My bedroom was just three steps across the hall, and I dashed inside it to finish getting dressed. Olivia wasn't wrong, if I didn't get a move on, I most definitely would be late for my first day.

Not a good impression.

A small Bluetooth speaker nestled on top of my Ikea dresser quietly played one of my favorite alternative rock songs with soft-spoken lyrics about a love as big as the solar system—my attempt to make today a little less nerve-wracking.

It wasn't working.

As quickly as I could, I dressed myself in black paper bag slacks that hugged the curves of my hips and offered a little extra support in my lower stomach, belted over a blush sleeveless bodysuit. A black oversized blazer added an extra dash of professionalism while my gently worn Converse low-tops told any onlookers I wasn't just a marketer, I was a *cool* marketer.

That was the goal, at least.

I paused for one final glance in the full-length mirror on my closet door, gently tugging on and then smoothing down the lapels of my blazer, then left my room. I turned down the hallway that led to the open-concept living area of our apartment. It was small, but in a cozy way. The living room was just large enough to fit the couch, coffee table, and TV stand Olivia and I had splurged on right after our lease signing. Beside it was a small, makeshift dining area that was barely big enough for a card table, but we made it work.

The centerpiece though, was the fully upgraded kitchen. State-of-the-art appliances, brand-new cabinets, and the most marvelous kitchen island I'd ever seen, topped with smooth white and gray marble. It was my dream kitchen. Well, my dream kitchen if I had about half the space.

"First day! You pumped for the new job?" Olivia asked from behind a cup of coffee, leaning her slim hip against said kitchen island as she blew across the top of the mug to cool down the scalding liquid.

She was already dressed to impress in a sleek black pencil skirt that hugged her in all the right places, paired with a white silk blouse and towering black Louboutins that added at least two inches to her five-feet-five-inch frame.

After graduation, Olivia had pursued a paralegal certification, eventually wrangling herself a job at one of the top family law firms in the state of New York. While she'd only been there for a little more than six months, her natural poise and general ease in all situations made adapting a cakewalk. When you catered almost exclusively to some of the city's wealthiest clients, you had to look and act the part. I'd be damned if my best friend, the same one I'd seen totally at home in stained sweats and an oversized hoodie, didn't look like she belonged there.

I breathed out slowly, unsure how to answer her question—partially because my brain was still fogged with a pre-caffeine haze and partially because my emotions were roiling too fast for me to keep up.

Was I excited? *Absolutely.*

Landing a job—my *dream* job—at a legit record company was the biggest accomplishment of my young life. But it also meant throwing myself into a brand new company, with brand new people, and brand new tasks to figure out. I'd be the new girl for the first time in two years.

Talk about terrifying.

I shook my head to stop my internal meltdown and noticed Olivia staring at me expectantly from across the kitchen, mug hovering a few inches from her mouth.

"Yeah, definitely excited! A little nervous too, not gonna lie," I answered breezily, already on my way to the Keurig behind Olivia to make a cup of breakfast brew. I leaned back against the counter across from my best friend while the machine hissed and steamed.

"It's gonna be great! They'll love you," Olivia said with her most confident smile and set her mug down on the counter to fight with a strand of chestnut brown hair that had fallen out of her high ponytail. "And if they don't, screw 'em and do a great job anyway."

I laughed loudly, some of the jitters from moments ago already fading, and smoothed my hands down my legs while coffee dripped slowly into my mug.

Olivia strode through the kitchen to place her own empty mug in the sink, then paused at my side, a gentle expression crossing her face. "But seriously, it's gonna be great. I can't wait to hear all about your first day when we get home from our *big girl jobs* tonight."

She gave my arm a little squeeze then brushed past me on her way to the door. "I better get going. We have a huge custody hearing coming up so my boss is in rare form." Olivia lifted and lowered her eyes meaningfully, grabbing her work bag and keys from the table beside her. She paused to add, "Actually, can it even be considered 'rare form' when this is his personality ninety-percent of the time?"

"Good luck!" I called to her, wiggling my eyebrows from where I carefully spooned sugar and cream into my steaming coffee mug.

"Right back at ya," she responded with a wink, her body already halfway through the open door. As it clicked shut behind her, silence descended like a thick fog in the apartment.

Imposter. What do you know about marketing for musicians? Your most recent clients consisted of a luxury clothing brand, a tech startup, and a chain of gyms.

I shook my head, trying to physically banish the intrusive thoughts, and took a long, slow sip of my coffee.

You've been working in marketing since you graduated college four years ago. Before you graduated, actually.

At Syracuse, I'd fought fiercely during my sophomore year to nab an internship with a sports and entertainment conglomerate in Philadelphia. Infinity Entertainment, which owned the two biggest event venues in the city, brought me on for two summers as a Digital Marketing intern, then hired me full-time as a Social Media Specialist when I graduated. I'd covered everything from coordinating and promoting live performances to partnership development for charity galas at Infinity before jumping ship to work for their marketing agency of record for two years.

But that was Philadelphia. This is New York. *This is a record label,* that little voice taunted.

I sighed, the whoosh of air making the liquid in my mug dance.

You're not brand new to the field. You're just new to this company.

The fast pace at the agency, one of the most decorated in the Philadelphia area, forced me to learn skills I'd never even dreamed about in school, from SEO and content marketing to social media and digital analytics.

But Rabbit's Foot? This was the big leagues.

I'd dreamed of nabbing a job in the music industry since I was twelve, when I read a Q&A with a publicist to the stars in an issue of *Cosmopolitan* I'd snuck from my mom's room.

In college, I realized a job in crisis PR probably wasn't the right fit, but I instantly fell in love with the marketing and advertising side from the very first class I took. After busting my ass in unpaid internships and barely paid entry-level positions, it was hard to believe I'd finally landed this job.

It *was* my dream.

So why did I feel like I was about to throw up?

You got this, I thought to myself. *They picked you out of hundreds of other applicants.* YOU *deserve this.*

But did I?

On less than sure footing, I stepped outside of a black Honda CRV as soon as it double parked outside of my destination: a towering high-rise lined with plate glass windows that reflected the street outside back at me in the sunlight rather than offering a glimpse of the mysterious interior.

Being my first day, I opted to grab an Uber into Lower Manhattan from my Brooklyn apartment rather than brave public transportation or risk my worst fear—an unfamiliar parking situation. All of my many rounds of interviews had been virtual, so this was my first time seeing the Rabbit's Foot building in person.

Sliding out my phone, I punched in a quick tip for my driver as he pulled away, probably already off to grab his next fare from among the many commuters and tourists scattered across the city.

"You got this," I breathed aloud to myself, the building's entrance looming in front of me. My feet were rooted to the spot, fast-walking passersby weaving around me, some not even bothering to glance up from their phones as they hastily moved toward their destinations.

After a fifth person trying to squeeze by on the crowded sidewalk almost barreled right into me, I forced my feet to carry me closer to the high-rise—past the marquee that boasted the names of all the businesses housed inside, Rabbit's Foot gleaming on it in bright silver script—and into the building.

I first noticed a small, posh waiting area straight ahead, all plush white chairs and low tables, that butted up to a small hallway and an alcove full of elevators.

My sneakers whispered against the smooth, polished floors—so shiny I could practically see my reflection in them—as I headed in that direction and found several large signs with company names and their corresponding levels listed on them.

"Rabbit's Foot—eighth floor," I whispered out loud to no one in particular, then punched the *Up* button.

The elevator arrived after a few moments and carried me with modern speed to the eighth floor, the stainless steel doors opening up to a wide reception area adorned with a few plush armchairs in assorted vibrant colors and a long hallway that trailed off in either direction.

At 8:45 in the morning, the office was already bustling with activity.

Small recessed lights in the ceiling arranged every few feet and pointing in various directions lit the space in a soft glow, a far cry from the harsh fluorescent lighting at my last office. The walls were lined with framed artwork and old band posters, each one a colorful expression of creativity that drew the eye.

Music pumped through an unseen sound system—something pulsing and rhythmic that had me involuntarily bobbing my head, the vocals sung in a language I couldn't quite place.

The place was chic but designed for comfort, focus, and a little fun, too—the polar opposite of the harsh lines and polish of the lobby below.

The soft sound of whispers drifting over the music drew my attention down one of the hallways where I spied a group of people gathered inside a sleek cubicle area. Their heads were bent over someone's laptop as they spoke to one another in low voices.

"Excuse me—" I interjected softly from behind the low cube wall that separated us. "My name's Hannah Maxwell, it's my first day here. I'm looking for Annabelle?"

Four heads snapped up at once, clearly caught off guard by my intrusion. Without skipping a beat, one of the employees—a girl with hair as dark as a raven who didn't look a day over twenty-three—tapped a key on the laptop to hide the windows from the screen and turned to me with a thin-lipped smile. At least, I thought it was a smile.

"Right, I'll show you to Annabelle's office."

She stood up fully from where she'd been crouched down in front of the laptop, bringing into view an outfit way more casual than mine: an oversized vintage Doors T-shirt layered over loose black jeans with holes carefully placed just above both knees. I immediately made a mental note to figure out the dress code for this place. Her wide-set, slightly hooded eyes were a beautiful russet color, each lined with a thin black wing that probably would've taken me at least an hour to get right. Her nearly black hair was knotted in two spunky space buns at the top of her head.

"I'm Mei," she said as she led me through a maze of low-walled cubicles. Some were full of people already working, large headphones over their ears, noses pressed to a computer screen, while others were empty.

"Nice to meet you," I said, struggling to match her swift pace even though my legs had to be at least three inches longer than hers, while my eyes wandered through the open office space. The maze of cubes in the open-concept workspace eventually ended, giving way to a row of three large offices that lined the far wall. Each one was enclosed by crystal-clear glass, offering passersby a glimpse inside.

Name plates adorned each one, hung on the wall just beside the door—the first two offices were inscribed with names I didn't recognize, their occupants nowhere to be found at this time of day. The third office in line, however, was already lit up, and I immediately recognized the woman behind the desk from my virtual interview as we approached. She looked up with a smile and moved to stand, gently closing her laptop.

"Hannah, so good to see you again!" the woman practically sang, her voice just as melodic as I remembered from the interview. Internally I wondered if she had landed in this business after attempting a singing career of her own.

"Annabelle, such a pleasure to see you again as well," I said in response, my voice sounding more nasally than usual next to her beautiful mezzo-soprano.

"I'll leave you both to it." Mei tapped the glass door of Annabelle's office twice with her knuckles before turning on her heel and heading back the way we came.

Annabelle easily had at least a decade on Mei, making her at least seven years my senior. I could tell by the steely confidence behind each word she uttered that she'd been with the company for a while, and the industry possibly longer than that.

I also noted ruefully that she was dressed much more similarly to me in high-waisted army green capris that tied in the front, black ballet flats, and a white blouse. I even spied a matching green blazer hanging from a coat rack in the corner of her office.

We could practically be twins, I thought to myself with a grimace, suddenly feeling much older.

"Something wrong, dear?" Annabelle asked, tucking a strand of bright blonde hair behind her ear as she caught my expression.

"Oh yeah, sorry, I uh...thought I saw a spider on my pant leg but it turned out to be a loose thread," I lied smoothly, offering her my best *I'm a great employee* smile.

Annabelle smiled warmly back at me then looked down to her large L-shaped desk where she began thumbing through stacks of paper and manila folders that littered the top. Everything in her office screamed modern, and the desk was no exception. A matte black tabletop floated above a set of cabinets and drawers painted to look like gray concrete.

I looked around the space, taking in the macrame wall hangers filled with greenery that seemed so at odds with the contemporary framed artwork hanging beside them.

Annabelle drew my attention when she plucked up a folder with a triumphant flourish. From where I sat, I could see the words WELCOME PACKET stamped in block lettering on the front cover, a sticky note with my name on it just below.

"I can show you to your new *home* here," she said with a tinkling laugh, already exiting her office. I had to move fast to catch up.

"We've got you set up with a laptop, dual monitors, charging dock, and all the accessories you should need," she said over a shoulder as I followed her through the maze of cubes. After about three turns, she stopped at one just across from where Mei and the others had been sitting this morning.

That entire cube was notably empty now. The laptop screens locked, but still lit up, indicating their owners had only recently abandoned them.

"Here we are!"

I returned my gaze to Annabelle as she set the manila folder down on a desk I presumed was now mine. If anyone had been here before me, you wouldn't know it. The cube area had been completely cleared out of any personal effects, left only with the standard-issue tools and accessories provided by Rabbit's Foot.

"I'll give you a few minutes to get settled in. Please make yourself at home," Annabelle said to me, the same warm smile from her office still dutifully stamped on her lips. "I'll be back in about fifteen minutes to do a quick tour of the office, and then we'll get started with orientation."

I smiled back at her, tearing my thoughts away from all the ways I'd like to decorate this empty space, and nodded my head once in understanding.

"Your computer login info is on a post-it note under your keyboard. There are a few forms in this packet—" she paused to point to the manila folder, "we need you to fill out before you leave today. The rest of the HR stuff has been digitized and there should be a link to it in your inbox."

Annabelle's words were fast and well-practiced like she'd delivered the same spiel dozens of times before. But something behind her eyes made me feel welcome.

"Perfect, thank you so much."

She gently patted me on the shoulder, giving it the tiniest squeeze before she turned on her heel and walked back to her office.

I took a large gulp of water from my tumbler and put my feet onto the side rails of the treadmill beneath me while it slowly powered down from my half-hearted jog.

"Calling it quits already, Maxwell?" Olivia asked from where she still jogged beside me, eyebrows drawn up. Glancing down at her treadmill, I knew she'd go for at least another mile if left to her own devices.

We were a pretty good pair, both in and out of the gym. I preferred lifting weights to cardio, but Olivia was one of the strongest runners I knew. We balanced each other out.

But when I had promised to meet her at the gym a few blocks down from our apartment after work, I had clearly forgotten how exhausting first days were.

My first eight hours on the job passed by in a blur of information overload. I mainly met with Annabelle as she explained to me the ins and outs of the business, how the marketing department worked, and introduced me around to some of the team and other key players in our office.

The rest of the day I spent holed up with Annabelle in a conference room, going through presentation decks, accountability charts, and recent reports, pausing only for lunch and a much needed coffee break in the afternoon.

It was already going on five o'clock when Annabelle dropped me off back at my desk for the day. Most of the cubes around me had already emptied out for the evening. I had to rush out of the building to meet Olivia at the gym on time and already felt like I'd run a marathon before we even started our workout.

I'd used the time in between nearly breathless sets to fill her in on my first day, and by the time we hopped on the treadmill, I had no wind left in me.

"Yeah, just not feeling it today. My body and my brain feel like anchors," I said between gulps of water, my chest still heaving up and down in shallow breaths.

I watched in mild shock as Olivia powered down her treadmill, ending her run early in solidarity. She tossed her long brown ponytail over a shoulder and grabbed a towel that hung on the arm of her treadmill to wipe the sweat from her forehead.

I had to stop myself from glaring when I noticed she'd barely even broken a sweat.

"Come on, let's grab some celebratory sushi and go crash on the couch," Olivia said as she stepped down from her treadmill, and I immediately perked up at the thought of food and rest, thanking my lucky stars for having such a perfect friend in my life.

Chapter 2

Annabelle sat opposite me at the long, rectangular conference room table, her expertly filed nails tapping out a note on her laptop keyboard.

Mei sat beside me, her facial expression bored. Her laptop sat open in front of her, angled slightly away from me, the screen empty except for the Slack app—Rabbit's Foot's preferred program for internal communication. GIFs lit up the open group chat, but I couldn't make out the names or faces of the senders from where I sat.

Mei's outfit closely resembled her ensemble from yesterday—another vintage T-shirt, another pair of ripped jeans. This time her dark hair was pulled back in a claw clip, loose pieces flanking her face.

We sat here waiting for my first client to arrive, and I realized Annabelle still hadn't told me the name of the band I'd be working with. Or what I'd be doing. It was only my second day with the company, but that didn't feel normal.

The conference room was moderate in size with decor that matched much of the rest of the office. The table itself was made of a large piece of custom-carved oak, lacquered and polished until it reflected like a mirror. The wall behind me was made entirely of glass, offering a panoramic view of the city outside and bathing the room in natural light.

A clock hanging from the far wall of the conference room ticked loudly as we sat in silence, my anxiety climbing with each passing second. The whooshing sound of an email being sent echoed in the quiet room making me jump. Finally, Annabelle looked up at me with her usual professional smile and closed her laptop.

"I'm sure you're wondering why we're here and what to expect from this meeting," she said, reading my mind. "I don't normally love throwing new hires in," she continued, crossing one leg over the other under the table. "But you came highly recommended from your previous employers, and we have a very big and very urgent opening to fill."

Flattery. Superlatives. This could not be good.

Mei let out a small snort when Annabelle paused, all but confirming my suspicions. Annabelle shot her a pointed look and Mei's eyes returned to her Slack messages, her smug smile vanishing.

"I appreciate the bode of confidence..." I trailed off expectantly, wishing she'd just spit it out.

"One of our longest-standing clients is about to go on tour in a few short weeks. The tour is important in its own right, but its true purpose is to tease the release of a new studio album early next year."

Annabelle paused, shooting a passing glance behind her at the clock on the wall before continuing. "We've been preparing a marketing strategy for this for close to a year now, and a lot of our campaigns promoting the tour itself have already launched... but to continue building buzz throughout the tour and leading up to the album's release, our strategy leans heavily on an active social media presence."

I nodded, hanging on to Annabelle's every word. *They want me to do social media? For a campaign that's already in motion? Piece of cake.*

"Unfortunately, the social media manager previously on this account..." Annabelle wavered for a moment, searching for the right words. "Well, she left to... pursue other endeavors."

At this, Mei choked on another laugh, even louder than before, making it impossible to ignore. I shifted in my chair and craned my neck to look directly at her, eyebrows raised.

"What Annabelle means is she got a little too close to a client and, as these things usually go, it didn't end well." Mei leaned back in her chair and crossed her arms over her chest, meeting my gaze defiantly.

My jaw fell open before I could help it. Was she insinuating someone slept with a *client*?

It was a huge no-no at my last agency, cemented permanently in the employee handbook. And judging by Mei's smug tone and the annoyed look on Annabelle's face, I guessed the label felt similarly.

"As you know, Mei, we deal in facts here at Rabbit's Foot. Not idle gossip," Annabelle said tightly, her expression and tone leaving no room for rebuttal.

Mei shrugged nonchalantly back at Annabelle as if to say, *sorry, not sorry.*

"The fact of the matter is, we are three weeks away from the first tour date and have no one to run the band's accounts," Annabelle continued, drawing the conversation and my focus back to the job at hand. "We need someone with experience in these platforms and who knows how to… handle client relationships appropriately." She leaned back in her chair, tenting her hands in her lap, and glanced at the clock again.

My mind raced. On one hand, this was the biggest opportunity I'd ever been given. It was exactly what I wanted when I first applied for this job.

But was I ready for this? Did this mean I'd need to physically *go on tour* with… I remembered the name of the band still had not been disclosed.

"The first half of the tour only lasts six weeks, and then you'd be back here for a three-month break before embarking on the second half," Annabelle said, once again reading my thoughts. Or some of them, at least.

I chewed on the inside of my cheek for a few long moments, my eyes drawn to the patterns and swirls of an abstract mural above Annabelle's head as I pondered her words.

Six weeks. Less than two whole months. When put like that, it didn't seem *that* huge.

My head swam with unspoken questions, so I latched onto the biggest, most important one floating around inside my brain.

"So who is—" I began to ask, but the words were cut off when Annabelle stood up, a wide smile plastered on her face that I immediately knew was reserved for *big* clients. Very Important People only.

I turned my head to follow her gaze, eyes landing on the now-open door. The doorway was filled with people I hadn't even heard arrive.

Annabelle warmly greeted the first person to walk in, a man who looked to be in his late forties. He wore a tailored gray suit with a powder blue button-down underneath. He looked like he may have once been handsome, but deep lines in his forehead and a receding hairline echoed years of a high-stress job.

This was the guy who ran off the last social media manager?

I shot a confused glance at Mei who seemed to follow my thoughts. *Just wait*, she seemed to say, her eyes widened knowingly.

I refocused on the door to the conference room just in time to see a group of guys—*definitely* younger than the man in the suit, but still possibly early 30s—shuffling in slowly.

The guy in the front of their pack had hair cropped just above his shoulders, its brown hue so dark it looked almost black. He wore a plain dove gray T-shirt that stretched tight across his chest and hugged his arms just above his toned biceps.

He was muscular, but not in a way you get from spending hours at the gym. And he was tall, at least six-foot-three from the way his frame filled the open doorway.

I continued slowly taking him in— the sinewy arms completely covered in tattoos, the prominent collarbones sticking out from the top of his V-neck collar, the expression on his face that looked almost... bored.

And then his gaze met mine.

Like his hair, his eyes were so dark they were almost black in the natural light of the conference room, but as he held my stare I noticed they were actually a dark amber—like the color of expensive whiskey. My breath caught in my throat as recognition flared in my mind, the sound of alarm bells only I could hear ringing in my ears.

To some, he may not be conventionally handsome. But there was a ruggedness to his features, a striking clarity in his gaze. One that had drawn me in from the very first time I saw him on my TV screen almost ten years ago.

I knew that chiseled jaw, lined with stubble from at least a few days of not shaving. If his Wikipedia page was to be believed, he had just turned thirty this spring, but there was an air of boyish charm to him as he stepped gracefully into the conference room.

How many times had I watched those full lips stretch and pout around a microphone, belting out the lyrics that carried me through part of high school and all of college?

My assignment wasn't just *any band*.

This band had been number one on my Spotify Wrapped every year for as long as I could remember. Because I listened to them almost daily.

My assignment was *Olympus*.

Mei must have seen the gears whirring in my brain because I felt her firmly kick my shin underneath the table, the sudden contact snapping me back to reality. The rest of the band shuffled into the room and settled in around us until we took up every seat at the eight-person table.

"Thank you for joining us in the office today," Annabelle began as I fiddled with my laptop, desperately avoiding eye contact with anyone in the band, lest they sniff me out as a superfan. "As you know, Camila recently left us for another opportunity, leaving the social media role vacant for your upcoming tour."

I risked a glance up and found the band's frontman still staring at me, a mischievous smile playing on his full lips. I quickly tore my attention away from him and faced Annabelle fully, forcing myself to focus intently on every word she spoke.

"With the start of the tour quickly approaching, we had to move fast to find a replacement," she smiled widely in my direction, lifting an exposed palm to me. "I'd like you all to meet Hannah. She came to us highly recommended from an agency specializing in communications and digital marketing, and has extensive experience in social media for clients of all sizes."

Because I had no other choice, I inhaled sharply and plastered a smile on my face as Annabelle began introducing everyone seated across from me.

But I already knew each of their names. Intimately. In fact, the only new name was that of the man in the suit: their manager, Ryan.

Each man waved as his name was said aloud, offering me small, polite smiles.

"Zach—" *Lead guitar.*

"Angel—" *Drums.*

"Peter—" *Bass guitar.*

"Ezra—" *Lead singer.* His eyes met mine again, but he didn't wave like the others. Instead, he bowed his head slightly in greeting, amusement dancing in his eyes.

I could only watch as he broke our staring contest to take in the rest of me. His gaze felt warm against my skin as it roved over me, from the top of my head to the lowest point revealed above the table, and back up again. I felt my cheeks start to burn under the intensity of that stare, the sensation only growing when Ezra's eyes rested on my lips for far longer than appropriate.

Right when I felt like I might pass out from sensory overload, Mei kicked me sharply underneath the table again, jerking me back to life. I turned back to my boss just in time to hear Annabelle and the band's manager turn the conversation to planning and logistics for the upcoming tour and subsequent album release.

I knew I should be paying attention—they were essentially discussing what the next six weeks of my life would be like—but there was a quiet humming in the back of my head that prevented me from taking in any new information.

It was only at this moment I realized I was never actually asked if I wanted to take on this new client. To travel around the country for the next six weeks.

In the end, I guess it was never really a choice. That was the job.

·♥·♥·♥·♥·♥·

"Wait. You mean to tell me that your first real assignment at your brand new job is to do social media for a band you've been low-key obsessed with for the last—I don't know—decade?" Olivia's eyes were wide as they pinned me over the half-empty boxes of Chinese takeout sitting between us.

She balanced gracefully on one of the rustic industrial bar stools that lined our kitchen island, one leg drawn up underneath her, gym clothes still hugging her athletic body.

I took a large bite of my shrimp lo mein and nodded, eyes focused down on my food as though the answer to life's greatest questions lay at the bottom of the carton.

"And you want me to actually agree with you, to *believe*, this isn't the greatest thing that's ever happened to you—besides me, of course?" Olivia pressed, chopsticks still hanging midair on their way to her mouth.

I glowered across the island at her in response.

"Honestly, Han. The only bad part of this I'm hearing is that you're going to be on the road, far, far away from me, for *six weeks* after we just finally moved in together," Olivia said, ignoring my glare. She finally brought that bite of food to her mouth, pausing only long enough to consume it before adding, "The rest of it sounds pretty freaking amazing."

I grimaced down at my food, stabbing my chopsticks into the container more forcefully than was necessary. "In that case, you're more than welcome to join me."

Olivia let out a mocking laugh, her eyebrows twitching. "Yeah right, Bruce would probably have a heart attack if I was gone for more than four days," Olivia scoffed, referencing her brilliant—not to mention gorgeous—boss.

Olivia reminded me at least once a week that, although he was an absolute powerhouse in the courtroom, he was also a complete pain in her ass, prone to random fits of neediness and micromanaging when he was at the office instead of in court.

She expertly grasped a spring roll between her chopsticks and brought it to her lips, then paused again, mouth gaping. "But maybe if you end up in a cool city for a few days, I could come out to visit."

Note to self, get the full tour schedule from Annabelle and convince Olivia to meet me on the road, I thought.

"Look, I know it's a big change, so it's probably a bit scary," she said around her spring roll. "But you know this band inside and out, not to mention you're in their target market. You're gonna ace this assignment."

"Okay, yeah I'd be lying if I didn't admit it's pretty freaking incredible. This is exactly what I wanted when I took this job. But—"

"But *nothing!*" Olivia practically shouted, dropping her chopsticks into her container. "You were made for this. You're literally manifesting your life's dreams. *Woo-sah* and all that." She wiggled her fingers mystically between us, earning a loud laugh from me.

"You're right, I know you're right. It's a great opportunity. It's just, I've been there for two days. Literally. It's way too soon. This feels like a trap." I finished the last bite of lo mein in my carton and pushed away from the island to discard it in the trash.

"It's not a trap. It's the universe answering your prayers." Olivia rolled her eyes and joined me at the trash can to toss her own empty carton. "Stop trying to deny the universe and its infinite blessings because it doesn't fit perfectly into your neat and tidy plan."

She turned around and leaned her back against the kitchen counter beside us to face me, crossing her arms over her chest. "Plus, aren't you in love with the lead singer or something?"

I staggered backward slightly, my back meeting the kitchen island opposite her. I'd completely skipped over the electric pulse that filled the conference room for my entire meeting with Olympus when telling her about my new assignment.

"I'm not *in love* with him! All I said was that he's mildly attractive," I managed to choke out, hoping the words sounded more convincing than they felt.

"If memory serves, I believe your exact words were, *he's extremely hot and talented,* and *his lyrics speak directly to the core of your being.*" She raised her eyebrows in my direction.

In that moment, I absolutely hated that she had a memory like an elephant.

"That was three years ago when they released their last album! I was just caught up in the moment and all the new music, that's all. Besides, this is my job. He is my client. There can be absolutely no funny business," I said, narrowing my eyes in her direction. "The last girl already lost her job for falling for his charms. I can't let that happen to me," I added quietly, lowering my gaze to the hardwood floor beneath my feet.

"Um, what? I'm gonna need a little bit more of an explanation than that."

I groaned and pinched the bridge of my nose between my fingers. "I don't know all the details, but one of my coworkers vaguely implied they started sleeping together at some point, and... it didn't end well. Obviously."

"It sounds like it ended great for you. Just not so much for her," Olivia said wryly. "Plus, that sounds like gossip to me. It sure as hell wouldn't hold up in court without some proof."

"Thanks, Judge Judy," I answered drily. "Either way, I can't make that mistake."

Olivia laughed loudly, reading straight through my holier-than-thou expression. "Okay, just because it was *maybe* a huge mistake for her doesn't mean it would end the same way for you. Plus, you don't even know if she boinked the lead singer. Maybe she has a thing for bassists."

I blinked meaningfully in her direction.

"Fine, fine," Olivia held up her hands in surrender. "No funny business."

Chapter 3

A paper cup half filled with coffee warmed my hands as I lifted it to my lips and took a long sip, nearly draining it in one gulp. *Was this my fourth cup of the day? Fifth?*

I'd lost count at some point, during the many trips back and forth from my cubicle at Rabbit's Foot to the well-stocked kitchenette on my floor.

I'd been at the label office since seven that morning, digging through all of Annabelle's files on Olympus. Combing through strategic plans for their upcoming tour, reading reports on the digital campaigns already in motion, and skimming press release drafts about their new album, releasing in March of next year.

Golden lances of late-day sunlight sliced through the office's many windows as the sun slowly crawled toward the horizon. A glance at the corner of my laptop told me it was nearing six. I guess I hadn't noticed the low murmur of the other Rabbit's Foot employees leaving for the day about an hour ago. Some maybe even earlier.

Had I eaten lunch?

It had been one week since I got my first assignment, being sent on a six-week tour following one of my favorite bands around the northeastern part of the country. It had been a week and *one day* since I started this job. There was a lot to catch up on.

"I know I said I enjoy being busy, but memorizing nearly two years' worth of marketing plans in a matter of days wasn't exactly what I had in mind," I mumbled quietly to no one. There was little risk of being overheard at such a late hour. No one around to think I was crazy for talking to myself.

Fortunately, due to the accelerated timeline, I hadn't been given any other major clients from Rabbit's Foot's robust roster. I'd had the opportunity to shadow a few other account managers, but Olympus was pretty much my entire life.

"Having fun yet?"

I jumped at the sound of a disembodied voice behind me and swiveled around in my office chair. My coworker Mei leaned up against the wall that opened into my cube area, a knowing smile tugging on her lips.

I hadn't been able to get a read on Mei since first meeting her. Mean Girl or a friend with a penchant for gossip and sarcasm?

I slowly exhaled the sharp breath I'd sucked in at her sudden presence and decided to give her the benefit of the doubt. "Oh you know, living the dream." I pursed my lips into a thin line, eyes widening with meaning.

She snorted and took a seat at the empty desk across from me, crossing her legs to make herself comfortable. "So did you know during the interviewing process this is what you were hired for?" I noticed when she spoke, she often cocked her head to one side, almost like a cat assessing its prey. I shivered slightly at the thought.

Shaking my head slowly, I answered, "Not exactly. The general job duties? Yes. This is what I signed up for. The fact that I'd be sent on tour immediately after starting? Not so much."

Mei nodded thoughtfully, understanding in her eyes, even as they were cast down at the floor.

After a few beats of uncomfortable silence, I decided to go for it. "What can you tell me about my... predecessor?"

Mei inhaled a deep breath like she knew this was coming and met my gaze. "Oh you know, the usual. She was young but ambitious. Pretty decent at her job, although a little too peppy for my taste."

I gave her a pointed look, inclining my head.

Mei sighed and started picking at a piece of lint on her pants, obviously stalling for time.

Oh no, you started this conversation. We're doing this.

I raised my brows and cleared my throat to get her attention.

She finally met my eyes again. "Fine. Her name was Camila. She had been here for about two years when she was assigned to Olympus's account—Annabelle had previously handled them personally, but after she got promoted to director and grew her team, she just didn't have the time anymore. It started pretty normally. Like I said, she was good at her job. Things were going well.

"At some point during campaign prep, Cami and Ezra became... close, I guess? I don't know the details—she was smart enough to keep it pretty under wraps—but there were signs. You could sort of... feel the charge in the air any time they were together. See them staring at one another, knowing looks on their faces. I couldn't tell you how many times I walked into the middle of one of their hushed conversations and watched them go totally silent at the interruption."

Mei paused, picking at her pants again. I couldn't help but recall the thick tension I felt in the air during the first meeting I had with Ezra and the rest of the band.

Caught in my thoughts, I hadn't noticed Mei's pointed stare in my direction. It was like she could see what was inside my mind. "The problem with getting involved with musicians, especially the ones you work with, is... they're unpredictable. And they're faced with a lot of temptation every day. My guess is things eventually went south between Ezra and Cami. At least, TMZ publishing a series of photos showing Ezra canoodling with some model sure made it seem that way."

"And Cami was fired?" I couldn't help but blurt the words. I needed to know—to hear the consequences out loud.

Mei just shook her head though, her lips twitching as she turned her attention to something out one of the windows. "Surprisingly, no. I'm not sure if Annabelle even knows the full story, or if she just doesn't care. Either way, I never heard any whispers that she planned to let Cami go, or that she was upset about any of it. But whatever it was that happened... Cami couldn't get past it and left."

Suddenly Mei hopped out of the chair she had commandeered and moved back toward the cubicle exit. When she reached it, she turned back to face me one more time, her expression serious.

"Look, Annabelle wasn't totally wrong the other day, when she called it gossip. None of us left here really know the details of what happened. I could be wrong." She shrugged, the look on her face reeking of unspoken words: *but I doubt it.* "I know I make jokes, but this is a good place to work and you seem like you could fit in well. So I guess what I'm saying is... why risk it, right?" Mei tried to keep her tone irreverent, but the darkness in her eyes belied the false humor.

Before I could think of a response, she rapped her knuckles twice on the low cube wall and disappeared.

The next two weeks passed by in a blur of long days at the Rabbit's Foot office and late nights working at the kitchen island in the apartment I shared with Olivia.

She'd only given me crap twice about my overzealous work ethic before Bruce, her authoritarian boss, pulled her in on a big case that had her working just as much. Or *nearly* as much.

I worked primarily with Annabelle or through Olympus's manager, Ryan, on everything. As Annabelle had mentioned during my first few days, most of the planning and logistics had already been handled, either by my predecessor Camila or by Annabelle herself when she was desperately trying to fill my position.

My time was spent editing and publishing scheduled content and confirming travel details. I hadn't seen Ezra since that initial meeting in the conference room. Things were starting to settle into a new normal.

The content the team before me had worked on wasn't bad. Ordinarily, I'd think it was good. But having been a long-time fan of Olympus myself—a detail I vowed to share with no one at the label—I felt it lacked some of their unique personality. The parts that made them special.

Although it hadn't been asked of me, I spent a lot of my free time poring through old photo albums or the band members' personal social media accounts from the past two years, trying to learn as much as I could about them without having to talk to them. You know, the stuff that would probably make me look crazy if I did it at the office.

The long days had me feeling weirdly energized, my confidence slowly rebuilding with each item I checked off my to-do list. As a result, I'd started altering some of the planned content ideas here and there to help some of that personality shine through, and happily watched our engagement rate climb.

The sound of light knocking on my cube wall drew my attention from my label-issued laptop, and I glanced up to find Annabelle beaming at me.

"Just about ready?" she asked from behind her cat-eye glasses. Her white-blonde hair was pulled back in an elegant chignon, an expensive-looking scarf knotted around her long throat.

She looked like an old Hollywood starlet.

"Yep, just wrapping up something real quick." I smiled back and saved a draft of the post I was working on, then tapped a few buttons on my keyboard to put my computer to sleep.

With the tour starting in less than a week, the guys had one more big media day to promote it before we took off. Annabelle had planned to handle it on her own—one of her final hurrahs with an old client—then invited me to tag along at the last minute so I could get to know the guys better.

Normally, I'd be stoked.

It was the perfect opportunity for me to start capturing my own content for our social media channels. Not to mention put in some face time with the client. After all, happy clients who share positive feedback with leadership mean big promotions and paydays later. But Mei's vague warning sounded in my head like an alarm as I gathered my belongings from my desk and followed Annabelle down the quiet hallway, my black-heeled booties tapping out a steady rhythm on the tiled floor.

As we waited for the elevator, I smoothed down the edges of my brown suede mini skort and picked a stray piece of thread from the black, patterned tights underneath. Though I'd never admit it, I spent a little extra time selecting my outfit and doing my makeup in preparation for today's excursion.

It looked a lot more polished than my everyday attire, but I caught Annabelle's small smile of approval when she eyed me in the mirrored elevator walls on our ride to the lobby.

The interview was at a mid-sized media studio not far from the Rabbit's Foot office. We arrived in an all-black company-owned vehicle before the band, using the extra time to briefly chat through logistics with one of the producers.

While Annabelle and the producer chatted like old friends—this clearly wasn't my boss's first time here—I let my eyes wander around the interior of the studio.

We were tucked somewhere backstage while a small, live audience was ushered into the studio to take their seats. Producers and technicians bustled around us, checking equipment and talking to unnamed colleagues through their headsets.

I tried to take it all in, but my mind buzzed with anticipation of Ezra's—*Olympus's*—arrival.

If I hadn't been so distracted, I might have noticed the tall, tanned man approaching our group before he stood right beside me. I had to hold back a jump at his sudden presence.

The man smiled at us, his crystal blue eyes dancing between Annabelle and myself. Recognition flickered at the back of my skull just as Annabelle crooned, "Tom! Lovely to see you as always."

Tom Wesley—the journalist interviewing Olympus today.

I'd watched his shows and read his articles a handful of times over the years, whenever he'd covered a band I liked. He'd made quite a name for himself as one of the most influential music journalists in the country.

And one of the best looking.

With his strong jawline dusted with just the right amount of stubble and the way his long sleeve, navy blue button-down shirt hugged his sculpted arms, cuffs rolled up to show off just a little bit of sun-kissed skin, I could easily see why.

"Been looking forward to this one for a while. I've been a big fan of Olympus since they released Cosmic View," Tom said to Annabelle and me.

At the mention of Olympus's second studio album, I inclined my head to meet Tom's gaze. I wasn't prepared to find his bright sapphire eyes already staring at me.

"Ah, I didn't realize you were a fan!" Annabelle chirped delightedly from my side. I had to bite back a laugh as I took her in from my periphery. She angled her body so it was mere inches from Tom's. With the way her head tossed back and her hand flew to her collarbones, she was practically in a swoon.

Tom held my eyes for a beat longer, something like amusement lighting in them, before he directed the brunt of that beautiful gaze to Annabelle. "Oh yeah, big fan. Made my research for this interview so much easier."

Tom offered her what could only be described as a thousand-watt smile and chuckled, the deep baritone echoing like a complex melody written just for me—*us.*

Yep, Annabelle was officially swooning now.

We exchanged introductions—Annabelle had of course already met Tom a handful of times, both of them being industry vets—and made small talk for a few minutes about some of our other clients, Olympus's tour schedule, and an op-ed Tom recently wrote for Billboard that I pretended to have read.

"If you'll excuse me, I've got a few last-minute things I need to knock out before we get started. It was lovely to see you, Annabelle." He extended his hand to her and she squeezed it gently with her own.

"And you, Hannah," he added in a low voice that registered in my core, his eyes dancing as his hand gripped mine. Something in the way he said my name echoed with unspoken promise.

My hand sparked at his touch, heat blooming in my cheeks that had nothing to do with the stifling, dry air in the studio. After a beat, he released my hand and turned around, off to some other room in the studio.

"Well, he's not bad to look at," Annabelle said, glancing meaningfully in my direction. "And if I'm not mistaken, I'd say he has eyes for you."

I laughed softly and ran one of my hands through my hair. "Yeah, right. He's an on-air personality, I'm sure he just knows how to work his charm."

This earned me a barking laugh from Annabelle, and my smile widened.

Annabelle's phone chirped in her bag and she fished it out to read the incoming message. "Perfect, the guys are almost here," she said, tapping out a quick response.

My body tensed at the news, muscles contracting in warning.

Work. This is your job. You need to do your job and you need to do it well.

"I should grab some video of them walking into the studio. You know, build some buzz ahead of the interview airing tonight," I said in a rush, digging my phone out of my shoulder bag.

"Great idea! I'll let them know we should be ready to get started soon."

Annabelle turned on her heel and headed deeper into the studio. I took a deep breath to steady myself and stalked back toward the front entrance to greet the band outside.

The bright light of mid-day was like a welcome shock to the system after spending a half hour in the shadowy, sunless interior of the studio. I glanced up and down the street in front of me just in time to see two of the record label's company town cars pull up, with what I could only assume was Olympus tucked securely inside. The cars stopped at the curb, engines cutting to a dull idle in the No Parking zone. Olympus's manager stepped out of the first one, followed by the drummer, Angel, and the bassist, Peter just behind him.

My pulse quickened as I eyed up the second car. The lead guitarist, Zach, stepped out first, lifting a hand to his forehead to shield his eyes from the sun's piercing rays. Ezra stepped out after him, a broad smile plastered on his face as he swaggered across the sidewalk to join the rest of his group. He said something under his breath to his bandmates, and they all laughed.

My lip twitched upwards involuntarily at the intimate moment. It reminded me they were more than just bandmates. They'd also been friends for nearly two decades. A fact I needed to do a better job of pretending I didn't know.

"Hi there... Hannah, right?" their manager Ryan asked uncertainly, even though we'd corresponded via email more than a dozen times. I held back the desire to roll my eyes. He offered me a tight smile when he reached my side, though I couldn't see his eyes through his opaque black sunglasses.

"Right, good to see you again," I murmured in response, flashing a broad smile back at him. No time like the present to make a great impression. "I was hoping to get some video of the guys heading into the studio to do some promotion before it airs, if that's okay? We've still got about twenty minutes until they're needed for the pre-show meeting." I gestured toward the phone in my hands, my camera roll cleaned out and ready to go.

"Ah sure, sounds good. I'll leave you to it then," Ryan replied, his mind already elsewhere as he scanned something on his phone. "Please send the guys my way when you're done."

I nodded and watched him walk through the studio doors, steeling myself for what came next. I could feel every eye of Olympus pointed at the space between my shoulder blades, their owners crowding in behind me, waiting for direction.

Taking a deep breath, I spun around to face them, my "customer service" smile plastered firmly on my lips. "Hey guys, great to see you all again—" I began, ready to leap right into my spiel about the video

I hoped to capture, the setup, framing, and all that, when Ezra cut me off.

"Hannah. Great to see you again." He smiled warmly, but there was something mischievous in his eyes as they met mine. He reached a slender hand out to lightly touch the outer edge of my shoulder, right where the short sleeve of my white bodysuit ended. The unexpected jolt of electricity from his skin on mine nearly turned me into a puddle at his feet, but I didn't let it show.

His speaking voice was melodic, so like the way he sang. I felt the tenor's rumble deep in my gut, and my skin suddenly felt like it was stretched too tight over my bones. He'd barely spoken in that first meeting a few weeks ago, certainly not directly to me. His attention felt like the light of a thousand suns beating down on me, so much stronger than the real sun blazing above us in the height of the August afternoon.

"Right," I said, trying to recover my professionalism. "I'm excited to get things rolling and figured we'd start with some quick promo for the interview."

I launched into a quick explanation of my ideas, what shots we'd need, what I wanted them to do. The guys nodded animatedly through all of it. My goal was to showcase the humans behind the music, maybe even pushing them out of their comfort zone a little bit.

They took my direction surprisingly well, their vibrant and playful personalities shining through in every take. At one point they even hoisted one another up on their shoulders—at Ezra's and Peter's prodding—and ran up and down the packed sidewalk outside of the studio, earning more than a few irate looks and shouts from the pedestrians they passed.

Seeing the light in Ezra's eyes, the freedom within every one of his movements, the evident bond between him and his bandmates, set my soul aglow. I had no control over my beaming grin, coaxed from me by the joy painting his features as he strut confidently up and down the street, waving to passersby, most of whom did not recognize him, surprisingly.

In one final take, they attempted to build a cheerleader-style pyramid, with Peter and Angel on the bottom and Ezra and Zach trying to climb up on top. With just four of them, though, there weren't enough bodies to make it work right, the pyramid collapsing each time in a fit of laughter and flying limbs.

"Come on Han, you be the top of the pyramid," Ezra had yelled to me during their last attempt. "*We need you!*"

Fortunately, they toppled over before I had to respond.

After just under fifteen minutes, I had everything I needed for the promos, plus a burning stitch in my side from laughing so much.

When we wrapped up, I followed Olympus through the threshold of the building for the pre-show meeting. Although I figured I wouldn't be needed for the introductions, I wanted to get some editing and posting done in the interim, and I recalled the producer mentioning a green room where I could hole up until things got rolling.

The guys branched off in the direction Annabelle disappeared to earlier, obviously more familiar with the place than I was. My feet followed their lead in hopes our destinations were one and the same, my curious eyes again scanning the shadowy environment as we moved through unfamiliar hallways.

I had been in studios before for past jobs, but none this modern. It was set up primarily for online streaming and the entire building had been converted to suit that format. Only one mid-sized stage was set up for filming, with an intimate section for a small in-studio audience facing it. The rest of the building was filled with high-tech production equipment.

Lost in my thoughts, I didn't notice when Ezra stopped walking in front of me, and my body collided with his with a loud *thud.*

"Woah there," he said, quickly swiveling in my direction and reaching his hands out to steady me. I could feel heat radiating from where his palms met my upper arms.

My cheeks grew red and hot under his gaze. "Oh my gosh, I'm so sorry. I guess I wasn't paying attention."

He chuckled softly, the corners of his mouth jutting up in a crooked smile, "No harm, no foul. You'll need a little more than that to take me down." He was still holding onto my arms as his amber eyes darkened. "But you're more than welcome to keep trying."

He winked and reached one of his slender hands up to brush a piece of strawberry hair off my cheek, carefully tucking it behind my ear in one smooth motion. And almost as quickly as it began, Ezra released me, spun in place, and strode off into the labyrinth of rooms to join the rest of the band.

I stood rooted to the spot, my jaw gaping, wondering what just happened.

Chapter 4

The clock on the wall of the production room showed half past three in the afternoon by the time the interview wrapped. My body ached from standing in the control room for so long—muscles used to sitting at a computer all day roaring in protest. The dull pain in my legs was well worth it though, for this behind-the-scenes glimpse at production magic.

"I think that went well," Annabelle mused from beside me. We'd stood side-by-side for much of the afternoon in companionable silence, catching every angle of the interview on a collection of screens on the wall.

Went well was an understatement. Tom had played off the guys perfectly. His questions were thoughtful and opened the door for a lot of compelling, and oftentimes hilarious, behind-the-scenes stories that the guys of Olympus were all too eager to share.

It could not have gone better.

I held in my internal monologue, only nodding in response to Annabelle as she reached over to squeeze my shoulder once in farewell. "I'm heading across town for a client meeting. Feel free to take a company car back to the office from here, or work the rest of the day from home if you'd like."

I watched Annabelle exit the production room, her manicured thumbs already flying across the tiny keyboard on her iPhone, and plotted my next move. Olivia wouldn't be home from work for a few more hours, so that meant little chance of interruptions there. Getting home before dusk for the first time all week sounded like heaven.

Hiking my work bag up over my shoulder, I exited the production room and wracked my brain, trying to remember the right path back to the exit. After what had to be at least two wrong turns, I heard the muffled sound of voices coming from inside a small room to my right. Maybe they could point me in the right direction.

I hesitated just outside the door, torn between not wanting to interrupt the occupants and being desperate for help. Eventually, my desire to get home won out and I slowly lifted a hand to knock against the doorframe, then immediately stopped, my arm frozen in horror. One of those voices belonged to Ezra. The other was higher pitched, definitely female.

They were talking in sharp, hushed whispers, making it hard to understand the words from my hidden position outside the room. It sounded a lot like an argument.

Curiosity got the best of me, and I leaned quietly against the doorframe, angling my body over just enough to make out the figures in the room.

Ezra stood opposite a woman that could only be described as gorgeous. Tall, thin but with a few curves in the right places. Bone structure that could start a war. She wore a burgundy dress that hugged her figure, her bright blonde hair pulled back in a claw clip with loose waves framing her face.

As I took in her features, I could immediately tell something wasn't quite right. Her eyes looked swollen and her cheeks shone with a thin river of teardrops.

It somehow only added to her beauty, and I felt an unnatural pang of jealousy. When I cried, I typically looked like a freshly washed tomato: bright red, wet, and blotchy. The complete foil to this movie heroine standing opposite Ezra.

"I'm going to be gone for more than six weeks, Andie." I could just barely make out Ezra's voice as he spoke. The woman he spoke to—Andie—choked on a quiet sob. Ezra reached out to gently squeeze her arm. "It's only going to get harder when I'm on the road," he added quietly. "You need someone who can be around."

"But I know there's something here, Ezra," Andie whispered through tears, almost too quiet for me to catch. "I'm willing to wait. To give this a real shot. Aren't you?"

"I... well, it's just... We've only been together for two months. I'm going to be gone for almost as long as our entire relationship."

Andie choked back tears again, her eyes cast down to the floor. After a few moments, she slowly lifted her head and reached out to gently grasp one of Ezra's hands tentatively in her own. "Let's just leave the door open. Talk when you get back."

Andie paused, then steeled her face with determination, visibly willing the tears to stop lining the corners of her eyes. "If you still feel this way in six weeks, then so be it."

Before Ezra could come up with a response, Andie dropped his hand and turned on her heel so quickly I barely had time to duck out of sight before she came barreling through the doorway. I managed to hide behind some random equipment stored off to the side in the hallway, my heart pounding in my chest at the fear of being caught eavesdropping.

I could no longer see him from my impromptu hiding place, but I heard Ezra sigh deeply. I could almost picture him raking his hands through his dark, messy hair. After a few moments of quiet, I heard his footsteps approach the door.

Faster and more gracefully than I thought possible, I hopped out from my hiding place, making it look as though I'd just come from down the hall. I grabbed my phone from my pocket, pretending to be entranced with something on the screen just as Ezra stepped into view.

He pulled up short when he saw me, giving me a long and careful once over.

Time to give the performance of my life.

I waited another beat before looking up from my phone, feigning surprise at the sight of him. "Oh, hey Ezra! I didn't realize you were still around."

Ezra's eyes raked over my face and it took all I had not to squirm beneath his piercing stare. "Right. Just had to grab something back here before we take off," he said finally, rocking back on his heels.

Phew! Nailed it.

My triumphant smile faltered when I noticed the usual roguish light in his eyes was absent. I felt the strange urge to comfort him, but I couldn't. Not without giving myself away. And not without crossing a very clear line in our relationship.

"Well, if you need anything, anything at all, please let me know," I said slowly, dropping the closest thing to a hint that I could manage. "I'll be around, editing some of the stuff we got today."

I couldn't help but feel for him. I only caught the tail end of it, but that conversation looked brutal.

Ezra smiled back at me, but it didn't quite reach his eyes. "Thanks, I uh... I'll see you around." With a final glance, he stepped around me and headed toward what I assumed was the front entrance of the studio.

Ah, so that's where I should have been going.

It was strange to see him so reserved, to compare this quiet shell of a man to our playful encounter earlier in the day. Even his shoulders were hunched. His presence smaller.

For the second time that day, I found myself stuck to the floor, watching him walk away.

"That dude is into you."

Olivia took a long swig of her beer, nearly draining the pint glass in her hands before setting it back down on the table with a flourish. We sat opposite one another at an oak-finished high-top table at a brewery a few blocks down the street from our apartment. It had quickly become one of our favorite places for happy hour—they always had decent beer on tap and the elevated menu of bar bites rotated weekly. Not to mention it was a short walk from home.

After the long day both of us had, we decided to bail on work a little early—well, on time for most people, early for us—and meet up for drinks. Since then, two hours had passed and we'd drunk probably a growler's worth of beer between the two of us.

"He just broke up with his girlfriend. Or, I guess, he kinda broke up with his girlfriend—" My mouth twisted in question. To be honest, I wasn't totally sure where he and Andie had left things, despite my eavesdropping. "Either way, he doesn't *want me*." I stabbed a french fry forcefully into a portion cup of ketchup and brought it to my lips.

"Okay, look," Olivia held up her well-manicured hand and started ticking off fingers. "Number one: he *mercilessly* flirted with you before the interview. Number two: he presses the pause button with his girlfriend later that *same day*. Number three: when she tells him she sees the two of them going somewhere, having a real future, he responds *I know*. Not, *so do I*. Not, *I want the same thing even if I need some time to think*. Just, *I KNOW*!"

She finished her speech with a pointed look, wiggling her three elevated fingers in my direction.

I rolled my eyes and began ticking off my own fingers. "One: as sad as it might be, he probably just wasn't that into that girl. It happens. There's an entire genre of romcom devoted to the topic. Two: he's *known around the world* for being a massive flirt by nature and probably acts that way with everyone. I'm not special, I'm a girl with legs and boobs just like the rest of 'em. Three: we *work* together. Just because Rabbit's Foot didn't make me sign anything saying I wouldn't date a client, doesn't mean they approve of it. The last girl who had my job may have quit because of it. Either way, it's a bad idea!"

I lowered my fingers, reaching out to grab my pint glass and take a long sip as doubt began to creep in. Was I making these points to convince Olivia, or to convince myself there was no chance of anything between Ezra and me? Growing up to meet your favorite musician, fall in love, and live happily ever after was a dream. A schoolgirl fantasy. It wasn't real. It didn't happen.

I was being practical.

Olivia's mouth twisted into a grimace. "Ew, okay wait. Do you think he slept with that girl from Rabbit's Foot while he was dating the model chick from today?"

Before I could emphatically respond, I felt a light tap on my shoulder and noticed Olivia's eyes widen at something behind me. Turning around, I was greeted by a familiar handsome face.

"Hey. Hannah, right?" The tall man behind me smiled widely, his clear blue eyes glittering like twin pools in the low light. "We met earlier at the interview."

He'd changed into something more casual—a black v-neck tee that dipped low on his broad chest, revealing just a hint of taut muscle and dark hair beneath, and dark gray straight-leg jeans—so it took me a moment to recall the name. But even through my slight beer haze, I managed to smile back, shifting in my bar-height chair to face him more fully. "Right! Tom. Good to see you again."

I could feel Olivia trying to catch my attention from across the table and did my best to avoid her, focusing my full attention on the music journalist before me.

Tom's hair was tousled in a way that only looked effortless, but in reality probably took a fair bit of upkeep to maintain. I'd never had a problem with guys who took care of themselves, though. Something about it was deeply appealing.

"The guys were great earlier today, the views are already rolling in on the interview," he said, leaning one of his elbows against the backrest of my stool until mere inches separated us.

I beamed, making a mental note to watch the stream as soon as Olivia and I got home.

"You getting excited for the tour?"

I opened my mouth to deliver a canned answer, then paused to consider. I realized that despite all of the work I'd been putting in at this job, this was the first time I'd been asked how I felt about it. About the tour, about being away from home for six weeks.

"It's hard to separate the nerves from the excitement," I answered honestly, surprising myself.

Tom chuckled, that same rumbling baritone from earlier, and I bit back my grin.

"But I'm really looking forward to seeing the country."

Tom nodded knowingly just as a booming male voice shouted his name from across the brewery. He passed a glance over his shoulder and waved off someone I couldn't see, then held up a finger to signal *just a second*.

He turned back to face me with a disappointed wince, ruefully gesturing back at his friend with a loose wave of his hand. "Unfortunately, I've got to get going. But now that you're at Rabbit's Foot, I'm sure we'll be seeing more of each other," he said, reaching into his back pocket for his wallet to produce a business card. "If you ever need to get in touch about a client, or a project, or... anything."

He flashed me one of his winning smiles and I noticed one tiny dimple poke out near his left cheekbone. I chewed on my lip to distract myself from how adorable it looked.

Tentatively, I reached out and took the business card from him, our fingertips brushing. "Thanks, maybe I will."

I watched him walk back to his table of friends, mostly to avoid the look on Olivia's face for a few passing moments.

"Um, who was that?"

I picked up my pint glass and drained the rest of my beer, buying myself time before responding. "Just some journalist I met at work today. He did the interview this morning with Olympus," I offered casually, trying to brush it off.

"I feel like I'm in the wrong line of work or something," Olivia responded, shaking her head and crossing her arms over her chest as she leaned back casually in her stool. "You meet a new hot guy every other day at that place."

I choked out a laugh and rolled my eyes, scanning the brewery to find our server. I needed another beer. "You work with hot guys all the time too—hot, *lawyer* guys, no less. Bruce is practically Greek god status."

After flagging down the waiter and giving him the international sign for *another round, please* I turned back to Olivia, wiggling my eyebrows suggestively at my reference to her hot boss.

I'd only met him once, when Olivia had dragged me to a work happy hour she swore she couldn't get through without me. I had to work overtime to keep my jaw from dropping to the floor when she introduced him.

He seriously looked like he'd stepped right off the runway and into the low-lit cocktail bar with his suit that probably cost more than my car, perfectly tailored to his muscular frame. Olivia said he worked out twice a day and occasionally biked to work. It showed.

Olivia blew out a breath of air and leaned back in her chair. "Bruce might be *Greek god status*, but he's also a Grade-A Asshole. And the bane of my existence."

She paused speaking while our waiter silently brought over two fresh pint glasses, waiting until he was halfway back to the bar before continuing. "All that to say, forget everything I said about Ezra. *That guy* was definitely flirting with you. And he's hot. Sure, his name is *Tom*," she wrinkled her nose a little snobbishly, "but I think we can work with that."

Chapter 5

My phone buzzed from my bedside table where it was still plugged into the charger. Glancing up from my open suitcase, I stretched out across my bed to read the name on the screen: Mom.

Crap, I thought to myself, straining to pick up the phone and unplug it from the wall.

We'd texted here and there over the past few weeks, but I realized with a sinking feeling in my gut we hadn't actually spoken since I got this assignment.

My mom had no idea I was going on tour for six weeks.

It wasn't that I was avoiding her on purpose, exactly. My life had turned into complete chaos in preparation for leaving, my days filled with prep work and my nights filled with packing.

"Hey, mom!" I said with too much enthusiasm when I picked up the call.

"Hannah! I'm a little surprised I caught you," my mom replied, already laying on the guilt trip, "I thought maybe I'd get your voicemail again."

"Yeah, sorry about that," I winced and sat down on the edge of my bed. "Things have been busy at work, you know...plus getting situated at the apartment—"

My mom broke in before I could finish. "That's actually why I called! I have a wide open weekend and I wanted to visit. I figured we'd get dinner and you could tell me all about your new job, and I could help with anything you had left to unpack."

My mouth twisted and I scanned the mess of belongings strewn across my bed, thankful my mom couldn't see me. "Oh wow, mom. I would love that, seriously, I would, but..." I trailed off, still trying to figure out how to tell her I wouldn't be around this weekend. Or the next six after that.

"What's wrong, you already have plans?" my mom asked, sensing my hesitation. "I could try and do the following weekend instead."

Shame crept up my neck. My mom usually volunteered at the local animal shelter on the weekends to stay busy, and they'd come to rely on her help. It must've taken some planning for her to get a free weekend.

Sighing, I ran a hand through my red-blonde hair and bit my lip. "Actually, mom... I got a big assignment at work and—" another short pause. "And I'll be going on tour with the band Olympus for the next six weeks." The last sentence rushed out of my lips in a nearly unintelligible flurry.

Silence stretched out on the other end of the phone line.

Finally, my mom spoke, her voice quieter than before. "Wow, I don't know what to say. That's great, honey." She paused again.

"Olympus... isn't that the band you like? The one we saw in concert when you were a teenager."

I bit back a smile that she remembered and nodded my head, then realized she couldn't see me. "Yep, that's them. I've seen them in concert like... five more times since then."

"Well, I guess you'll be seeing them about a hundred more," my mom joked and I exhaled a sigh of relief. "Seriously, honey. I'm happy for you, and so proud. I just wish you would've told me a little sooner! Six weeks on the road is a big deal." My heart nearly cracked at the dull sadness in her voice. "You know me! I'm going to be worried sick the whole time," she added, trying to make herself laugh, though it felt forced.

I forced my own laugh in response, trying to lessen the tension. "I know, I know. I'm sorry, really. It all happened so fast. I've barely had time to make peace with it myself, but I promise I'll be super safe and well-cared for. The label is putting me up in nice hotels every night, and we'll have plenty of security on the road," I added, only partially telling the truth. I knew I'd have comfortable accommodations every evening—Annabelle had tasked me with doing all of the bookings myself—but I had no idea what security would be like during the trip. Despite all my research and preparation, that was one area I'd neglected.

Rabbit's Foot wouldn't send one of their bigger clients out into the wild without protection though, right? By association, I should be fine.

"I want you to at least text me every single day, so I know you're okay," my mom replied, her tone going from disappointed to matronly in a matter of seconds. "But a phone call would be nice once in a while, Hannah."

I couldn't help but roll my eyes, immediately feeling like a kid again. "I know, I know, mom. I will, I promise."

"I love you, sweetie. I really am so proud of you. Your dream job, at age twenty-six!"

I felt my lip quiver and closed my eyes, trying to stop the tears threatening at the corners of my eyes. "Thanks, mom. That means a lot."

"Tell Olivia I said hello. And don't forget to text me!"

I breathed out another laugh, swiping at the tear trailing down my cheek. "I will. Love you."

When we hung up, I threw my phone down on my bed and followed it. I'd earned a few minutes to lie down and breathe.

I was officially going on tour with my favorite band.

Olympus's first show was tonight.

How was this real life?

Fortunately, tonight's show was pretty local—at an amphitheater in Jones Beach, about an hour's drive outside the city.

Still, after tonight I'd spend nearly every waking moment with Olympus. With *Ezra*.

I had to admit, it was getting real. Things were ramping up, and the content I'd created the other day with the guys was blowing up.

As I laid there on my bed, staring at the stark white ceiling above, I couldn't help but wonder how I stacked up against my predecessor. So far, all the feedback I'd received from Annabelle was glowing.

And yet at least once a day I'd pause in the middle of whatever I was doing, a strong sense of Impostor Syndrome pressing down on me like a weight. Like this dream life could be ripped away at any moment, and there was no way in hell I knew what I was doing, or even deserved to be here at all.

Those kinds of intrusive thoughts had me working overtime, watching trends online every spare second I had and brainstorming new content ideas to take our efforts to the next level.

Sighing out a long exhale, I forced myself to stand up and finish packing. I had only an hour before I had to meet the tour bus.

As I was piling the last of my toiletries on top of my filled-to-the-brim suitcase, my phone buzzed from the bed where it was buried underneath a pile of discarded clothes. I struggled for a moment to get my case zipped, only turning my attention back to my phone when it was finally shut.

I noticed the text was from an unsaved number.

`Looking forward to tonight`

I stared down at my phone for several seconds, a puzzled look twisting on my face. The tour started tonight, so I know I didn't make plans with anyone. Wrong number, maybe?

`Who is this?`

The typing bubble popped up almost immediately.

`Hannah Banana, that hurts! Didn't even save my number?`

Then after a few more seconds of typing, another text came through.

`It's Ezra, in case you hadn't guessed.`

My eyes nearly bulged out of my head, my thoughts whipped through a sea of emotions: first embarrassed for not having my own client's number; then excited by the prospect of *Ezra Freaking Bell* texting me; then annoyed at the childish nickname he'd branded me with; then smug thinking about the small dent I just made to his ego.

He could afford it.

The next thing I knew, my fingers were flying across the keyboard and pressing send before my mind could catch up. I simply couldn't help myself.

    Ezra…? You'll have to be a bit more
    specific.

He fired back three laughing emojis almost immediately.

    Ouch! She bites.

    Let's just say, the only Ezra in your life
    who matters.

I rolled my eyes and hammered my thumbs against the keyboard.

    Okay "VIP" Ezra. New rule: no Hannah
    Banana nickname.

    Touché. See you soon

The typing bubbles stopped after that message, and I decided to leave it at that.

Did I just flirt with Ezra Bell?!

The sound of air brakes screaming to life had me taking an involuntary step back as it startled me out of my thoughts. I glanced up to find the Olympus tour bus slowly making its way to a stop a few feet from me in the otherwise empty back section of the parking lot I'd been waiting in.

No matter how many times I tried to push them away, the memories of my few exchanges with Ezra crept into my thoughts when I was alone. I'd need to get a handle on that if we were going to spend the next six weeks shoved together in close quarters on the road. I had to keep this relationship strictly professional. It was, quite literally, my job.

I was relieved to find out the tour bus was mostly for carting us and our belongings around and *not* a place we were expected to sleep each night. Despite how large the bus was as it filled my entire line of vision and took up several parking spaces in the empty lot, it was still far too small for that with five of us, plus a driver, in tow.

This first leg of the tour was primarily on the East Coast, with the largest distances between shows no more than a six-hour drive. The bus would take us to each city, but I had a hotel reservation with my name on it each night.

It also meant no flights necessary for this first leg. That would come later when the second half of the tour brought us to the West Coast

As the tour bus let out a loud screech I could only assume was the parking brake locking into place, I closed my eyes for a second and breathed in and out through my nose. Opening my eyes again, I reached down for the handle of my lilac wheeled suitcase.

I guess I'm doing this?

I wheeled my suitcase to the door of the bus, reaching it right as it flew open wide, the steel staircase descending with a mechanical whir. Expecting our middle-aged bus driver, my jaw fell open when it was Ezra bouncing down the steel steps instead, one of his hands already stretched toward me.

"Need a hand?" He hopped off the bottom step, sending his shaggy hair bouncing around his temples, and stopped directly in front of me with just a foot or two separating us. His wide-set mouth was set in a wry smile, the bright sunlight overhead reflected in the dark pools of his eyes.

I had a split second to decide how I was going to handle this weird back-and-forth tension between us. To decide who I would be on this tour.

The shy, timid girl Ezra first met in the conference room three weeks ago, totally shell-shocked sharing space with her celebrity crush. Or the confident woman he'd texted this morning, who could care less about his platinum record deals, or the tip of a tattoo that peeked up just above the waistline of his joggers when he stretched or moved too quickly.

Looking up at Ezra from beneath lowered lashes, one corner of my lips tilted up in a half smile.

"I'd love that," I said smoothly, then thrust my suitcase in his direction. "If you could just stow this one, I'll keep the other bag with me."

I waited just long enough to see the surprise and amusement light in his eyes before I sidestepped him and climbed onto the tour bus.

Just past the driver's area, the top step of the bus opened to a space that seemed much larger than should be physically possible, outfitted with overstuffed couches sheathed in black leather on either side of a center aisle.

Beyond the pseudo-living room, there was a small kitchenette on one side of the bus, a stainless steel sink in its center, flanked by a Keurig coffee machine on one side, and a toaster oven on the other. A small microwave clung to the wall above it. A small booth and table formed the bus's only dining area directly across from the kitchenette.

That was as far as I could see from the very front of the bus. Beyond the kitchen, the center aisle came together where a half wall blocked my view of the sleeping area tucked at the far back of the bus.

Content with my mental tour-for-one, I turned my attention back to the overstuffed couches and the three band members lounging a little *too casually* on them, purposefully not looking my way.

Zach, the guitarist, pretended to read a magazine, but he was flipping through the pages too quickly to possibly know what he was reading.

Peter and Angel were across from him, playing some sort of video game on one of the flat screens mounted high on the wall. Judging by how entrenched they were in the game, it's possible they truly didn't notice me.

"Hey guys," I said, forcing my voice to be lighter than I felt. *You can acknowledge me now.*

Zach closed his magazine and dropped it to the couch, glancing up at me in feigned surprise. "Oh hey, Hannah! Didn't even hear you climb aboard. Welcome to the Olympus-mobile!"

"Make yourself at home! Our casa es su casa," Angel added from his spot beside Peter with a smile. His eyes never left the TV screen.

Peter merely offered me a quick wave of his controller, his concentration focused solely on the game. Judging by Angel's significantly more relaxed demeanor, Peter was probably losing.

I returned Zach's smile and made my way toward the middle of the bus and decided to make the little booth my home. I dropped my work bag to the seat facing the front of the bus and smoothly slid in beside it.

"Everybody ready to roll?"

I looked up slowly, feigning disinterest at Ezra's voice echoing from the doorway. He stopped at the top of the steps, clamping a hand down on the shoulder of our driver, a broad grin stretched across his lips. The rest of the guys started whooping and hollering, Peter and Angel even pausing their game to join in.

It was hard not to laugh along with them.

Our first stop of the tour brought us to Wantagh, NY, a relatively small but affluent town on Long Island and the home to a pretty cool outdoor amphitheater right on Jones Beach.

I was immediately blown away by the venue.

Even in the bright light of a late summer afternoon, I could picture how cool the show would look in this setting. The stage of the amphitheater backed up to the water's edge, the stadium-style seats fanned around it on the opposite side, giving concertgoers in the far right and left seats a view that was equal parts stage and glittering ocean.

The amphitheater itself seated about fifteen thousand, and based on a text from Annabelle I'd received en route, every single one of those seats—even the standing room on the lawn—would be filled.

Closing my eyes, I could practically hear the roar of the crowd in my ears, mingled with the opening chords to Olympus's first song on the setlist: "Galaxy."

A quiet voice and the billowing scent of citrus and sandalwood pulled me from my thoughts. "Pretty cool, isn't it?"

I turned my head to the side to see Ezra standing just behind me, his gaze trained out on the ocean behind the stage.

"This is probably one of my favorite spots on the East Coast," Ezra added thoughtfully after a moment, then directed his attention to me. Warm amber, like a glass of whiskey, pooled in his eyes as they reflected the sunlight. There was a tentative smile playing on his full lips.

I nodded at him once then turned back around to face the stage and the water behind it. "I imagine it must look pretty cool lit up at night." My voice was quiet too, afraid we'd ruin the spell whispered by the calm, blue sea.

"Being able to hear the sound of the waves crashing behind us in between songs is next level," Ezra said reverently, and I could hear the awe in his voice. Before I even looked back, I knew his smile had widened.

Unable to resist seeing it for myself, I turned around to face him fully for the first time since we'd arrived, nervously wrapping my arms around myself. "It seems cliché to ask, but are you ready for tonight? It'll be your first live show in—what? Three years, right?"

It sounded dumb as soon as the words left my lips, but I was genuinely curious what it felt like to pick back up and perform in front of so many people after a long hiatus.

Was it thrilling? Or terrifying? Or both?

Ezra's eyes caught mine and held them, a few moments of silence stretching out between us. I wasn't sure what he found there in my gaze, but it prompted him to answer.

"It's been a long road of practicing, getting back into the groove. Can't deny that," he started, the words exhaling from him like a long sigh. "But I think we're ready. I'm excited to get back out there—the energy of a crowd feels like home to me."

I couldn't help but let out a grunt of a laugh, picturing myself out there in front of a crowd of thousands. "I can't imagine performing in front of that many people—I think I'd die."

Ezra chuckled, laugh lines etching themselves around his mouth. The way his smile lit up his handsome face made my breath catch in my throat.

"I think you'd do just fine," he whispered, tilting his head to one side as if he needed to look at me from another angle—like one would stare at a painting on the wall of a museum. The movement caused a strand of his dark hair to spill across his forehead.

My cheeks heated under the intensity of his gaze and my mouth all but dried up. I coughed to expel the thick feeling in my throat, and the sudden noise seemed to set both of us in motion.

"Guess I better go grab the rest of the guys for soundcheck," Ezra said quickly, raking his fingers through his dark hair as he glanced behind him. As if he expected the rest of the band to be standing there, watching us.

Fortunately, they were not.

"Yeah, of course!" My voice was too loud, too bright after our hushed conversation. "I'll be out to join you guys at some point—to grab some pre-show video," I added, trying to sound cool, casual.

Like I know what I'm doing.

Ezra flashed a smile, one of his eyes winking as though he could see the gears whirring in my head and, with a half wave of his hand, he turned back to find the rest of Olympus.

I caught myself watching him walk away. It was only the feeling of my phone buzzing in the back pocket of my jean shorts that eventually jerked me back to the present. I freed it and glanced down to see four missed texts.

Three of them were from Olivia.

Hey! Did you make it out there yet?

Helloooo? Starting to think your bus is toppled over in a ditch somewhere…

Okay, now I'm getting worried. If I need to plan a funeral, I'm going to be so pissed.

I rolled my eyes and quickly tapped out a response.

I'm fine! Bus is fine! Everyone is FINE! We made it here a little bit ago, sorry it took me so long to respond. The place is pretty cool so I got distracted. I'll send you a video.

I pressed send on the text and pulled up the fourth message, from my mom.

Hope you made it safely! Please call me when you get the chance.

Love you,

Xoxo Mom

I chuckled. It always made me smile, the way my mom felt the need to sign off her texts like an email.

I texted her too, assuring her I was safe in Wantagh and promising to call her later that evening. Then I switched over to my camera app to take a quick panoramic video of the venue, spending a little extra time on the area where it looked like the ocean water met the back of the stage.

Not one minute after I sent the video to Olivia, my phone buzzed again in my hand.

Holy shit! Your job is so cool. I might have to find a reason to come visit you…

I laughed loudly to myself and sent back a series of emojis that appropriately conveyed my excitement about Olivia joining us on the road. Then I returned my phone to my pocket and started the walk back to the bus.

·❤·❤·❤·❤·❤·

The rest of our afternoon in Jones Beach passed in a blur of sounds, lights, and colors—literally. We spent the majority of the afternoon running checks on everything needed for tonight's performance.

First, the sound checks.

I wasn't sure what I had expected—maybe a few times yelling "testing, testing, 1, 2, 3" into a microphone? The reality was like watching an intimate, live performance where I was the only one in the crowd.

Well, if you didn't count the techs running around behind and in front of me, ensuring everything was in working order.

After a few minutes of playing around on stage—Ezra and Peter yelling the occasional inappropriate phrase into their microphones, Zach strumming through chord progressions from his favorite non-Olympus songs, and plenty of rambling drum solos from Angel in the back—the band launched into some of the songs from their setlist.

Most of the time, they didn't play them the entire way through—sometimes pausing to make adjustments or talk to the sound techs and equipment managers about notes for the real performance. But getting a glimpse of them performing this close, with no crowd behind me was... surreal.

I found myself more than once getting completely lost in the music, in the sound of Ezra's voice, when I was supposed to be working. He still sounded every bit as good as when the band released their platinum debut album a decade ago.

Somehow, I managed to break the enchantment long enough to capture a *few* clips of them playing, plus many, many more funny shorts for social.

After a particularly hilarious video of Ezra belting out an old Mariah Carey ballad, which he dedicated entirely to a beet-red Zach, the four of them decided they had what they needed for the show and packed it in, each of them dispersing in different directions.

I lingered in one of the blue folding seats of the amphitheater for a few minutes, watching back the same clips on my phone over and over without actually seeing them... because my periphery was following Ezra's movements instead. I couldn't help it. My eyes were drawn to him like a magnet.

He stepped off the stage and slowly walked along the outermost path of the amphitheater, stopping every few feet to greet the technicians, event coordinators, and various other people he passed, offering them broad smiles, handshakes, or the occasional clap on the back like they were longtime friends.

Curious, my gaze trailed his path, not toward the labyrinth of rooms at the back of the amphitheater where the others had gone, but toward the exit. Before I knew my body was in motion, I stood and followed him.

I kept a careful distance behind as Ezra wove his way through the maze of passageways that connected the stage area of the amphitheater to an outdoor plaza filled with concessions stands, merch tables, and a large bar. After being in the shade offered by the amphitheater, the heat from the blazing afternoon sun beating down on the plaza hit me like a brick wall. I lifted a hand to my brow to shield my eyes from its bright light, cursing myself for leaving my sunglasses in my laptop bag.

Just turn around now before he catches you stalking him like a lunatic, I thought to myself.

I was surprised to find him still moving at a steady pace, past the concession stands being cleaned and stocked ahead of the crowd that would soon pass through, toward the front gate. His gait was easy, unrushed, but gave the air of someone with a destination.

From a few yards behind, I watched Ezra carefully pick his way through the temporary fencing that wove between the security gates at the entrance and the main lot of the venue, an area that would soon be filled with anxious patrons waiting to get inside.

He passed by a few security guards with nothing more than a wave, none of them bothering to stop him or ask where he was going as he continued toward the main section of the parking lot just beyond the entrance. Like they were used to this type of thing.

With still a few hours remaining before the doors opened, only a small group of eager tailgaters had arrived. They posted up beside their cars in the very front of the lot with ten-by-ten tents, yard games, and coolers to help pass the time. One of the cars, I couldn't tell which, blared a Florence + The Machine song from its speakers.

Hanging back partially in the shade offered by a makeshift security tent at the gate, I watched Ezra make his way over to a group of four women who looked to be in their late twenties, though it was a little hard to tell from my vantage point. They were dressed for the height of the afternoon heat in tank tops, shorts, and sunglasses, each with a sweating bottled beverage of choice in one hand as they chatted animatedly with one another.

At first, they spared the approaching man only a passing glance, not bothering to pause their conversation. A moment later though, one of the women sprang from her seat on top of a wide blue and white cooler, gesturing wildly to her companions. I could tell even from several yards away what she was saying to them, why they were all springing up from their seats and pointing.

Ezra's tousled, dark hair blew faintly in a passing breeze as he reached them. Half of his face was obscured from my view, but I could just make out the mischievous grin curving his lips as he spoke to the women.

And I could certainly make out the way they leaned toward him, the way they giggled as he spoke.

I kept my gaze narrowed on the five of them as one of the women produced a phone from her back pocket. Ezra smoothly pivoted around and leaned his back toward them, a casual arm slung around the small of their backs as they took a selfie.

Everything about the interaction felt intimate, inviting.

The way he gently squeezed their shoulders before sliding his arm back to his side, the sensuous curve to his smile as he bade his farewell to move on to the next group of fans in the lot.

The way one of the women fanned herself, practically in a swoon behind Ezra's turned back.

It took every ounce of my being not to roll my eyes.

It wasn't that I was jealous. That would be stupid.

Ezra was nothing to me, nor I to him, other than colleagues at a work event. He was just out here, interacting with his fans. Doing his *job*.

But a niggling voice in the back of my head couldn't help but wonder what that was like. How it would feel to have his attention on me that way. To feel the gentle stroke of his fingertips against the curve of my spine.

I coughed to clear the intrusive thoughts then backed away slowly, taking cover behind a pillar. With no more than a quick wave or a nod to any event workers I passed, I hustled my way to the small but well-furnished green room set deep within the building behind the stage.

Chapter 6

My back relaxed into the plush cushion of the sage green couch beneath me, my feet propped up on an antique-looking coffee table crafted from polished cherry wood that had been repeatedly scuffed and worn down by boots and sneakers and time. When I first sat down, I wondered what famous musicians had once found comfort in this exact spot before me.

Beside me, my laptop played a trending TikTok on a continuous loop while I cut together video clips on my phone, trying to emulate the trend on Olympus's account. My eyes stung from staring at the two screens for so long as I struggled to get the timing just right, my neck aching from being hunched over in the same position without relief.

When I finally finished the draft, the door to the green room burst open with a flourish and Peter—the bassist—rushed in with a wide grin plastered on his face. He fisted a water bottle in his left hand, his large palm and thick, muscular forearm making the object appear comically small.

"The crowd's piling in now! It's gonna be huge out there tonight," he shouted to no one in particular. Clearly, he hadn't yet adjusted his volume after leaving the loud din of the shadowy alcoves directly behind the stage.

It was the first time I'd seen one of the band members since I'd half stalked Ezra a few hours ago—all of their pre-performance duties kept them busy. I looked up from my phone after ensuring the video draft was safely saved in our account and offered him a timid smile.

Peter collapsed onto a matching couch opposite mine and took a long swig from his water bottle then turned his gaze on me. "The first act will probably start in about thirty minutes. If you want to head out there to get some content, I can show you the easiest way to the side stage," he offered, dragging a hand through his cropped black hair. It fell directly back into place like it'd just been styled by a professional in that infuriating way only men ever seemed to be blessed with.

I lit up immediately at the idea, leaning forward to brace my forearms on the tops of my thighs. "Yes!—" I said a bit too energetically, then tried to tone my voice down. "Uh, yeah. That would be great. Thank you."

I was looking forward to checking out their opener, Lucid Dreams—a trio of women, all about my age, with a roaring indie rock sound and ultra-poetic lyrics. They were the real-life version of what I imagined in my head growing up when I sang into a hairbrush in front of my mirror. My pre-teen dream personified.

Peter grinned and nodded at the enthusiasm I failed to hide, then sank back into the couch. I could just barely make out small beads of sweat glistening above his brows as almost every muscle in his body seemed to uncoil in unison against the cushions beneath him.

As fun and incredible as the job seemed, it also looked exhausting.

We'd arrived at the amphitheater over five hours ago and the guys had been going non-stop ever since. To have to put on a show well into the evening after all that? Intense.

I watched silently, clicking the screen off on my phone, as Peter closed his eyes and lolled his head back to expose the ridges and curves of his neck. It shouldn't be possible, or even allowed by nature, but every member of Olympus was good-looking—albeit in very different ways.

Peter was what I'd describe as conventionally handsome.

Where Ezra was lithe muscle honed from life's adventures, Peter was solid. Broad, packed muscle. If he didn't play bass, I probably would've pegged him as a professional athlete.

His smooth, fair skin juxtaposed against his dark hair only accentuated the emerald green of his eyes. And when they were open and focused on you? The combination was nothing short of hypnotic.

If you were into that kind of thing.

Yes, Peter was objectively good-looking. But for some reason, I still felt my eyes drifting to the green room door every few seconds... searching for someone else.

Because I was staring at that closed door, I didn't notice when Peter's eyes had opened and zeroed in on me.

"Expecting someone?" he asked, amusement in his voice. I could sense the upward curve of his smirk before I turned my head to face him.

Play it cool.

"What? No, I just... I was thinking about heading out there. It's getting louder so I thought maybe Lucid Dreams was about to come on."

Nailed it.

Finally returning his gaze, I noticed his long limbs were still relaxed against the couch, but I had been right about the knowing smirk playing on his lips. He eyed me quietly for a few moments more, searching for something. It took every ounce of will I had not to wither beneath his gaze.

Eventually, he sat upright and set his water bottle down on the table decisively. "Alright, let's check it out."

Only a little too eagerly, I jumped up off my own couch and tucked my phone into my back pocket. I never told Olympus this—and they'd probably never thought to ask, given how *highly recommended* I came—but this would be my first time side stage at a concert, and every single one of my nerve endings hummed.

Peter opened the door and led me through a maze of passages toward the stage, the din of the crowd outside growing louder and louder with each step.

Random people passed by us in a blur—sound techs and engineers and various other industry experts, I guessed, working overtime to bring this show to life.

One of those people stopped to latch onto Peter, grasping one of his thick arms to grab his attention in the organized chaos. Peter waved me on, holding up a finger to signal, *one moment, please*, while he faced the tech beside him.

The humidity hit me like a wall when I reached the opening to the side of the stage. It was the tail end of August and the East Coast was experiencing one of those intense, late summer heat waves. The combination of the sun's early evening angle, the crush of bodies in the audience, and the nearby ocean made it feel like noon in July.

My jaw fell open when my eyes found the audience.

Seeing fifteen thousand people packed into an amphitheater was a totally different experience than imagining it.

The roar of voices carried across the open air, mashing together in a kind of song. There was something thrilling about being able to see all these people, nearly hear their conversations drifting on the merciful evening breeze, and know they couldn't see me.

Ezra wasn't exaggerating earlier—even tucked away beside the stage, I could hear the crashing of waves and the calls of the gulls flying overhead in search of their next meal.

Just thinking about him summoned the scent of citrus and sandalwood to my nostrils, and I inhaled deeply, letting my eyes close for a moment so my other senses could take control. The center of my chest warmed when his image flashed behind my eyelids.

"Pretty amazing, isn't it?" The sound of a silvery voice in my ears forced my eyes open, and I turned my head to see Ezra standing just behind me, mere inches separating our bodies.

I sucked in a sharp inhale, my muscles tensing at the surprise. Ezra only shot an encouraging smile in my direction. For all my immediate panic, his gaze disarmed me.

Offering a small smile back, I inclined my head toward the gathering crowd. "You weren't kidding earlier. This place is insane."

He chuckled lightly in agreement and the sound rang in my ears like a long-forgotten song. Without control over it, my smile widened to a grin, the corners of my eyes crinkling with amusement.

"Hey, there she is," Ezra said, drawing my attention back to him. I shot him a quizzical glance, one of my eyebrows arching in question.

"I was starting to think you forgot how to smile. You know... for real. Not one of those polite customer service things you use on us normally," Ezra joked, rocking forward to bump my arm with his.

The motion closed whatever small distance had been between us. "Next we'll work on getting a real laugh out of you."

I rolled my eyes at him but couldn't stop myself from grinning wider. "Might want to lower your expectations. Start small, like with a light chuckle?"

"Ah, yes, of course. Maybe a soft chortle?" he shot back in mock seriousness, scratching his chin with two fingers as though deep in thought. This time I did laugh loudly, the sound coming out like more of a snort. I quickly covered my mouth with a hand trying in vain to stifle the noise.

"Hey, progress!" Ezra shouted approvingly, earning another playful eye roll from me.

We stood so close that every slight movement from either of us caused our hips to bump together. I could practically feel his breath against my cheek on every exhale.

Ezra noticed our proximity at the same time I did and his lips parted slightly to speak, then closed again.

Instead, he reached a hand up to brush a few stray strands of his dark hair away from his face, his amber eyes boring into mine from behind a sultry gaze. Nervously, I bit down on my bottom lip and drew part of it into my mouth. Big mistake. His eyes immediately shot down to my lips, the amber in his irises becoming pure, molten heat.

He looked... he looked like he wanted to kiss me.

But that couldn't be right.

My heart fluttered in my chest and a shiver raked its way up my spine, the muscles deep in my core clenching. I felt myself leaning toward him, just a half an inch, my body operating completely on autopilot.

Noticing the small movement drawing us even closer, Ezra's eyes shot back up to mine, the look in them both slightly surprised and a little reckless, too. It made my toes curl in my sneakers.

Ezra reached a hand up to gently brush his fingertips against my cheek. So slowly, he continued trailing them up the curve of my cheekbone to tuck a loose piece of hair behind my ear. He paused there—his broad hand stretching to cup my jaw.

A breathy sound escaped my lips at the pulsing heat of his hand against my flushed cheek, the sound lost to the whipping sea air surrounding us.

"There you guys are!" a booming voice barreled into us, immediately breaking the spell we'd cast.

Peter.

Ezra dropped my jaw like it had burned him, shoving his hand into his pocket and taking a step back from me in the same movement. I was struck with a feeling of relief mixed with... disappointment?

That couldn't be right either.

I *didn't* want Ezra to kiss me—it would complicate everything and make my job that much harder.

I'd seen him with those women earlier—the way he managed to flirt with every single one of them without even trying, without ever learning their names or memorizing their faces.

No, this was good. I should thank Peter for the interruption.

"Lucid Dreams is going on now, we've got about forty minutes until we're expected in the staging area," Peter said mostly to Ezra when he reached us.

"Got it. I've just got to check on one thing quick with Zach, but I'll meet you there," Ezra replied, forcing a smile at his bandmate.

Most of the heat had left his eyes, the irises cooling to their typical dark hue. His smile didn't reach them. He clapped Peter firmly on his shoulder in both greeting and farewell, then strode off into the labyrinth I'd just come through not ten minutes earlier.

Peter watched Ezra take a few steps, only turning to me when he disappeared around a corner.

"So... what was that all about?" Peter asked quietly, forcing a casual tone that didn't quite take.

My gaze snapped up to his face, my expression a mix of question and... fear. Fear about what Peter saw. Or, more appropriately, what he *thought* he saw. What he might say to other people.

"We were just talking about the amphitheater—Ezra said it's one of his favorite places to perform," I replied, careful not to let my voice climb too high or sound too defensive. I turned my attention back to the crowd in front of us to emphasize my point.

It was true, if only partially.

"Really?" Peter asked, skeptical.

I kept my eyes on the crowd, afraid of what I might give away if I faced him.

"It's just pretty crazy that you were able to talk about the venue while staring so *deeply* into each other's eyes. You guys must have superpowers or something."

At the mocking tone, I couldn't help but roll my eyes. I crossed my arms over my chest and turned back to Peter.

Oh great, his smirk was back.

"It's called peripheral vision, Peter. Google it," I replied defiantly, inclining my chin.

Peter cackled loudly in response, the sound booming around me despite the cacophony of noises coming from the crowd. It made my muscles unclench, my body easing out of fight-or-flight mode.

Peter replied after he was done laughing, "Ah, right. My mistake." He coughed once into his fist and then dropped his hand to his side, his expression turning serious. Well, serious for Peter.

"In that case, I'll just say one thing—be careful around *the venue*. It truly is a great *venue*, but it can be... temperamental. While it may look one way on the surface... well, it's got a pretty robust past, some of it not so pretty."

The slight pauses and stumbles as he found the right words mixed with a kind of boyish earnestness in his eyes. I knew his intent was good, his words were genuine.

"That sounded a lot like three things," I whispered, trying to make it sound like a joke. It fell flat.

Before Peter could respond, the stage lights dimmed and Lucid Dreams made their entrance from the opposite side, drawing my attention.

Within moments, the sound of guitar riffs and pulsing drum beats overtook the roar of the crowd. I watched in awe, immediately forgetting my awkward conversation with Peter in the rush of excitement at seeing the band play from so close.

While I stood transfixed by the moving melodies coming from center stage, l felt a gentle squeeze on my shoulder and looked back to see Peter leaning in close to my ear. "Just think about what I said, okay?"

Despite our closeness, he had to practically shout the words so I could hear them over the music, but the message landed.

I paused for a few moments to sort my thoughts out, unsure how to respond. While I considered, I could feel an empty space growing behind me as Peter left to find his bandmates.

Chapter 7

The pulsing beat of amplified rock music reverberated throughout the entire amphitheater as I struggled to hold my balance from my hidden corner on the side stage. Olympus had taken the stage minutes before and were about halfway through their second song, but sweat already beaded along my forehead. Despite the absence of bright overhead sun, the August heat and humidity from the water behind us pressed down on me like a weight.

I'd been hiding out on the side stage since Lucid Dreams walked on for their set. Because it was a great location to watch the show and secretly capture stills and videos on my phone. Definitely not because I was avoiding Ezra and Peter after our earlier encounter.

With the help of some production assistants who found me struggling to get closer to the performers without walking in front of them, I found a hidden passage that linked the left and right sides of the stage to provide discreet transport back and forth, giving me unparalleled access from shadowy alcoves on either side.

Seeing Lucid Dreams perform from such a short distance away had been a mind-blowing experience. I felt the music in my bones more than I heard it as it pulsed through the floorboards beneath my sneakered feet. I made a mental note to find the band after the show, if just to tell them how amazing they'd been.

As much as I loved them, it was nothing compared to seeing Olympus live.

Though I'd never tell the guys this, I'd been to at least five of their shows before landing this job. After all, they were one of my top three bands of all time. But seeing them this close, where I had a perfect view of the sweat beading on their skin, could see Ezra's chest rise and fall as he inhaled between verses, was another level entirely.

I bit down on my lip hard, trying my best to avoid focusing on Ezra too much... but resistance was futile when he was on stage. It always had been.

The grace with which his lithe body moved to the rhythm of each song. The way his mouth widened and his eyes closed while his voice climbed up and down the octaves. The way his slender fingers elegantly cradled the microphone to his lips.

It felt... intimate. Each roll of his hips, seductive. Every movement timed perfectly to the music. Heat pooled in my cheeks, my chest, my core as I watched him. He knew exactly what he was doing—the embodiment of a rockstar.

From the very first song, the crowd was electrified.

I had to capture their energy.

As the guys crescendoed through the fifth song on their setlist, I carefully inched my way out to my new favorite spot near center stage where I could remain mostly hidden from the audience behind a grouping of speakers if I crouched down.

From my hideaway, I braced my forearms against my knees for support and pressed record on my camera app. The stabilizer locked around my phone had to work overtime to prevent the vibrations in my arms and legs from ruining the video as I panned out over the first few rows of fans.

They screamed every single lyric back to me in perfect unison. I couldn't hear them from my position on stage, the phone's mic only picking up the pounding rhythm of Olympus to my immediate left, but it didn't matter.

When the next song started up, I closed out of my camera app and prepared to carefully crabwalk my way back to the safety of the side stage, but as I turned, my eyes caught on Peter and Angel and I stopped dead in my tracks.

Even through their concentration, their faces were lit with pure joy as they played, heads bobbing to their shared tempo, eyes dancing with the thrill of performing in front of a live audience again. *This* was what their fans wanted to see. I had to capture this.

Inhaling a determined breath, I steadied the wild beating of my heart then made my move.

Being the closest one to me, I slithered shyly up to Peter first. Though I stayed out of his way as much as I could, I caught his eye as I stepped into his peripheral vision, and—all remnants of our tense conversation from earlier were gone. He grinned broadly in my direction, the smile lighting up his handsome face, even under the dancing stage lights.

I breathed a sigh of relief, my confidence building as I captured a close-up video of his nimble fingers flying across the frets of his bass, each one of them effortlessly creating a driving undercurrent for the melody.

While I stood there, mere inches from Peter-Freaking-Campbell, bass guitarist for my favorite freaking band, I fought the urge to pinch myself.

Peter winked at me when I waved him my thanks for indulging my close-ups, and then I was on the move again.

I picked my way carefully around the stage, stopping briefly at Angel first. If Peter's bass playing formed the driving undercurrent to the raging river of Olympus's song, then Angel created the bedrock foundation that kept everyone in line. I watched in awe as his foot stamped in time to the boom of the bass drum, the heavy sound resonating against the snapping of the snares. He made it look easy, his head thrown back in a breathless laugh when he caught me filming him. Angel may have been here to do a job, but it was clear drumming was a passion for him, an outlet for his pent-up energy.

I had to cross the hidden passageway behind the stage to pop up beside Zach on lead guitar next.

Unlike the two showboats before him, Zach smiled shyly at me as I crouched beside him for a close-up view of his guitar. He truly was a gifted musician. Like Angel, Zach made every note, every chord look effortless—the way his fingers flew across the frets maniacally, but the rest of his body remained loose and still.

I didn't realize I was grinning like a madwoman until I caught a quick glimpse of my reflection on my phone screen. My cheeks and jaw ached, the muscles in my legs spasming from being crouched for so long, but I didn't care. It would be worth it to post these videos. To set myself apart as more than just a newbie at Rabbit's Foot.

A sudden roar of high-pitched screams filled my ears, drawing my attention to the front of the stage... where I was greeted by the toned, bare back of Olympus's frontman.

I knew he often removed his shirt while performing—had tried to prepare myself for it in advance. But nothing compared to the raw sight of the powerful muscles of his back and arms flexing as he cradled the microphone stand to his body.

His bare skin glistened with sweat, droplets tracing patterns on his back that were almost as intricate as the tattooed surface beneath them. It was hard to make them out completely from my vantage point, but the theme was clearly nautical—a small cluster of towering palms protruding from a sandy surface set within a body of water, a sun descending toward the horizon on his skin, and a lighthouse far off in the distance.

It wasn't like I'd studied them on Google Images before or anything.

Too many seconds passed before I realized I was gaping at Ezra while he sang—was it just a coincidence that he now belted out one of my absolute favorite songs, all while the ladies in the crowd screamed and writhed before him? *For* him.

Struggling to regain my composure, I snapped my jaw shut and turned back to Zach, praying he was too focused on playing to have noticed my stare. If he had caught anything, he didn't let on, his eyes instead cast down at his guitar as he strummed through a particularly tricky riff.

At least it hadn't been Peter.

· ♥ · ♥ · ♥ · ♥ · ♥ ·

By the time the show was over my legs burned from crouching for so long and thick beads of sweat dripped from every pore in my body.

More than once, I could've sworn I caught Ezra watching me while he sang, his eyes seeming to follow me from spot to spot like a portrait in a haunted mansion.

I probably imagined it.

Anxiously, I waited backstage for the final lights to dim out front, my eyes locked straight ahead on the small passageway I knew Olympus would walk through at any moment. Finally, the four of them stepped out of the darkness, arms thrown around one another's shoulders, broad grins stretched across their bright and shiny faces.

Seeing the happiness in their eyes, in their body language, my own lips curved upwards and parted to exhale a breathless laugh.

"That will seriously never get old—never!" Peter's booming voice carried over the noise of the crowd still reeling in the amphitheater behind them.

"You know what *has* gotten old? You missing the second entrance in 'Patterns' because you're too busy showboating around with Ezra," Zach said from beside him, his tone more playful than accusatory as he referenced a song they'd played about halfway through their set.

"Ehh you're just jealous of my sweet moves. Plus, nobody noticed! That crowd was electric," Peter replied swiftly, curling his bulging bicep more tightly around Zach's head, pulling him in to press a sloppy kiss to his temple.

All four of them laughed boisterously, Zach rolling his eyes in what could only be called brotherly love as he shook Peter's arm off.

Then the weight of eight eyes settled on me in unison.

"Well... what'd you think?" Ezra asked, his tone quiet, reserved. He tucked his hands into his pockets and sucked his full bottom lip into his mouth.

In my excitement, I'd almost forgotten he didn't know I was a fan.

I wanted to play coy, tease him, especially after our earlier encounter, but I couldn't muster up anything other than, "Amazing. You guys were amazing."

"No lie? You're not just saying that?" Peter pressed, cocking an eyebrow as he folded his large arms over his chest, his muscles straining at the tight fabric of his plain black T-shirt.

"I swear on your... bass guitar—"

Peter cut in quickly, "Woah, bringing Sally into this, eh? She must be serious." He took two sidelong glances at the friends around him, who nodded unanimously in response.

"Come on, let's get moving. This old man needs beauty sleep," Ezra joked at his own expense with a smile, unlinking his arms from the shoulders of his bandmates to fall into step beside me.

I kept my gaze ahead while we walked, trying to ignore the heat coming from my left side. When we turned a corner, I noticed the three members of Lucid Dreams still wearing their stage attire while they helped pack up some of their things. I halted my steps down the passageway, eyeing them up.

Would it be weird if I walked up to them and said something?

They'd been so incredible, I had to tell them. Would they be annoyed if I just aimlessly fangirled after such a long day, though?

Ezra felt my pause and stopped, angling his body to look at me. Following my gaze with his eyes, realization sunk in and one corner of his lips turned up. "You want me to introduce you?"

I turned to look up at him—he was so tall—and he cocked an eyebrow. The rest of Olympus had already sidestepped us and continued on to finish their night.

Offering him a polite half-smile, I nodded. "That would be great, actually. Thanks."

Ezra gently grasped the crook of my elbow, leading me to where Lucid Dreams stood chatting amongst themselves.

"Hey, Marina—" he started, turning to one of them—the singer and lead guitarist if I wasn't mistaken. "Jess—" his head tilted to nod at who I thought was the drummer. "Kat—" he nodded once more at the bassist. "Great show tonight." I knew he was saying their names solely for my benefit.

All three women smiled back at him, pausing what they'd been packing to greet us.

Ezra added, "This is Hannah, she's... she works with us."

I offered a small wave to the women standing before me, trying not to pick up on Ezra's slight stumble when introducing me. *Was he thinking about Camila?*

I brushed off the thought, unwilling to let it ruin this moment. "I just had to say, you all were amazing. That last song? Hearing it live was a life-changing experience."

Marina let out a soft, tinkling laugh that floated through the air like a spring breeze, all three women beaming graciously back at me.

We talked to the trio for a few more minutes before we had to bid them goodbye or risk a riot from the staging and production teams still flitting around us, eager to get home. First about their set—Marina promised to get me a copy of their setlist before the next show. Then about their merch—I was already eyeing up at least two shirts and a can koozie.

Afterward, Ezra led me back through the labyrinth of hallways toward the Olympus green room, his gait relaxed and smooth despite the late hour and the exertion of his live performance.

"Don't let me leave here without grabbing some merch from their table," I said to him as we walked slowly through the near-empty hallways.

Ezra chuckled beside me, his hands slung casually in his pockets. "I'm sure they're about cleaned up for the evening..." He glanced sidelong at me just in time to see a disappointed frown twist my lips. "But maybe we can stop by tomorrow before showtime and you can have your pick?"

My frown immediately became a small, appreciative smile and I nodded right as we reached the door to Olympus's—*our*—green room. As Ezra opened the door, sounds of laughter and excited chatter from three booming male voices filled my ears. I had to look down at my feet to hide my own widening grin and the laughter threatening to bubble up.

The amphitheater felt oddly quiet as I followed the passageways that led to the exit, my footsteps sounding too loud against the concrete floor. The heavy roar of the crowd and the music from the speakers still pulsated in my ears like tinnitus, hours after the show had wrapped.

I ended up being one of the last of our little crew to leave. Despite the chaos of four grown men talking—more like yelling—around me in the green room, I immediately plopped down on the same green couch from earlier to edit and organize the photos and videos from the show.

As the rest of my group was leaving for the night, Ezra had hovered at the door to the green room and lifted his brows and the corners of his lips in my direction. "We're going to stop at the hotel bar and grab a drink before lights out. Are you in?"

I offered a polite smile and shook my head. "Gotta get these videos edited, but thank you."

This may have been my first time touring with a band, but my instincts told me we needed to hype up this first performance as much as possible.

When I finally climbed out of an Uber at our hotel—thank you Rabbit's Foot AMEX—my eyes burned from lack of sleep and my body was heavy with exhaustion.

I stepped up to the front desk of the empty lobby, happy to find someone sitting there despite the late hour. I offered up the details of my reservation and glanced around while the front desk attendant furiously tapped against his keyboard.

The hotel itself looked a little antiquated—like the furniture still clung to memories from decades past, but in a way that felt intentional. Opulent leather armchairs clustered around wooden coffee tables were tucked into a corner of the room lined with Victorian tea rose wallpaper to form a small lounge area. A plaque on the wall above declared the hotel first opened its doors in 1941.

Well, that explains a bit.

The sound of the front desk attendant's voice snapped me back to reality. "You'll be in 304, one of our Deluxe rooms. The elevator and stairs are just around the corner to the left."

He gave me the typical hotel spiel—when breakfast would be served, where to find the ice machine, how to dial the front desk—and handed over my room key, which I was surprised to find was an actual brass key and not a keycard like the modern chains used.

As I turned to head toward the elevator, the front desk attendant reached down underneath his desk and pulled out a large brown paper bag.

"One of our other guests left this for you," he said, drawing my attention. I looked quizzically from him to the bag and back again, and the attendant merely shrugged once and pushed the unexplained package in my direction.

Too tired to ask questions, I grabbed the bag by its handles and hooked it around my elbow. It was surprisingly light given the size.

"Have a good night," the attendant said from behind me as I towed the bag and the rest of my luggage to the elevator and eventually up to my room.

The room's interior matched the décor of downstairs. A queen-sized, four-poster bed sat squarely in the middle, small wooden end tables flanking either side with matching antique lamps resting atop each one.

The dresser sat against the wall opposite the bed. It was made of the same wood as the bedside tables and topped with a massive mirror. The only modern touch to the room was a mini fridge and small coffee maker, tucked discreetly into the corner beside the dresser.

I threw my stuff and the mystery bag down onto the bed with a flourish. We'd only be here for tonight, so there was no point in unpacking. Instead, I grabbed only what I needed for the night and the next morning from my suitcase, haphazardly tossing my toiletries into the room's adjoining bathroom while I got ready for bed.

Dressed down in my pajamas—an oversized Def Leppard T-shirt I'd inherited from my mom, soft with age, and loose drawstring shorts—I sat down on the side of the bed and pulled the mysterious paper bag into my lap. Fighting the urge to shake it like a wrapped Christmas present, I tentatively peeled the slice of tape off the top that bound the bag's sides together and peered inside. It looked like... clothing?

That didn't make sense.

Tentatively, I reached my hand inside the bag and pulled out the first item on top. It was a soft, black tank top with a hot pink design on the front and... *Oh my god.*

I quickly dumped out the full contents of the bag onto my lap to confirm my suspicions and my jaw fell open.

Inside the bag was every piece of merch Lucid Dreams was selling on this tour—there had to be at least four shirts, two can koozies, and even a couple of stickers lying on top of the pile.

I stared and stared at the clothes in shock wondering where it could have come from when I spied a small piece of folded paper tucked amongst them. Gingerly, I grasped it between my thumb and forefinger, my heart already racing in my chest.

As I unfolded the piece of paper, the scent of citrus and sandalwood caressed my nose and I bit my lip, knowing immediately who this surprise was from.

I couldn't decide which one you'd like best, so I got them all.

Hope this brought another REAL smile to your face. We'll work on the laugh later.

Don't work too hard.

E

I read and reread the note at least five times until I could practically hear Ezra's voice thrumming in my ears over each word.

Gently, I dropped the note back onto the pile of merch and moved to grab my phone from where it sat charging on the bedside table. I scrolled to find the texts from—*could it really have been just that morning? It felt like a lifetime ago*—Ezra, his number still unsaved in my phone. As if that one act would be too defining. Too monumental.

`Thank you` was all I typed, pressing send before I could lose my nerve.

`Of course` came the response a few seconds later, like he'd been waiting up for my reaction.

As I placed my phone back down on the bedside table, I caught a glimpse of myself in the mirror across the room. I was smiling—a *real* smile, just like he'd wanted.

Chapter 8

Days passed in bursts of blistering afternoon sunshine and cool evenings on the road.

After the opening night in Jones Beach, the tour led us to two more stops in New York, then further north for a week traipsing through cities in Connecticut.

In a given week, Olympus typically had three shows, which meant the random days in between were used for travel, resting, and working.

For the guys, that meant rehearsing together, messing around with potential new music, and tweaking their setlists so every single show was a little bit different.

For me, it meant triple confirming hotel reservations, emailing the staff at each venue about schedules and security, and checking in daily with Annabelle about our content plan and performance reports from the road so far. Oh, and of course, everything that went into actually enacting that content plan. Each show provided me with tons of content, keeping me busy editing and scheduling posts during whatever free time I had left over.

There were some days last week when I barely left the hotel room during the day, only sneaking out at night like some sort of corporate vampire to catch the show.

Because I was busy. Definitely not because I was avoiding anyone.

Our first show after Jones Beach, I had been on edge. Every time Ezra and I were in the same room, I waited for the shoe to drop.

But it never did.

I started to wonder if he'd forgotten about his gift. I should've been relieved, but my heart tightened as the days stretched on. I realized I wanted him to bring it up. To explain why he left it for me in the first place.

Stupid.

The entire week in Connecticut was utterly uneventful. Unless you thought listening to the guys playing Call of Duty on the tour bus was exciting.

I did not.

As the tour bus carried us over highways and byways toward Rocky Hill, Connecticut—*no, wait... we were heading to Boston now* from *Rocky Hill, right?*—I holed up at the small booth across from the kitchenette. For the past three weeks, the space had become my impromptu office when we traveled. I never once actually ate a meal here, unless you counted snacks scarfed down over a paper towel while I worked.

"Emails still emailing?"

I peered over the top of my laptop to find Ezra watching me, his long body leaning casually against the tall pantry that formed the backrest for the other half of the booth. When he had abandoned his video game and crept back to where I sat, I had no idea. I hadn't been able to hear him over the sound of my furious typing.

I could still catch the sounds of the game in progress, the occasional shout from either Peter or Zach or Angel depending on the outcome. Which meant Ezra and I were alone together. For the first time in nearly two weeks.

"Oh yeah, you know. Lots of irons in the fire I have to circle back on," I joked when I realized too much time had passed after Ezra's question.

Ezra smiled at my corporate lingo quip and slid into the seat across from me, tenting his hands together on the table. I watched him for a few moments, expecting him to continue. When nearly a minute of silence passed, my eyes drifted helplessly down to my laptop screen, fingers already inching back toward the keyboard.

"I ask this with as much respect as possible," Ezra interrupted before I could settle back in. "Do you ever do anything besides work?"

I blinked. Once, twice, three times. My head cocked to one side as I narrowed my gaze at him.

"Don't get me wrong, I know how busy things are on the road," he hedged quickly, exposing his palms to me. "It's just... you're traveling the country. Or part of it, anyway. Don't you want to, I don't know, go see stuff?"

Taking a moment to consider it, I chewed on my bottom lip and shrugged. "I mean, yeah I'd love to get out there more. It's just tough with a stacked schedule."

Ezra nodded and said, "Well, good news. We've got a few free days coming up in Boston—"

He saw me opening my mouth to deflect and held up one long index finger to keep me quiet.

"No excuses. If you don't have enough pictures or videos or Tic-Tacs by now—" he waved a hand wildly through the air, "I don't think you ever will. Take a break. Live a little."

His eyes danced in the natural light coming in from the window beside us, a small, knowing smile playing on his lips. I had to pull my lips into my mouth to keep from laughing at his blatant mispronunciation of TikTok, to hide the smile threatening to break across my face.

Instead, I nodded and tapped a key on my laptop to close down the email I had open.

"I can't make any promises. But I will try."

"Han, you can't just sit around in your room all day. You're traveling the country on essentially an all-expenses paid vacation. Get out there and live a little," Liv's voice echoed in my ear, my phone pressed tightly against it by my shoulder as she repeated the same words Ezra had spoken to me the afternoon before.

I had to strain to hear her—the reception in this Boston hotel was terrible, and she sounded a bit like she was at the bottom of a well. Still, her message hit home.

I sat on the edge of the unmade bed in my hotel room, elbows resting on the tops of my thighs, and stared out at the view of the city from my window.

"You're in freaking Boston. Go do some touristy things!" Liv continued as if she knew where my eyes were focused.

I *had* somehow gotten caught up on all of my work on the bus ride the day before. My inbox was at zero—an unprecedented feat since my start at Rabbit's Foot. Yesterday, Olympus had killed it at their first and last show in Massachusetts for this tour, and we weren't due at our next stop in Rochester until Monday when the guys would do a couple of Zoom interviews about the tour thus far followed by a show that night.

That left me with a wide-open schedule for the day before we were on the road again bright and early tomorrow.

"You know what? You're right. I am going to go out and be a full-blown tourist while I'm here," I said, determination I only half felt in my voice.

"That's the spirit!" Liv cheered from the other end of the line. "Okay, I've got to run—meeting with Bruce in ten minutes. Love you, bye!"

The line crackled then went dead. I put my phone down on the bed beside me and pulled my laptop onto my thighs from where it had been asleep in my bag on the floor.

The reception may have been terrible, but the free hotel Wi-Fi worked surprisingly well. The screen cast my face in a sea of light and shadow when I opened up a Chrome browser tab, typed in a search for "Boston things to do" and pressed enter.

My quick Google search offered a plethora of ideas, but with just over twenty-four hours left in the city, I had to be picky. After a few minutes of deliberation, I settled on a walking tour led by a Benjamin Franklin impersonator at ten, a stop at the famous *Cheers* bar on Beacon Street immediately after, and a quick tour of the

Samuel Adams Boston Brewery to round out the day. I'd return to the hotel afterward for dinner in their restaurant.

It was already after nine, which gave me under an hour to cross town to the tour meeting spot.

"She lives!" A booming voice echoed from across the hotel lounge when I exited the elevator on the ground level. My head swiveled on my shoulders to find the source and landed on a collection of early-thirties males sprawled comfortably across a few couches. From the center of that group, Peter Campbell waved a muscled arm lazily at me, a goading grin plastered on his lips.

Crap. I'd hoped to exit the hotel unseen, but no such luck.

I shifted my eyes covertly down to my watch then back up. I was down to just over thirty minutes to make it to the tour on time. Forcing a smile to my lips, I reluctantly made my way to where Peter, Zach, Angel, and Ezra sat.

"We were starting to get a little worried about you, squirreled away in that hotel room all day," Peter teased.

Great, now him?

"Oh, you know. Annabelle's been keeping me busy," I hedged, waving off his words. "But actually since you brought it up, I'm on my way out now to do some touristy things."

None of the guys said anything, but all four sets of eyebrows arched in my direction. Ezra inclined his head.

"Right, um, the first stop is a Revolutionary walking tour through the city, led by none other than Ben Franklin himself. Then a stop at the *Cheers* bar, you know, where everybody knows your name. And last, but certainly not least, a tour of the Sam Adams brewery." At some point during the spiel, my voice took on the tone of an infomercial salesman, earning a few smiles and chuckles from the band in front of me.

"Anybody interested in joining me?" I added, mostly as a joke, before I could stop the words from coming out of my mouth.

Peter, Zach, and Angel all took turns looking away, staring at the floor, the ceiling, the walls, basically anything that wasn't me.

As expected.

Surprisingly Ezra answered, "Yeah, I'd love to tag along if that's cool."

My mouth fell open and it took every ounce of client services training I'd undergone in my career to regain my composure. "Really?"

"Yeah, why not? We're in Boston with nothing on our itinerary." Ezra shrugged casually and looked around at the rest of the guys, who were now also gaping at him.

"Oh. Yeah, okay. Cool," I said, feeling anything but. "The tour starts in thirty minutes, so we'll have to hustle."

My insides felt like a volcano ready to erupt. This would be our first time alone together since walking the halls of the amphitheater that night in Jones Beach. The night we never talked about again.

"Let's do it!" Ezra stood up from the couch with a flourish and stepped around the end tables to join me. For a moment, it looked like he was going to offer me his arm, then decided against it, instead shoving his hands into his pockets.

In a truly unexpected twist of events, the two of us spent the entire day together. Alone.

What I thought would have been a day riddled with awkward silences and tension turned into one of the best days I'd had in a while.

He cracked just the right amount of jokes during our walking tour to come across as charming. Maybe it was thanks to the blacked-out Ray Bans he wore the entire time, or maybe we'd simply gotten lucky that the Sunday morning crowd had consisted primarily of octogenarians and young families, but not a single soul recognized him. Not even Ben Franklin.

I was pleasantly surprised to find he'd seen a few episodes of the television show *Cheers*, because when we arrived at the landmark bar and restaurant he shouted, *"Pour me a beer, Sam!"* The show had been a favorite of my mom's and I'd been forced to watch it against my will so many times I eventually started to enjoy it.

After offering the slightly confused bartender, who was most definitely not named Sam, a sheepish smile, Ezra and I stayed just long enough to enjoy one beer each at the crowded bar before hopping into an Uber to our tour at Sam Adams, arriving just five minutes before our ticket time.

"You ready to taste some brewskis?!" Ezra asked enthusiastically from my side as we stepped out of our Uber in front of the large brick building that housed the Boston brewery. He clapped his hands together, rubbing them back and forth eagerly as he took in the massive structure before us from behind his sunglasses.

"Okay new rule, you can never say the word 'brewski' again." I cringed in his direction, wrinkling my nose as we approached the entrance side by side.

Ezra tossed his head back in a roaring laugh, his shaggy dark hair cascading over his toned shoulders. Although I rolled my eyes in response, I smiled, my gaze lingering on the soft curve of his full lips and the way the corners of his eyes crinkled with amusement.

Pulling himself together, he shot me a sidelong glance and said, "You know, you make an awful lot of rules."

"Well, I wouldn't have to if you weren't so ridiculous *all the time*," I shot back, the retort rolling off my tongue before I could think better of it. *Must still be buzzed from that beer.*

"Fair enough," Ezra said sheepishly, palms raised until he was distracted from our conversation by something much bigger. Literally.

"Oh, take a picture of me in front of it!"

A giant wooden barrel that had to be taller than two men stacked one on top of the other was built into one side of the building, emblazoned with the Sam Adams logo and an advertisement for their tours. Brushing right past the entrance, Ezra bounced over to stand beneath it, lifting his arms to the nearly cloudless sky above.

"Make it look like I'm holding the barrel up," he commanded and twisted his face into a goofy smile.

Holding back a snicker, I did as requested, standing back far enough so, at the correct angle, it looked like Ezra was supporting the full weight of the barrel above him. I snapped a few photos on my phone, then tucked it away in the back pocket of my jeans before striding up to join him at the brewery entrance.

"Those are definitely going on the band's official Instagram account," I joked, wiggling my eyebrows comically.

"No way! Those are all mine, I call dibs," Ezra argued, moving sideways to bump his hip against mine. My side warmed at the touch. "Text them to me."

I pulled out my phone to do just that then stopped, replying, "Later, we have to get inside or we'll miss the tour."

"Wait! Don't you want a picture with the barrel?"

I hesitated. Something about the idea of Ezra taking my photo made my stomach flip, and my mouth run dry.

"*Why yes, Ezra. I would love a picture*," he said for me in a high-pitched voice, tugging on the sleeve of my shirt to place me in front of the barrel against my will with one hand and wrestling my phone out of my hands with the other.

I didn't put up much of a fight.

"Say 'Ezra is the best singer ever and a musical genius and a gift to the modern era of rock,'" he crooned as he angled my phone for the picture, and I laughed. A real, full belly laugh, like one I hadn't felt in... I couldn't remember how long.

Ezra snapped what had to be at least two dozen photos while I cackled, a soft summer breeze gently tossing tendrils of my wavy hair through the air. I stopped laughing long enough to smile and pose for at least one real photo, and then Ezra was walking slowly back toward me, his eyes focused down on the phone screen in his palms. He stared at it quietly for a few moments, his lips twitching upwards, and my stomach flipped again.

Tentatively, I extended a hand for my phone and said, "Come on, we're going to be late."

Ezra shook his head, clearing his thoughts, and handed my phone over, the screen still open to what he'd been staring at. As I followed him into the brewery's front entrance to join our tour, I looked down to see the photo on the screen, one of the dozen he'd taken while I laughed.

In it, my cheeks were flushed, my smile wide and genuine, my hair gently brushed back from my temples by the breeze. It was a photo, not of someone who spent their evenings writing reports and conducting market research, but of someone who knew how to laugh, how to have fun, how to get the most out of life.

Something inside me cracked open just a little as I stared down at that photo, completely missing whatever introduction our guide offered the group huddled inside the brewery entrance. A small seedling taking root in a barren land.

The two of us spoke in hushed whispers and breathless laughs as the hour-long tour wound us and a group of five others through the brew house, careful to keep our voices low so as not to interrupt our guide as he told us all about the brewing process at every step.

Despite the rule I set before starting the tour, Ezra managed to squeeze the word "brewski" into *at least* seventy-five percent of our conversation.

By the time the tour ended, my head and body felt lighter than it had in years. Due, in no small part to the three beers we tasted along the way.

But it wasn't just the beer that had me buzzed.

No, I would've felt this way stone-cold sober.

During that one-hour tour, I started to realize that was the effect Ezra had. On me, on everyone he encountered.

His carefree energy was infectious.

Being with him made me temporarily forget who we were, that we were here in Boston for any reason other than to spend time in one another's company. I forgot about my job, and why I absolutely, positively could not fall for this guy. Why it was dangerous to even be spending time alone with him.

Every moment that passed between us, I lost more and more of my sense and reason.

It felt *good*.

The sun had sunk lower in the cloudless, early evening sky by the time our guide left us to our own devices in the tasting room. Delaying our inevitable parting when we returned to the hotel, Ezra convinced me to stay a little longer at the brewery to enjoy one more pint glass.

He swiveled back and forth on the barstool beside mine, slowly sipping from his lager, stretching out time at this last stop on our adventure whether he meant to or not.

"This was fun."

I looked up from my own pint glass, which had just two fingers' worth of amber beer still in it, and smiled warmly at him. I may have been drinking slower than usual.

"It was."

"Great thing I suggested it, right?"

My eyebrows arched so high on my forehead they nearly kissed my hairline, my mouth twisting to one side. "I'm sorry, *you* suggested? Ezra, I planned this entire day."

He set his pint glass down on the bar top and turned his stool around so he was facing me fully, then reached out a finger to gently nudge my eyebrows back down into their normal place.

I scowled instead, trying to ignore the electric shock that coursed through my entire body at his touch.

"Sure, you planned the activities. But if I hadn't goaded you into giving up work for one day, we never would've ended up here," he explained, folding his arms over his chest decisively. "*My* idea."

I rolled my eyes but decided not to argue. After all, he had a point.

•♥•♥•♥•♥•♥•

"Guys, come on!" Ezra crowed from where he sat cross-legged on the floor of the tour bus, his bandmates and myself crowded around him on the couches. He'd traded in the dark wash skinny jeans and white striped, V-neck shirt that showed off his tattoos from earlier for his typical ensemble of a loose cutoff tank top and moss green joggers.

"We're halfway through this tour, we've played eight killer shows so far, and we don't have to leave for Rochester until Tuesday."

It was Sunday evening and Ezra had pulled us all from our respective hotel rooms for a "family meeting" in the bus, which turned out to be a ploy to get us to go out for drinks in the city before we had to leave.

The beers from earlier must be clouding his judgment, I thought to myself.

"How many beers did you have at that brewery, dude?" Zach asked, reading my mind.

"No, come on—no. For your information, my head has *never* felt clearer. But that's beside the point." Ezra kicked his legs out in front of him and stretched back to rest on his hands. The pose accentuated his defined triceps, and without meaning to my eyes began tracing the lines of toned muscle and tattooed skin on display.

"Well it's actually been nine shows, so sorry if I don't trust your judgment," Zach shot back, a ghost of a smirk on his lips.

"Nine? All the more reason we need to *get out*!" Ezra recovered quickly, his eyes dancing between everyone else huddled in the bus interior. "The point is, we've been busting our asses for the last three weeks and it's time to cut loose."

"Hey man, I'm in. Let's do it!" Angel grinned from across the bus, drumming his hands on his thighs.

"Yeah, what the hell? I'm in, too," Peter said, standing up from beside Angel and stretching his thick arms overhead. "Just give me some time to go back in and change."

"Oh yeah, gotta make sure you gel your hair just right for the ladies," Angel said to him with a wink. Peter just rolled his eyes and turned toward the couch where Zach and I were huddled, eyebrows arched in unspoken question.

Zach shot a final pleading look in my direction, but I quickly turned away. My gaze immediately locked with Ezra's instead. He made his dark eyes appear doe-like, his full lips just the right amount of pouted.

Out of the fire, into the frying pan.

"Are you in, Han?"

I paused, biting down on my bottom lip as I weighed my options.

On one hand, exploring the city that day had been some of the most fun I'd had in months. Maybe longer.

But on the other hand, I knew I shouldn't be getting this close to the guys. We were coworkers, not friends. This was my job, not a frat house.

Coworkers go out for drinks together.

Hush up.

I must've been taking too long to respond because suddenly Ezra shot forward so he sat on his knees in front of me, hands clasped together like he was begging at the feet of a king. Or a queen.

"Come on, Han... please? For me?"

My cheeks heated at the sight of him kneeling before me, the darker recesses of my mind imagining a similar scenario where the bus was empty except for the two of us. One where he was begging for an entirely different reason.

Through sheer willpower, I pressed the thoughts away and turned back to Zach, pasting an apologetic look on my face. "I think we're outnumbered. And if you can't beat 'em..."

"YES!" Ezra shouted triumphantly and shot to his feet, his six-foot-three frame towering over me in such close proximity. He wrapped his long, toned arms around me, pulling me in for an embrace.

My senses overloaded with the scent of him as my head crashed against Ezra's hard chest. The skin not covered by his loose-fitting tank top was warm, almost fiery, where it pressed against my cheek.

I forced myself to look up at him but the movement only made my chin rest against his pecs. I felt myself slowly smiling up at him, that same airiness from the brewery tour returning to my head, my muscles, my bones.

He grinned widely down at me and from this angle, with his slender hands pressed into the small of my back, I felt something snap between us.

The pad of his thumb began tracing small circles on my back and a wicked feeling stirred low in my core then radiated further down, turning my legs to liquid.

Ezra tilted his head down slightly and a piece of his dark hair fell loosely against his temple. I had to fight the urge to brush it behind his ear as I took in every inch of his beautiful face. My eyes betrayed me, blinking down toward his full lips as though drawn by a magnetic force.

My heart nearly stopped when I noticed how close they were to mine.

The same thought must've crossed Ezra's mind, because his gaze slowly trailed down my cheekbones, my jawline, eventually landing on my mouth. In that moment, all of time and space seemed to stop around us. Challenge lit behind his eyes, his piercing stare pinning me to the spot.

"Dude—" voices swirled around us, but they were muffled. Like I was trapped underwater, but the feeling wasn't suffocating. No, it felt warm and freeing.

I don't know how long Ezra and I held each other, locked in an embrace that was way more than friendly. It could've been seconds or hours.

"Hey, are you guys coming?" Peter's voice finally broke our trance and I jumped back, pinning my hands down at my sides like I'd been doused in cold water.

How long had Peter been standing beside us? What had he seen?

I turned sideways, my eyes cast down to the floor of the tour bus to avoid looking at either man. Willing the heat in my face to subside, I inhaled a deep breath and tucked a loose strand of hair behind my ear. I said nothing.

"Yeah, sure. We're right behind you," Ezra answered softly from beside me instead. I could feel his eyes burning holes in my flushed skin, but I refused to make eye contact with him again, afraid of what I might find there. Of what might happen.

Instead, I watched Peter, Zach, and Angel walk down the steps of the bus to head into the hotel, still carefully avoiding Ezra's gaze.

He waited a few more moments for me, still staring in my direction with parted lips as if he wanted to say something but couldn't form the words. After the silence stretched between us, he gave up and climbed down the bus steps himself to trail his friends, leaving me alone with my thoughts.

I swore I saw a fleeting look of disappointment on his side profile as he walked away.

Chapter 9

I waited several minutes to ensure the guys were safely tucked inside the hotel before carefully picking my way down the bus steps, through the mainly deserted parking lot and to my room. My skin was still flushed, warm to the touch from Ezra's embrace, even after my slow stalk through the cool September evening air. I cranked the thermostat way down in my room, the dull rumble of the A/C unit whirring to life oddly comforting in the otherwise stuffy silence.

What was I thinking, letting Ezra get that close to me? I knew nothing good could come from it... but it was like my brain lost control of my body every time he was around.

I took a seat on the bed for a minute, now freshly made thanks to the housekeeping staff who'd quietly entered and tidied up while I was away, waiting for my heart rate to return to normal. I probably only had about twenty minutes until they'd be expecting me.

Inhale. One, two, three.

Hold. One, two, three.

Exhale. One, two, three.

I had to repeat the cycle three times before I felt somewhat recentered.

Glancing down at my phone—somehow five minutes had already passed!—I sprang up from the queen size bed and raced to the adjacent bathroom to rummage through my makeup bag.

Like the first hotel, and every other since, I hadn't fully unpacked my belongings. Didn't feel a need to, not when most stays lasted no more than one night at a time. In fact, this may have been the first hotel we'd stayed in two nights in a row.

In record time I managed a decent smokey eye using the one eyeshadow palette I'd brought with me, the areas where I'd messed up my winged eyeliner miraculously hidden by my thick, coated lashes.

Dropping the mascara tube in the sink in my rush, I darted for my suitcase where it still sat, half open on the floor in front of my bed, to dig for my favorite pair of black jeans—the ones worn in just enough to be comfortable as soon as they slip on, with frayed holes in and around the knees. I paired them with a high-necked, sleeveless black crop top.

My iPhone screen lit up after an insistent tap from me, showing the time: eighteen minutes had passed since I'd reached my room. I gave it two more minutes before every member of Olympus was pounding on my door, much to the chagrin of our temporary neighbors.

Running back to the bathroom, I slicked a dark red lipstick onto my rosebud lips, the deep color making them appear more plump and striking than usual, then tugged on my black Converse low tops.

I had to pause for a moment when I caught sight of myself in the room's full-length mirror. I was far too humble a person for self-praise, but when I saw the way the dark clothing hugged my body, the way the smokey eye and red lip pairing contrasted my fair skin, even I thought I looked pretty damn hot.

Who are you trying to look hot for?

Shut up.

As I headed for the door, I told myself I was dressing up for myself. You know, in case I met someone cute at the bar. And because I'm a professional, I needed to keep up appearances.

It was most certainly *not* for the lead singer of Olympus.

"First round's on Ezra!" Angel shouted as we entered the bar, thumping both of his hands down on Ezra's shoulders to give him one of those strange, bro-acceptable squeezes.

I hung toward the back of our group, giving myself some time to catch my bearings. I found out on the walk over that a girl Peter and Angel had met at our hotel the day before recommended this place for a casual night out. At first glance, it looked like a typical dive bar, like one of many I'd visited with Olivia during our college days.

Random photos and old posters littered the walls and the air smelled a little like spilled beer and the stale, secondhand smoke that clung to someone's clothing as they came back inside. The overhead lights were already dimmed for the evening crowd, the bar lit primarily by rainbow-colored accent lights aimed down at the shelves of bottles. As I made my way to the bar where the rest of the band was already crowded, I turned my head to the right and saw a small stage tucked back against the far wall.

I wonder what that's for. This place isn't big enough for legit performances.

I was still staring at the stage when I felt a warm presence at my left side. I turned my head just in time to find Ezra unceremoniously holding up two shot glasses in his hands and guessed one was meant for me.

"Whiskey?" he asked, confirming my suspicions. One corner of his mouth turned up while his eyes danced in the low light of the bar. Wisps of his hair fell loosely against his temples, distressed like he'd been running his hands through it. Something about the way he looked reminded me of the first time I'd seen Olympus in concert with my mom. The memory brought a smile to my lips.

Ezra caught it and assumed I was accepting his offer. His answering grin lit his handsome face.

I didn't normally shoot whiskey, but I had a feeling I'd need it to make it through this night. I inclined my head to meet his gaze, emboldened a little by the dim lighting of the bar, and reached out to take the shot glass with a casual shrug of my shoulders, "Sure, what the hell."

Our fingertips brushed as I grabbed for the glass, and I knew I wasn't the only one who felt the tingling sensation where his skin met mine when I caught Ezra breaking our eye contact to gaze at our hands.

He let his fingers linger on my glass for a few moments longer.

"Salud," I said when he finally dropped his hand, and we clinked our glasses together before downing the amber liquid in one smooth gulp. It burned the back of my throat with a welcome heat—a distraction from the unnatural warmth I felt standing in Ezra's orbit.

He winked at me then took my shot glass, making to return it to the bar right as an overhead speaker crackled to life.

"Weeeeelcome everybody to Karaoke Sunday!" a male voice boomed over the speakers drawing the entire bar's attention to the small stage across the room.

Karaoke! So that explains it.

Oh no.

I loved karaoke, but there was absolutely no way I could sing in front of my favorite band. Immediately, I felt bad for the rest of the poor suckers here tonight who had no idea they'd be watched by a group of legit, touring musicians with more than five studio albums under their belts.

"Ooooh boy, it's karaoke night!" Peter said from over my shoulder, an almost maniacal grin on his face as he eagerly clapped his hands together. His ability to sneak up on me despite his six-foot-five frame continued to amaze me.

"You think anyone will do one of ours?" Zach mused thoughtfully from beside him, taking a sip of his craft beer—a stout, judging by the near-black hue of the liquid in the low lighting.

"Oh, 100%. We are grade-A karaoke material," Ezra answered, nodding his head seriously.

Yeah, I definitely needed more booze to get through this.

I gently pushed past Peter to get the bartender's attention, tuning out the rest of their conversation to order whatever hazy IPA they had on draft. When I could finally enjoy the first drag of my beer, the bubbles and foam warming me gently from the inside, I turned around and leaned my back against the bar to take in my surroundings from a safe distance.

Back on the stage, I saw a small blonde girl who couldn't be a day over twenty-one nervously grabbing for the microphone. The opening notes of an old Taylor Swift song I recognized blasted through the speakers and I had to bite back a laugh. Not out of any disrespect to the song or the performer—I wouldn't go so far as to call myself a Swiftie, but many of her songs often found their way onto my playlists—but because of Zach's question moments ago.

Stepping forward, I placed each of my palms on Zach and Ezra's shoulders, patting them comfortingly. "Unless you guys covered a T-Swift song I don't know about, I'm guessing this isn't your crowd."

I couldn't suppress the cackle this time as it bubbled up, amused by the stricken expressions on the guys' faces.

About two and a half hours after that first performer took the stage, I found myself leaning up against an old barstool, my second beer warming in my hands. Sometime between the fourth and fifth singers, the guys and I migrated to an old pool table tucked in the back corner of the bar.

An antique stained glass pendant light suspended from the ceiling above it, casting a dull glow around the area. Ezra and Zach were currently playing each other, but each of them only had a few balls left to sink before going for the eight.

My foot tapped to the rhythm of the song playing from the stage—this time a guy who looked to be in his late twenties was crooning out a surprisingly good rendition of "Mr. Brightside."

The rotating cast of amateur singers had proven me wrong, albeit only slightly. There were a lot of Taylor Swift, Britney Spears, and Adele fans in the audience. But there'd also been plenty of heavier anthems too, including one weirdly impressive cover of Metallica's "Enter Sandman" from a timid-looking young girl that I had not seen coming.

Since arriving, Ezra had *gently* peer pressured all of us to do, not one, but two shots. I choked down one of them and knew I couldn't get through a second. Fortune shined upon me when our beautiful, curly-haired bartender saw my pleading expression and swapped out my second "shot of vodka" for water instead.

The liquor I did drink, along with the two beers I'd already finished, were casting that gooey, comfortable haze over my body and mind. I was not drunk by any means. But the easy buzz came on quickly after the beers I'd tried earlier that day at the brewery.

It felt nice. Disarming.

This entire day had felt that way. A content smile tugged on my lips as the day's events replayed in my mind. What started as another morning alone with only my thoughts and my laptop to keep me company turned into an adventure. My first in a while.

I felt a presence looming at my side and I glanced up to find Peter standing there, his eyes also focused on the stage.

He probably thought I was smiling up at the performer. *Good.*

"I guess you were right, Han," he said after a few moments, pulling his gaze from the Brandon Flowers wannabe to offer me a tight smile. "No one's going to cover us tonight."

My smile faltered. I knew he wasn't really disappointed—none of them would be. For being highly successful men in their early thirties, they were surprisingly normal. Down to earth. Even if half of them were shameless flirts.

Yet for some reason, his words hit me like a blow.

Maybe it was the alcohol fogging my brain, or the general sense of joy radiating from my bones after a genuinely great day. Whatever it was, I found myself standing up and chugging down the rest of my beer.

"Maybe we can fix that," I said to Peter, handing him my now-empty glass before trudging my way to the stage.

I had to move quickly before I lost my nerve.

Before I knew it, I stood in front of the DJ in charge of karaoke night. Truthfully, I didn't know what I'd do if there was still a huge line of people to perform ahead of me—even with the beer I'd just chugged, there was no way my false bravado could hold up that long.

Leaning in close to the DJ, I cupped my hands around my mouth to shout out the Olympus song I'd chosen on my walk over. It was one of their most popular songs to be sure, but by far the most karaoke-friendly. Not to mention I'd sung it a few times before at karaoke nights just like this one, out at the bars with Olivia and our other college friends.

The DJ nodded emphatically to me and immediately queued up the song, pointing from me to the occupied stage as he mouthed the words, "You're next."

Oh boy.

I shot one glance back toward the pool table. Peter watched me through a narrowed gaze, one eyebrow quirked high on his forehead, my empty glass still in his hand. Fortunately, it didn't look like he'd had the stroke of consciousness to clue in any of his bandmates yet.

From my vantage point, I could see Ezra and Zach were still wrapping up their game, eyes focused intently on the table in front of them. Angel leaned back against the wall behind them, talking animatedly to another male bar-goer I hadn't met.

The final chords of "Mr. Brightside" rang out in the room and I forced myself to look up at the man performing and offer my applause, trying what I could to distract myself from my nerves.

"Alright, everybody give it up one more time for Austin!" The DJ crooned into his microphone as the performer walked off the stage to a few shouts from his friends in the crowd.

"Next up, please put your hands together for Hannah!"

I whispered words of thanks under my breath that he didn't mention the name of the band or the song.

It didn't hit me until that very moment that I might be revealing myself to the guys. Olympus still had no idea I was a fan.

I couldn't blow the performance. I was too proud for that.

Maybe I could play it off—say that I'd seen them perform this song so many times on tour the past few weeks that I'd somehow mastered it... without practice.

Somehow I didn't think they'd be that stupid. I didn't think *Ezra* would be that stupid.

I walked onto the stage to the sound of polite applause, taking my place in front of the microphone just before the opening chords to the song boomed through the speakers. My hands shook as I grabbed for the microphone stand. I needed something to ground me.

Immediately, realization dawned clear as day on Peter's face from the back of the bar. The wide, boyish grin that turned up his lips and lit his emerald eyes was all the confidence I needed to carry on.

I launched straight into the first verse and it was like riding a bike. The peaks and valleys of the notes, the powerful lyrics—it all came back naturally to me as if it was just another night out back at school with Liv. "Here With Me"—it was a song from their second studio album, one I'd sung probably more than a million times to myself since it was first released eight years ago.

As the chorus crescendoed to life, I risked a glance back at the pool table. This time, Ezra and Zach had completely abandoned what was left of their game and stared up at me. Even Angel had stopped talking to his new friend, his jaw slack and his head inclined as he watched me through wide eyes.

Someone in the crowd directly in front of the stage joined in on the chorus, shouting out the lyrics as he clapped his hands together to the drum beat. My tentative half smile widened into a grin and I turned my eyes to him, silently encouraging him to keep going as much as I could.

I moved through the song, confidence building with every line, and a few more people from the crowd joined in when they knew the words. As I started on the final chorus of the song, I risked one more glance at the band in the back of the bar.

This time, they all smiled.

Peter clapped his hands together rhythmically while Angel drummed out the beat—*the one he created*—on the tops of his thighs. Even the usually stoic Zach nodded his head along, his fingers flexing as though reaching for his guitar.

Ezra—I could see the amusement dancing in his eyes from clear across the bar as he fought the urge to belt out his own lyrics. His arms were folded loosely against his stomach, his hip relaxed against the side of the pool table. His eyes never left my face, but repeatedly raked over me from my temples to my jawline—from my eyes to my lips. Waves crashed and roiled in my stomach, and it had little to do with my nerves about performing.

In what felt like an eternity and no time at all, the final chords of the song rang throughout the packed bar, and I returned the microphone to its stand as the crowd erupted into applause and cheers.

"Give it up one more time for Hannah!" The DJ's voice reverberated around us and he pressed a button to blast an air horn sound through the speakers. My cheeks were hot, my smile wide, my heart pounding when I exited the stage.

Almost immediately after I stepped into the main area of the bar, I felt a hard chest press against the side of my face and broad arms envelope my entire upper body.

"That was incredible!" Peter yelled above me and I realized he was responsible for my sudden captivity.

My face crushed even harder against his chest when more limbs and bodies pressed in around us. I was pretty sure the entire band was hugging me now.

"You absolutely killed that song." I thought that was Zach's quiet voice chiming in from somewhere behind me.

"Yeah, Han! I didn't realize you had pipes," Angel added from somewhere over my right shoulder.

"Thank you so much guys but... I'm having trouble breathing," I squeaked out from beneath the crush of their bodies.

All at once cool air rushed in against my body, into my lungs, as they released me and stepped a few feet back.

The reprieve only lasted a few seconds before Peter clapped his hand gently onto my shoulder again, his grin wide and mischievous. "It might be time for a new lead singer." He wiggled his eyebrows at Ezra and I forced myself to look squarely at the Olympus frontman for the first time since exiting the stage, bracing for his reaction.

His smile was small, but I could see where it shone brightly in his eyes, the dark amber smoldering in the dim bar. I bit my lip, anxiously waiting for him to say something. *Did he hate it? Did I just irrevocably embarrass myself in front of him? Is he weirded out that I knew the song so well?*

His eyes broke our staring contest to drift down to where my teeth tugged nervously on my bottom lip. I could've sworn I saw those eyes darken when I bit down hard.

When he finally spoke, it was to say, "It would be my honor to be replaced by someone so talented." His lips stretched wider, laugh lines wrinkling adorably at the corners of his mouth.

The guys behind me cheered and laughed, clapping each other on the back.

"I say we owe this girl a drink," Peter said from over my shoulder and immediately pressed his way toward the bar, towing me along by my hand. His towering frame and broad shoulders easily sliced us through the roaring crowd, but the center of my body felt like it was being pulled backward by a magnetic force.

I glanced back over my shoulder to see Ezra where we'd left him, still staring at me, and I knew he was the source of the tug in my gut.

·♥·♥·♥·♥·♥·

"This seat taken?" a disembodied tenor asked from over my left shoulder.

I glanced up from where I'd been staring into my warming beer to find Ezra behind me, brows lifted in question and a tentative curve on his lips. For the first forty-five minutes after my performance, I couldn't escape the claps on the back, high-fives, and side hugs—most of them from the four members of Olympus.

But eventually, they'd all once again trickled off to find their own merriment at the little dive bar. Thankful to be out of the spotlight, I'd picked out a stool on the emptier end of the bar to nurse what I knew would be my last beer of the night.

It seemed my alone time was now nearing an end though, yet I didn't mind the company.

I offered him a polite smile and gestured a hand toward the empty stool beside me, Ezra happily taking it a split second later. A companionable silence stretched between us, each of us taking small sips of our drinks in turn.

"You truly are an enigma, Hannah Maxwell. That was very impressive up there," Ezra said eventually, swiveling slightly on his bar stool to direct his knees toward me. "Really gave me a run for my money."

I laughed softly and wrinkled my nose, my knees involuntarily turning toward his until they brushed. "Yeah, right. If you got up there right now, I think everyone in this entire bar would forget I existed."

Ezra chuckled encouragingly and shook his head. "I doubt that. I certainly wouldn't."

A chill raked up my spine. "So how did you get your start, anyway?" I blurted.

His lips quirked up as he dragged his fingers through his hair, mussing up the tousled waves even further. "Funny story, actually. When I was a kid, I never even thought about a career in music. I didn't even learn to play an instrument until I was like—what? At least fourteen." He paused, glancing sidelong at me with his trademark mischievous smirk then clarified, "I wanted to be an artist."

I arched an eyebrow. "An artist?" The words came out slowly, like I was sounding them out.

Ezra nodded and said, eyes twinkling, "Yep. A painter."

"Alright then, why art?"

"Easy, my mom." He took another sip of his beer.

I furrowed my brows, willing him to continue.

"She's an artist. Has been since well before I was born. And she's not just an artist, she's... incredible. Crazy talented. I grew up watching her create the most amazing things out of nothing."

Ezra spoke with his hands, using them to enunciate every word, like simply saying them wasn't enough to convey his thoughts. I watched his expression turn wistful, his amber eyes glazing over slightly in that far-out way that told me he was knee-deep in a memory engraved deeply in his heart. The corner of my lip twitched up at the sight.

"Our house was always littered with half-started canvases, palettes of dried paints, broken-off hunks of charcoal, and just about any other artist's tool you could imagine," he continued with a grin, eyes still focused on the back of the bar. "I would sit there and watch her work for hours, mesmerized by her face as she concentrated, seeing the pure joy there when she finished a project. And I knew immediately that was how I wanted to spend the rest of my life, living in those emotions, creating them for others."

Then he leaned in closer to me, hovering his lips just inches from my ear and in a conspiratorial whisper added, "Problem was, I was a shit painter. And a terrible drawer, and a mediocre at best sculptor."

I couldn't help it, I laughed. Loudly. "I find that hard to believe."

"Oh, believe it. I was garbage. It was soul-crushing." He pouted slightly at me and laid a hand against his heart, but his eyes danced with the type of self-deprecating humor only the very well-adjusted could pull off.

I shook my head, still smiling. "Fine, so your dreams of becoming the next Van Gogh are crushed. Then what?"

"I wasn't kidding, it was devastating at first. I had all this pent-up creative energy, but there was no way I could settle for being mediocre. Not for anything," he went on. "My mom, she saw me struggling and bought me my first journal. Told me to write down everything I was feeling and then some."

"She sounds amazing," I said softly, the words leaving my mouth before I could stop them.

Ezra beamed, and the full force of that broad grin on those full lips, the tiniest hint of a dimple blooming at one corner, the way his amber eyes lightened to the color of the most expensive glass of scotch you could find, it nearly knocked me off my stool. "She is. She's totally crazy, you know—artists and all that. But she's also wise, and really good at reading people. In that moment, she knew exactly what I needed and how to help me through it."

Ezra shrugged then and took another swig of his beer, the bottle sweating into his palm as he held it.

"So I started writing. At first, it was just wild rambling about my day, all of the crazy thoughts floating around in my brain. Then it became like... lyrical poetry. I couldn't stop. I wrote in that journal all hours of the day and night, most of it trash that will never see the light of day." At this, he winked at me and I rolled my eyes good-naturedly.

"Soon I filled that journal and needed a new one. Then a new one after that." He wet his lips, then drug his teeth against the bottom one thoughtfully and I had to fight the urge to reach out and touch them. "It wasn't until I was hanging out with Zach one day, listening to him mess around on his acoustic that I realized what I'd been writing weren't poems at all. They were songs. All they needed was the right music to back them up."

I sucked in a slow breath and let it out through my nose, marveling at his story. I'd listened to interviews with Olympus over the years with vague ruminations of how the band got its start. Those interviews had none of this detail, this personal anecdote. I craved more.

Ezra returned my gaze as his trip down memory lane came to an end, a timid smile now tugging at the corner of his lips, as though he wasn't quite sure about all he had revealed to me.

I couldn't stop myself from reaching out a hand, resting it gently against his forearm for a beat. In the dim light of the bar, I thought I saw the circle of honey-gold rimming his pupil turn molten at the touch, and I forced myself to pull my hand away again.

"From there, we strong-armed Peter and Angel into joining our merry band of morons and the rest is history," Ezra said, a note of forced brightness in his tone that wasn't there before I'd let go.

·♥·♥·♥·♥·♥·

It was just after midnight when we finally left the bar, although we practically had to drag Peter out and away from a girl he'd been chatting up half the night.

"Pizza! Need. Pizza." Ezra crowed, his voice hoarse from trying to talk over the loud din of the dive bar. He threw one of his arms around my shoulders to tuck me in against his side as we crawled through the small parking lot and toward the main road at a snail's pace.

All of my limbs had that weightless feeling I typically only got after a long workout. I blamed it on the hours of standing, playing pool, and bobbing along to the music that rang throughout the bar after karaoke ended. It most definitely had nothing to do with the heat of Ezra's strong arm cradling my shoulders as we walked.

I wasn't sure when we'd become so comfortable with one another.

After my song, the drinks flowed liberally. I didn't pay for a single beer, but there was always a fresh one in my hand.

I found myself sneaking water from the very kind and *very* discreet bartender who had served us most of the night. I made sure to leave her a very nice tip on my measly two-drink tab.

We started as one big group—all of us laughing and sharing stories over our drafts. But then slowly, one by one, each of the bandmates wandered off to find their own amusement.

Peter spied a cute blonde girl sitting a few stools down from us and, with a wordless salute and a wink in my direction, made his way over to talk to her.

Angel and Zach decided to pick up a game of two-on-two pool against a couple of guys who looked to be about my age and had been running the tables all night, mumbling something about showing them who's boss.

That left Ezra and I sitting beside each other. Alone.

Despite the noise pressing in from all sides of the crowded bar—there were a few timid Olympus fans who mosied up to us here and there to ask for photos or autographs—it felt like we were the only two people there.

He regaled me with stories about past tours they'd done together across Europe and Asia. I listened in wonder as he described the different people they'd met and the experiences they'd shared along the way. Ezra and his bandmates had done nearly everything I could imagine—climbed the Great Wall of China, meditated in Thailand, rode the renowned Eye of London, and countless other adventures I'd only dreamed about.

In turn, I told him about my time in college and my best friend Olivia. Despite my stories sounding average and dull to my own ears when compared to his jet-setting around the world, he listened intently to every word, asking me thoughtful questions and making poignant observations about my life.

Before I knew it, hours had passed.

Ezra's arm tightened around me as we hobbled less than gracefully toward a pizza shop down the street that was miraculously still open at the late hour.

He and I dropped into the first open booth we saw, Angel and Peter falling in across from us. Zach, by far the most sober of our group, made his way to the counter to place our order.

A man who had to be in his early sixties bustled back and forth between the register and a large, roaring pizza oven behind him, both taking orders and helping to make them all in one fluid dance. He had dark hair and dark eyes and tanned skin, an apron dusted with flour hanging loosely over his t-shirt, which looked like it proudly displayed the name of the pizza shop—Amore's. Although his face was wrinkled and lined with age, I could tell he was once handsome. Still was, by some standards.

Even though he'd clearly been here working hard for hours, he still greeted each customer with a broad smile, chatting with each of them like they were an old friend he hadn't seen for a while.

As the older man, who I pegged as the owner of the shop, paused his dance long enough to take our order from Zach, a younger man who looked like he could've been his twin—minus forty years—stepped out from the back to bring a steamy, large pizza to a booth full of college-age guys seated in the aisle opposite us.

"I need all of that in my belly. Right now," Ezra groaned from beside me, gazing longingly at the pizza. He inhaled deeply and moaned with hunger, the sound stirring something inside of me.

Imagine if you were the one eliciting that sound from him.

I stamped down quickly on the traitorous thought.

The young man carrying the pizza deposited it carefully on the table, the guys appreciatively digging in right away, and turned around just in time to see the look of pure euphoria on Ezra's face. The server looked like he wanted to laugh, but tried hard to hold it in.

"It's okay, you can laugh at him. I do," I said to him with a lopsided grin, earning me a light-hearted jab in the ribs from Ezra's elbow.

The server smiled politely at us and looked like he was about to turn away when something lit behind his eyes. He turned and looked at Ezra more closely, searching. Ezra blinked slowly back at him.

"This is going to sound crazy but... you look just like Ezra Bell from Olympus," the server said eventually, realizing he'd been staring in silence for too long.

"You know, that's one of the least crazy things I've heard all day," Ezra replied, his sleepy smile turning mischievous. "I am Ezra Bell."

The server's mouth fell open and his eyes scanned the rest of the table, taking in Angel and Peter sitting across from us. Then Zach returned to our table and I thought I was going to witness this guy's head explode right in front of me.

"I feel like I missed something..." Zach trailed off, eyes darting between Ezra and the server.

"Wow, sorry that probably came off so weird. I'm a big fan of you guys!" the server said, trying to regain his composure. "I can't believe Olympus is here, in my pizza shop."

Understanding washed over Zach and he smiled widely back at our server, clapping him gently on the shoulder as he inclined his head to look him in the eyes. "Thanks man, it's always great to meet a fan. What's your name?"

"Tyler," the server responded, then after a moment added quietly, "Would it be possible to get, like... a picture with you guys?"

"Of course, dude!" Angel chimed in from his seat while the rest of the guys nodded reassuringly.

We all stood up from the table while Tyler pulled his phone out of his back pocket.

"Here, let me," I said to him with a smile, already reaching for it. Tyler nodded appreciatively and handed it over, already open to the camera app.

The guys lined up in a surprisingly neat row considering the booze they'd consumed, with Tyler squarely in the middle, grins wide and arms slung around one another's shoulders like they were all the best of friends.

I didn't realize I was beaming back at them until it was over.

Despite the mad frenzy that was sharing a pizza with the four members of Olympus, I managed to put back two slices and a handful of fries before the food littering our table was completely gone. Although Tyler and his dad refused to let us pay for our meal, we made sure to leave them both a very generous tip to make up for it.

With full bellies, lazy smiles on our lips, and sleep heavy in our eyes, the five of us slowly walked along the cracked sidewalk leading back to our hotel. Dawn was still a few hours off, and the night sky loomed large over our heads. The brightest stars in the sky peeked out from behind their black veil to shine down on us, even with the light pollution from the city. The leaves of small trees that lined the vacant street rustled in a cool breeze that sent a shiver up my spine.

Peter, Zach, and Angel were at least three yards ahead of where Ezra and I loped slowly side by side, drawing out each step to make the night last a little bit longer.

I knew I shouldn't allow myself to get this close to him, but there was a small part of my brain that was desperate to keep digging in.

The man I'd spent hours talking to at the bar was a far cry from the flirtatious, playboy rockstar persona I'd seen him play so well on stage.

I wanted to know more. To open up his head and peer inside. See what he thought about the world... what he thought about me.

There can never be anything between us.

"Does it ever get weird?" I blurted out to shut out my thoughts. Shut out the empty feeling pooling in my gut.

Ezra glanced at me, brows arched.

"Being approached by fans in public—does it ever get weird, knowing your life could be interrupted by a total stranger at any moment?"

Ezra lowered his brows in understanding and tilted his head back to look up at the dark, cloudless sky. He took the time to consider my question.

"Weird probably isn't the right word to describe it," he spoke at last, gaze still pointed at the constellations above. "It can be a bit of a shock sometimes, sure, but not in a bad way. We've been in this game for—what? A decade now. And I can honestly say it never gets old."

Ezra tore his gaze from the sky and turned his head to look at me fully, his steps slowing further. I slowed my pace to match, hanging onto his words.

"I don't think I could ever take that for granted. The idea that something I wrote or that we—" he waved his hand in front of him, gesturing at the fading forms of Peter, Zach, and Angel, "—dreamed up in a studio resonated so strongly with someone that they were willing to spend their hard-earned money to support us? That is the absolute coolest thing ever." Ezra's eyes sparkled as he explained, emotion lighting up his dark irises.

"But when you're out trying to live a normal life or spend time with your family, doesn't it ever feel disruptive?" I couldn't help but prod.

"Sure, it can be a little inconvenient to be recognized out in the wild when I'm not expecting it. I still forget that my face lives rent-free on the Internet." Ezra chuckled and I smiled indulgently, unable to imagine the feeling of millions of people knowing my name or face. *The way I'd known his before we'd even met*, I thought.

"But those people are the ones who matter. Being able to make that connection with them is such a... privilege," he added in a quiet voice, turning contemplative once again. "I could never turn them down for a picture, or an autograph, or whatever it takes to make them feel half as special in that moment as they make me feel every day."

Listening to him talk was more intoxicating than any of the alcohol I had that night. The man standing beside me, hip bumping mine every couple of steps, was not who I'd expected. I wet my bottom lip then tugged it gently into my mouth with my teeth, forcing myself to meet his gaze again.

It was at that moment I realized we'd stopped walking completely and stood in front of the entrance to our hotel.

"Well, when you put it like that..." I trailed off, my voice floating up into the brisk, early morning air as I tried to ignore the pull of the tightrope going taut between us.

Feeling like I needed something to fill the void, I said, "I have to admit, hearing about it all tonight, your life sounds pretty amazing. I've always wanted to travel the world, but never made it farther than

Florida." I rasped a laugh, my throat raw from talking and shouting so much to be heard over the roaring din at the dive bar. "I did almost study abroad once during college, in Spain, but never saw it through."

"Why didn't you?" The words weren't accusatory like he thought I was weak for bailing. Just genuinely curious.

"Money, for one," I answered honestly, earning a soft snort and a nod from Ezra. I turned to gaze out at the horizon just behind Ezra's shoulders. "It's always been me and my mom at home. The two of us against the world. My dad left when I was barely old enough to walk, so I've always felt like... like I'm all she has." I shrugged, then went on, "At the time, it felt hard enough to be just one state away at school. I guess I couldn't handle the thought of being across an entire ocean."

I tore my eyes away from the horizon to meet Ezra's gaze. "I always thought: what if? What if something happened, or what if she needed me and I wasn't there? I don't know, it probably sounds like a stupid excuse."

Ezra slowly reached a hand up to tuck a stray strand of my hair behind my ear and I shuddered at his touch, the way it felt like we'd been building to it after all these hours dancing around each other. "No, it doesn't sound stupid. It sounds to me like, as much as you may have wanted to travel the world, you had something else you wanted even more."

His fingertips gently grazed my ear lobe, then traced soft lines down my jaw, the movement bringing our bodies closer until there was no more than a hand's breadth separating us. "There's nothing wrong with that."

He studied my face in the dim, pre-dawn light and I fought the urge to look away. I watched his amber eyes turn molten as they traced circles over my skin, the heat in them like a physical touch. Suddenly, his eyes stopped moving when they caught me chewing on my bottom lip.

Those dark eyes became almost feral.

"Is it crazy that I want to kiss you right now?" Ezra asked softly. His hand, I noticed, was still gently cupping the place where my jaw met my ear.

If I wasn't still standing, still breathing, I'd have thought my heart stopped beating in my chest. The sound of crashing waves—or was that my blood rushing?—echoed loudly inside my head.

Do it! Let him kiss you!

No! You have to stop this. It's not real.

My mind was at war with itself.

"Crazy probably isn't the right word to describe it..." I whispered after a long pause, echoing his words from our conversation a few minutes ago.

"I sense a *'but'* coming."

"*But*... it's late. And we've got a big day of traveling in the morning. We should probably get some sleep."

And if this goes south, we still have several weeks of tour left to get through. I'm not prepared to deal with that level of awkwardness.

"You make a strong case. It's hard to argue with someone as smart as you, Hannah."

My heart skipped and I gave him a pointed look, my willpower depleted to almost zero.

"Hey, can't blame a guy for trying." Ezra gently stroked my jawline one last time then dropped his hand to his side. "You head up—I left something in the bus I want to grab," he added, already taking a few steps backward in the direction of the parking lot.

If I wasn't mistaken, I'd say he looked wounded. He hid it well with a boyish grin, but guilt reared up inside of me. Guilt and my own sense of disappointment.

"Goodnight Ezra. Thank you for a truly amazing day," I said softly, then turned back to walk inside the hotel.

It depleted the last ounce of willpower I had not to turn back and run into his arms.

Chapter 10

My phone buzzed from inside my bag while I cradled my chin in one of my palms, elbow propped up against the table in front of me. I sat hunched over the small dining table in the Olympus tour bus, my usual office, trying to get work done while we coasted easily toward our next stop in Rochester, New York. A half-empty bottle of Gatorade rested on the table next to my company-issued laptop, the screen bright against my hooded, sleep-deprived eyes.

I'd woken up feeling mildly unscathed from last night's festivities—no raging nausea or anything like that. But my body was not used to staying up until five in the morning anymore, and no amount of Advil or caffeine had managed to fight off the intense headache I had from lack of sleep and the mix of liquors in my bloodstream.

Even after I'd left Ezra at the front door of the hotel and returned to my room, I couldn't fall asleep for what seemed like an eternity. Instead, the events of the night replayed like a film in my mind.

Spending all day traipsing around Boston with Ezra.

Singing at the karaoke bar in front of the guys.

Spending practically all night with Ezra, laughing and joking and telling stories like we'd known each other forever.

Ezra admitting he wanted to kiss me outside of our hotel.

Me nearly letting him.

When I did finally fall asleep against the soft down pillows of the hotel bed, my rest was fitful at best. I awoke just a few hours later, spurred to action by my anxiety.

I raced to pack my belongings up for another day of travel, determined to beat the rest of the guys to the bus so I could post up in my favorite side of the booth and pretend like nothing happened.

It almost worked—until Ezra climbed up those steps.

My brain screamed at me not to look up from my computer, not to make eye contact. But the air between us hung heavy with an invisible electric current and my eyes betrayed me. As soon as I looked at him, my toes curled as flashbacks of the night before replayed in my head.

My traitorous eyes slowly raked over his features: the soft, dark hair falling in loose waves around his face, still damp from the shower he must've just taken. His amber eyes, flecked with hints of gold right around the pupils, assessing me from across the bus. His aquiline nose, slightly crooked at the bridge from a break he never properly reset years ago—or so he'd confessed to me last night.

And finally, his full lips—lips that softened delicately when he ran the tip of his tongue over them during breaks in conversation.

I shivered at the thought.

After I finished taking him in fully, I noticed his normal lopsided grin was nowhere to be found—instead a smile that didn't quite reach his eyes hung where it should be, his jaw set tight.

The hint of apprehension only made him more attractive.

Silence stretched between us like a tightrope corded through our hearts, waiting for one of us to tip over and fall to our death. Ezra opened his mouth like he wanted to speak and my heart sped up, waiting, then—

"Come on man, stop blocking the door."

A moment later, Peter shoved Ezra forward to make his way up the rest of the steps.

The electric current in the air died and I returned to my laptop. I stared down at the same email to Annabelle I'd been working on—and failing miserably at—for about the last fifteen minutes.

Hey Annabelle!

Everything is going really well on tour. As you can see in the attached report, our follower counts and engagement rates are both up significantly over last period.

Our followers are loving the behind-the-scenes clips, so I'm scheduling out more of those over the next week.

Oh, by the way—I nearly made out with Ezra last night and literally can't stop thinking about him. I think I'll plan a June wedding. You're invited, of course, being the one who connected us!

I groaned under my breath and deleted the last paragraph then slammed my laptop shut in frustration.

"Trouble at work?" a quiet voice asked from beside me. I was so caught up in the email draft that I hadn't felt the warm presence looming over the booth or caught the scent of sandalwood hanging in the air. When I glanced up in mild surprise, Ezra slid easily into the booth beside me, a wary smile on his lips.

"Something like that," I replied, praying he hadn't been able to read the last part of my fake email before I deleted it.

It was the first time we'd spoken since last night. Part of me was terrified he'd bring up the *almost* kiss and another part of me was concerned he'd ignore it completely—pretend it never happened, the way we'd never once spoken about his gift the first night of tour.

I couldn't decide which would be worse.

My phone buzzed again from inside my bag, this time indicating two text messages, and the sound drew my attention temporarily away from Ezra's penetrating stare. I decided to ignore them—probably just Annabelle waiting on that email I couldn't bring myself to finish this morning.

"It's the lead singer of that band you work with, isn't it? I heard he's a real piece of work..." Ezra trailed off, one corner of his mouth twitching.

I breathed out a laugh that sounded more like a whoosh of air and dropped my elbows to the table, steepling my fingers above them. "You're not wrong. He's actually *the worst*." I gave him a pointed sidelong look from the corner of my eye.

Ezra laughed loudly, the sound reverberating through me. "At least I heard he's good-looking. Like, really, really ridiculously good-looking."

I cocked my head to look at Ezra just long enough to roll my eyes and deadpanned, "Did you just catch your own reflection in a spoon or something?"

Ezra's eyebrows shot up on his forehead, his mouth falling open in surprise at my volleyed *Zoolander* reference. He closed his mouth in time for the corner of his lips to twitch upwards, bowing his head at me in silent praise.

Dozens of unspoken words hung between us, sucking all the oxygen out of the bus until I thought I might pass out.

Ezra broke first. "So listen, uh...I wanted to talk about last—"

My phone buzzed loudly in my bag again, this time indicating an incoming phone call. Instead of ignoring it, I jumped at the chance to avoid this conversation.

"Sorry, I better get this. It could be Annabelle with something important," I said to Ezra by way of explanation, already fishing my phone out of my bag.

"Hello, this is Hannah," I answered in my typical work voice, not even bothering to look at the caller ID.

"Oooh, your customer service voice is so hot," my best friend Olivia sang in my ear and my mouth fell open in a small O of surprise.

"Liv? Why are you calling me?" I asked, then winced at how rude that sounded. I felt Ezra intently watching me, his eyes leaving a warm sensation on my skin in their wake.

"I had to call! You weren't answering any of my text messages and this couldn't wait," Liv answered, thankfully not calling me out for my severe greeting.

"What couldn't wait?" I asked, chancing a sideways glance in Ezra's direction. He was sitting close enough to me that if he strained, he could hear both sides of our conversation. I prayed Olivia didn't bring up anything I'd told her about him, or ask how things were going.

I hadn't yet had the chance to tell her about the night before. I was dreading that conversation, in fact. It felt too big, larger than life, to convey via text or even on a long-distance phone call.

"I was hoping your offer to join you on the road for a few days still stands because... I booked a hotel in Chicago! I'm flying out on Wednesday," Olivia squealed from the other end of the phone.

An immediate sense of relief washed over me, and not just because she didn't bring up my awkward encounters with Ezra right in front of him.

After nearly a month on the road, I was finally going to see my best friend again! I smiled into the phone, my eyes absently staring out the bus window without seeing any of the farms and fields passing by us at sixty-five miles per hour. "Of course it still stands! I've been dying to see you since I left."

"Great, because this ticket is non-refundable," Olivia answered breezily and I couldn't help but laugh. It was very on-brand for Liv to act first and ask questions later.

My sleep-addled brain immediately began making mental calculations. It was Monday and we were already on our way to Rochester for an outdoor show there tonight. Tuesday morning it was back on the road for a stop just outside of Cleveland, then we'd have another early start Wednesday morning to make the five-hour drive to Chicago. If my calculations were correct, that would put us there just before Olivia's plane touched down around dinnertime.

I told her as much over the phone and we hashed out some of the logistics. By some stroke of luck, Olivia had managed to book her room at the same hotel we were staying at. We made plans to meet there as soon as her flight landed.

When we finally hung up, my cheeks hurt from smiling so much. My head swam, already trying to plan all the activities we could squeeze in between shows.

"You look a lot happier now," Ezra observed from beside me, snapping me from my trance.

I turned to face him, a content smile still plastered on my face. "I am. My best friend is meeting us in Chicago."

"Oh no, there's going to be two of you?" Ezra's eyes widened comically, his mouth stretching into an exaggerated grimace, and I knew we were back to our typical banter.

My muscles relaxed back into the comfortable booth behind me.

After giving it as much thought that morning as I was willing to, I realized I wasn't ready to have a serious conversation with Ezra. I wasn't ready to talk about my feelings—these feelings I didn't even understand. And I sure as hell wasn't ready to hear what he thought about the whole thing.

"Brace yourself," I said to him conspiratorially, casually bumping my shoulder against his to release more of the tension from earlier. "Olivia is like me on steroids."

Ezra shuddered beside me. "I better go warn the guys."

He gave me a final pointed look that I returned, then unfolded his long body from the booth and disappeared toward the front of the bus.

·♥·♥·♥·♥·♥·

Our time in Rochester and Cleveland passed by in a flurry of sound-checks, practicing, performances, virtual interviews, and... work.

I had expected the few days leading up to Olivia's impending arrival to drag with agonizing slowness. But with just two weeks left before our break and the upcoming West Coast leg that would pick up in January, Olympus's schedule was the busiest it had been all tour.

Outside of the shows each night where I snuck around the stage and pit area trying to find some unique angle or shot I hadn't already captured to share with Olympus's online fandom, I barely even saw them until we were packing up our things and climbing onto the bus again each morning.

And for me, it was probably better that way.

When I said the days were filled with work, I meant Legitimate. Hard. Work.

Capturing the band during their performances was the fun part. It challenged me creatively—and physically. Running around the venue in the dark, trying to stay out of the way while also getting close-up content of the guys was the toughest workout I'd ever done. Even Olivia's demanding workouts at the gym had not prepared me for this.

It was the part that came *after* the show that I hadn't fully visualized when I took this job.

Editing what felt like a million hours of video on a tiny phone screen, my neck and upper back aching from leaning forward for too long; trying to come up with a witty caption or on-screen text to draw attention and make people laugh or even care enough to pause their doom scrolling; and of course, the most time-consuming but rewarding part of it all: responding to hundreds of comments.

I had been given a brand guide when I first agreed to represent Olympus and it mentioned the importance of personalization and talking directly to the fans. It was standard, boilerplate stuff I'd read and created myself a million times before for past clients. My outlook changed though, after that night at the pizza shop and my conversation with Ezra, when I truly started to understand what that personal connection meant to him, to this group.

As a result, I'd redoubled my engagement efforts online ever since.

When I reached the summit of the bus steps Wednesday morning and stopped to scan the faces of each member of Olympus in view, they looked like... zombies.

Peter was sprawled across the couch, his eyes shut while his broad frame dwarfed the sofa beneath him in a way I might ordinarily find funny if it wasn't for the tight knit of his brows and the dark circles underneath those closed eyes.

Zach and Angel waved a tired greeting to me, their eyes similarly dark and hollow, before disappearing to the two small beds at the very back of the bus.

True to form, Ezra laid across the floor, right in the middle of the only walkway.

His toned arms were tucked behind his head in a makeshift pillow, his eyes closed. His beautiful face was loose, relaxed, though I knew the hard floor couldn't possibly be comfortable.

Seeing them so burnt out instantly dried up any thoughts I had about being exhausted myself. At least I didn't have to get up in front of a crowd of thousands every night and put on the show of their lifetime.

"Can't take your eyes off me, huh?" Ezra slowly peeked one eye open, a corner of his lips turning up in a smirk that made my blood boil instantly within my veins.

I screwed my face into what I hoped was my deadliest scowl, already regretting my empathy from two seconds ago. "Actually, I was trying to imagine how it must feel to be self-centered enough to lie in the literal middle of the only walkway on the bus."

Peter snorted from his spot on the couch but kept his eyes shut, trying not to engage.

Ezra opened both of his eyes, the smirk replaced by a sweeping, teasing grin aimed squarely at me. "In my defense, Zach and Angel beat me to the beds. I had no other choice."

"Don't bring us into this!" a muffled shout came from the back of the bus—Zach, I thought, but his voice sounded like it was coming from inside a pillow.

Realizing Ezra wasn't going to move and our driver was politely, albeit impatiently, waiting for me to get out of the way, I chucked my bags across the aisle, into the small booth behind and opposite Peter's couch. Oh so carefully, I toed one foot at a time over Ezra's prone form to join them, silently willing myself not to trip and crash land on top of him. A chance glance down at Ezra's lips and the broadening smirk on them told me his mind had plummeted in the same direction.

After making it safely across the man-sized obstacle in my way, sweat beginning to bead on my brow from the concentration and blush that flared across my neck and cheeks, I sat down in the booth just in time for the bus to jolt forward, slowly carving our path out of the hotel parking lot and toward the highway. I shifted my work bag to my lap, fully meaning to pull out my laptop and begin another long day of work during this five-hour ride. Instead, my gaze drifted out through the window to my left, aimlessly watching our slow crawl toward the highway as my mind wandered along with it.

I was unable to recall exactly when my relationship with Ezra had made this shift—from polite, strictly business communication about travel logistics and social media content to the back-and-forth banter of long-time friends. Or possibly more.

Maybe it was that day in Boston, or the would-be kiss at the hotel later that night.

But I had the niggling feeling this winding road and the path we now walked down had started long before that.

Cars and roads and trees and buildings blurred past my unseeing eyes as I stared through the bus window for the better part of the drive to Chicago.

Olivia's plane was in the air for the latter half of the trip, and my phone remained quiet where it was tucked into my saddlebag. I'd managed to get a little bit of work done during the drive, even after spending most of it daydreaming. None of the guys made a peep the entire ride, every last one of them fast asleep with pure exhaustion, offering a rare time of peace and quiet, with nothing to fill my ears but the roar of the road beneath our wheels.

After a daunting five hours, we slowed to take the exit off the highway. As if by a cosmic pull, my phone vibrated in my bag once, alerting me to a new text. Smiling to myself, I reached into my bag for it while the bus cut a path through clogged city blocks toward our hotel. Olivia's message lit up my face as I scanned it—she had just left baggage claim and was waiting for an Uber. I tapped out a quick reply to let her know we were getting close to the hotel, then tossed my phone back in my bag and returned my gaze to the window.

It was just before rush hour as I stared eagerly out the window at the busy streets of Chicago. People busied themselves bustling through the city—some with coffee cups clutched in their hands, others with noses pressed down to their phone screens. Modern high rises rubbed elbows with squat brick buildings. Curtains and blinds were pulled back from their windows, lights on inside to reveal men and women at work or already in a state of respite for the evening. Everywhere I looked teemed with life. We rounded corner after corner, halted at stoplight after stoplight, the congested city traffic slowing our progress. It reminded me a bit of New York, but that didn't quelch the feeling of butterflies fluttering in my stomach. A new place to explore.

"Ever been here before?" Ezra's disembodied voice asked from my right. I had no idea how long he'd been standing next to me while I was lost to the city outside.

I shook my head, grinning enthusiastically, and tore my gaze away to face him.

Ezra's wavy brown hair was more mussed than usual from sleep, and there were faint red lines zigzagging his cheek where it had pressed down into the floor. He smiled lazily at me, his amber eyes soft.

"Nope, never made it out this way. You?" I asked, though having been a touring musician for more than a decade I was pretty sure of his answer already.

"Oh yeah, loads of times," he answered breezily then slid into the seat across from me. "It has its perks but... I'm more of a beach person. The water. Wide open spaces. Warm weather." Ezra shrugged and looked through the window himself. I tried to imagine how congested and overwhelming the throngs of people and buildings must look through his eyes.

I'd never been able to figure out if I was more of a city person or a… whatever the alternative was—country person? Suburb person? Nothing seemed to fit.

I always seemed to long for whatever was different from my day-to-day. Growing up in a really small suburban town, I dreamed about going to college in a big city. But when I was at school, I longed for the tree-lined drives and sprawling green yards back home.

The beach—that did sound nice, though.

I heard the hiss and pop of the Keurig machine whirring from the kitchenette, signaling the rest of our group was starting to wake like their collective subconscious knew we were close. Inhaling deeply as the delightful smell of fresh dark roast filled the air, I made a mental note to find the closest coffee shop when we arrived and order the largest size they had.

Ezra drew my attention again when he asked, "Your friend here yet?"

I nodded my response, unable to stop the grin from spreading on my lips. "She touched down a few minutes ago."

"So Miss Tourist Girl—it's your first time in Chicago. I assume you've got big plans?" He smiled wryly at me and winked.

I rolled my eyes half-heartedly and laughed. "Of course! Olivia is even more of a planner than I am. We've got a full itinerary ready to go, complete with reservations and annotations." I paused to narrow my eyes at him. "And before you ask, no you are not invited."

Ezra let out a quiet chuckle and exposed his palms. "Wasn't gonna ask, I promise."

"Did I just hear you have a friend joining us?" Peter popped his head in from the kitchen, a steaming mug of black coffee in his hands. The dark circles beneath his eyes had faded considerably with his nap. "Is she hot?"

My jaw popped open, my eyes widening menacingly at Peter. Ezra just cackled across from me.

"What? It's a valid question," Peter added, sliding into the booth next to me. His broad frame took up nearly the entire seat, squeezing me as close to the window as I could go.

"Yeah, you know our boy here is *painfully* single," Ezra chided, wiggling his brows at Peter.

Peter grimaced and dragged a large palm down his face. "Being around Angel when he baby talks to his phone screen every time he FaceTimes his girl back home is killing me."

I smiled indulgently, then my eyes glazed over for a moment while I remembered the *breakup-not-quite-breakup* Ezra had just before we left New York. Emboldened by our new friendship or flying high from sleep deprivation, I cocked my head at him and asked, "And you? Are you *painfully single*, too?"

Peter sucked in a breath beside me, regret about starting this conversation washing over him. I wasn't sure why I'd even asked. Why that simple joke cracked open a small hole inside me. Something about Peter's frame crushing in beside me reminded me of that first night of tour—the warning he gave me just before the show started.

I'll just say one thing—be careful...

Ezra registered the change in my tone and his smile faltered. He hesitated a few moments, eyes darting between me and Peter several times before he focused the full weight of his attention on me. His amber irises darkened as he studied my face.

I faltered under his stare and had to drop my eyes to my hands where they were folded in my lap.

"I wouldn't describe the situation as *painful*, but... yes. I am not currently engaged in a romantic relationship," Ezra said slowly, carefully enunciating every word.

"So you and Andie are..." Peter trailed off quietly next to me and my body went rigid.

"—Friends," Ezra cut in sharply, and for the first time I heard venom lace his words.

"You said *what*?" Olivia shouted at me over the rim of her wine glass, her voice carrying throughout the spacious wine bar and seeming to echo off the wall of windows that separated our table from the busy street outside.

"Shh!" I hushed her in a sharp whisper, though I couldn't stop my lips from turning up slightly at the corners. "Keep it down, we're not the only ones here." I shot a covert glance around the wine bar—it was still before the dinner rush, so only a few tables near us had occupants.

As soon as we checked into the hotel, I made an excuse about meeting Olivia and bolted, nearly sprinting the three blocks to a nearby Starbucks just to burn off the nervous energy pulsing through my body. And fill said body with more anxiety-inducing caffeine. *I'm only human.*

I had been sitting at a small dining-height table tucked in the back of the Starbucks stewing in my own roiling emotions, cold brew in hand, when Olivia asked me to meet her at a wine bar a few blocks away. More than happy to trade my caffeine for booze, I didn't hesitate to join her.

Since sitting down, I had been regaling her with the events from the past few weeks, all leading up to what happened on the tour bus earlier that day.

"Very bold, I have to give it to you." Olivia shook her head and took another sip of her wine then set the glass on the table, red liquid sloshing toward the rim. "And then Peter brought up the girl?"

I nodded, the small smile that had started to form on my lips faltering at the mention of Andie, Ezra's maybe girlfriend? *Well, not according to him.*

"I'll give that bassist something. He's got balls," Olivia commented, leaning back slightly in her chair. "And it seems like he's genuinely looking out for you, which is a pleasant surprise." She paused for just a moment before adding, "Is he hot?"

I snorted loudly midway through a sip from my glass of Pinot Grigio, and the chilled liquid burned in my nostrils. It took me a few seconds to gather myself before I could respond, "Funny you should ask—he actually wanted to know the same thing about you." I shot her a meaningful look, eyebrows wiggling.

"Okay, let's come back to that later. I see you trying to change the subject," Olivia shot back and I winced. "So I can see from here how that may have been awkward, but..." Olivia trailed off as our server returned to the table to silently top off both of our wine glasses.

We both waited for him to exit before speaking again.

"But..." I prompted, then took another sip of wine. This time, thankfully, it didn't end up in my nose.

"*But* the guy says he's not seeing this girl and you have no compelling reason to believe otherwise. He's hot. And he's clearly into you. I'm not seeing any problems here," Olivia said with a shrug. She made it sound so simple.

"Okay, say I'm willing and able to set aside the Andie thing, to accept that they really are just friends and Ezra is ripe for the taking," I started, leaning across the table to drop my volume. As the words came out, I found that, deep down, I *did* want to believe that. I wanted to believe that Ezra was into me. That he'd rather pick the average, small-town girl with big dreams over the hot model dressed to the nines in designer. I wanted to feel *wanted*.

But this was real life.

"The *problem*," I continued, drawing out each syllable in the word. "Is that he is, for all intents and purposes, a coworker. This is my job—a very big, new job, by the way, that I cannot afford to mess up. We already know what happens when you get personal with the client—"

"Actually, we don't," Olivia cut in quickly. She leaned forward, bracing her elbows against the table to steeple her fingers together in a stance I could only imagine intimidated anyone unlucky enough to be on the receiving end of it. "All we've got are a few vague whispers and half stories. Rumors. We don't really know what happened with the last girl. None of that would hold up in court."

Camila.

I blew out a long breath, gripping my wine glass just to have something to do with my hands. On one hand, it felt pretty clear from Mei's warnings that something had gone down. And considering Ezra's track record, I felt pretty sure I knew what that something was.

On the other hand, Olivia had a point. I didn't know the truth, if or how Ezra was involved, or why Camila left Rabbit's Foot. And the guy I'd been getting to know over the past few weeks simply didn't reconcile with the image of him plastered all over the media. The image I'd even believed before we'd become close.

Olivia moved her head to try and catch my gaze, which had drifted off into space as I considered what she was saying. "Look, as your best friend in the entire world, can I ask you a serious, radically candid question?"

I inhaled a deep breath and said, "Like I could stop you."

"Fair," she said, then cleared her throat and narrowed her eyes at me. "Hannah, why are you so adamantly against this? I feel like you've thrown yourself so hard into work, even before landing this particular job, to avoid a personal life—" Olivia held up a manicured hand when she saw my mouth pop open, ready to protest. "You haven't been in a relationship, or even casually dated anyone, in what? Four years?"

"There is nothing wrong with being focused on my career!" I interjected before she could silence me, trying unsuccessfully to keep the defensive edge out of my tone. "You work even longer hours than I do sometimes."

"But I'm not using work as a way to put off *living*. I go on dates, play the field, and have fun. I take risks and sure, sometimes it bites me, but then I get back in the saddle again."

I took another breath. Then another. "I don't know. It just seems like too big of a risk."

"What feels like a risk, though? And what is *at* risk?"

I combed a hand through my hair and looked away, eyes gazing unseeingly out the window beside us. "The risk of losing my job. The risk of throwing away everything I've ever worked for."

"So you're telling me if the job wasn't an issue, if Ezra was just some random hot guy who flirted mercilessly with you instead of your client, you'd feel differently?"

"Yes! Well... maybe? I don't know!"

Olivia's voice softened to a tone I knew she rarely used with anyone other than her closest friends. So, me. "Tell me what's really going on."

I chewed on my lip, still trying to avoid looking into her eyes. I watched people pass by on the street outside the bistro for seconds. Minutes.

Finally, I opened my mouth to say so quietly I wasn't sure she could hear me, "What if I put myself out there and he turns me down? Or what if I end up just another notch in the exhaustive conveyor belt of girls in his life? What if he just leaves too, like..."

"Like your dad?" Olivia supplied gently.

I nodded, my bottom lip wobbling against my will.

In one smooth movement, Olivia reached a hand across the table to gently grasp mine, giving it a small, reassuring squeeze. "Han. You are an amazing, intelligent, beautiful, loyal to a fault, marketing whiz kid, sweet baby angel. If anyone, and I mean *anyone*, chooses not to see that, not to love that, they aren't worth a second of your time. Don't dull your sunshine for those people, and don't *ever* hold yourself back over *what-ifs*.

"Take a chance, go on a date, have sex—hot, intense, passionate, hands-on-the-headboard sex! It doesn't have to be love right away. It doesn't need to be Ezra, either. But you deserve a chance at your own adventure, your own happiness, whatever that may look like. If you like this guy and think there could be something between the two of you, you owe it to yourself to find out, consequences be damned. We can deal with the fallout later, together. Because no matter what happens, I'm not going anywhere. I promise you that."

I could feel tears brimming in the corner of my eyes and willed them not to spill here, in the middle of this restaurant. In my heart, I knew Olivia was right. She was annoying that way.

It didn't need to be anything serious. Maybe I could explore this thing between Ezra and me without strings, without consequences, without Annabelle ever knowing. Have fun without giving up every single piece of my heart, without giving up my career.

"Okay, okay…" I said after a few moments of silent consideration, earning me a wide, beaming grin from Olivia that lit up her beautiful face, lit up the entire room. "I'll give it a chance."

"This week. You'll give it a chance this week, in Chicago," Olivia added, blinking innocently in my direction.

I groaned and threw my head back to look at the ceiling, "Fine. I will give it a chance this week, while you're still here. Which is perfect, because you can pick up the pieces when I find out he has absolutely zero interest in me and I've been totally overthinking it this entire time."

Olivia howled with laughter then said, "Shut up, it's going to be great."

"Can we be done talking about me now?" I asked, mirroring Olivia's innocent blinking from moments earlier.

"Of course, let's move on to my favorite subject: me. Tell me more about this bassist…"

Chapter 11

"Okay, okay! I admit it, they're pretty good." Olivia held up her hands from her seat beside me. We sat side by side in an empty row of seats toward the middle of the house, watching Olympus during their soundcheck.

"*Pretty* good?" I asked incredulously, eyebrows hitched high over my widened blue eyes.

"Fine, they're really good! Whatever," Olivia finally relented, though one corner of her mouth tugged up.

I grinned triumphantly and turned my full attention back to the band on stage, my high ponytail bouncing against my shoulders. The amphitheater for tonight's performance was again situated beside a span of water, in this case Lake Michigan. The combination of the tranquil, aquamarine water butting up against the towering Chicago skyline was breathtaking. Almost as good as the view that first night at Jones Beach.

With how busy things had been lately, this was the first time I'd made it to one of their sound checks in nearly two weeks. I'd forgotten how different it was to see them play in such an intimate setting, without the roar of the crowd nearly drowning out the music. Aside from the small snippets of songs I got to hear, my favorite part was the sound of them bantering with each other over the sound system.

"Wait until you see them tonight," I whispered to Olivia in between songs.

I heard Olivia suck in a sharp inhale just before Olympus launched into "Push," one of my favorite songs off their third studio album. "Speaking of, I wanted to talk to you about that."

My spidey senses tingled at the way her voice had dropped an octave, and I turned reluctantly to look at her. She bit down on her bottom lip, considering what she was about to say. I blinked back at her expectantly.

"As you know, I only have a few days here in Chicago with you before I have to fly back to New York," Olivia began. I nodded along, fear surging in my gut. *Don't tell me Bruce called you back early.*

"And while you know I would absolutely *love* to go to Olympus's show tonight, I was hoping maybe the two of us could go out together instead. You know, since our time together is so limited. Plus, you've seen them do this show like a hundred times already, and you said it yourself that you had so much content—enough to keep you busy for weeks."

Olivia was starting to ramble, throwing more and more reasons at me until I finally held up a hand to pause the avalanche of words. Her eyes bored into mine pleadingly, the picture of innocence. It was a look I'd become familiar with over the years.

Releasing a slow sigh from between my lips, I glanced between the stage and Olivia then said, "Fine, fine. You picked a good night. Rabbit's Foot is sending someone from their photo team to take stills for the upcoming album jacket. I still need to check with the guys to make sure they won't need me, but as long as they're okay with it, I think I can sneak away for just one night."

Olivia cheered and threw her arms out, pulling me in for a tight embrace over the low armrest that divided us. "Thank you, thank you, thank you! I already have everything planned. I promise it'll be worth it!"

"This is what you were excited about?" I asked skeptically, arms folded over my chest.

Olympus had been more than fine with giving me the night off to spend with my best friend when I'd asked. The only clue Olivia had given me about our plans for the evening was to "look hot." Not very helpful, but very on-brand for Liv.

Things were starting to add up as we stood outside of an old warehouse that had been gutted and turned into a nightclub, judging by the line of eager patrons in various states of dress—or *undress*, in the case of a few of them—already queuing up outside the front door.

I already had the faintest buzz from the one glass of red wine I'd had at dinner, but not enough that the idea of bodies pressing in against me at a packed club felt remotely appealing.

"Come on! We haven't had a messy night out since college. We're still young, we need to live a little," Olivia crooned, bumping her hip against mine. "This place had great reviews."

I blinked at her, but before I could respond, Olivia grabbed my hand and pulled me into the back of the queue just as a bouncer emerged through the looming front doors to begin checking IDs.

"Oh good, it's ladies' night," I read aloud from a whimsical A-frame sign propped just outside of the entrance while we waited for our turn in line.

"I know! No cover," Olivia replied, not picking up on my sarcasm.

Soon I was handing over my ID to the burly bouncer guarding the entrance. He was probably the same height as Peter, I noted, but not nearly as broad, and I had to suppress a snort at the idea of Peter here running security at a packed nightclub.

Knowing him, he'd probably love every second of it.

Taking in my odd expression, the bouncer eyed me, then my license, then me again, his eyes looping back and forth for what felt like an eternity. Just as Olivia started to get that impatient look on her face that never ended well, the bouncer handed my license back and moved on to the group behind us with no more than a gesture of his thumb in the direction of the door.

No turning back now.

Two hours later, sweat beaded on my brow, the cold water in my plastic cup sloshing up and over the rim as I raised it above my head, waving it back and forth in time to the pulsing music blaring from every direction.

Though I'd never admit it to Olivia, I was having a pretty decent time. I had just finished my second tequila soda and opted to take a quick break with water for a bit.

Dancing lights in every shade shone down from the rafters to cut through the darkness, bouncing off the walls, the bar, the bodies packed into the room, and making everything look hazy. From atop a platform at the front of the large dance hall, the DJ played hit after hit, keeping me moving in time to the endless string of songs he expertly wove together.

But Olivia had been right. This was fun.

As the song smoothly transitioned into another, I closed my eyes and tilted my head upwards, allowing a wide grin to spread across my lips. Liv's arms circled me as we danced, our bodies gliding together in perfect harmony. It had been ages since I'd danced like this, but my hips easily picked up where they'd left off, circling and swaying to the beat.

I opened my eyes to catch Olivia glancing back over her shoulder toward the entrance to the cavernous dance hall, a motion I'd seen her repeat several times throughout the night.

"What do you keep looking at?" I asked, shouting to get her attention over the music.

Olivia's eyes snapped back to me, but her expression remained blank. "Huh? Oh, nothing. There's just some cute guy back there. I thought he was checking me out," she answered breezily.

I gave her a pointed look that screamed *I don't believe you* but she shrugged and threw her hands toward the ceiling, twirling in place in perfect time to the melody. Deciding to ignore it, I took a large gulp of my water and mimicked her movements.

Suddenly, Olivia leaned in close to my ear to yell, "I'm going to grab another drink! Stay here so I can find you." By the time I opened my eyes, she was already weeding her way through the crowd toward the bar, the sea of bodies parting for her then swallowing her back up again in the blink of an eye.

Shaking my head at her disappearing form, I took another sip of my water right as the DJ transitioned into another song. It was one I recognized from my college days and immediately my body picked up the familiar rhythm. My smile returned, my earlier thoughts forgotten as I twirled and swayed in place, eyes closed to the world around me.

"Nice moves," a melodic, masculine voice rumbled from behind me right as the warmth of a long torso pressed against my back. Whirling around, my mouth snapped open at the sight of Ezra Bell standing behind me, two drinks balanced expertly in his slender hands.

"Ezra! What, what are you doing here?" I stammered, complete shock in my voice and on my face.

He chuckled softly and inclined his head to gesture behind him. Following his direction, I spied Olivia leaning casually against the large bar in the heart of the dance hall, a plastic cup lifted in the air toward me in a toast. Then I noticed Peter leaning against the bar directly beside her, so close their arms pressed together.

My shock was replaced with intrigue and I nodded back at her, lifting my now-empty water cup in response. Clever girl. A night away from Olympus, huh?

Touché.

I forced myself to turn away from Olivia, tilting my head back to look up at Ezra. "How..." I started to ask, unsure how to form the words.

"Liv told us where you'd be tonight and invited us to meet you after the show," Ezra cut in, sensing where my thoughts were headed. "And before you yell at me for the surprise, I was sworn to complete and utter secrecy by your friend over there." Ezra leaned in conspiratorially, his lips hovering next to the shell of my ear. "Just between us, she scares me a little."

I let out an involuntary barking laugh, my head thrown back with the sound, an image of Olivia's piercing stare from the other day flashing through my mind. She certainly knew how to intimidate.

Dropping my eyes down to the two cups in his hands, I arched a brow, "Double-fisting tonight, are we?"

Shifting as though he'd completely forgotten about them, he gestured one of the cups in my direction. "Oh! This one's for you. Liv told me what you liked."

"Did she, now?" I mused quietly, allowing my eyes to dart back to the bar once more. Now, Olivia and Peter had their heads pressed together, trying to hold a conversation over the din of the club, the sides of their arms completely flush with one another as they leaned in.

I turned my gaze back to Ezra and added, "Liv is just full of bright ideas tonight, isn't she?" Nevertheless, I reached out to take the full cup from him, lifting it to my lips to take a deep swig.

Ezra's warm, spicy scent filled my nostrils when he took a step closer, leaning in again to whisper in my ear, "You look like you're having a good time."

My eyes widened, my brain going fuzzy at his nearness. The only blessing was he couldn't see my expression standing so close. "What makes you say that?"

"I just meant with Liv here in Chicago. Seems like you're enjoying yourself, that's all." Ezra shrugged, the movement shifting him even closer to me so our bodies touched as we swayed slightly back and forth to the rhythm. The DJ had shifted his set to a series of throwbacks from the mid-2000s, the pulsing beats nostalgic. "Plus, I saw you dancing on my way through the crowd and I gotta say, you've got some pretty sweet moves. You've been holding out on me."

I laughed in spite of myself, shaking my head so my hair bounced loosely against Ezra's shoulder. I decided to ignore the compliment. "Oh yeah, it's great to see her. I don't think I told you, but we're roommates. We just moved in together when I started this job," I explained between sips of the tequila soda he'd bought me. I knew I should slow down, the slow burn I felt curling through my core telling me the liquor was doing its job to dull my senses, but the sipping kept me from fidgeting too much in Ezra's presence.

"No way!" Ezra shouted over the song, then shifted a few inches back to take a sip of his drink—a whiskey coke by the look of it. "That must've been tough, having to hit the road so soon after moving into a new place."

I nodded thoughtfully, just barely able to hear him over the noise of the club. I glanced around the packed dance hall, the crush of bodies showing no signs of slowing down despite the fact that it had to be going on one in the morning. An oddly companionable silence fell over us as our bodies subconsciously swayed back and forth to the music.

Eventually, Ezra leaned in toward me again and brought his lips to my ear. "So listen, uh... the main reason I wanted to come out here tonight—" he cut himself off to take another rallying sip of his drink.

Sensing exactly where this conversation was headed, I stiffened beside him. I knew I'd promised Olivia I'd give this a chance. But right now?

"Well, we haven't really had the chance to talk since that night, after karaoke—" he continued.

"Oh wow, I *love* this song!" I interjected, my voice overly enthusiastic. I moved to sidestep Ezra, planning to mask my running away with what I hoped would be a graceful twirl to the music.

As soon as I zigged, Ezra zagged and my left shoulder careened straight into his solid chest. The shock of his solid frame against my limp arm had me tripping and then falling toward him. Ezra reached out his hands to steady me before I could hit the ground, forgetting about the still half-full whiskey coke in his hand.

I felt the shock of ice and chilled liquid splashing down the front of my shirt before my brain caught up and realized what had happened.

"Oh Han, I'm so sorry!" Ezra's mouth gaped open in horror.

Why had I decided to wear white tonight?

Slowly, I looked down at my shirt and winced visibly at the sight of it. It was completely soaked through.

"It's okay, I uh... I just need to get to the bathroom and try to clean this up." I tried again to step around him and make a break for it to the nearest ladies' room.

Just before I bolted, Ezra caught my arm, gripping it firmly, but not painfully, in his strong hand. "Wait! We brought the bus down here—it's out in the warehouse lot. I can help you clean this up and get you a clean shirt to borrow."

Before I had time to think, he was tugging me toward the club exit.

·❤·❤·❤·❤·❤·

"Here's some towels. I'll dig up a clean shirt from my spare bag and be right back," Ezra said, thrusting a whole roll of paper towels at me before he sprinted toward the bedroom area at the back of the bus. Why they'd decided to bring the entire tour bus out to this remote warehouse district I didn't know, but I was grateful for a quiet place to hide.

I stood in the small kitchenette next to the booth I'd worked from so many times over the last several weeks it almost felt like home. While Ezra rustled through a bag in the back of the bus, I started dabbing at the stain on my shirt. It had spread on the walk from the nightclub to the tour bus, the thin fabric of my crop top completely soaked through.

"Got one!" Ezra crowed, hoisting a ball of black fabric above his head triumphantly as he emerged from the bedroom area and jogged back toward me. "Ugh, that's so bad. I'm really sorry," he added when he took stock of the dark, spreading stain. "Here, let me help."

Without thinking, Ezra grabbed the lump of paper towels from my hands and began dabbing at my shirt, trying desperately to sop up the spilled liquid. I bit down on my lip, my arms frozen at my sides as he firmly patted the towels up and down my torso. Heat bloomed in my cheeks, spreading down my neck at each touch that pressed the cold fabric into my skin.

"Um, Ezra—" I tried to say, but struggled to form the words.

"We should probably just get this off and try soaking it in the sink," was all he said in response, completely disconnected from his hands on my body, his focus entirely on trying to undo the damage.

"*Ezra*—" I said more firmly and he finally looked up from my shirt to see my wide blue eyes blinking slowly beneath my arched eyebrows. I watched his eyes dance between my shirt and my face as his brain caught up, then widen in horror.

"What am I doing? I am so sorry, Han, I don't normally just... I don't know, grope people like this! I just felt so bad about the drink and wanted to help, but this was probably not the best way to go about it and—"

Ezra finally stopped his rambling at the sound of a low, bubbling giggle filtering from my lips, the sound slowly growing louder and louder as my foggy brain processed the ridiculous situation unfolding between us.

"You're... laughing," Ezra said slowly, his expression cagey, like he thought maybe this was a trap. My laughter grew louder still, the sound becoming a cackle that echoed in the otherwise quiet, empty tour bus.

Then Ezra was laughing along with me and the beautiful sound of it nearly stopped my heart. My face softened when our eyes met, our laughter slowing, then stopping, until all that remained were tender smiles curving both of our lips.

My eyes traced a pattern along his face, taking in the five o'clock shadow coloring his jawline and the way he chewed on his bottom lip nervously. Unconsciously, I licked my lips and I could've sworn Ezra stopped breathing for a moment. The intensity in his amber gaze pierced through me, rooting me to the spot. All I could do was watch as he took one slow step toward me, then another, the sweet and spicy scent of citrus and sandalwood flooding my senses and making me dizzy.

With every ounce of willpower I had, I forced myself to step backward, away from Ezra's advancing form, until I felt the cushion of the booth seat against my knees. "Ezra, I... we can't." The words were breathless and lacked conviction, but I willed them to come out just the same.

"*Why*?" Ezra pressed, throwing his hands out to his sides. "I know this can't be all one-sided. I know you feel this, this... this *thing*, too. Why ignore it?"

"Because!" I exploded back defiantly, irritation rearing up in me like a lion that had been caged for far too long. "Because we *work together*. This is my job and I take it very, very seriously. Because I don't want to end up being the next Camila!"

My hands balled into fists at my sides, my chin inclined with a determination I didn't feel. I knew I had told Olivia, promised her in fact, that I'd give this a chance. But I couldn't. Not yet, at least. Not until I knew the truth about what happened to my predecessor, what could happen to me if this all went south.

Rather than arguing with me like I expected him to, Ezra's brows arched high on his forehead in question, his mouth twisting in confusion. "Camila? What on earth has she got to do with us?"

I sighed deeply and looked down at the floor, then hugged my arms around my middle as though I could physically hold myself together for this conversation I'd been putting off for weeks.

My bravado faded as quickly as it had come. Eventually, in a barely audible voice, I explained, "Don't play dumb. I know something happened between the two of you. You got close, started seeing each other? I heard it ended badly and that's why she left Rabbit's Foot... why I got this job in the first place."

I could feel Ezra's intense stare on my face, but I avoided it. Silence stretched between us for one, two, three seconds...

Then Ezra laughed.

No, he didn't just laugh. He *howled*.

Incredulously, I looked up at him, my mouth gaping wide. "Why are you laughing about this?" I demanded, hugging my arms even tighter around my torso.

"Sorry, I—" Ezra wheezed, trying to speak through his cackling. "I know I shouldn't laugh, but—" he tried again, but couldn't finish.

I merely glared at him, blinking back the rage firing up in me again.

Finally, he regained some semblance of control over himself, his expression turning serious—well, as serious as Ezra could be. "That's what you think happened with Cami? You think she and I started hooking up and then—what? She dumped me or something and ran off to California?"

California. So he kept up with her whereabouts? Odd for them to keep in touch after such a dramatic ending to their affair, but it could check out if they'd been close.

But wait, did he say she *dumped* him?

"No, no. Well, yes, but you got the last bit wrong," I stumbled, waving my arms in front of me as if that would clear things up. "*You* dumped *her* after you got bored, and she left the label in disgrace."

As the words tumbled out of my mouth, I started to consider them against the man I'd come to know over the past month. It just... didn't add up. My defiance faded, replaced by the sinking feeling of skepticism and embarrassment. And guilt.

Ezra's smile faded, too. As he tilted his head to look at the floor, I could see my accusation had hit a nerve. After a moment, he huffed a steadying breath and looked up to face me fully. His amber eyes gleamed with earnestness in the dim light of the bus and I knew what he was about to say would be the truth.

"Cami and I did become close during her time as our social media rep," he started, his voice so soft I had to strain to hear him. "Really close, but not in the way you *assumed*." There was the tiniest hint of venom in that last word.

"We became close friends," Ezra started again, "and yes, we started spending a lot of time together outside of work. Cami's a cool girl." He shrugged, adding, "But she wasn't interested in me like that. Her type is like... the complete opposite of me." Ezra chuckled, lost in his thoughts, and reached a hand up to scratch aimlessly at the back of his head. It ruffled his shaggy hair even further, a look that only seemed to make him more attractive.

"I guess I don't get the joke. Gonna need you to elaborate a little further on that," I said, trying to keep the bite of frustration from my tone.

He sighed again and forced himself to meet my eyes again. "I probably shouldn't be telling you this. It's not my place to say, but given the circumstances...."

I lifted my eyebrows in his direction, silently willing him to keep going.

"When Cami and I were spending so much time together, she made friends with some of my friends. In particular, she started spending a lot of time with my best friend, Lexi. *They* became very close and—" he trailed off, his eyes widening slightly, mentally willing the dots to connect in my head.

And then they did.

"Oh, oh, oh my gosh, I—" I stuttered, my mouth falling open. Heat immediately rose to my cheeks once again at my mistake and I reached up to rub a hand over my face, trying to scrub away the last five minutes of my life.

Ezra smiled politely at me when he knew I understood and reached out a gentle hand to squeeze my arm. "Anyway, things started to heat up between them. They fell in love. The only issue was Cami hadn't exactly told her family about her... about that part of her just yet. She and Lex were at a crossroads in their relationship where it was either take the next step or call it quits. Lex is an all-or-nothing type of girl." On his last sentence, he smiled and the corners of his eyes wrinkled adorably.

I barely noticed. I bit down nervously on my bottom lip, my mind trying to jump forward to the end of the story, jumping to the worst possible conclusion.

"Cami decided it was time to talk to her family. She wanted to be with Lexi. Wanted her to become part of her family one day. They went back to Colorado—where Cami's from—to see her parents."

I sucked in a sharp breath, afraid to hear what came next. I didn't realize I was biting down so hard on my bottom lip until I tasted metal.

At once, Ezra sensed my unease and reached out both of his hands to lightly grasp my shoulders. "No, no, no! It went well, it went well! Cami's parents were great, and they loved Lex, like I knew they would. I am an excellent judge of character."

I laughed at his attempt at a joke, feeling tears pricking at the back of my eyes. I probably looked crazy. Ezra must've noticed them, too, because he slowly reached up a hand to brush his calloused thumb tenderly against my temple.

"Anyway, after that, Cami decided to move in with Lexi, in her apartment in San Francisco. I'm pretty sure she's working at a small, indie record company under the Rabbit's Foot umbrella thanks to a glowing recommendation from your boss."

So Annabelle had helped Cami get a new job? I thought back to the brief conversation we'd had when she first put me on this assignment. Her clipped tone and vague explanation… at the time, I'd assumed it was due to the nature of what went down. But the more I thought about it, Annabelle never admitted or agreed that Cami had slept with a client. In fact, she shut down Mei's accusations immediately.

No, I read into all of that because of what Mei had said. Or implied. Annabelle's look of ire was because Mei's accusations were *wrong*, not because they were scandalous. At the end of the day, she was just protecting a former employee's privacy.

Shaking off the memories, I mustered up a small smile for Ezra, feeling strangely connected to these two people I never met, and to him, for telling me the truth. "So you're saying you didn't hook up with Camila?"

Ezra snickered softly, his thumb now tracing gentle circles against my cheek. "I'm saying she would be mortified and grossly offended you even suggested such a thing."

I laughed loudly, the sound coming out a little wet, and thought I probably would've liked Camila if we'd ever crossed paths.

"Hey, there she is," Ezra said softly. We were standing so close now that I could feel the tingle of his minty breath, warm against my cheeks. "A real laugh."

Immediately, I remembered the words written in his note from weeks ago—that first night in Jones Beach when he'd bought me every piece of merch his opener was selling.

My heart swelled as I stared at the man before me. This kind, light-hearted, beautiful man I'd come to know over the last month on the road. He was so at odds with the playboy, showboating rockstar I'd pictured in my head when I first took this assignment.

So much had happened in that short time. Between us. Within me.

And now I *wanted* him. So deeply, I wanted him.

Ezra opened his mouth to break the silence that had fallen between us, but before he could, I lunged.

Chapter 12

My mouth crashed into his and I was surprised to find how soft his lips were beneath the ferocity of my kiss. Slightly coarse, like they were just the tiniest bit chapped from singing earlier that night, but full. Accepting. Just the right amount of reciprocating pressure despite my sudden attack.

Heat coursed through me, a desire stronger than any I'd ever felt before flaming through my bones.

Ezra pulled back to search my face, a ring of honey-gold rimming his pupils, which were wide in the dim light of the bus. When he found no sign of hesitation—nothing but the breathless longing etched there—his long, slender fingers twisted gently up into the loose waves at the nape of my neck, and then his mouth was on mine.

His kiss was deliberate, filled with intention. He took his time, tasting and teasing with a laziness that almost frustrated me. Like we had all the time in the world here, together.

Ezra's warm lips easily parted mine, his tongue sliding in to meet my own. I arched against him instinctively and felt the arm he'd cradled around my back tighten, bringing me even closer to his lean, muscled body. A breathy moan escaped me at the sudden contact, our bodies burning where they joined. I could've sworn I heard his breath catch in his throat when my hips rolled tentatively against his, the sure sign of his arousal firm and telling against me.

I thought my head was going to explode.

There was a soft tug at the back of my head and I followed it, exposing my neck. Ezra's mouth quickly found the sensitive spot just beneath my earlobe. Unable to contain it, I moaned again, the sound echoing in the empty room with nothing pressed against my lips to muffle it.

"Make that sound again. I liked it," Ezra commanded breathily in my ear and sparks flew behind my closed eyelids—like I might come undone right then and there, pressed between Ezra's hard body and the table behind me.

Ezra's hand slid down along the curve of my spine, his fingertips somehow hot and cold at the same time as I felt them through the thin fabric of my shirt. I realized I was still wearing the stained and soaked crop top, but the thought flittered out of my mind as fast as it had come when I felt Ezra's strong grip on my bottom, hoisting me first up against him, then to perch on top of the table.

He stepped smoothly between my legs, his knees gently edging mine apart so he could fit flush against me, and inclined his head to meet my lips with his own. I met his pressure willingly, deepening our kiss until all I knew was the spicy and sweet scent of him and the tantalizing feel of his mouth on mine.

My arousal climbed and raged within me and I clawed hungrily at his back, gripping the soft fabric of his T-shirt in my hands to pull him closer still. There was no longer any evidence of where his body ended and mine began. Ezra loosed a groan when his long hardness met the soft pulsing heat between my legs, reassuring me my desire wasn't one-sided.

Oh so slowly, Ezra began to press gentle kisses down along my jawline, his tongue tracing lines and patterns more intricate than the tattoo lining his back along my skin as he moved down, down, down until he was kissing and nuzzling the base of my throat.

"Hannah..." he breathed against me, halting his kisses to rest his forehead against my collarbone, the very edge of his teeth scraping against the flushed, sensitive skin there as he spoke. I could feel the shallow breaths escaping his parted lips, little whispers of fiery wind against my chest. I arched my back, lifting toward his painfully still mouth, willing him to continue his pleasant trek down my body.

Instead of obeying my silent command, Ezra pulled back to face me fully. He only put a few inches between us, but I shivered at the shock of frigid air where his mouth had just been. I felt the absence of his embrace like a phantom limb. Desperate to close the distance between us, I pressed forward.

Gently gripping the side of my hip bone to still me, Ezra again whispered, "Hannah..." His voice was thick and hoarse, like tires crunching on gravel. It forced my eyes open. He reached up to grip both of my hands in his, resting them palm-side down on the tops of my thighs. His breathing was still shallow as his dark eyes held mine.

"Noooo," I crooned softly, unable to keep the whine from my voice. "You're stopping, why are you stopping?"

Ezra slowly untwined his fingers from mine and slid his palms up my bare arms, leaving goosebumps in their wake, until they came to rest on my shoulders. He leaned in again, just enough to press his forehead to mine. "I want nothing more than to take you right here, on top of this table. And then again on every single surface of this tour bus," he started, and liquid heat pooled between my legs, that desire raging once more through me like a roaring lioness.

"Please don't say 'but' now. Just end your sentence there and we can make all those wants a reality," I cooed, lifting my head in another attempt to press a kiss to his lips. He turned a fraction of an inch at the last moment so my mouth caught the edge of his stubbly jaw instead. I pulled away, mouth twisted in a frustrated pout.

"*But—*" he emphasized and I scowled. "I want more than that, too. I want to know this is real. I want to know it's not just the tequila soda talking, or some reaction to being caught up in the moment with a ridiculously hot, irresistible guy."

As I opened my mouth to object and parry his self-indulgent joke, he gave me a pointed look and lowered his voice to a seductive rumble to add, "And I want you to have full control over all your senses when I explore every single square inch of your body and make you feel things you've only dreamed about."

I swallowed hard. "Confident, are we?"

Ezra chuckled, and the sound brought a faint smile to my lips.

I knew I wanted him—beyond a shadow of a doubt. Our earlier conversation had sobered me, the fog of the tequila and the wine before that gone.

Deep down, I knew he wasn't just pushing me away, either. I could still feel the very full length of him pressed against my inner thigh, proving to me this longing wasn't one-sided.

But I also knew he was right.

What was that old saying, *nothing good ever happens after midnight*?

Jumping into this would probably only lead to a messy morning, and we were due at the venue before lunchtime for soundcheck. Not to mention the fact that Olivia and Peter could come walking up, looking for a ride home at any minute only to find us here. That was a bridge I was far from ready to cross tonight. Or possibly ever.

We had time. And the way his eyes gleamed as they stared into mine told me it would be worth the wait. So I huffed out a reluctant sigh and inclined my head to look at the ceiling. "Fine, but it better be epic after all that bravado."

Ezra laughed, louder this time, and stepped back from the table I perched upon, extending a hand to help me down. "Oh, you have absolutely nothing to worry about. I'm gonna blow your mind," he teased with a wink. I rolled my eyes at him and we fell right back into our typical banter.

It didn't feel like we were washing away the last hour or the line we'd come right up to and then crossed here in this tour bus, though, as he tossed innuendos and wiggling eyebrows my way and I parried back with stinging one-liners of my own.

It felt like us.

Ezra escorted me back to our hotel, ever the gentleman when he held open the door to the Uber for me and helped me step out of the car. We opted to leave the tour bus behind for Peter and Olivia, the driver still dutifully waiting at the lounge in the front of the nightclub with his Coke and lime.

On our way out of the bus, we'd remembered at the last second that I still needed a fresh shirt to replace my now *very* stained white top. Ezra had gallantly offered me his, and somehow the oversized, threadbare Local H shirt looked intentional with my black shorts and Converse.

"Tonight was…" I trailed off when the elevator doors slid open, depositing us on our quiet hotel floor.

"I know," was all Ezra replied and when his fingers brushed mine as we trudged slowly down the long hallway to my door, he gently intertwined them, our arms dangling loosely between us the rest of the way.

When we reached my room, I stopped in front of my door and spun around to face Ezra fully. "I guess I'll see you tomorrow. We leave at eleven for soundcheck—don't be late," I said, mustering up my most matronly voice.

Ezra loosed his slender fingers from mine to hold his hands up be-tween us defensively, his whiskey-colored irises glowing. "Wouldn't dream of it."

Playfully, I rolled my eyes, then bit my lip nervously. After every-thing that had happened—god, could this really all have taken place in the span of an hour?—I was less sure now where we stood with one another than ever before.

Reading my thoughts, Ezra gingerly tucked a stray piece of hair behind my ear, allowing his fingertips to trail along the sensitive skin there. I shivered at the contact.

"Dream of me," he said with a mischievous grin and I fought the urge to swat at him. "Goodnight, Han," he added in a softer voice.

Ezra leaned in slowly and pressed a gentle, chaste kiss to my lips that said so much more than words ever could.

Still half-facing Ezra's receding form in the hallway, I struggled to insert my hotel key card into the lock without looking. Finally, I heard the familiar whir and beep that told me it'd found its mark, and the bolt slid open. Reluctantly, I offered Ezra a final wave, which he returned with an animated air kiss, and pushed open the heavy door to my room.

Weird, I didn't think I'd left the lights on.

"What was that all about?" a voice rang out in the room that should've been empty and my heart leaped into my throat. Tentatively, I peered around the wall that jutted out to separate the doorway from the bedroom to find Olivia perched expectantly on the edge of my bed.

"Geez, you scared me!" I shouted at her, hand clutching at my throat and eyes as wide as saucers. My lungs struggled to suck down air from the shock. "How'd you even get in here?"

Olivia waved a hand, glancing at the closed door and then back to me. "I got my own key card from the front desk. That receptionist is gullible. It wasn't hard to convince him I was you."

Yeah, probably because he thought you were hot and he might have a chance, I thought. Olivia had a way of getting whatever she wanted out of the opposite sex, her goddess-like beauty combined with her quick wit was enough to turn any man into putty in her hands. I cocked my head in her direction and blinked slowly, willing her to realize how creepy it was that she snuck her way in here.

She didn't.

"Soooo what happened with you and Ezra?" she asked instead, a feline grin curving her plump lips. Despite the late hour, she still looked incredible—her makeup as fresh as it was when we'd left earlier that evening.

I noticed she'd changed into loungewear, at least, but even that looked elegant on her lithe form.

I groaned and stalked over to the bed and flopped down on my stomach beside Olivia, cradling my forehead in my hands. "Do we have to do this now?" I whined, my voice muffled against the fluffy down comforter beneath me. "It's almost three in the morning." Then I lifted my head with a start, eyes bulging in realization. "Oh no, we thought you and Peter were still back at the club. We told the bus driver to wait."

Olivia reached a hand out to gently pat my back, "Don't worry about it, I'll text Peter to deal with it. And in exchange, I want every sultry detail from tonight."

I shot my best friend a glare that she answered with dancing eyebrows even as she typed a message on her phone.

"*Tomorrow*, of course," she parroted back to me. "Now scoot over, I'm staying here tonight."

She pushed her manicured hands firmly against my prone form, making room for herself in the king bed. Knowing there was no way around this, and secretly looking forward to the quiet comfort of my best friend, I rolled over onto my side to give her enough space to curl up beside me.

Within minutes of Olivia reaching over to switch off the bedside lamp I was asleep, thoughts of soft lips and sexy lead singers filling my dreams.

Chapter 13

"Come on! It's almost time for soundcheck!"

I could hear Zach's voice clear through the walls of my hotel room, along with the sound of his fist banging against a door.

Remind me to ask for a room on a different floor next time.

From the sound of it, he was knocking on Peter's door. His room, I remembered, was two down to the left. Fortunately, I'd already been up for a few hours, my adrenaline still pumping from the night before.

With Ezra.

We kissed.

And I had wanted more. So much more.

A shiver raked up my spine at the memory, the feeling not wholly unpleasant.

Olivia had stayed in my room that night, both of us sleeping soundly tucked together beneath the oversized down comforter. When we woke up a little before eight, she'd pressed and begged me for details until I spilled everything like a schoolgirl with a crush, clutching a paper cup of chalky hotel coffee between my hands.

About an hour into our conversation, after she'd already had me run through the *events* on the tour bus in excruciating clarity at least twice, she'd been summoned by her boss for a video call. With an eye roll to rival all eye rolls, she reluctantly left my room, grumbling something about him pulling his head out of his ass.

Textbook Liv.

I used the alone time to take a burning hot shower, precisely do my makeup, and wax philosophical about what to wear. What says *we made out last night and it was amazing and I'd like to do it again, but also I'm totally chill and not desperate at all and we can keep things super casual?*

Ultimately, I'd settled on an old Aerosmith T-shirt from the late 90s my mom had given me, tucked into charcoal paperbag shorts. It went perfectly with my winged eyeliner that I most certainly did not need to fix with a Q-tip. Twice.

Tentatively, I peeked my head out of my door as the knocking down the hall continued. Sure enough, Zach was standing outside Peter's door, hands on his hips. Exasperated.

"Have you always been the mother hen of the group?" I asked him, a small smile curving my lips.

His head stirred at my voice, but his shoulders relaxed when he recognized me. "I swear, they are the reason I have gray hair at thirty-one."

I couldn't help but laugh. Fortunately, Zach chuckled softly too, some of the tension melting from his body just as Peter's door swung slowly open in front of him.

Peter looked more than a little worse for wear, his black T-shirt unusually rumpled. The bags under his eyes were prominent enough to see even from my position at least ten yards away. I watched him look slowly from Zach to me and then back, his foggy green eyes blinking with sleep.

Apparently he'd partied a little harder than I realized when he met Liv at the club last night. Maybe it should've been me interrogating my best friend this morning. As I stood there I vaguely recalled the familiarity with which she'd said, *I'll just text Peter to deal with it*, when I confessed we'd left our poor bus driver behind.

"Not a word," was all Peter said to both of us, breaking my train of thought. He hiked his black bag up over a broad shoulder and stalked past Zach, aimed for the elevators.

"I think they have Gatorade downstairs!" I shouted after his receding form, the teasing tone in my voice echoing down the hallway.

Without looking back, Peter threw his middle finger in the air, aimed squarely at me, before he disappeared around a corner. Zach just shrugged my way in a half-apology then offered a small wave before jogging after his bandmate.

I chuckled and threw him a small wave in return. As I rotated back toward my room, I heard the click and whoosh of another room opening nearby and hesitated just in time to see Ezra step into the hallway.

My mouth went dry when our eyes met. He looked ruggedly handsome—the stubble on his jawline had grown a bit more overnight, making him look every bit the rockstar. The tattoos adorning his toned arms were on full display in a loose tank top, the neckline dipping low on his chest to offer an uninterrupted view of the strong column of his throat and collarbones.

Could collarbones be considered sexy? Was that a thing? Because on Ezra, it was.

I tucked a loose lock of hair behind my ear nervously, offering Ezra a small smile. "Morning."

He grinned broadly back at me and closed some of the distance between us in just a few steps. "Morning," he said back, his voice soft in the expansive silence of the hallway.

"You just missed some of the guys. Peter's looking a little worse for wear," I offered awkwardly, inclining my head toward the elevators.

Ezra grimaced. "Great, tonight should be a fun one."

I laughed and relaxed a little against the doorframe. I could feel Ezra's eyes raking hungrily over me and it took all of my focus not to wither beneath his appraisal.

"So listen, tonight I was thinking—" Ezra started to say when the click and whoosh of another hotel room door opening cut him off.

"Freaking Bruce, I swear to God," Olivia huffed, stomping over to me, phone still in her hand. "He swore up and down he'd be fine without me, but I'm gone not two days and he's all over the place," she continued when she reached me, then when she realized we weren't alone added, "Oh, hey Ezra."

Ezra offered her a warm smile and nod, then said, "Better leave you guys to it. Soundcheck and all." He gestured with a thumb behind him. "But you'll both be at the show tonight, right?"

"Oh yeah, wouldn't miss it," Olivia answered for us, glancing down at the phone in her palm when it buzzed with a new message. Bruce again, judging by the bulging vein on her forehead.

I shrugged and gave Ezra a small, apologetic smile as he took several slow steps back toward the elevators, his eyes pinning me to the spot until he had to round the corner.

·♥·♥·♥·♥·♥·

Olivia and I stood huddled in a corner on the right side of the stage, carefully peeking our heads out now and again to watch the crowd. It was in between the first act and Olympus's show, and most of the concertgoers casually milled around, chatted eagerly with friends, and sipped on beer that had probably gone warm by now from the heat of the sweltering September evening.

It was Liv's last night in town before she flew back to New York, and she'd promised to watch Olympus's entire show with me, to make up for playing Cupid last night. I'd been dying to share this experience with her, reflecting on the last four weeks of shows.

The buzz of electricity in the air. The building anticipation.

The press of hundreds of bodies moving in sync to the first song.

My reverie was broken by a light tap on my shoulder and I turned around to see Ezra rocking back and forth on his heels behind us. His near-black hair seemed to shine beneath the moving overhead lights, which cast him in long shadows. He wore his signature dark green joggers that taper at the ankle—exposing a small piece of the tattoo winding from his foot to his calf—and a white, loose-fitting tank top that showed off the taut muscles underneath.

It was only after taking this mental catalog that I realized Ezra was waiting for me to respond to a question I never heard. Thankfully Olivia seemed to be paying attention, answering, "Yeah, it's been so cool! I can't believe our girl gets to do this every night for *work*." On her last word, she threw me a playful smile and stepped sideways to bump her hip against mine.

Our girl. I knew the title was intentional.

Ezra didn't seem to notice. Inclining his head toward me, one corner of his lips lifted as he narrowed his eyes. The deep amber color seemed to glow as he said slyly, "I have a feeling you're going to like tonight's show."

My eyebrows furrowed in confusion and I could feel Olivia's gaze on me when she asked him, "Don't you guys do the same thing every night?"

Ezra chuckled and stuffed his hands casually into his pockets, keeping the full brunt of his focus on me. "Oh no, we like to mix it up a little bit. The heart and soul of the setlist doesn't change much, but we've got a few tricks up our sleeves." Amusement played across his lips, the wicked gleam in his eyes opening a pit in my stomach.

What did he have planned?

Before I could ask, the rest of Ezra's bandmates hurried up behind him, ready to take their places.

"It's showtime!" Peter shouted over the din of the crowd, clapping both of his broad hands down on the backs of Ezra's shoulders, a voracious grin curving his lips.

The lights lowered over the stage, electricity building in the air as the audience in the pit surged forward, those with seats suddenly on their feet. Under the cover of darkness and to the sound of a backing track, the band took their usual places on stage as the crowd roared.

Even Olivia shouted along with them from her place beside me, her delicate hands cupped around her mouth to carry the sound. She wasn't necessarily a fan of Olympus, but we'd been friends for nearly a decade and I'd forced her to listen to them more than a few times. Seeing her now, enjoying this experience with me, brought a wide grin to my face. Ezra's strange hints were already forgotten.

No matter how many times I'd watched Olympus open their set, it never got old.

The stage remained dark as Zach expertly strummed the opening chords of their first song, overhead lights flashing as the music layered in. When Ezra's voice finally sounded, everything on the stage lit up. Several large screens hung on the stage walls behind them flared to life, flashing between dazzling geometric patterns timed to the music and video of their performance so the folks way back on the lawn didn't miss a single thing happening on stage.

As always, they looked completely at home in front of the crowd. Ezra's hips swayed to the rhythm, his eyes closed as he belted out the lyrics to a song off their first studio album. It was like no time had passed since its release, his voice every bit as precise and ethereal as it was a decade ago.

Feeling Olivia bobbing back and forth to the rhythm beside me, I allowed myself to get lost in the song—if only for a short while.

Their set chugged on like a well-oiled machine. They'd swapped out a few songs on their setlist for some they hadn't played since the first night in New York, but there'd been nothing unusual in their performance. If my mental math was correct there was just one song left before the encore.

So much for surprises tonight!

The venue was practically boiling, between the heat of late summer in Chicago and the press of hundreds of bodies swaying in place. Even the breeze off the lake behind us wasn't enough to cool things down, despite its best efforts.

Ezra's shirt came off about eight songs ago, as it usually did.

Despite still having a staff photographer out there tonight doing most of the work, I'd managed to sneak onto the stage a few times to capture some of my own content. Olivia didn't seem to mind my disappearing act, but I still tried to keep the excursions to a minimum. I couldn't stop my mind from whirring with different ways to use the videos I'd taken, though. My gritty, first-hand content would break up the beautiful images from the photographer nicely, creating an eclectic mix on their feed that was so wholly Olympus.

As Olivia and I silently waited for the band to launch into the next song, I opened up the photo app on my phone to check the lighting on the last video I'd captured. It was only after I closed out of it, satisfied with the quality, that I noticed the music had stopped and Ezra was talking to the crowd.

Okay, that was a little odd.

They didn't normally break at this point in the show. I carefully tucked my phone into my pocket and looked toward center stage just in time to catch the tail end of Ezra's sentence. "...try a little something different for you guys tonight. We've got a funky cover we think you're going to love. You wanna hear it?"

The crowd roared its answer back at him. It was an unintelligible cacophony of voices—a mass of noise, but it was clear the answer was a resounding *yes*.

Ezra's smile widened and he shot a look in my direction, holding my eyes for a few beats. His full mouth curved into a seductive smirk, a small yet adorable divot appearing at the corner of his mouth. When he finally tore his gaze away to face the audience, my heart started to race.

Oh no.

What was this? What was he doing?

Why did he look at me like that?

Olivia looked over at me, her eyebrows so high on her forehead I thought they might disappear into her hairline. All I could do was shrug back at her, just as much in the dark about Ezra's antics as she was. At the last moment, I decided to pick up my phone and press record, just in case this surprise ended up being a great marketing opportunity for the next tour date.

The band picked up the rhythm of a song, but I couldn't immediately place it. It wasn't one of their usual covers.

It had a fun groove to it and sounded like it was from a different genre—maybe hip-hop?

Finally, Ezra started singing and my jaw dropped to the floor.

I watched in mute horror as his hips rolled in time to the melody of Ginuwine's "Pony," my eyes wide as they took in every tantalizing thrust.

Olivia gasped beside me, then started cackling like a hyena. She grasped one of her hands firmly on my shoulder to keep herself upright, her laughter threatening to double her over and bring her to the floor.

"Damn, your man's got *moves*," she crowed.

"Shut up!" I hissed at her as she buried her face in my shoulder, still managing to peek out at the show with one eye. Olivia wasn't the only one amused. The crowd completely lost their minds—especially the women up front. The song may have been from the late 90s, but it was a classic. One that had been remixed by artists from nearly every generation; repurposed for movies and television shows and even TikTok trends.

When the chorus kicked in, Ezra paused his audition for *Magic Mike,* running the fingers of one hand through his hair while the other firmly gripped the microphone stand.

I'd never witnessed such a huge genre leap at a live show before, but somehow this song just... worked for them? The dark, slightly edgy punch of the electric guitar paired with the groovy bassline that was Olympus's signature style added a depth of sound that perfectly complemented the original arrangement.

At some point Olivia had made it through her laughing fit and was now dancing animatedly beside me, tugging on my arm to convince me to join her.

But I was still frozen to the spot.

The song entered the second verse and Ezra's body slowed once again. His sure and practiced hands grasped the microphone stand like a lover as he rocked his hips leisurely back and forth. The muscles in his abs rippled with each movement, his torso glistening with sweat.

My cheeks burned as I watched. I was sure I looked like a ripe tomato even under the cover of darkness.

When they reached the bridge, Ezra stopped rolling his hips and looked directly at the side stage—directly at *me*—holding my eye contact while he sang the suggestive lyrics.

My breath caught in my throat.

He smirked at me from behind the microphone, one of his hands stroking a painfully intimate trail from his chest down to his muscled stomach and then back up. I shuddered watching him, my body becoming liquid against my will.

This is not happening.

Trying desperately to regain what little composure I had, I closed out of the camera app on my phone—my hands were shaking so badly the video would've been useless anyway—and took a deep breath. With defiance in my darkened blue eyes, I returned the full force of his gaze, willing my lips to form a smirk of their own. As nonchalantly as I could, I tossed my hair over my shoulder in a way that I prayed screamed strong, confident, and completely unfazed. Basically, the opposite of what I felt.

His amber eyes held mine a few moments longer, but all traces of his cocky attitude had vanished, replaced by something far more primal.

Ezra was the first to break our little struggle for dominance, turning back to the crowd to wrap up the song. It was like a bucket of cold water dropped on me, the second his heated gaze left mine.

Like the bonfire I was standing next to suddenly went out.

"What *the hell* was that?" I shouted as I stormed into the green room after the show.

"Oh, hey Han," Peter said slowly, forcing me to stop my charge and take note of the packed room, filled with every member of Olympus.

I'd left Olivia behind when the lights dimmed, taking off in a run when the show ended to get back here to... do what, I wasn't quite sure. Confront Ezra? Jump his bones? At this point, my brain was such a muddled mess that all bets were off on which side of my psyche would win out.

Seeing the wide eyes of all four band members staring wordlessly at me gave me pause, my roiling emotions fizzling down to a dull simmer almost as quickly as they had sparked. I closed my mouth, which had been bobbing open like an angry fish, and folded my arms over my chest, doing my best to force what I hoped was a friendly smile to my lips. "Hey, Peter—everyone," I said, giving him, Angel, and Zach a pointed look that said *get the hell out of here before you're caught in the crossfire of whatever comes next.*

The three of them blinked slowly back at me, obviously not catching my drift. *Okay, guess I need to be a little more direct.*

"I think Olivia may have gotten lost somewhere backstage... could you go and make sure she's okay?" I lied, carefully enunciating every word to convey the hidden meaning.

Peter's brilliant emerald eyes lightened with understanding. "Right, yes. Angel, Zach, why don't you come help me?"

Apparently he was the only one picking up what I was putting down because Zach's face twisted with annoyance. "All of us?"

Right as my eye started to twitch and I opened my mouth to rage again, Peter cut me off, "Yes, dude. All of us. Let's go." His voice was the sternest I'd ever heard it, the glare he gave his friends leaving no room for argument.

Zach rolled his eyes, but both he and Angel followed Peter through the green room door and into the labyrinth of hallways behind the stage. For a second, I felt bad for abandoning Olivia in such an unfamiliar area. Then I remembered the way she cackled during Ezra's little show and stamped a mental foot on that guilt.

I waited until the door was fully closed before rounding on Ezra, flames burning in my sapphire eyes. In two long strides, I closed most of the distance between us, jabbing a finger toward his face. "You said you wanted to take things slow. And then you go out there and tell me you've got some big surprise you think I'll like, which turns out to be *you*, shirtless, practically humping a microphone stand?"

Ezra grinned at his own cleverness, but the pointed look I threw his way had him turning the expression into a cough, bringing one of his fists up to his mouth to cover it.

"So, did you?" he asked timidly after a stretch of silence, somehow looking up at me through lowered lashes despite being almost a foot taller.

I cocked my head to the side, trying not to be disarmed by his charm. "Did I *what?*"

Ezra's lips spread wide in a feline grin, his eyes dancing with mischief. "Did you like it?" His voice was a seductive rumble I felt in my gut.

I blinked slowly back at him, chewing on the inside of my cheek to fight off the slow smile that threatened to spread across my lips. *He was such an ass sometimes.*

But he also made me want to laugh. To live—for more than just my career. I swallowed that thought.

Don't get ahead of yourself, Hannah.

At the end of the day, when the tour was over and Olympus returned to their normal lives and I to mine, I would be just another blip on the radar. I had plans for myself, ambitions. I loved working with Ezra, and Peter, and Zach, and Angel, but I wanted to move up at Rabbit's Foot, to prove myself. And that meant more clients, new clients, longer hours, *the works.*

A bitter taste rose in the back of my throat for a split second. I swallowed that down, too.

There was no time for anything serious, but maybe we had time for... other things.

"How about this," I said, folding my arms over my chest and cocking a hip to one side. "If you want the real answer to that question, you know where to find me tonight."

Ezra's amber eyes widened in mild surprise and I smirked.

Catching him off guard was so vindicating.

Before he could reply, I turned quickly on my heel and flounced through the door, careful not to look back.

Chapter 14

A quiet knock sounded on the door to my room, drawing my attention from the window that looked out over the city. I hadn't been looking at anything in particular, my nerves were too shot for that. But staring out at the expansive night sky and the few stars visible through Chicago's light pollution was far better than watching the minutes tick by on the bedside clock.

Which I most definitely had not done for twenty minutes after I first arrived.

I inhaled a deep, clarifying breath, letting it whoosh audibly out of my mouth, and rose from my spot on the hotel's large four-poster. Shaking hands smoothed down the front of my ribbed tank top and adjusted the tie on my lounge pants as I willed myself to relax.

Nearly two hours had passed since I walked away from Ezra, each minute slipping by at a painstakingly slow pace, draining my internal fire along with it. As I approached the door, another knock pounded through the heavy wood at my delay, and I struggled to reignite the confidence I had felt the moment I confronted Ezra in the green room.

"Hannah, open the damn door," a sharp but distinctly feminine voice commanded and my mouth twisted. When I rushed to swing open the door it was Olivia, not Ezra, standing there with her arms folded over her chest, one foot tapping impatiently on the carpeted floor.

With a sweeping glance, she took in my modest pajamas, the loose hair styled to hang down my back and frame my face, and my makeup—touched up from earlier to give my face a fresh and dewy glow. One corner of her mouth ticked up.

"Peter told me you left the venue hours ago, I just came to make sure you were alright..." she trailed off, leaning her lean body against the doorframe. "But it looks like you were expecting someone else?"

Her ability to read me like an open book was getting old.

"I don't have time to explain right now, but I *promise* I'll fill you in tomorrow," I answered in a sharp hush, already waving my arms to shoo her away. "After all of your pushing, I may or may not be waiting on one very hot, very single lead singer to meet me."

Olivia sprang from the doorframe and clapped her hands together, surprise mixed with delight shining in her eyes. You'd have thought she was the one about to get laid.

"Get it girl!" she squealed, reaching out to give my shoulder a light squeeze. "Text me tomorrow when it's safe to come over. I want to hear *every* detail." Olivia wiggled her eyebrows suggestively and even though I didn't want to laugh, my mouth betrayed me.

"Fine, fine, *now go!*" I replied, pushing her back into the hallway. I didn't wait to make sure she was on her way to her room before quietly closing the door. I puffed out another long exhale that rustled the strands of hair framing my face, then leaned my back against the door. Seeing Olivia had been a nice distraction, helping to simmer off some of my nerves.

I took a step toward where my phone perched on the night-stand—maybe Ezra had been held up at the venue and texted me to let me know?—when another knock sounded on my door.

"Damnit, Liv," I mumbled under my breath, eyes rolling as I turned around. I flung open the door expecting to see my very sheepish best friend with a *very* good reason for disturbing me yet again.

Instead, I was met with the very hot, very single lead singer I had been waiting for.

"Hey, Han. Sorry, I know it's late. We decided to stay after and sign some autographs," Ezra explained mildly, a small, apologetic tilt curving his full lips.

My gaze caught on those lips, lingering there for just too long to be casual, before I responded, "Of course, yeah! No problem," in what I hoped was a breezy, totally relaxed way, and leaned my left shoulder against the doorway.

Silence stretched between us as Ezra's amber eyes gave me a tantalizingly slow once-over, leaving flushes of heat on my skin in their wake.

"Can I come in?" he asked softly when his eyes met mine again.

I sprang to life, taking a wide step back to give him room. "Right, yes, sorry. Please, come in."

"Please, come in"? What is he, a vampire?

Ezra shot me a grateful look and stepped into the room, politely pretending to take it in. Like it didn't look almost identical to his own down the hall. I took longer than normal to close the door behind him and check the lock, using the extra time to still my racing heart.

Where was all that bravado now?

"So..." I started, leaning my back against the door and folding my arms over my chest to hold myself together. We both knew why he was here, why I had been waiting for him. Who would be the first to break?

"So..." Ezra said, taking one tentative step toward me. Then another. Electricity snapped in what little space remained between us with each whisper of his foot against the floor.

When I checked into this hotel, I had been elated at the size of the room—the gaping window overlooking the city skyline, the gigantic spa tub in the attached bath, the large vanity pressed against one wall, the king-size bed in the center that was all mine.

Now with Ezra standing in here, it felt like a shoebox: positively claustrophobic. The walls pressed in on me, forcing us closer.

With just one more step, Ezra closed the space between us entirely. He reached a calloused hand up and I thought he was going to grab my face and kiss me again, the way he did on the tour bus the night before.

Instead, he pressed the flat of his large palm against the door, just above my head, so his six-foot-three frame arched over me. Caging me in. I pressed my thighs together, trying to stifle the heat growing between them at his nearness.

BookTok would be screaming right now.

"You were a little... heated earlier, in the green room," he purred, a wicked half smile on his lips.

"You told me to watch out for a *fun* surprise and then did a strip tease on stage. How was I supposed to act?" I shot back quietly.

Ezra's shoulders shook with silent laughter, the movement bringing him even closer until mere inches separated us. "How about appreciative? Awed? Aroused?"

With a snort, I rolled my eyes and added an A-word of my own, "Annoyed?"

I knew he was teasing me, but the way his quirked eyebrow matched his smirk nearly drove me mad. My answering smile was smug, self-satisfied at my own cleverness.

Ezra chuckled, the beautiful timbre of it echoing through the cavernous room and immediately evaporating some of my anger in a way only he seemed capable of. His other hand reached up, palm pressing against the door on the other side of my face. The intoxicating aroma of citrus and sandalwood washed over me and I breathed it in deeply, not bothering to care if he noticed.

"Just admit you enjoyed it," he coaxed, his minty breath tickling my ear as his face hovered a fraction of an inch closer to mine.

I inclined my chin to catch and hold his gaze, not ready to break for him. Ezra merely slid one of his hands off the door to cup my chin. When our eyes locked, I saw something shift in him.

Ezra closed what distance remained, stepping one of his knees in between my thighs, and pressed his mouth to mine. The pressure of his kiss forced me firmly against the door. Willingly, my lips parted for him and his tongue swept in—tasting, teasing, exploring.

He tasted even better than he smelled, the deep herbal notes amplified a thousand times over.

I unlocked my arms from around my chest and reached up, thrusting a hand into the hair at the nape of his neck. The soft strands slid through my fingers like silk. My other hand found his hip, gripping him tightly to pull his taut body flush against mine.

Ezra deepened our kiss, his free hand curled around the base of my spine while the other cradled my jaw. The hand I rested on his hip couldn't stay still for long as our breathing grew heavy, full of want. It slid up over his threadbare shirt, caressing the planes of his abdomen before coming to rest flat against his sculpted chest.

With a quiet groan—so quiet I almost couldn't hear it—Ezra broke our kiss to move his lips down, grazing them along the sensitive skin just beneath my earlobe. He knew exactly what that would do to me after our too-brief liaison the night before. My moan was involuntary and my body arched into his. I felt something hard press against my lower stomach and the muscles in my core clenched, damp heat blooming between my thighs.

Ezra's hand traced idle circles along my spine, then moved around toward the front of my body, first brushing a soft touch against my hip, then moving up along my stomach, underneath my tank top. A rush of blood thundered in my ears.

Slowly, he moved that hand of his up my abdomen until the tips of his slender fingers grazed the bottom of my breast. The fabric of my bralette was thin, but still the obstruction felt like too much.

I wanted his bare skin on mine. I wanted *more*.

Ezra's teeth grazed my earlobe and I couldn't stifle another moan before it escaped my lips. The breathy sound encouraged him, his teeth clamping down gently on the delicate skin there. I sucked in a sharp breath at the mixture of pain and pleasure, fisting the fabric of his T-shirt just to get a grip on something, anything, in my haze.

As he continued to nibble and kiss the sensitive skin around the shell of my ear, his nimble fingers found their way inside the elastic band of my bralette. I shivered when he brushed a thumb over my pebbled nipple, another groan breaking past my lips. Without thinking, I tilted my head back against the door to expose my throat to him, my body silently willing him to replace that gentle hand with his mouth.

I waited for alarm bells to sound in my head, the whispers to *stop!* or the shouts of *What the hell are you doing?* to distract me from the feeling of Ezra.

None came.

Even my subconscious wanted to sleep with a rockstar.

My fingers unwound themselves from his shirt and slid around his back, then lower, dipping into the loose-fitting waistband of his joggers. He shivered at the brush of my chill fingertips against his bare skin, grinding his hips into mine at the same moment.

Stars flashed behind my closed eyelids and I gasped. Ezra lifted his face at the same moment, muffling the sound with another fierce kiss. Our tongues danced to a silent melody, the kiss yielding just long enough for me to tear his tank top over his head, tossing it carelessly to the floor behind him.

Eagerly, my hands roamed the length of his torso, exploring the dips and planes of his pectorals, then heading south across his defined abs.

I never realized quite how muscled he was until I could feel it beneath my palms.

Ezra's hand slid out from beneath my shirt so he could pull back just enough to look into my eyes right as my adventurous fingertips found the front of his waistband and brushed against the hardness waiting for me underneath. I bit my lip at the sheer size of him, my cheeks heating under his gaze. The low growl that escaped his lips was filled with want. Desire flamed within me and, eager to hear him make that sound again, I caressed my fingers once more over the front of his briefs.

Ezra groaned, even louder this time, and closed his eyes for a moment, biting down hard on his bottom lip as though that might help him regain control. When his eyes reopened, they were nearly black, his lids heavy. He leaned forward to rest his forehead against mine and asked, "Are you sure?"

"Yes," I breathed without hesitation, my husky voice unfamiliar to my ears.

Ezra's answering grin was carnivorous and his hands were steady when they reached for the bottom of my tank top, ripping it up and over my head in one smooth motion, followed shortly by my bralette. In a sweeping glance, he took my bare torso in fully for the first time, his gaze sweeping from the moon phase tattoo along my rib cage, curving up toward my swollen breasts and peaked nipples, begging for his touch.

He licked his lips hungrily and then his mouth was on me.

Tenderly, he kissed his way down from my collarbone, his mouth carving a slow path over the tops of my breasts as he carefully walked me away from the door, toward the king-size bed in the center of the room. As we moved, his tongue swept slow, delicious circles around my nipple while his hand palmed my other breast.

The feeling of him on my bare skin was euphoric. Better than I ever imagined on the few late nights I dared to let my thoughts and desires wander freely.

My knees buckled against the edge of the bed, but Ezra caught me with one hand behind my back, gently laying me down atop the soft, down comforter. Raising my hands above my head, I interlocked my fingers and arched my back, putting myself on full display for him as his tongue continued to tease and taste every inch of my breasts.

His hand trailed down my abdomen and, with practiced surety, he slid my lounge pants down to below my knees with one hand, until I could easily kick them off the rest of the way. His delicate fingers walked their way back up my leg, up over the peak of my knee, then down the soft curve of my inner thigh, until his thumb brushed a teasing circle over the top of my underwear. There was no hiding how ready I was, the slickness beneath his touch giving away everything I felt.

Ezra groaned with satisfaction and grazed his teeth against my nipple. My answering pulse of pleasure had me bucking my hips, panting loudly as I willed his hand to touch me again.

More, more, more.

"So impatient," he teased breathlessly, grazing his teeth against my breast again until I shuddered beneath him.

Had I said that out loud?

My eyes were shut tightly, my head tilted back into a soft pillow, when I felt Ezra pull his mouth away from my breast. The sudden absence of him felt like the sun being blinked out by a storm cloud on an otherwise perfect day.

In a panic I snapped open my eyelids, ready to protest, just in time to see that beautiful mouth of his poised over the apex of my thighs. I gasped at the sight of Ezra Bell between my legs—the legendary rockstar, the playboy, the king of the stage now worshiping at my altar. The heat from his breath against me threatened to send me into orbit.

Ezra held my hungry gaze, his dark eyes gleaming with lust. His calloused fingers gingerly pulled my black, lacy bikini underwear down the tops of my thighs, over my knees, and past my ankles, his fingertips driving me wild as they caressed my skin the entire way.

"You have no idea how long I've wanted to taste you," he murmured against the soft curve of my inner thigh, pressing a kiss to the same spot.

I licked my bottom lip then sucked it into my mouth, unable to look away as he continued a trail of kisses higher and higher on my thigh.

"Please," I begged, the sound more air than an actual word.

He hooked one of my legs over his shoulder and flicked his tongue against my center. Colors flashed in my vision, my eyelids slamming shut at the sudden shock of pleasure that rocked through me.

On his second stroke, my hips threatened to buck us both right off the bed. Ezra placed a broad palm flat against my lower abdomen, pinning me to the spot.

On his third taunting stroke, I opened my eyes to look down at him, my desire edged with impatience that he continued to tease me despite knowing exactly what I wanted. In spite of it, actually. He tilted his head and chuckled against the soft flesh of my inner thigh, mere inches from where I *needed* him, then began pressing a trail of soft kisses down and up one leg, then over to the other, purposely avoiding where I craved him most.

"You are the worst," I whimpered without conviction. He barked a laugh, then pressed his tongue flat against my center, dragging it slowly up until it was exactly where I wanted it. With smooth, precise circles, he tasted every inch of me. With every expert stroke of his tongue, every muscle in my body seemed to tense and thrum, drawing closer and closer to the edge until I finally tumbled over completely.

My hands fisted the blankets beneath me, my head thrown back as I tried desperately to hold in my screams of pleasure. Ezra's tongue worked through every roll of my hips, carrying me to the edge of the earth, to the edge of the galaxy, where shooting stars danced behind my eyelids and my breaths came in short, ravenous gasps.

It wasn't until my body slackened, my chest heaving with exertion despite having done nothing but enjoy the ride, that Ezra's mouth delicately pulled away.

The absence of him was short-lived as he began to place a trail of gentle kisses up my lower belly. A satisfied smile curling my lips, I watched as he kissed his way up the flesh of my stomach, one of my hands twining loosely in his hair to massage his scalp. He flashed me a boyish grin that made me giggle—*actually* giggle, *who does that?*—when his trail of kisses led him to the curvy underside of my breasts. There, he resumed his earlier work.

In an instant, arousal flared within me again. I gently tugged at his hair, urging his lips to mine. His answering kiss was hungry, his lips easily parting mine until I could taste myself on his tongue. With a roll of my hips against his taut body, I realized, much to my chagrin, that his pants had yet to come off.

That simply will not do.

Greedily, I reached both hands down, fumbling with the waistband of his joggers until I could push them and his boxers down to his knees in one fell swoop. Chuckling good-naturedly at my clumsiness—or maybe the desperation in that movement—he gracefully kicked them both off the rest of the way.

His mouth never left mine as he whispered, "Eager girl. I like that."

I nipped at his bottom lip in mock reprimand and snaked an arm around his bare back to pull him flush to me. I groaned when I felt the full length of him press against my inner thigh—this time nothing separating us. When he adjusted his hips so the tip of him teased the apex of my thighs, sparks danced behind my eyelids. He was so close to where I wanted him.

Suddenly, my eyes sprang open in a panic, my lips and tongue pausing their dance with his.

"Wait, do you have..." I trailed off, my words nearly consumed by his kiss.

Ezra pulled back a fraction of an inch, eyebrows raised in question.

I blinked slowly, my eyes flicking down to the nonexistent space between us and back up. "Protection," I whispered and rolled my hips the tiniest bit to emphasize my point. I thought his eyes were going to roll back in his head at the unabated touch, his breath hissing out and tickling the tip of my nose in a gasp.

Ezra managed to pull it together enough to nod, propping himself up on one hand and using the other to gesture a "hold, please" signal in my direction. Quickly, yet somehow gracefully, he crawled over to the edge of the bed where we had discarded his pants and fished a condom out of his pocket.

When he climbed back up toward me, I arched a brow in his direction as if to say, *expecting something tonight, were we?*

He simply shrugged, a coy smile playing on his lips.

In one swift motion, Ezra rolled onto one side next to me and expertly slid the condom on, allowing me to take in his impressive length for the first time.

That... is going in me?

I shuddered, Ezra breaking my thoughts as he trailed a caressing touch up and over the curve of my hip.

"Are you sure?" he repeated gently, those slender, nimble fingers tracing invisible patterns up and down my ribcage.

He was so patient and gentle. I knew with one hundred percent certainty if I asked him to stop right now, he would back off without question.

Instead, I tugged him back on top of me, allowing my legs to fall to either side of him, before wrapping them securely around his hips. He shivered when his hardness brushed against me, the center of my thighs slick with want.

I thought I had never known true pleasure until Ezra's mouth was on me mere minutes ago.

But I was wrong.

So, so wrong.

Nothing compared to the feeling of Ezra Bell inside me.

My eyes rolled back into my head when, with a painfully slow roll of his hips, he pushed into me. It took me a few moments to adjust to the full length of him. And when I did, I matched him thrust for thrust, rolling my hips to meet his rhythm. Wanting—*needing*—more of him, I bucked my hips and managed to roll the two of us over until I sat soundly on top, setting the pace as I rode him.

"Hannah," he breathed, his eyes snapping shut, dulling all other senses until all he could feel was me around his length, our bodies moving in perfect sync. "You feel so good."

The sound of my name on his lips echoed around us like the chorus to a song we were writing together in the center of that hotel bed. One that only we would ever hear.

It felt like only moments had passed when I approached the brink once more, though it had to be much longer, judging by the tiny beads of sweat trickling down my temples and spine.

When I couldn't contain myself any longer, I threw my head back and bellowed his name at the ceiling, at the sky, at the solar system above us, and he joined me.

<h1 style="text-align:center">Chapter 15</h1>

"How do you always smell so good?" I asked, my voice thick with gratification and the type of exhaustion I usually only felt after a tough sweat session at the gym with Olivia.

After we mustered up the energy to bring each other to the peak of ecstasy a second time—well, Ezra's second time, my third, if we kept score—Ezra had immediately made himself at home in my bed, pulling me against his side so my head rested on top of his tattooed shoulder. One of my bare legs draped casually over his thigh, resting snugly between his knees.

I felt Ezra lower his head to peer down at me and inclined my own to meet his gaze, noting just a little smugly that his amber eyes were also hazy.

"Me?"

I nodded and took in a deep inhale against his neck for emphasis, a sated smile curving my lips. He smelled like a day at the beach where the water was just cool enough to feel refreshing, where the sand was like a warm caress against your skin instead of a third-degree burn, where no seagulls tried to steal your last french fry. He smelled like a vacation at a five-star resort you weren't footing the bill for. He smelled like... a place I never wanted to leave.

I stiffened at the thought.

Fling, I reminded myself firmly.

No romance.

No relationship.

He exhaled deeply, one corner of his mouth twitching, and tickled the side of my cheek with his index finger before dropping his hand to trail idle circles around my exposed shoulder. "What can I say? I've got excellent taste in soap."

I huffed a laugh, allowing my eyes to flutter closed as I breathed in his warm, spicy scent one more time. Ezra leaned his head down a fraction of an inch to press a chaste kiss to my temple and I felt like my heart might burst from being so full.

If this somehow turned out to be my last night on Earth, I'd be totally content with that.

"Tell me what you're thinking," Ezra whispered against the top of my head as if he could hear my thoughts churning.

My eyes snapped open, suddenly worried mind reading really was a thing. Maybe it was for Ezra. He was a man of many talents.

Confess that my last thought was about dying in his arms, after no dates and having sex *one time*?

Oh no. Absolutely not.

Think. Think. Think.

"I'm thinking... that I've never felt so exhausted before in my entire life."

Ezra snorted into my hair, his hand pausing on my shoulder just long enough to poke me gently in the ribs.

"No, no, no. You're not getting off that easy," he started and I lifted my head to give him my best, that's *what she said* look, earning me another laugh. "I'm serious. Tell me... your deepest, darkest secret. I want to know everything, starting with the juicy stuff."

A shiver raked up between my shoulder blades.

I had never been that interesting of a person. Certainly not one to have a juicy secret. But I had to give him something. More than that, I wanted to give him something. A piece of me, however small.

I chewed thoughtfully on my bottom lip, my eyes scanning the room in search of ideas. When they landed on the carefully locked door to the bedroom, my lips curled as I remembered the way I awkwardly invited him in.

"Okay, here's something only Olivia knows about me," I started, turning my gaze on Ezra's body, still partially covered with mine. I stared a hole at the spot where the white hotel sheet draped across his lower abdomen, just barely obscuring what rested below.

"I know you may be thinking, *wow, that Hannah is so smart and worldly. She must only watch artsy films and documentaries in her spare time—*"

Ezra interrupted me with a loud *pfft* sound he couldn't contain, which I kindly returned with a light pinch to his upper pectoral.

"The truth is, I *love* soapy dramas. And supernatural dramas," I went on, stroking my fingertips over the area I just pinched. "My all-time favorite show is one that came out when I was in ninth grade called *The Vampire Diaries*. It's the best piece of television excellence I've ever seen. On a scale of one to ten, it's a hundred. The characters? The drama? The soundtrack? Amazing. Incredible. Inspiring. I rewatch it at least once every year."

"*The... Vampire Diaries*," Ezra sounded the words out like he'd never heard them before.

I shot up, bracing a hand against Ezra's sculpted stomach to support myself. When his eyes immediately dipped down to my bare chest, I wrestled the sheet up just enough for some semblance of modesty.

"You've never heard of *The Vampire Diaries*?! It's a cult classic!"

"I don't think it's been around long enough to be considered a classic, Han," Ezra debated, cocking an eyebrow. "You're not *that* old."

I playfully swatted his shoulder. "Fine, whatever, maybe not a classic. But it has a cult following, and I just so happen to be a member. I've seen it probably a dozen times and the series finale *still* makes me bawl my eyes out. I can't even listen to the soundtrack without tearing up."

"Wow, I feel like I need to see this just to understand what could possibly make the great Hannah Maxwell burst into tears," he deadpanned, but I could see amusement dancing in his whiskey-colored eyes.

I rolled my eyes and settled back down against him, our bodies fitting together like two adjoining pieces of a puzzle. "Your homework for the foreseeable future is to get some culture and watch the show."

He chuckled, the sound making his chest vibrate against my cheek. "Fine, fine. I'll watch the show. But that hardly counts as a secret, even if Olivia's the only one who knows. Other than me now, of course."

I opened my mouth to protest, but Ezra cut me off to clarify, "You said it yourself, it has a cult following. Half the world loves this show.

Hardly newsworthy. Or secret." He leaned down to place his lips close to my ear. "Hannah Maxwell, I want something personal."

I shuddered at the way my full name sounded on his lips, the four syllables taking on a seductive quality I'd never heard before.

He wasn't going to make this easy on me. I chewed over my thoughts as they ricocheted around my brain. I grasped onto one and took the plunge.

"I do have a bit of a confession to make..." I began, trying to adopt his mischievous tone to mask my embarrassment at what I was about to share.

"Uh oh, you're not about to tell me that was your first time, right?" he joked and I playfully swatted at his stomach.

"*No*," I enunciated sternly, though he could probably hear the grin in my voice as I tried to hide it against his skin.

"The truth is, this tour..." I hesitated for just a moment longer, then decided to rip off the bandage. "This tour wasn't the first time I've seen you guys play live. The band, I mean. In fact, I've been a fan of Olympus since I was sixteen, when your first album came out. I've probably been to, like, five of your shows before I landed this job."

I felt Ezra's jaw fall open against my head and started to get nervous when he didn't respond right away. Tentatively, I peeked up at him, already wincing at what I might find there—shock and outrage that I had lied (omitted, really)? Embarrassment that I had been jamming out to him as a young and awkward teenager (just over four years separated us in age, but when you're a kid like that, it makes a big difference)?

Instead, I was greeted with a wide, boyish grin that made him look exactly how he did in Olympus's debut music video, even a decade later. "You sneaky little—" he crowed, hugging his arm around my shoulders until my body was pressed so firmly into his side I couldn't tell where I ended and he began. "I *knew* there was no way you had that 'Need You Here' karaoke down so perfectly after just a few weeks on the road with us."

He tried to screw his face into his most serious expression to add, "I can't believe I just slept with a liar. My pure body and soul are tainted forever." Ezra shook his head slowly, feigning disappointment, but the corners of his mouth tugged up in a way that gave away the punchline.

"Shut up!" I yelled, swatting at his chest again. "I didn't lie. I just... withheld information. Information you didn't need to know at the time."

I stuck my tongue out at him and in a flash, he leaned down to suck it into his mouth. What started as a joke quickly turned into a passionate kiss that threatened to have us climbing back on top of one another if left unchecked.

"Okay, okay, your turn," I breathed into his mouth, trying to keep my voice light as I broke our kiss.

Ezra pulled back just enough to look into my eyes, the tip of his nose tickling mine. "I have no secrets, Han. I'm an open book. You probably know all about me already, having been a fan for ten years. They write about me in the tabloids every other week. Pick your poison." He kept his tone casual, joking, but I could see the way his irises clouded, hear the biting edge to his words as he deflected.

Oh no, I wasn't having that.

I shoved a palm against the broad plane of his chest, pushing him back until he rested against the headboard. "Ezra Bell, if everyone knows it, it's hardly newsworthy," I parroted back at him. "I want something personal."

Ezra laughed quietly, that armor he'd worn for years cracking just enough for me to see through. "Personal, eh? Hmm…"

For a few quiet moments, his eyes took on a far-off quality. Then they slid back to meet mine. There was a kind of steely resolve in them that hadn't been there a minute before. I swallowed hard, waiting.

"Okay, here's something I don't think anyone really knows," he started, dropping his hand to pick at a loose thread on the sheet, his gaze following. "Our very first show after we went platinum with Infinite Horizons, we went on late. Like, really late." Ezra paused, the corners of his lips turned up in a ghost of a smile. "Everyone thought it was an equipment issue, that's what we told them, at least. In reality… I was backstage puking my guts out."

My eyes bulged but I held my tongue, willing him to go on.

He abandoned the thread he'd been picking at and met my gaze. "I was so nervous to perform in front of a crowd that size I actually vomited from nerves. I didn't even know that was a thing people did in real life." He snorted softly, his nose wrinkling at the memory.

I gasped in mock horror. "I'm sorry, you mean to tell me Ezra Bell gets nervous? And here I thought you were born with a microphone in your hand and a stage beneath your feet."

He rolled his eyes but his smile widened, the humor finally reaching them. "That's what I *want* you to think. What I want everyone to think, really. I'm always nervous, though. It's gotten better with time and practice. Obviously, I'm not vomiting anymore, but sometimes my hands are shaking so badly before a show I can barely hold the mic."

He lifted and dropped his shoulders, then added, "People think this comes easy to me. The music and the singing and the writing.

And honestly, that used to be fine. I put on a show and hustled so hard in the early days so they would look at me and think, *wow, that guy's got it*. So I pranced around on stage and I flirted with the girls in the audience and did all the things I thought I was supposed to do. And it worked. People started seeing me as someone who could walk on stage with no practice, put on a show, entertain the world, and then spend the rest of my time goofing off or partying or sleeping around."

I winced almost imperceptibly at his last words. Thankfully Ezra didn't seem to notice.

"In reality, it's hard. Getting stuck on a lyric, or hung up trying to find the right chord progression, or even just the mental marathon of being crammed into a small room with your best friends for so long you start to wonder why you started hanging out with them in the first place." He let out a soft laugh and shook his head. "When we first started out, I wanted nothing more than for everyone to think I had it all together. Now? Sometimes it feels like I'm waiting for someone to figure it out. To call me on it."

I nodded, unable to find the right words. It was impossible not to relate to everything Ezra had confided in me. He probably had no idea just how much I empathized with his struggle. How a dull ache had begun to build in my chest as my own struggles with impostor syndrome were reflected right back at me.

How hard had I worked to make everyone, even my own mom, think I was born for this career? That I was smarter and more driven and more qualified than anyone else. That I deserved to be here, when in reality, my own biggest critic has always been me.

The ache in my chest sharpened as I looked at Ezra, really looked at him.

How could Ezra *Freaking* Bell feel this way?

How could people believe this guy was as shallow as a kiddie pool?

A veritable rock god and yet here he was, showing me the same fears and the same feelings of inadequacy I'd been facing down every morning since landing this job.

I reached out to take one of his hands in my own, giving it a tight squeeze. Then another. He offered me a small smile, squeezing back.

I wasn't ready to confess my own uncertainties. It would be dangerous to do that, to fully let him in. And yet I wanted him to know he wasn't alone. That he was seen, even if it was just by some girl at his record label who probably meant nothing.

"Well, now at least one person knows the truth: that you're just as lost as the rest of us peons."

Ezra let out a breathy laugh and shook his head, the light slowly returning to his dark eyes. For a moment, he looked like he wanted to say something more. Instead, he reached his hand up to cup the side of my face and leaned forward to press a hard kiss to my lips.

My entire being melted into his kiss, my lips parting around his. Ezra swiftly looped his arms around my back, sliding them down to cup my bottom in his hands so he could pull me into his lap. My legs fell easily to either side of him, our chests crashing together as his tongue met mine. One of his hands snaked up into the hair at the nape of my neck, tugging it gently, while the other traced slow circles up and down my spine. My own hands cupped his face, holding on for dear life as though one false move would send me careening off the edge of the Earth.

It would be so easy to surrender to him again. To let him lay me down against these fluffy down pillows. Things had already progressed too far too quickly tonight, though. Any further and I'd risk an attachment I wouldn't survive.

Reluctantly, I broke the kiss and rested my forehead against his. My chest rose and fell in rapid succession, my lungs trying desperately to suck down air. "You should probably get back to your room," I whispered, my lips nearly touching his as they formed the words.

In reality, I wanted him to stay. I didn't want this night to end. Going back to our regular lives tomorrow felt oddly like an ending. A death sentence.

"You're kicking me out?" Ezra asked, indignantly. "Come on, I thought I was pretty good!"

He leaned in for another kiss and I lifted a hand to press two fingers to his lips, suppressing a giggle. Slowly, I scooted back from him and sat up straight, pulling the crisp, white sheet along with me to keep my still-naked body somewhat covered. Ezra, on the other hand, sat up fully beside me and made no moves to hide himself, his lithe figure with muscles in all the right places very much on display.

Half-heartedly, I pushed on his shoulder with my palm, nudging him toward the side of the bed. "It's late and you have to get back before the whole world realizes you're here."

He cocked an eyebrow at me, folding his arms over his bare chest. "Excuse me, are you trying to hide me? Am I an embarrassment to you?"

Rolling my eyes, I shoved him again, this time more forcefully, and used my other hand to keep the sheet tugged tight against my body. "I'm not hiding you, I'm just not ready for prying eyes and ears and voices to butt in on this." I waved my free hand vaguely in the space between us. "Olivia is going to be in here at the crack of dawn so we can enjoy one last breakfast together before she heads back to New York and if she finds you in here, the entire hotel will know within the hour."

Never mind that I planned to share the entire evening's events with her myself, sparing absolutely no detail.

He didn't need to know that.

Ezra sighed and pouted one more time in my direction, but when I didn't budge, he unfolded his long, lean form from the bed and began the painstaking process of collecting his clothing. Each article was strewn about the room in a careless path between the bed and the doorway.

I tried to tear my eyes away, but watching the dips and planes of his muscular chest each time he bent and stood, the way his triceps strained as he pulled his shirt over his head, and the way he had to shimmy ever so slightly to slide his pants up over his firm backside was slowly becoming my new favorite pastime.

When he was finally clothed, he knelt one knee down on the bed before me and leaned in. He was so close I could see the gold flecks in his eyes. "So, what exactly is *this*?"

I groaned, unable to stop myself, and leaned back against the headboard to put a little bit of space between us. I could barely think straight when he was within kissing distance. He followed me with his body, using one hand braced against the bed on either side of me to hold himself up.

"Do we have to put a label on it right now? Can't we just... I don't know..."

"Enjoy it?"

"Yes! Enjoy it."

His smirk deepened. "So, you're saying you liked it, huh?"

I groaned again, snared in his carefully laid trap.

He laughed and leaned in the rest of the way to press a slow kiss to my lips. Without thinking, I opened for him. We kissed slowly, purposefully, taking our time with one another in a way we hadn't been able to before. Until my heart was fluttering in my chest, my breathing ragged, heat pooling between my legs.

It was Ezra who had the good sense to break the kiss this time, drawing back just enough to rest his forehead against mine. "Something to leave you wanting more."

My cheeks flushed and I sucked my bottom lip into my mouth, trying to stave off the want rising in me.

With one final chaste kiss pressed to the tip of my nose, Ezra stood and crossed the hotel room in a few long strides. He offered me a final wave of goodbye as he stepped into the hallway, and then slid the door shut soundly behind him. When I was certain he was gone and not coming back, I released the breath I'd been holding in a gasp of air and slid down until my head rested comfortably against my pillow.

It was partially true, what I'd told him.

Olivia knowing was one thing. With Liv, I could control the narrative. She wouldn't be here the next two weeks, prying into every encounter, reading into every look Ezra and I shared. After everything Peter had said to me back in Jones Beach, and how weird he had been on the bus the other day, I wasn't ready for the rest of Olympus to know how far things had gone between Ezra and me.

And I sure didn't want anyone at Rabbit's Foot finding out.

Besides, based on every romantic comedy I had ever watched, most *friends-with-benefits* situations were best enjoyed in secret.

Chapter 16

"Well, good morning to you," Olivia boomed from her seat at a table for two in the hotel's restaurant the next morning. I blinked slowly back at her, eyelids heavy with sleep, and slid into the chair on the opposite side.

She reached out to gently push a steaming cup of coffee toward me with two fingers. "Figured you might need this. Looks like you've had a long night."

I lifted an eyebrow, ignoring her hidden meaning, but secretly I was grateful for the coffee. She was right, I did need it. With sluggish hands, I picked up the mug and brought it to my lips, taking a long swig even as the hot liquid burned my lips and throat.

My night with Ezra left me reeling and I hadn't been able to fall asleep until nearly five in the morning, which made this eight o'clock wake-up call pure torture. I was happy to see my best friend, though. And disappointed this breakfast meant she was leaving. So, I tried to put on a brave face.

"Speaking of, how *was* your night?" Olivia's tone dripped with suggestion.

"Good."

"Good?"

"Yep, good."

Olivia scoffed.

I took another large sip of my coffee and picked up a menu, suddenly very interested in their selection of pastries.

Olivia reached out a hand to pin the menu to the table and glared at me. "Han, I'm your best friend. We tell each other everything. Now, how was your night?"

I sighed and let go of the menu—I knew what I wanted anyway, and it wasn't a pastry—and met her glare. I took a deep breath, then let it out. "Ezra and I hooked up."

There. It was out in the open, the first hurdle behind me.

Olivia's face lit up. I think she may have even let out a high-pitched squeal. "Tell me *everything*."

So I did. For the most part anyway. There were a few details about Ezra I wanted to keep for myself.

Like that guttural moan he makes right before he—

I had to pause twice in my recounting of events, once when the waiter took our order and a second time when he brought back two heaping plates of eggs, sunny side up *of course*, sausage, home fries, and toast. I scarfed mine down in record time, the sound of gasps and *oohs* and *aahs* from Olivia across the table serving as a soundtrack.

Three orgasms in one night had me positively famished.

"Wow," Olivia marveled when I finished, pushing around a sausage link on her plate with her fork. "When I told you to go out and get some, I hadn't expected *that*."

I laughed quietly and sipped my coffee, the liquid gone cold during our conversation.

"What does this mean for you two now?"

My stomach dropped and suddenly I wished I hadn't eaten so much, the food turning over in my gut. "Why does it have to mean something? Why can't it just be a thing we did? Something that happened. Do we have to define it?"

Olivia's eyes widened. "Uhh... yeah maybe that works for a one-night stand from Tinder. But the two of you work together. You can't leave things open-ended. It's impossible."

I bit my lip. "He's a rockstar, Liv. I'm sure it didn't mean anything to him." Just saying the words felt like a kick to the ribs, but I was determined to keep things casual. "He did imply he wanted to do it again, though."

"Oh my god, my best friend is basically dating Ezra Bell."

I raised my hands, eyes going wide. "No, no, no. No dating. We are just... I don't know, what are the cool kids calling it these days? Hanging out?"

Olivia cocked an eyebrow, her gaze narrowing. "So, what? You're like, friends with benefits?"

I shrugged, feeling out the phrase a little more. On one hand, I didn't want to put a label on this at all. But on the other hand, friends with benefits felt like a good fit. Something casual, easy.

"Damn girl, get it." Olivia laughed and leaned back in her chair, draining the last of her coffee. "Friends with benefits with a bonafide rockstar. My little girl's all grown up."

I rolled my eyes but couldn't contain my smile. "If that's what it takes to keep my work life with my work life and my... after work life with my after work life, then sure. Friends with benefits it is." I made makeshift boxes in the air with my hands as I spoke, trying to fit my words into neat little containers.

"Your ability to compartmentalize is—"

"Enviable? Astounding?" I cut in with a satisfied smirk.

"I was going to say, second only to mine," Olivia shot back, lifting her eyebrows as she put a hand over her heart.

I breathed a laugh, then my expression softened. "I'm going to miss having you here. Are you sure you can't stay for another week?"

It was Olivia's turn to roll her eyes. "Yeah, right. Bruce would have a freaking heart attack. Or charter a private jet to come out here and take me prisoner."

"Being taken prisoner by a hot, rich attorney? With a private jet, no less? Sounds like you're the one with the exciting life."

Olivia flashed me a feline smile and winked as she said, "Not even Bruce could handle me."

The sound of my laughter was cut off by the insistent vibration of my phone on the table. Ezra's name flashed across the screen, first one incoming message, followed in quick succession by another.

"Is that him?" Olivia leaned across the table as far as she could, trying to catch a peek.

My heart started to race.

Was he messaging me to say it had been a mistake? That he never wanted to see me again and would be calling Annabelle immediately to get me fired?

```
Hey! Hope I'm not waking you. I can't stop
thinking about last night :)

I have a Zoom interview this afternoon,
but I was wondering if you wanted to get
dinner together after?
```

My heart stopped.

He wasn't brushing me off, or embarrassed about our hookup, which was great.

But a *date*? My experience in friends-with-benefits situations was nonexistent, but this felt against the rules.

My phone vibrated again in my hands, another text from Ezra.

`It doesn't have to be anything formal, like a date. Just food.`

I let out a breath I didn't realize I was holding.

`Food sounds great! You pick the time and place.`

I set my phone down and could already feel Olivia's unspoken questions hanging in the air.

"We're going to hang out later. Get some food."

Olivia made that squealing sound again, wiggling in her seat. "I have a feeling you'll both be eating a little more than deep dish tonight."

Saying goodbye to Olivia was hard.

Like, harder than hard.

My heart was a lead weight in my chest when I helped her load her suitcase into her Uber after breakfast, the pang of missing her already starting to ache before she was even gone.

Ezra proved to be a nice distraction, though.

That night, he took me to his favorite spot in Chicago for deep-dish pizza—was Olivia psychic or something?—claiming I couldn't really say I had visited the city without trying it at least once. I had always been partial to Neapolitan. One could argue it was a prime motivator behind my decision to go to school in, and eventually move to, New York.

But I had to admit, Ezra wasn't kidding when he told me deep-dish was an orgasmic experience. The thick, buttery dough; the heaping layer of robust sauce; the ooey gooey cheese. Oh, the cheese.

It was life-changing.

Or maybe that was what we did after dinner, tangled up in the sheets of my hotel bed one last time before we hit the road for our second to last week of shows.

How is that even possible?

"Ezra, come on, we have to get to sleep!" I crowed halfheartedly through a fit of giggles as Ezra pressed a row of featherlight kisses down the back of my neck. I could feel the rumble of answering laughter in his chest where it pressed against my back. His arms snaked tighter around my naked body as I tried to slide out of his grip. Resistance was futile.

The clock on the nightstand read half past two in the morning. Even though I knew we needed to sleep, my body was a live wire, every nerve ending firing where Ezra's bare skin met mine.

"We have to meet the others in less than six hours," I whispered, but my eyes were already falling shut, my body relaxing into his touch. A breathy moan escaped my lips when Ezra's teeth nipped playfully at the spot where my neck met my shoulder. His fingers splayed across my lower abdomen, pinning me to him, and I could feel his growing erection pushing against my behind, ready for round two.

I almost gave in.

Almost.

"Ezra," I breathed, my voice light but firm, and he paused his teasing to prop himself up on one elbow so he could lean over me and meet my gaze.

"We don't know if the bed in Ohio is going to be this comfortable. We need to make the most of it while we're still here."

I shook my head and said, "All the more reason to *sleep in it.*"

"Can't I just enjoy having you all to myself one more time before we're stuck on a cramped tour bus?"

I laughed. "I'd hardly call that tour bus cramped. It's almost the size of my apartment."

"It's going to feel cramped tomorrow when Peter's giving both of us the silent treatment for the entire ride to Cuyahoga Falls."

I twisted my spine to peer back at Ezra over my shoulder, eyes narrowed. "Why would Peter give us the silent treatment?"

"Oh, you know Peter," Ezra replied, lifting and dropping one of his shoulders. "Hates being left out. He was extra petty when I told him you and I were having dinner solo tonight, and he was *persona non grata.*"

My eyebrows jerked up. I blinked slowly.

Ezra took that to mean my knowledge of the Latin language was lacking. "You know, persona non grata... he was unwelcome... not invited to tag along."

"Yes, I know what persona non grata means, but why did you feel the need to tell him we were having dinner together in the first place?"

Ezra's eyebrows lifted this time. "I couldn't not tell him we had plans. Zach and Angel usually have their own thing going on, phone calls and FaceTime with their ladies back home and all that, but

Peter and I typically spend most of our free time on tour together. He wanted to know why I couldn't hang with him."

"Okaaaay..." I said slowly, not quite willing to concede the point. I rolled over until I was lying on my other side to face Ezra fully, his long frame easily adjusting to the change in position. "What exactly did you tell him? How did you say we were having dinner together?"

Ezra cocked his head, the movement throwing pieces of his hair across his temple. "Why are you getting all weird and sweaty about this?"

I flushed, trying to figure out if I could check for actual sweat on me without him noticing. "I'm not getting all sweaty or whatever. I just... We haven't really had *the talk* yet. About what this is. And I'm not saying we need to. In fact, I'm pro not saying anything. About anything. To anyone."

Ezra blinked slowly.

"It's not like we're dating or anything serious," I cut in to fill the silence.

His lips drew together, a muscle in his jaw feathering. His amber eyes stayed on me, but it was like they were looking through me, focused on something else entirely. "Right," he grumbled eventually.

Was he upset about this?

Impossible.

"I mean, we can't really, right? You're a client. I basically work *for you*. It would be a huge breach of... ethics, or something." I could feel myself starting to ramble, but couldn't stop the word vomit. I chewed on the inside of my cheek when I saw his eyes darken.

Ezra's eyebrows knit together until they were almost one, somehow still an adorable brown unibrow. "Right," he said again, even quieter than the first time. "Sure, I get that."

"I'm just saying, I think it would be in both of our best interests to keep things quiet and casual between us. Friends, plus…"

As suddenly as it had vanished, some of the light was back in Ezra's eyes. It was still much dimmer than before, but his pout faded and one corner of his mouth twitched up slightly. I'd take it.

"You mean friends with benefits?"

"Yes!" I cut in with too much enthusiasm. "Exactly, great suggestion."

"I wasn't sugg—"

I cut him off by pressing a swift peck to his lips. "*Light*," I whispered, emphasizing my point. "Casual," I breathed against his lips, then pressed another quick kiss to them. "No strings. No prying eyes. Just fun." I pressed two more soft kisses to the same spot then left my mouth there until I could finally feel a real smile curving his lips.

Ezra snaked his arms back around me, one of his hands coming to rest against the nape of my neck while the other cradled my lower back. "This might take me some getting used to," he murmured against my mouth, his teeth grazing oh so lightly against my bottom lip. "I'm going to need lots of practice time with you."

I shuddered within his grasp, eyelids falling closed as I breathed in his warm scent. "Agreed. And we should probably set some ground rules, too."

He laughed breathily then nipped more firmly at my bottom lip, making me squirm. "You and your rules."

"The world would be chaos without my rules."

He rubbed the tip of his nose against mine then pulled back far enough to look at me. "Okay, lay them on me."

I grinned like the Cheshire cat and sat up straighter in bed, Ezra following my lead to sit beside me so we were shoulder to shoulder, our backs pressed into the squishy down pillows we had propped against the headboard. It was more like my shoulder to his bicep given how much he towered over me, but it worked.

"Okay, rule number one," I ticked off a finger. "No PDA."

"Was never a fan of the stuff anyway. What's next?"

"Rule number two," I paused for a few seconds to think, tapping my extended finger against my lips. "No telling anyone about us."

Ezra arched an eyebrow at me. "Anyone?"

"Anyone."

"So you haven't already told Olivia every gory detail?"

I froze. "Best friends hardly count as *anyone*."

"I can't tell Peter! What if he's my best friend?"

I shot him a look. "Pick a different best friend. Ideally one who doesn't know me, or where I work, or that we work together."

Ezra held up his hands defensively. "Fine, fine. Pick a different friend, got it. What else?"

I thought back to every *no-strings-attached* romcom I had ever read or watched. Then, I smirked.

"Just one last rule," I whispered, leaning over until my lips hovered over Ezra's. "Try not to fall in love with me."

Ezra grinned against my lips and leaned in to close the millimeter of space between us, giving me a soft kiss in answer. He lifted his hands, running them up and down my bare arms while deepening the kiss at the same time.

Heat bloomed in my core as his tongue slid smoothly into my mouth, a gasping moan emanating from deep within me. The sound snapped something in Ezra, his hands sliding down to cup my bottom and pull me into his lap. He was hard and already slightly slick where he pressed against my lower belly. The feel of him, the knowledge that *I* was the one who did that to him, was like a drug.

His fingertips traced tantalizingly slow circles along my back, curving against my spine and drawing me in until my bare breasts crushed against his chest in a way that made me see sparks.

We had slow, euphoric, delicious sex—so different from the fervent, needy hookup on our first night together.

When it was over, I curled my body against his side and fell into a peaceful sleep, my head resting comfortably on his chest.

My last thought before I was completely lost in dreamland was that I may have already started to break my own rule.

Chapter 17

"How's life on the road treating you?" my mom asked, her warm voice bright and clear through the phone line, even hundreds of miles away. It instantly relaxed me, the way it always had growing up. Then she added, "It's been almost a week since your last call, I guess work must be keeping you busy?" and I felt an instant twinge of regret.

Had it been that long?

She initially proposed we talk on the phone every day. I told her that would be impossible, especially on show nights, and she had relented... to phone calls every other day.

Up until now, I had stuck to my promise.

Things had gotten a bit chaotic over the last week in Ohio. When Ezra and I spent nearly every spare moment we had together. Sending each other flirty text messages from opposite ends of the tour bus while we traveled from town to town. Stealing kisses backstage when no one was around. Exploring every inch of one another beneath the rumpled sheets of whatever hotel we were at for the night.

His bed, my bed. It didn't matter.

I lost track more than once when some of my clothes ended up left behind in his room. Or that time he brought his toothbrush, along with his very fancy and *very* expensive hair care products—one reason he smelled so damn good all the time, I discovered—so he could sneak in a shower before a particularly early morning start.

Mmm, that was our first time together in the shower, I recalled. Thank God for years of yoga classes. Ezra was surprisingly limber considering his height.

Every stolen moment with him was heady. Like the rush from a drug I never tried before but couldn't imagine giving up now.

I was treading on more dangerous ground than I thought.

"You there, sweetheart? I said work must be keeping you busy," my mom repeated when I became lost in my thoughts for too long.

"Among other things," I thought to myself.

"What was that, honey?" my mom asked. "I couldn't quite make it out."

Crap, did I say that out loud?

"Nothing, mom. Just that you're right, work has been really busy. I'm sorry I've been MIA, but things should ease up soon. This is our last night in Ohio. After that, we've got a show in Pittsburgh, a show in Philly, and then we're on to Atlantic City for the big finale."

"I saw online you guys were coming to Philadelphia soon! I don't think I told you, I tried to get tickets but it was already sold out."

"Mom! You don't have to buy tickets. You've got someone on the inside now. I could've hooked you up."

"Ah well, I already told the rescue I would take a volunteer shift that evening. We'll just have to plan a weekend for me to visit when you're back home."

I smiled, though she couldn't see me. "That would be great. I miss you, Mom."

Her voice was like warm honey when she answered, "I miss you too, Hannah. I don't think I say this nearly enough, but I'm proud of you. So, so proud of you. The first in our family to go to college, and now look at you! On tour with your favorite band, working at your dream job. I always knew you'd go far. Ever since the day you corrected that little boy in preschool when he called a spider an insect."

My cheeks colored at the memory and I was pleased she couldn't see me. She had a penchant for telling this story to any unsuspecting stranger who would listen.

"You looked that boy dead in the eye and said, 'Actually, spiders are arachnids' at the age of four! Using a word like arachnids before you were even in kindergarten." I could hear the pride in her voice, it was always there when she recounted my achievements. I could picture her shaking her head in awe like she always did.

"And here I always thought I disappointed you for not going into something science-y after that, like entomology," I joked. Like I always did when we ran through this routine.

She laughed, right on cue. "Oh no, sweetie. It never mattered what you did, just that you found something you loved. Something that would keep you safe and secure and well cared for."

I sighed, a pang of homesickness I hadn't felt in weeks stabbing me in the chest.

My mom had always pushed me, not to be *the* best, but to do *my best*. Her kind and caring support was what carried me through late nights studying for the SATs, and the all-nighters in college as I worked toward my degree.

She was my lighthouse in uncertain weather. Someone I could look toward and find my way through any storm.

I felt a tear prick the corner of my eye and shook my head, snapping myself back to the present. "As soon as I'm settled back in New York, you're coming to stay with us for the weekend. Olivia will be glad to see you again. We'll go to all your favorite restaurants in the city, walk through Central Park, all the touristy stuff you love."

"I'll be counting down the days."

"Are you okay?" Peter asked me in between bites of the biggest bowl of Cheerios I had ever seen. It looked like he grabbed a stainless steel mixing bowl out of the cupboard, probably the only one we had, and filled it with an entire box of cereal.

We sat opposite one another on the tour bus as it carried us to our next stop in Cleveland. I tore my eyes away from the bus window I had been staring blankly out of for... *how much time had passed?*

Shaking my head to dispel the fog, I turned my attention back to Peter to find him blinking expectantly at me, eyebrows arched high on his forehead. I hadn't even noticed when he sat down, my thoughts trailing off into the distance with each passing mile. I was supposed to be working, but I was having a hard time concentrating.

The entire past week, I had a hard time concentrating.

"You had this weird look on your face and I swear you haven't blinked in like... longer than normal," Peter explained slowly, putting his spoon down and tensing up as though he might need to spring across the table to stop me from having a fit.

I barked a laugh I didn't quite feel and waved my hand dismissively. "Oh yeah, I'm fine. Just didn't sleep well last night. Exhaustion must be catching up to me."

It wasn't a lie. I bit my lip as my thoughts drifted once again, this time remembering the way Ezra's teeth felt when he tugged on my earlobe, the way his week's worth of stubble tickled when it dragged across my inner thigh, the sound he made when I went down—

"There! You just did it again," Peter exclaimed, breaking my reverie before it could get too far.

My cheeks reddened and I had to look down at my lap, pretending to pick a piece of lint off my black leggings. "I just need a giant cup of coffee, then I'll be good as new."

Peter nodded, lips pursed together while he considered, then shrugged with what I assumed was acceptance. He stood, taking his giant bowl of cereal with him, and moved toward the front of the tour bus where his bandmates were already entrenched in a video game. All I could make out over their shouting were the sounds of explosions and gunfire.

Before I could return to my very important duty of staring out the window and replaying the events of the last week in my head, my still half-open laptop started to ring, the sound of an incoming Zoom call bleating from its tiny speakers. I rushed to throw it open the rest of the way, my worst nightmare playing out in stark reality as Annabelle's name and perfect headshot flashed across the screen.

As quickly as I could, I reached for my laptop bag, pulling out pens and business cards and scraps of paper with long-forgotten notes on them, digging for my headphones.

I couldn't find them.

There was no time. The call had already been ringing for far too long. I sucked in a deep breath and spared one more glance at the guys in the front of the tour bus. They were too entrenched in their game to notice me, not if I kept the volume low enough. And prayed the background noise suppression feature did its damn job.

"Annabelle! How are you?" I asked when my boss's face popped into view, forcing what I hoped looked like a bright and totally at ease smile to my lips.

"Oh good, I was hoping I'd catch you," Annabelle answered with her own thousand-watt grin, her white teeth stark against the fire engine red of her lipstick. "Sorry to call unexpectedly. I was in the middle of typing an email to you and thought this would be easier."

I lifted my eyebrows slightly. "Of course, what can I do for you?"

"I was hoping to get a quick update on your content plan for the rest of the tour. As I mentioned in my email last week, we're looking for something big to cap things off now that we've got just over a week until the break. Something that will engage the fans, keep them wanting more, just in time for us to tease the new album."

Oh my god. She had *asked for something big.*

I had completely forgotten to put together a pitch. But I still had time! That wasn't due to her until... I glanced down covertly at the calendar on my laptop. Today.

The pitch was due today, and I had fumbled it. No wonder she was calling me.

Think, think, think.

I opened my mouth, closed it. Then opened it again, willing something—anything—to come out.

I had nothing.

I had barely even given it a passing thought over the past week. It was taking all I had just to keep up with the content cycle, filling the daily pipeline with videos and stills from each show, because...

Because I was spending every spare moment I had with Ezra.

And when I wasn't with him, I was thinking about him. I was just doing it now, right before this call. And I was probably going to do it again after we hung up.

"Hannah? Are you still there? It looks like you might be frozen." Annabelle's singsong voice snapped me back to reality. Unfortunately, it still wasn't enough to give me a brilliant content idea.

"Yes, yes, I'm still here. Sorry, the WiFi in the bus can be a bit spotty when we're moving," I stalled.

"Of course, of course," Annabelle nodded on my laptop screen. "If you could just give me a quick rundown of your ideas here, we can hop off so you can kick the details over via email."

"Right, yes. My ideas," I said slowly, still trying to buy time. "So my idea is... well, what I was hoping we could do was—"

"Hey, Annabelle!" Ezra's voice boomed in my ears, cutting off my pathetic blundering. He slid into the booth beside me, reaching a hand out to turn my laptop until he was in the frame. "Looking radiant as always."

I could see Annabelle's blush through the video screen and resisted the urge to roll my eyes. Even with the momentary distraction, it was still *me* in the hot seat, not her.

"Ezra! So good to see you," she preened. "I trust you've been taking excellent care of our Hannah."

Her tone was light, playful, no more than friendly banter. Only Ezra and I knew the hidden implication in her words. My hands started to sweat, my every nerve ending acutely aware of where Ezra's body touched mine as we sat side by side.

"Of course! She's been keeping us in line," Ezra replied smoothly with a wink that had Annabelle beaming. "We're all pumped about her idea."

It took every ounce of restraint to stop my jaw from falling open. My *idea*? What *idea*?

I shifted my eyes to shoot a horrified glance at Ezra who merely returned it with another, almost imperceptible, wink and a slight upturn to the corner of his mouth.

"That's actually why I called!" Annabelle answered, completely unaware that I was internally melting. Could one die from lack of preparation and stress? If so, I was for sure a goner.

"Oh, the Instagram Live Q&A? Yeah, we love it! We've never done anything like that before, and it seems really in line with the direction we've taken lately."

Ezra's lips were moving, I could hear the words coming out of his mouth, and yet it was like my brain registered them in another language.

"But what sold it was her idea to give away all-access passes to Nowhere Fest to four lucky participants in the Q&A, plus a private meet and greet. She really gets how important the fans are to us, how much we want to build those personal connections whenever we can." When he finished, Ezra slung a casual arm around my shoulders, like we were old buddies, and beamed at the camera lens on my computer.

All I could do was blink. My mouth opened and closed like a drowning fish.

Ezra was... well, he was rescuing me. There was no other way of putting it.

And his *idea*.

It was brilliant.

It was something I would have thought of. Something I *should* have thought of, had I been giving my actual job any attention whatsoever this past week.

Annabelle was saying something to us, but I could barely hear it. "—love it! I'm sure we can accommodate the expense. I think there's time for a meet and greet right after your acoustic set on the first day. Oh, this is great! Dominic upstairs is going to love it. The whole exec team will."

I forced a smile to my lips, trying to act like this wasn't a total shock. Like it had been my idea all along.

Through the blood pounding in my ears, I managed to make it through the rest of the call. Thankfully, it wrapped up pretty quickly after Ezra saved my job. My *life*.

I promised Annabelle a more detailed write-up of the plan via email later that day, saying I needed the additional time to incorporate her *brilliant* suggestions before it would be ready to present to our Chief Marketing Officer.

The bus was just pulling into the parking lot of our hotel in Cleveland when I clicked the End Meeting button to close the video call. Before I could shut my laptop, Ezra grabbed my hand under the table to give it a squeeze.

"That was amazing! We make a pretty great team. Maybe I should quit the band and be your assistant or something," he joked, lips stretched wide in one of his trademark handsome grins.

My lips tugged down as I avoided his gaze, pulling my hand free from his and shoving it into my lap.

Ezra's eyebrows furrowed, his grin faltering. He leaned in closer to me, trying desperately to meet my eyes. "Hannah, what's wrong?"

"Can you scoot out? I think I need some air."

"Hannah, come on. Talk to me." His whisper was hoarse. Concerned.

I pushed lightly against his shoulder. "Just, please. Let me out."

Frowning, Ezra stood from the booth, stepping back just far enough for me to slide out. As I moved toward the front of the bus, I heard the others groan when I crossed their field of vision and blocked the television for half a second. At least they hadn't heard my painful call with Annabelle, too.

In a daze, I stomped down the steel steps and didn't stop when my feet hit asphalt. Somewhere, it could have been miles behind me, I heard the sound of heavier footsteps following me.

"Hannah, wait!"

I kept walking toward the empty back half of the parking lot, willing myself to calm down.

"Hannah, come on! Just stop and talk to me. Tell me what I did wrong!"

I could feel the fiery pit of anger and shame opening up in my gut. I knew I should ignore it. Quelch it. Keep going and keep my mouth shut.

It was too late.

"You didn't do anything wrong!" I exploded, whirling on the spot to face Ezra.

He pulled up short behind me, his hands shooting up in front of him, as though the look on my face was enough to knock him to the ground.

"I'm the one who screwed up," I clarified in a softer voice, my gaze going distant as it slid toward the horizon.

"Hannah," Ezra breathed, taking one tentative step forward. Then another. Until he could reach a gentle hand out to touch my shoulder. "You didn't screw up."

I cocked my head to the side, eventually meeting his eyes again. The empathy and concern within them almost brought me to my knees. "I did. I missed an assignment. A *huge* assignment. That call was five seconds away from ending in complete disaster. If you hadn't stepped in—" Tears pricked at the back of my eyes and I blinked them back, unable to finish my sentence. I couldn't afford two mental breakdowns today, especially not in front of this man. My *client*.

"But it didn't, Han. Annabelle *loved* the idea. She's happy. She says Dominic is also going to be happy, whoever the hell that is. They all think you're some sort of marketing wizard. So what if you got a little help? You've done so much for us these past few weeks, I'm only glad I could finally repay the favor."

Ezra's thumb traced idle circles against my shoulder, trying to relax away the doubt and self-loathing that crept up my spine. That dark, intrusive voice inside me had me shrugging Ezra's hand off and taking a step back from him. His face fell at the distance I put between us.

"I shouldn't need you to swoop in and save me, Ezra. I appreciate you jumping in, I do. And if I had the presence of mind to ask how you came up with such a brilliant idea right now, I would. The problem is that *I* should be the one coming up with brilliant ideas. I should've been putting in the work, focusing more on Annabelle's assignment this past week." I paused and dragged a hand through my hair, looking just past Ezra's shoulder. "This is exactly what I was worried about when I said we had to keep things light and casual. This is my job. I can't screw it up. I can't afford any distractions."

Ezra recoiled from me as though I'd slapped him, his amber eyes darkening until they were nearly black. "Is that what I am to you, a distraction?" There was a tightness in his voice I so seldom heard, it was enough to send me backpedaling.

"Ezra," I whispered, taking a slow step toward him. When he didn't retreat, I advanced another, until I could reach out and rest my hand against his bicep. "I didn't mean it like that," I gave his arm a gentle squeeze. "I was telling the truth before, *you* didn't do anything wrong. This is my fault. I just need some time to cool down."

Ezra bit down on his bottom lip, his dark eyes trained on the ground. I could feel the muscles in his arm tense underneath my loose grip. His jaw feathered as he contemplated what I said, what I was offering to him again. The only thing I could offer him.

His whole body seemed taut, like there was a wave cresting inside him, waiting to crash down upon us both. Silence hung thick like fog in the air as the seconds ticked by.

Finally, he nodded without a word. His eyes didn't even lift to meet mine, but I sighed with relief just the same. Grateful this was over and we could move on.

I moved forward, arching up on my toes to press a kiss to Ezra's lips, but he pulled away before I could reach him. In one smooth motion, he turned on his heel and walked toward the entrance of the hotel, leaving me alone at the edge of the parking lot.

Chapter 18

My relationship with Ezra grew more strained during our time in Ohio and Pennsylvania.

As promised, and with a little help from Mei back at the home office, we coordinated the Instagram Live Q&A the day after the Pittsburgh show. The hotel we were staying in fortunately had a spare meeting room we could use, for a hefty rental fee.

Ezra helped too, like he said he would. He convinced the guys it was the right move, helped figure out the time and place, and even worked with me on some last-minute training to get every member of Olympus prepared for a more hands-on style of interview.

Despite some minor technical issues at the very beginning of the livestream, the promo had gone swimmingly.

As usual, the guys were amazing.

Peter, Angel, and Ezra's boisterous personalities translated so well to the interactive format. Even the usually introspective Zach enjoyed himself. He lit up like a switchboard when fans asked technical questions about his writing process and his inspiration for some of their most popular songs—and a few deep cuts, too.

The fans ate up every second of it.

More than a hundred thousand people submitted questions for the Q&A, and at its peak, more than two hundred thousand tuned in to watch. I needed Annabelle's entire team back in New York to help me sift through and select questions, and to decide on the four lucky winners of the VIP passes after it was over. The executive team at Rabbit's Foot had been so thrilled with the results, they even decided to foot the travel bill for our guests.

After the blunder I was so sure would cost me my job, everything was back to looking up at work. Annabelle called to congratulate me on a job well done at least four times.

As good as things were going for me in my career, that's about how bad they were with Ezra.

I could still feel the static charge in the air any time we were in the same room. That shock to the system when we locked eyes, like every hair on my body stood on end, something deep within our cores drawing us together like magnets.

Yet he made fewer and fewer excuses to abandon his bandmates and make his way to my hotel room in the evening. When he did show up, our trysts were fiery, desperate, torrid; but brief. He no longer stayed the night after we were done, when our bodies were so spent from sensuous sex it ached to even move. No longer came to my door with his toothbrush and hair care products in hand, offering us more time together.

I told myself it was a good thing.

It was what I wanted.

Thanks to his great idea, I was busier than I had ever been. Less time spent sneaking around with Ezra meant more time devoted to my number one priority: my job. Still, my heart sank every time I watched him hastily gather his clothes and make his way through the door without so much as a passing glance my way, let alone a goodbye kiss.

He didn't even come to my room later that night, after the Q&A was over, to ride the high of a job well done.

So much for being a team.

So, as the bus carried the four sleeping members of Olympus and myself toward our next and final destination, I ran through logistics one more time in my head.

The next few nights, Olympus would join forty other acts of all shapes and sizes at Nowhere Fest, an alt-rock music festival near the beaches in Atlantic City. Today—Friday, I reminded myself—they had an intimate acoustic set on a smaller stage in the early afternoon. Afterward, they would stay behind in the pit for the private meet and greet with our lovely sweepstakes winners. On Saturday, Olympus was one of four headliners that evening. Sunday, the last day of the festival, they had one more smaller set in the afternoon and then it would all be over.

The tour.

My situationship along with it, it seemed.

One small ray of sunshine in my otherwise cloudy disposition: Annabelle sent me an email late the night before to let me know Rabbit's Foot was sending a staff photographer and videographer to the festival—they had a few other clients performing and wanted to get additional content—and encouraged me to "take it easy" and enjoy the weekend's festivities.

Despite all the weirdness happening with Ezra, I was excited.

Aside from Olympus, I was a fan of at least ten other bands playing, including Lucid Dreams who were making their festival debut after opening for Olympus the past six weeks. I planned to take Annabelle up on her offer.

That was about the only ray of light I had to look forward to. At the end of the day, this last stop signaled an ending. I had gotten so used to seeing Ezra every day. To seeing Peter, Zach, and Angel, too.

What was going to happen when they all went back to their regular lives and I had to return to mine?

Sure, we were booked for another leg, but that didn't start for three months. Three months was a *long* time for a situationship. Especially one currently hanging on by a thread, built on a collapsing foundation.

Ezra and I technically lived in the same city. But New York was massive and we hardly ran in the same circles. At my request, we never defined what we were to each other. Would he simply forget about me when the thrill of being shoved together on the road wore off?

My eyes drifted toward the front of the bus where Ezra lay on one of the leather couches, one ankle crossed over the other. Even in slumber, one foot bounced in time to a rhythm I couldn't hear.

I watched him in silence for a minute, chewing on the inside of my cheek, then dropped my gaze.

It was going to be a long weekend.

· ❤ · ❤ · ❤ · ❤ · ❤ ·

A bright sun blazed overhead, baking the ground beneath my feet as I trudged through the festival grounds. As soon as our bus arrived and parked in the secure area where only performers and their crews were allowed, the band immediately set to work meeting with sound techs, huddling over the setlist one final (dozen) times, and making sure everything was in order.

Olympus had been on the scene for nearly a decade and played plenty of festivals, especially in their early years working like grunts to make it in the industry, but Nowhere Fest was huge, even for them. To headline it?

Everyone was excited, but there was an edge to every sidelong glance shared, every hushed conversation, every impromptu practice session on the bus.

Although we made great time on our arrival and Olympus still had about an hour or so before their acoustic set, the guys didn't waste a second. I was used to the hustle and bustle—craved it, even—but Annabelle's email floated through my mind like a devil whispering on my shoulder, telling me to *chill out* and *have a good time.*

I decided to follow the advice and disappeared into the already crowded grounds where festival-goers dressed in everything from flannel to rave gear milled about from stage to stage, merch table to merch table. With a glance down at my watch, I clocked about thirty minutes until I had to meet Ian and Leah, the photographer and videographer Rabbit's Foot had sent to cover the festival.

Plenty of time to orient myself.

The festival area was actually an old municipal airport, made up of grassy expanses bisected by large stretches of tarmac. The main stages were arranged in misshapen rows and semi-circles, flanked by a packed campground on one side and a grass parking lot on the other, each section separated by makeshift gates topped with colorful flying banners.

My feet crunched over the short clipped grass as I dodged smiling people near the merch tables, many of them supporting large plastic cups or tall cans of beer in their hands, my head on a swivel to take in my surroundings. In my haze, I bumped elbows with a tall, rail-thin man sporting a fuschia mohawk and a silver hoop through his nose. He offered me a wide, apologetic grin and reached out with a steadying grip to keep me from tumbling to the ground on impact, and then he was on his way again. Everyone at Nowhere Fest was blissful. Energized. Happy to be here, to be alive.

Through the crowd, I could just barely make out the assortment of tents and motorhomes on the far side, their owners streaming in and out as they packed supplies for the day into bags and slung them over their backs.

I'd never been to Nowhere Fest before—camping was not my style and there was no way I could afford the jacked-up hotel rates in this area on my part-time wage in college—but it had always been on my bucket list. An all-expenses-paid trip where I essentially had a golden ticket to go where I pleased because I was *with the band*?

After I'd taken my fill of the festival layout, I hesitated under the cool canopy of an info tent. The next show I wanted to see was straight back in the direction I'd come, at a stage a little ways off from where Olympus would perform in just over an hour. If I turned back now, I could make both set times with minimal walking in between.

My eyes darted between the merch tents and the packed bar a few yards away. I didn't typically advocate for drinking on the job, unless it was a corporate event.

Annabelle did encourage me to enjoy all the festival had to offer, though...

Before I could make a decision, a vaguely familiar face waded into view, interrupting my mental ping-pong match. "Hannah! Hey, I hoped I might see you here," a low baritone rumbled in my direction as a tall man with light olive skin approached. He wore a simple dove gray, half-button Henley that hugged the planes of his chest and arms. He was sunkissed in a way that hinted at long days spent outdoors and perfectly complemented his sapphire eyes.

It took my brain a few seconds to catch up, my eyes going wide when it did. "Tom! What a surprise," I started to say when he extended his hand to me in greeting. I took it in my own, mustering the most business-professional handshake I could. "But of course, you're covering the festival. Duh."

He chuckled obligingly as his firm palm slid out of mine to tuck into the pocket of his jeans. "Yep, I go where the beat takes me. No pun intended," he replied with a wink that had my cheeks heating.

I laughed too loudly in response, trying—and failing—not to be distracted by the dimple that poked out just under his right cheek.

"You're here with Olympus, right?" he asked before an awkward silence could stretch between us.

Maybe I didn't need that beer after all, my brain was already fogged enough. I nodded and forced a confident smile to my lips. *I can do this.* "Yes! They're doing an acoustic set today, then a headline show tomorrow. But between you and me," I leaned in conspiratorially—a huge mistake, I realized, when the delicious, masculine scent of his expensive cologne filled my nostrils, "I'm hoping to scope out a few other acts this weekend."

Tom nodded seriously, going along with the joke. "In that case, maybe we should check out a few of those acts together. You know, it's safer in numbers and all that."

My stomach flipped and I was once again thankful I hadn't had that beer. If I wasn't mistaken, I'd think Tom was flirting with me.

He *had* given me his number all those weeks ago at the brewery. But there was no way. Right? *Right?!*

I swallowed hard, my thoughts sliding to Ezra. We hadn't defined our relationship. We were just having fun. And as of late, we weren't really doing much of that, either. And still, the idea of spending time with another guy felt like an act of betrayal.

My smile tight, I avoided direct eye contact with Tom and said noncommittally, "Yeah, sure. That would be great." I forced myself to look at him again, all one hundred percent, grade-A, hot inch of him. "But hey, I've got to run and meet a few photographers from Rabbit's Foot that should be arriving soon, give them the lay of the land and all that. It was so great seeing you again."

Tom's winning smile faltered just slightly at my gentle rebuff, but he rallied quickly and reached out a hand to half-squeeze my shoulder. "I'll be in the media area most of today. Come find me when you're free."

· ♥ · ♥ · ♥ · ♥ · ♥ ·

After my encounter with Tom, I tapped out a quick text to the lead photographer on site asking him to meet me at the stage where Lucid Dreams was about to perform, ready to fully commit to this *enjoying myself* thing.

There was just enough time for me to stop off and grab a bottle of water—I had to say *no* to the beer; with Tom, Ezra, and my colleagues from Rabbit's Foot all here, I needed to keep my wits about me—and make it to the stage just in time to find Ian and his colleague Leah for a quick debrief before they were off to do their content curation jobs while I enjoyed the show.

Suckers.

From an unobtrusive hideaway at the back of the gathered crowd, I watched in awe, a broad grin plastered on my lips, as the female-fronted band launched into "Vacant Hearts" to begin their set. Time fell away as I stood there. The indie rock music carried back to me on a slight breeze that tickled up my spine and along the back of my neck, offering a small morsel of relief from the late September sun slowly making its descent toward the horizon.

When the band launched into my absolute favorite of their songs, "Lost in Hesitation," I allowed my eyelids to gently close, my body swaying to the melody while reality drifted further and further away. As Marina crooned mournfully about the frustration of pursuing a relationship with someone unsure about what they truly wanted, a warm, beachy scent encircled me on a phantom wind. It was followed closely by a press of warmth at my side, the feeling somehow at odds with the late afternoon heat.

I blinked open one eye, then the other, to find Ezra standing quiet and still beside me.

His eyes were cast up at the stage, hands loosely intertwined behind his back as he watched Lucid Dreams perform. I had no idea if he was a fan like me, already familiar with the song long before Lucid Dreams joined them on tour as their opener, or if the arrangement had been made entirely by the label. Did he hear the hidden meaning in Marina's words, too—the couple she described in some ways so similar to the two of us?

I was probably overthinking it. Classic Hannah.

We stood there together in companionable silence as the song came to an end, neither of us daring to break the moment. If he made the same connection I did, he didn't let on.

As Lucid Dreams launched into their final song of the set, the two of us hidden in the very back of a bouncing crowd, Ezra's hand slowly inched toward me, across that small gap of air separating our bodies, until his fingers twined loosely with mine.

Chapter 19

It was like the quiet before the storm as I walked through the empty festival grounds Saturday morning. Although the camping area was already buzzing with sound—the distant shouts of friends waking up one another inside tents and campers, someone's battery-powered boombox blasting what I thought might be "Fire Alarm" by Castlecomer—patrons weren't allowed into the main festival grounds until eleven.

Thirty more minutes of peace, I thought to myself, a knowing smile tugging at the corners of my lips as I passed by the merch stands. Most were already occupied by sleepy-eyed vendors, stretching their arms toward the sun and setting up their wares for another profitable day.

I arrived back at the festival grounds around ten in the morning, hitching a ride with Peter and Angel from the hotel. Energy pulsed from both of them like lightning the entire ten-minute drive, their banter more subdued as they focused conversation entirely on Olympus's headline show that evening.

During yesterday's acoustic set, the two of them were mostly off the hook, except for a few songs that called for Angel's skills on the maracas or bongos. They got plenty of attention at the private meet and greet afterward with our Q&A winners, but for all intents and purposes, tonight was their festival debut. If Paramore's headline show last night was any indicator, the crowd would be massive—packed in like sardines to fill every square inch of the pit.

We went our separate ways upon arrival. Olympus was doing an impromptu autograph signing at their merch table at noon and then would spend the rest of the afternoon preparing for their set. I, on the other hand, thanks to the help from the content curators at Rabbit's Foot, had nowhere to be. No real work to do. The big end-of-tour promo was done. My schedule was filled with white space and freedom.

It was unsettling.

Already, my fingers fidgeted, itching to type an email or check my Slack app. But my inbox could wait and nothing urgent screamed for my attention.

It was a weekend for those regular nine-to-fivers back home, after all.

I took a deep breath as I neared Olympus's merch tent, willing my body to adjust to the speed of... nothing. When I reached it, I was surprised to find two unfamiliar women bustling behind tables lined up end to end at the front of the space. The women looked to be about my age, a far cry from the usual crew: two older guys from Olympus's management company, Gabe and Ricky. They told the best dad jokes ever. I had grown quite fond of them over the past six weeks.

Tentatively I approached the booth, but my small presence wasn't enough to draw the women's attention. They already had most of the sample merch hung up on the wall in the back, each one numbered and labeled with the available sizes to make ordering convenient. The tables themselves were lined with thick black tablecloths printed with Olympus's logo and topped with a few samples of smaller items for sale—beer koozies, stickers, hats.

I observed silently as the two women busied themselves tearing open and arranging boxes, murmuring to one another about where things should go to make fulfillment easier. They moved with a practiced grace I wouldn't have expected from two newbs. At one point, the shorter woman with raven black hair and deep bronze skin whispered something in a snarky tone I couldn't quite hear, making the taller blonde next to her scream with laughter.

The way they danced around one another hinted at their closeness, my watchful eyes taking note of the way one would gently press a palm against the other's back when she needed to squeeze by in the crowded space; the way they'd lean in close to whisper into each other's ears conspiratorially so no one else could hear what they said in the eerie quiet of the festival grounds. Each touch was intimate, every smile speaking volumes. Heat filled my cheeks—I was a veritable creep standing there, watching them.

I cleared my throat to break their quiet dance, earning me narrowed looks from both women. I nearly wilted under their glares.

The blonde moved toward me, stopping at the edge of the table separating us and held a hand up to shield her eyes from the sun. "Hey, sorry but this area doesn't open up until eleven. We're still setting up now, but if you come back in a bit, we should be ready to go," she explained, her lilting voice doing wonders to cover up any annoyance she felt at the interruption.

So I was right, we hadn't met before.

I stepped forward, stopping just a foot away from the edge of the table so I wouldn't have to shout. "Hey, sorry to interrupt. I don't believe we've met. My name's Hannah, I work for Olympus's label." I jerked my thumb vaguely over a shoulder as if the tour bus and the band would materialize behind me.

Understanding dawned in the blonde's eyes, her mouth opening slightly. She dropped her hand back to her side just as her raven-haired companion spun around to face me.

My eyes followed the brunette as she quickly closed the distance between us in two strides until only the width of a table separated us. She gave me a once over, taking me in from head to toe in a passing glance, then met my eyes. Her pretty face split into a slow grin as she said, "So, you must be my replacement."

I couldn't think fast enough to stop my jaw from falling open, my eyes glued to the brunette before me.

Up close, I could see that her slightly baggy attire of an Olympus T-shirt and loose jean shorts couldn't hide the soft silhouette of her body. Her chestnut brown eyes were rimmed with long, black lashes and shone especially bright against her bronze skin. Even cracked in that wide grin, I could see her lips were full, accentuated by a coat of dark red lipstick.

She was gorgeous. And I realized almost a beat too late that she had extended her hand to me in introduction as she said what I already knew, "I'm Camila Ramirez."

I took her proffered hand and gave it a tentative shake, her grip firmer than my own. My voice sounded too quiet as I said, "Hannah Maxwell."

Which meant the tall blonde must be—

"Great to meet you, Hannah. I'm Lexi," she supplied, right as my brain caught up. Any sign of annoyance was gone, a welcoming smile now curving her lips in greeting.

Calling both women gorgeous would have been the understatement of the year, but they were beautiful in different ways. Where Camila was petite, all delicate curves, Lexi was tall and athletic, hard angles and taut muscles softened only by the light dancing in her hazel eyes.

Camila tucked one of her hands into her pocket and cocked a hip as she asked, not unkindly, "How's the job treating you?"

My shoulders lifted in a casual shrug and I turned my body so it was partially shaded by the tent in front of me. Despite being nearly October, it was shaping up to be another hot one. "It comes with its challenges. I wasn't expecting to leave for a tour after just starting, but it's been some of the most fun I've had in my life."

Camila chuckled knowingly and sorted through a stack of stickers on the table in front of her. "That sounds about right. Annabelle always was the *sink or swim* type."

"You've got some tough shoes to fill," Lexi joked, bumping her hip against her girlfriend's as she tossed her a wink. Camila rolled her eyes, but the way they kept their bodies close told me she loved the compliment... and the woman it came from.

I couldn't fight my smile around them. Seeing their closeness, how comfortable they were, made me want to keep the conversation going. To be part of their world. "I should actually be thanking you. All the documentation you left behind was a lifesaver those first few weeks. Pulled more than a few all-nighters getting caught up."

Camila snorted at the flattery but I thought I saw her cheeks flush as she bent over to fish a new box of stickers from underneath the table. "And how's the road been treating you? Talk about all-nighters, right?"

I froze, thoughts immediately sliding to my late nights with Ezra.

My silence was deafening. I could feel Lexi's eyes on me, curious and calculating as she caught my hesitation. Even Camila paused her work with the stickers to eye me up, her brows arched in question. "You know... because the shows go so late and then there's like a billion and one tasks to wrap up afterward."

Slowly I nodded, relieved.

"Ah, right. Yeah, it took some getting used to. Fortunately for me, I've always been a bit of a workaholic. Not afraid to put in a little overtime," I tried to joke, but it came out flat.

That was true at the start of the tour—I spent nearly every minute of my free time working when we first hit the road. Going above and beyond every day. Sneaking around with Ezra these last few weeks though, I had barely kept up with the bare minimum. And it almost cost me major points with Annabelle. Potentially much, much more, if Ezra hadn't bailed me out.

Reflecting back on it, I expected to feel guiltier for my lapse in judgment.

What I did feel guilty about though, was my reaction to Ezra's help. The way I shouted at him in Cleveland after the video call. My eyes shuttered at the memory.

He didn't deserve that.

Camila grunted her understanding, but Lexi must have seen something in my face. When she caught my eye across the table, I was met with an assessing stare. I tried to shake it off, feigning interest in one of the stickers on the table.

"And how is our good buddy Ezra?" Lexi fished.

I sucked in a sharp inhale, keeping my eyes trained on the table to avoid giving too much away. "I think he's enjoying being on the road again, being close to the fans."

Vague enough. I replayed my conversation with Ezra the night we ran into the fan at the pizza shop.

The night he told me he wanted to kiss me.

Shut up, shut up, shut up.

Camila smiled knowingly. "That sounds like him. Always restless. Only happy when he's in motion."

In spite of myself, I smiled. "Right? I think I'd probably die if I had to sing to fifteen thousand people, but he always looks so at ease up there." I fought—and lost—to keep the admiration out of my voice.

Camila laughed, nodding her agreement while Lexi lifted a brow. Damn, she was observant.

"I heard he's finally single..." There was an unspoken question there. One I wasn't prepared to answer.

Fortunately, Camila snickered and took the pressure off me, her eyes rolling so far back in her head I thought they'd get stuck. "It's about time he got off the hamster wheel."

Lexi's face twisted in mock admonishment and she gently nudged her girlfriend in the ribs with an elbow. Camila shot back a playful smack across the bicep that somehow turned into the two of them linking arms.

They were so at ease with one another, content. I felt a pang in my chest, a longing that hadn't been there in years. Possibly ever.

Why couldn't I have that?

Another vision of Ezra filled my head. That night in the hotel when he asked me why we had to hide. His amber eyes had pooled with unspoken promises: days filled with laughter and adventure, traveling the country and the world; a deep and true love with someone who made me feel alive.

The certainty I had felt that night evaporated like dew on a mid-July morning.

I didn't know how long we chatted, only that my cheeks ached from smiling—it was nice having someone new to talk to, someone female. I didn't realize how much I missed Olivia since she left me alone on a tour bus filled with testosterone.

And Ezra was right. I did like Cami and Lexi.

During our conversation, they confessed Ezra had no idea they were here—Peter helped them coordinate the whole thing as a surprise.

We were in the middle of brainstorming ways the two of them could make their grand reveal, each idea getting a little crazier than the last, when voices carried on a morning breeze filled our ears. With a glance down at my watch I realized it was already after eleven and today's crowd was beginning to stream in through the front gate.

And that meant I was late.

"I've got to get back to the tour bus before things get crazy. I'm supposed to meet up with the content curators before they start their day."

"Do us a favor when you get over there and send Ezra this way, will you? I think it's time for the big reveal." Lexi winked, a wide grin splitting her face.

"So I guess we're not going with my baby goat plan, then?" Camila asked, feigning disappointment. Her most recent outlandish idea involved acquiring a baby goat from a local farm and tying a note around its neck announcing they were here. Never mind we had no access to a baby goat. Or a collar for it. Or the means to train it to find Ezra.

With a breathless laugh, I nodded and darted across the grassy lane in the direction of the tour bus, right as the first group of festivalgoers reached the merch tent.

My mind raced with possibility as I made my way past a few of the stages on this side of the old airstrip. Thankfully all of them were still empty, save for the techs and engineers in charge of setup. Sure, I'd send Ezra their way. But first, we needed to talk—about our situationship, about our future, about what we both wanted.

About everything.

Chapter 20

At a gazelle's pace, my feet crunched over old tarmac and sun-baked grass. Some of it was still slightly brown in spots from the unseasonably hot summer, despite the festival organizers' attempt to treat it before the event. Without having to dodge tipsy concertgoers, I was making great time back to the tour bus, my body propelled on autopilot so my brain could focus on the task at hand: plotting exactly what I was going to say to Ezra when I got there.

I couldn't tell if my heart raced because I was nearly sprinting down the winding lane in front of me or because I was about to bare my heart to a guy I'd been crushing on since I was sixteen.

Not just *any guy.*

Ezra. Freaking. *Bell.*

Over the past six weeks he let me peer behind the mask, look beyond the facade he built around himself like a wall. The one no one else bothered to question. The one I had known for weeks now wasn't real, despite what I tried to tell myself. I saw the type of man he could be—who he truly was, despite the picture the online media had painted.

Someone kind and smart. The kind of guy who would stick his neck out for you when you needed help.

Someone fun and goofy. The type of man you could count on for a laugh on a bad day when all you wanted to do was cry.

Someone who cared so deeply for those around him and for the millions of people at home who found themselves lost in his lyrics. Who maybe felt like they weren't so alone, because he was there.

My worn Chuck Taylor's scuffed against the ground as it turned to gravel, bringing me closer and closer to what I was about to do. What I had to do. Sure, things were a little weird between us since I stupidly, so, so stupidly, called him a distraction.

But if my words hurt him so badly, it had to mean he wanted more, right?

The pang I felt in my stomach every time he looked at me from across the crowded bus and then looked away, eyes shuttering. The pain in my chest when he quickly gathered his clothes and walked out of my hotel room instead of holding me through the night.

I missed him.

More than that, I *cared* for him. More deeply than I had ever cared for any man before. I didn't know if it was love, not yet, but it was something. And I wanted more.

He needed to know that.

I knew in my heart he might still reject me.

Maybe I was too late. Maybe I dug my own grave that day in Cleveland. Maybe that look I saw in his eyes the first night we spent together was never really there. Maybe I made it up. Maybe he really was just looking for a fling to pass the time.

Or maybe he resolved himself to it after I had been the one to tell him we couldn't be anything serious.

A small voice in the back of my head whispered *no*. Told me to keep going.

Olivia's voice echoed in my head, joining that whisper. Telling me I had to at least try.

The long side of the tour bus took shape before me, my stride faltering for just a step before I recovered. Only ten yards separated me from my destination. Then five.

The point where everything could change looming larger with every desperate step.

Where it *would* change, either way. No matter the outcome.

I paused a few feet from the steps to the sound of voices—two of them, one masculine and one higher-pitched, feminine. *Did Ian and Leah beat me here?*

A quick look at my watch told me I was only a few minutes late to meet them. I didn't know them very well, though. Maybe they were early birds.

A slight hitch to the plan, but I could still recover. All I had to do was get them started on their assignment and possibly kick the rest of the band out if they were hiding in there. Then Ezra and I could talk.

We had hours left until their headline show. Plenty of time to... take fate into my own hands? Grab the bull by its horns? Start a new relationship with a rockstar?

Jesus, what had I gotten myself into?

The sound of voices inside the bus got louder—still not loud enough for me to make out what they were saying—then stopped completely. Slowly, I crept up the steps to the closed door, the new steel completely quiet underfoot. With one final deep breath to brace myself, my hand shook as I reached for the handle and pulled back. The door silently opened for me like it had countless times over the summer.

"Hey guys, sorry I'm late, I got—" my voice choked and then sputtered out completely when I reached the top step to find the source of the voices. And the reason I no longer heard them speaking.

Not Ian and Leah.

With eyes as big as saucers I stared across the bus to the two figures embracing near the window, the uneven sunlight pouring in beside them casting eerie shadows across their bodies. They were intertwined so closely, their lips locked so I could barely tell where one person ended and the other began.

But it wasn't enough to stop the recognition from dawning. If only it had been.

If only there was something that would have spared me. Prevented me from seeing this.

Ezra.

But... who was—?

No.

I swallowed so loudly the sound filled the quiet space and took a tentative step back. My mouth gaped like a fish out of water. Realizing they were no longer alone, the woman in front of me untangled herself from Ezra. The sound of their lips parting with a *smack!* echoed through me like a gunshot.

In my frozen state, my eyes managed to take her in: the bright blonde hair cascading down her shoulders in loose waves; the bone structure that could start a war; the way her short, black dress hugged all the right places.

The way one of her delicate, perfectly manicured hands was still loosely tangled in the scruff of hair at the nape of Ezra's neck, even as she pulled back to face me.

Andie.

Ezra's ex.

·❤·❤·❤·❤·❤·

I didn't spare a passing glance at Ezra. I couldn't look at him, not after what I'd just interrupted.

Without a word, I turned on my heel and practically fell down the steel steps of the bus in my rush to escape—to get away from *them*. My heart pounded so loudly in my ears that I couldn't hear anything else. I trudged blindly back toward the main stage, hearing nothing, seeing nothing. Not the voices and laughter of the crowd around me, not the gulls cawing and flapping their wings overhead. There was nothing but the blood rushing through my veins and the taste of bile stinging the back of my throat.

Ezra.

With his ex.

Kissing.

How could I have been so stupid? So naive to think this was anything serious to him?

My legs carried me across the same grassy lane I had just walked mere minutes ago, when my heart was full of hope. Now it was a lead ball in my chest, threatening to pull me under.

The sudden grip of two strong, steadying palms on my shoulders broke my stride and held me in place. It was a chore to force my chin to incline, to look up at the source of my restraint. Peter. His emerald eyes were round with concern, his mouth was slightly ajar like he wanted to say something, then saw the state of me and thought better of it.

I couldn't stop it when a small, sardonic laugh escaped my lips at the thought of what I must look like. The shock and shame of the last five minutes had to be written all over my face. Peter's eyes widened further at the breathless, bitter sound, so far from my usual demeanor.

"Woah, Hannah. What's going on, where are you going?"

The look on Peter's face, in his eyes, was almost enough to soften the lead ball inside me.

Almost.

Until I remembered his warning to me all those weeks ago. He knew this would happen. He tried to protect me from it, but I was too stupid to believe him.

I shook his palms off my shoulders and took a step back. Despite the extra foot he had on me, I managed to tilt my head up and look down my nose at him at the same time as I said, "You were right. About Ezra. About everything. You were right."

My voice was bitter, unrecognizable. But it felt good to let some of the anger and disappointment out.

Peter didn't deserve my disdain. I knew that. It wasn't his fault. And the bewilderment in his eyes told me he had no idea what I was talking about. The look of regret and pity on his face threatened to bury me. I had to get away—get out of here.

With a shake of my head and a passing glance at Peter, I edged my body around his broad frame, sidestepping until I was lost to the crowd. Before I knew what I was doing, my phone was in my hand, then against my ear, the soothing dial tone singing against my head.

"You're calling me? This must be serious," Olivia joked from the other end of the line, and the sound of her familiar voice, that warm and sarcastic tone I loved, had tears stinging the back of my eyes.

I opened and closed my mouth to speak several times, but the words wouldn't come out.

"Hannah, what's wrong? Hannah, are you there?"

"Liv, I—" My voice broke on a sob I couldn't hold back any longer.

"Hannah Maxwell, tell me what happened right now."

I did. As I waded through the crowd streaming in for the start of the festival, I told her everything. About the way I'd yelled at Ezra back in Ohio when he had just tried to help me. About meeting Camila and Lexi, and seeing how happy they were, how it made me realize I wanted something more with Ezra, more than a fling, more than friends with benefits. And how I found him in the tour bus, lips locked with his model ex-girlfriend, like I'd been nothing to him. Meant nothing.

After I finished recounting the story from start to finish, Olivia was deathly silent on the other end of the phone. When she finally spoke, all she said was, "I'm coming. I'll be there in two hours," and then the line went dead.

My hands shook as I slowly lowered the phone from my ear and tucked it into the back pocket of my shorts. People wound around me, smiling and laughing with one another, excited about a day filled with music and soaking up the early Autumn sunshine. In the middle of the lane, I was a tiny rain cloud ruining their fun.

I have to get out of here.

Olivia had always been a speed demon on the road, but even with her lead foot and supernatural ability to avoid speed traps, I knew it would take her at least the two hours she'd promised to get here from Brooklyn. Far too long to stay at Nowhere Fest where Peter or Camila or Lexi or Ezra might find me. Where I might completely fall apart in front of them.

The hotel.

I needed to pack and check out anyway if I was leaving Atlantic City for good. And Olympus had that autograph signing before their set today, guaranteeing none of them would find me before I was already gone.

With a plan in place, I became laser-focused. I pulled out my phone to order a ride to the hotel a short drive away, then switched over to my email app, typing out a quick excuse to Annabelle to explain my sudden absence at the festival.

I felt guilty lying to her, but she couldn't know—wouldn't understand—the real reason I had to get out. Away. Fortunately, I'd been all but dismissed for the weekend thanks to the help from...

Crap. Ian and Leah.

In my haste to escape, I never met up with them.

I tapped a quick message to them both on my Slack app, offering up the same excuse I fed Annabelle. They were professionals, had worked here the day before. They could figure this out on their own.

My ride arrived right as I pressed *send* on my vague excuse. With a passing glance over my bare shoulder at the front entranceway to Nowhere Fest, its bright collage of flags waving happily in the wind like the world wasn't caving in entirely, I climbed into a blue Honda Civic driven by my five-star driver Hugo and let it take me away. Away from this mess I got myself into after so many years of avoiding it like the plague.

Remind me to never take advice from anyone again, ever.

Chapter 21

EZRA

The world around me slowed to a crawl. I could see Andie's lips moving, knew she was talking to me, but I couldn't hear anything over the sound of crashing waves inside my head.

Hannah.

I hadn't meant for this to happen—not any of it. I never expected to feel the things I did over the past six weeks. Not from this girl—this woman—who in many ways was my total opposite.

Laser-focused where I was laid back.

Career-driven where I would be content to lay in the sand on a remote beach with nothing but a guitar to keep me company.

A type-A planner with the next five years of her life perfectly laid out in black ink on crisp white paper. A life I had no part in. She had no time for a guy like me. I would only waste it.

Yet when it mattered most, I couldn't resist her. Couldn't stop myself from falling. Because she was so much more than that. More than those things she hid behind.

Fiercely loyal to those she cared for.

Smart as a whip. Creative, too.

Passionate. Kind. Smoking hot, and she didn't even know it.

She was the most beautiful person I had ever met.

And I just screwed it all up.

"Ezra? Helloooo? Earth to Ezra," a shrill voice prompted beside me. I realized with a sagging heart that Andie was still standing there. Still talking.

My face twisted in a grimace and I stepped back, putting as much space between us as I could in the tour bus. It felt cramped. Too small. When Andie tried to close the gap, my hands shot up defensively.

"What are you doing here?" I asked her. The words came out far more forcefully than the first time I said them, when Andie first stepped onto the tour bus and kicked out those photographers from the label.

I couldn't even keep my eyes on her as she tried to answer. Couldn't listen to her response. All my thoughts were on Hannah, my eyes trained on the door as though I could will her to come back, to let me explain.

Andie kissed *me*. Not the other way around.

I didn't want that. I didn't want her. I didn't invite her here.

Would Hannah believe me? After the way I acted these last few days, the distance I put between us after Cleveland. When she had nearly broken my heart in that parking lot.

It didn't matter if she believed me right away. I would explain myself again and again until I was blue in the face. I just needed to get to her, to make her understand.

Andie was still talking, her slender hands gesturing wildly, those big blue eyes I once thought were so alluring wide with sincerity and lined with silver.

I couldn't hear any of it.

"Andie, I'm sorry," I cut her off, already inching toward the exit. "I thought we left things pretty clear back in New York. We're over. I moved on and it's time you did, too."

I knew I sounded more callous than I intended. I sounded like the asshole everyone believed me to be. It didn't matter. My brain was stretched in too many different directions to be gentle. Being gentle back in New York was what got me into this mess in the first place.

Why did she pick that moment to show up?!

Andie was crying now, tears and mascara running down her cheeks in black rivers, but I was already reaching for the door handle.

I could send Peter in here, he could calm her down. Get her to leave. He would hate me for it, but he'd help.

I had to find Hannah.

Chapter 22

HANNAH

Two hours and five minutes.

That was how long it took Olivia to reach me from our apartment in Brooklyn.

It would've taken the average driver more than two and a half hours to make it to my hotel in Atlantic City from Brooklyn. But not Olivia. Not my best friend. I didn't even want to know how fast she drove to make it in time, how many laws she had broken to rescue me.

I sat with my knees curled up to my chest, angled oddly in the passenger's seat of her sleek black Audi A6. Olivia cruised easily in the passing lane of the Garden State Parkway. I noted with a passing glance she managed to obey the speed limit now that I was safely tucked in beside her. Despite my near-constant assurance that I was fine, I could feel her eyes sliding over to look at me every few seconds. Checking to make sure I was still there. That I hadn't broken into a million pieces and left shards of glass and dust all over her leather interior.

Olivia had taken one look at my face when I climbed into her car and let me sit in silence for the first leg of the drive home. Let me process the events of the day. Something I was still trying to do.

Thirty minutes.

That was how long it took for my phone to start ringing... after.

The first call came while I was packing my belongings haphazardly into my suitcase—dirty clothes tossed in with the clean ones, makeup and toiletries dumped carelessly in the mesh compartment, spilling out of their cases.

There was no time for order, no room in my wild thoughts for organization.

When I heard the rough vibration coming from across the hotel room, I leaped up and over the still-twisted sheets of the king bed to lunge for the nightstand where I left it. I figured it had to be Annabelle calling to ream me out for abandoning my post.

Or, even more horrifying perhaps, Olivia calling to say traffic was gridlocked on the expressway and there was no way she could make it.

My breath caught in my throat when Ezra's name flashed across the screen instead.

Biting down on my bottom lip, I stared at the phone where it vibrated in my hand, unable to move. The call ended itself after five unanswered rings.

Next came the texts—

`Hannah, please pick up.`

`Please, I need to talk to you.`

`Hannah, let me explain.`

`Call me.`

`Hannah, where are you? Let me come find you.`

Then five more phone calls, all of them unanswered.

I started sending them straight to voicemail after the third. Either Ezra got the hint that I wasn't ready to talk or he was pulled away for the band's autograph signing at the festival. My phone was silent for the rest of the day, save for Olivia's periodic text updates from the road—by some small miracle traffic was light and she would *definitely* make it to me, she promised—and one email from Annabelle telling me to take whatever time I needed.

Two very, very small silver linings amid the blackest of rain clouds.

I adjusted my position in Olivia's car as the leg curled beneath me in the seat started to tingle and go numb, daring a glance in her direction. I could tell by the agitated rhythm she drummed on the steering wheel that whatever time I had left to avoid talking about it was running out. From the corner of my eye I saw her open her mouth and then close it three times.

"Just say it."

Olivia winced—caught. "Are you... sure? About what you saw?"

I cocked my head to look at her and blinked.

She was never one to beat around the bush. Her candor could be brutal, but I usually appreciated it. I knew she would never hide things from me. Never lie for convenience.

"All I mean is, you said you ran out of there pretty quickly. Is it at all possible what you saw was just... two old friends having a quick hug to say hello?"

I barked out a humorless laugh and Olivia winced again.

"I'm sorry, Han. I just..."

I smiled, the first real one in hours, and reached a hand over to gently grasp hers where it rested on her lap. "I know, and that's why I love you. Thank you, seriously, for coming to get me."

Her warm returning smile radiated down on me like the sun. It was the first time I felt warm in hours. "Anything for you."

With the expert skill of someone who had been my closest friend for nearly a decade, Olivia kept my mind off of Ezra and Andie and Olympus for the rest of the drive home. I knew once we got there, once I settled in, she'd want me to talk about it. To figure out what was next, where to go from here. But for now, I was content to let her regale me with stories about her crazy clients at the law firm, her devilishly handsome but douchey boss, and what was happening in her favorite HBO dramedy, *Succession*.

I even let her bribe another smile out of me when she pulled off the highway to buy us both Taco Bell—our comfort food of choice.

Olivia rarely let a moment of silence fill the meticulously clean cabin of her car. Each time it did, I thought of Ezra. Of us.

But what *us* was there?

I was the one to tell him we couldn't have a real relationship, that we had to hide it.

It had been my idea to keep things light. Casual. My exact words to him over and over when he pushed me about it.

And when he offered me a lifeline that day on the bus ride to Cleveland, not only saving me from sure embarrassment in front of my boss but also making me look positively amazing at my job, how did I repay him?

By telling him to back off.

It was hard not to think I was the one who pushed him straight into Andie's arms. Hard not to blame myself for what happened.

It didn't make me any less angry, though. *Hurt.*

By the time we circled the block three times and found a parking spot for Olivia's car near our building and climbed the three flights of narrow stairs to our apartment, the clock on the far wall by the window showed five. Olympus's show started in just one short hour.

The last one before their three-month hiatus, and I was missing it.

For a fleeting moment, I let myself wonder if Ezra was thinking of me. If he felt bad about what happened, if he regretted choosing Andie.

Part of me, the conscientious, workaholic part, prayed he wasn't. It would only be a distraction, something to make putting on a great show even harder. The part of me that was just a girl, a girl who finally felt ready to let someone else in, to peek behind the walls—break them down entirely, even—she felt differently.

I didn't hear from him again for the rest of the evening.

"Han, if you look me in the eyes right now and tell me Ezra is the biggest piece of shit ever, and that we hate him from now until the end of time, then I will personally help you burn all of your Olympus tees," Olivia was saying over a spoonful of peanut butter straight from the jar. "No one will be more supportive than me. All I'm saying is to sleep on it first."

She passed me the jar from her place huddled up beside me under a blanket on the blue-gray suede couch we spent way too much of our savings on. I dug in with my spoon and said, "I'm not ready to start lighting things on fire just yet, but I'm glad to hear you have my back."

Olivia batted her eyelashes playfully at me then turned her attention back to the TV. A cool breeze drifted in through the cracked window across the room—the mild day had turned into a seasonably chilly evening, reminding us that fall was here.

Fall in New York was always my favorite time of year. The leaves changing colors; the crisp and earthy scent of Autumn hanging in the air; the pumpkin spice lattes available at all my favorite coffee shops.

Would my favorite season now be tainted with the memory of my colossal mistake?

It was nearing midnight and Olivia and I had already blazed our way through half a season of our favorite comfort show: *Gossip Girl*. I still hadn't been able to convince her to watch *The Vampire Diaries* with me. Her passion for supernatural romance was severely lacking.

This had to be something like our fourth rewatch of the series, so we were only half paying attention. In between arguing about my love for Dan Humphrey despite all his flaws—which Olivia just *loved* pointing out every chance she got—she found small ways here and there to break the ice. To get me to open up about Ezra and what happened in Atlantic City.

While I did, I was surprised to realize how much of the past few weeks I had hidden from her—whether that was intentional or if I had just been waiting to see her again, I wasn't sure.

I could feel Olivia's attention back on me before she spoke. "Speaking of me always having your back, which I most definitely will..."

"I'm sensing a 'but' coming on."

"*But*," she emphasized loudly as she grabbed the peanut butter jar back from me, "Are you sure there isn't more to the story? Don't you think you should at least, I don't know, hear him out? I mean, he called you a billion times after you ran off."

I shrugged noncommittally. "Maybe. At some point. I don't know. I'm just not ready to hear what he has to say, I guess."

"Go on," she pressed.

I sighed. "I've thought it over a hundred times, sitting in my hotel room, on the drive home, even now on this couch. Yes, there is a chance it was all some sort of misunderstanding and there's a very good explanation for it and it'll be like 'Cool! Mystery solved, Scooby Gang. Let's go get ice cream' or whatever. But there's also a pretty significant chance he's just not into me. Or maybe he was sort of into me at first, but got tired of the game when I brushed him off last week."

Olivia paused, dropping her spoon back into the jar of peanut butter to pour all of her focus into me. "Okay, candid best friend question. Are you walking away right now because you actually think it's best, because he actually played you and is getting back together with his ex, or are you using this as an excuse to cut and run before you're fully invested?"

"Is it okay if I don't have an answer to that yet?"

Olivia's lips turned up as she reached a hand out to squeeze my shoulder. "Of course it is. As long as you give it some thought. Eventually."

As another episode of *Gossip Girl* rolled into the credits, Olivia shifted her body to face me fully, those tanned and graceful legs still tucked underneath her lithe frame. "So if you do officially call it quits with Ezra now, what are you going to do about your job?"

I cocked my head to give her a sidelong look and curled my blanket tighter around my shoulders. "What do you mean?"

Olivia looked down at the peanut butter jar in her hands, digging her spoon through it but not taking a bite. "Well, Olympus is your client. *Ezra* is your client. Even though the next leg of their tour doesn't start for three months, you're going to have to talk to him eventually. See him, take videos of him, promote him. All that jazz." She waved her full spoon through the air to emphasize her point.

I chewed on the inside of my cheek, my brain already whirring. I guess I hadn't thought that far ahead.

While they were on hiatus, I could probably do most of my job without interacting with the band at all. I'd done it before, in the beginning. Dodging the interviews and media appearances shouldn't be that difficult. Annabelle would likely trust my judgment if I convinced her the publicity team could handle it. But what could I do about the tour?

I couldn't ask Annabelle to take me off the account, that would give too much away and it wouldn't be a good look for me either.

A slow smile spread across my lips.

"I know that face. That face scares me," Olivia said, her eyes narrowing.

"I've got some work to do."

·♥·♥·♥·♥·♥·

Dull light crept in between the blinds of the small window above the old Ikea desk in my bedroom, telling me the sun was beginning to wake from its slumber beneath the distant horizon. Despite the late hour, or early hour, depending on how you looked at it, the occasional car still cruised past on the dusky street outside. Whether they were getting an early start to their Sunday or slowly making their way home after a raucous Saturday night, I couldn't say.

Stretching my arms overhead, I closed my eyes and let out a yawn—at least my fifth one this hour, but officially I'd lost count a while ago—then reopened my eyes to stare at my laptop again.

It had been just after midnight when I said my goodbyes to Olivia, brewed a fresh pot of coffee, and set to work. She seemed reluctant to let me go at first but eventually relented when I fervently promised her a lazy Sunday together.

My proposal wasn't perfect—not yet at least. It would take some editing before I could present it on Monday. But I had a good feeling I could pull this off.

I flashed a final satisfied smile at the computer screen after my eyes had finished their slow crawl across the clean presentation deck. Then I shut it and heaved my tired bones up out of my desk chair. I twisted my torso once, slowly to the left, then slowly back the other way, my back cracking gloriously with each turn. The muscles flanking my spine were cramped from sitting in the same position for so long, the breath huffing from between my lips stale with the taste of the three cups of coffee.

The down comforter and Egyptian cotton sheets set I'd splurged on right before moving into the apartment coiled around my body like a glove as I finally crawled into bed.

Home.

With everything that happened today, I hadn't even let myself appreciate being able to sleep in my own bed for the first time in nearly two months. Gone was that slight twinge of unfamiliarity I felt the first few nights I laid here. The little voice that woke me up in the middle of the night whispering *where are you?* was quiet.

After six weeks on the road, dealing with noisy hotel hallways and clunky wall A/C units, this bed in this room truly felt like home.

I was asleep as soon as my head hit my pillow.

Chapter 23

EZRA

Bodies pressed in on me, halting my procession across the grassy path that bisected the main stage area. Some of them were already visibly tipsy and stumbling through the makeshift lane, but I tried not to let my irritation show, head trained on the ground to avoid recognition as I tried desperately to find a hole, any hole, in this mass of people. Normally, I'd relish the opportunity to be in a group of fellow music lovers. To have the chance to meet our fans. Today, I couldn't afford anything that might slow me down.

Hannah hadn't answered any of my calls or texts, and I'd sent what felt like hundreds. My only chance was to find her before our autograph session. The only problem: I had no idea where to look. I didn't even know where I was going in this maze of tents and stages and masses of people. I just knew I had to keep moving.

If I stopped moving, I would implode.

Finally, I saw a path to freedom—a spot where the crowd thinned out between the stage and the pathway to the vendor tents on the opposite side. I sidestepped a group of giggling girls, tugging my baseball cap further down on my head until I was sure it obscured most of my face, and cut like a knife through the last throng of festival goers to pour out the other side like a tidal wave.

The vendor tents.

Maybe she was at our merch table, prepping for the autograph signing.

A man on a mission, I lengthened my stride. My feet carried me across the makeshift walkways at full speed, carefully dodging discarded beer cans and cups that hadn't found their way into a trash can with each step.

I pitied the crew who had to clean this mess up.

The blazing sun beat down on my bare shoulders from its home in the noontime sky—why was it still so damn hot in late September?—as I bobbed and weaved past a few more stragglers. I could feel sweat beading along my hairline and beginning to trickle down my back.

Fucking global warming, I thought to myself, almost grateful for the momentary distraction it provided.

Colorful banners indicating the entrance to the vendor area dawned before me, waving cheerfully in a slight breeze that wasn't nearly enough to make a dent in the afternoon heat. It felt like they were mocking me.

I lifted and dropped a shoulder, shrugging it off. No time for negative self-talk. I just had to find the Olympus tent.

Note to self: next time scope out the festival layout on day one so when you inevitably screw something up royally on day two, you know where you're going.

As quickly as I could without drawing attention, I continued down the lane, my eyes cast down at everyone's shoes, lifting only long enough to scan the sea of tables for a familiar tent, a familiar face.

"Ezra!" a low-pitched, feminine voice carried across the lane, halting me in place. My head swiveled back and forth above my shoulders, eventually coming to rest on a tall, athletically built blonde standing just inside one of the vendor tents. *Our* vendor tent, I realized when I glanced above her head at the large banner brandishing our logo. The blonde's companion, a slightly shorter and much curvier woman with hair as dark as night and creamy bronze skin, was busy helping the line of patrons queuing up in front of the tent.

It took an embarrassing amount of time before recognition dawned in my anxiety-riddled brain.

What the hell is—

"Lex?" I called to the blonde, already bobbing and weaving my way through the massive queue.

Shit, are all these people here for the autograph signing?

There was absolutely no way I wouldn't be recognized in front of my own merch tent. Oh well, it was worth the risk.

Lexi leaned across the table to wrap her long, toned arms around me, pulling me into an embrace so tight I nearly choked. "We were wondering when you were finally going to show up! We sent the new girl back for you over half an hour ago."

"What are you doing here?" I rasped through her stranglehold.

And did she say, 'new girl'?

"Surprise," Camila deadpanned from beside Lexi while handing change back to a customer. Her round, chestnut-colored eyes danced in my direction briefly before she moved to help the next person in line.

Lexi finally released me from her grapple and stepped back to examine me from head to foot. I didn't even want to know what she found in my frayed expression, the hunched defeat of my shoulders. Watching the beaming grin fade slowly from her pretty face, replaced by knitted brows and a tight jaw was clue enough.

"What's wrong?"

I reached up to ruffle the hair at the back of my head that stuck out beneath the rim of my hat. "Have you seen Hannah—" I started to ask sheepishly, then clarified, "The *new girl* who works for Rabbit's Foot. In Cami's old job."

Lexi's eyes narrowed and my cheeks heated under her calculating stare. She'd been able to read me like a book since we were kids. Good to see some things never change. Or maybe not so good. "What did you do?"

I winced at her flat, accusing tone and shielded my face from her glare with my hand, pretending to block out the blistering sun. The gesture had the added benefit of semi-hiding me from the group of festival goers to my left, who were thankfully busy talking to Cami about what shirt they wanted from the selection of samples on display.

Even with my impromptu disguise, I could already feel the questioning eyes of one of those fans on my back, staring right between my shoulder blades.

Kill me.

"Can we go somewhere private?" I murmured, trying my best to avoid someone recognizing my voice as I shot a pointed sidelong glance at the queue.

Lexi followed my gaze, understanding dawning a millisecond later. With an almost imperceptible nod, my best friend since kindergarten pressed an intimate squeeze to Cami's shoulder to silently let her know she was stepping out then beckoned me around to a quiet alcove behind the tent used to stash extra boxes from the vendors in this row.

When we were safely hidden by the back flap of the tent, Lexi turned on me, her arms crossed over her chest, eyebrows raised expectantly.

I sucked in a steadying breath. The shade the tent offered made the alcove at least ten degrees cooler than it was directly beneath the sun's rays, and I needed a second to enjoy the drop in temperature. "I messed up," was all I said eventually as the shade and slightly stifled breeze began to evaporate the sweat on the back of my neck. "Actually, Andie messed up."

Lexi's eyebrows only arched higher on her forehead, as if to say, *I'm gonna need more than that.*

I groaned and dragged a hand down my face, avoiding eye contact. "I take it you met Hannah already?"

Lexi nodded. *Go on.*

"Have you seen her within the last fifteen minutes?"

A blink. *I'm not answering your questions until you answer mine.*

With another groan, I turned my focus back to Lexi and told her everything. About the last six weeks on tour, the last six weeks with Hannah. About Andie randomly showing up today, *completely unannounced by the way*, and kissing me in the tour bus. Trying to rekindle a relationship that was over before I even left New York.

Lexi already knew that part. *I never liked Andie,* her eyes seemed to say, though her lips remained a thin line. She didn't interrupt me even once. That, in itself, was indication enough how deep I was in it.

"I need to find Hannah and explain what happened," I said with finality when my story was spent. "Have you seen her?"

Lexi cocked her head, not inclined to answer me too quickly. "She stopped by the tent earlier this morning and we talked for a while—" I perked up at that. "But she hasn't been back since then. I thought I may have seen her heading toward the gates about fifteen minutes ago, but it was hard to tell. We were getting mobbed."

My heart sank and my eyes glazed over.

The gates.

If she had left...

"Look, I like Hannah. I only spoke with her for twenty minutes or so, but she seemed cool. Like someone I might get along with," Lexi started, pulling me back to the present. She was unable to resist throwing that small dig at Andie—at all of my past relationships.

Fair. I didn't have the best track record when it came to dating.

"So if you're not serious about this, I think you should let her go. It'll suck for the rest of the day, and probably for a week or two after. But in the long run, you'll both be better off."

Tough love. Lexi's specialty.

I chewed on the inside of my cheek, trying to picture the next few weeks without Hannah in them.

I couldn't.

My mind was an inky blackness so empty and cold it seeped into my bones. There was nothing there without her.

"I'm serious."

Lexi hesitated, taking in my hollow eyes, my drawn face. Whatever she found there had her nodding. "She couldn't have gone far. Out here you've got the festival, the tour bus, or the hotel."

The hotel!

Though her tone remained stern, I could see the ghost of a smile curving on Lexi's lips when she saw me instantly perk up.

Approval. *That's a first.*

"You've got the autograph signing soon and then you need to get through this performance. Give her room to breathe, then find her. Tell her how you feel, but let her decide where to go from there."

I chewed on my bottom lip, some of my confidence waning again. *What if it didn't matter? What if she didn't care what I had to say?*

I shook my head. If she was at the hotel, it meant I had a chance. I could fix this.

·❤·❤·❤·❤·❤·

Trying to wade through a performance while my head and my heart were somewhere else was a new form of torture I hoped never to endure again.

More than a few times, Zach shot me a sidelong glance from his place beside me on stage, his dark eyebrows perpetually arched high on his forehead, silently questioning what I was doing.

Out of all the guys in Olympus, I'd known Zach the longest. We were the founders, the originals. It was amateur hour back then, messing around in our parents' garages. We saved up every penny we had to purchase guitars and drums and sound equipment. Our blood, sweat, and tears poured into the music. We were dreamers, but we put in the work to get here.

When you've played with someone that long, they know when you're off your game.

Zach was only part of the issue. I had to completely avoid Peter's glowering stare the entire time we played for that massive crowd. I could still feel it like a third-degree burn on the side of my face.

Before I could track him down and beg for his help after my conversation with Lex, he found Andie on the tour bus. It was easy for him to put two and two together. Like I knew he would, he stepped in to smooth things over for the time being. As pissed as he probably was at me, he was a good guy. Always had been.

To be honest, I never really understood why Andie wanted to date me. I had been passive about our relationship at best, and a bit of an asshole at worst. Peter, on the other hand, had always been kind.

When our show finally came to a close, I exited the stage faster than usual—partially to escape the piercing questions I knew my bandmates were itching to throw my way, and mostly to haul ass to our hotel.

The town car our manager ordered me took an eternity to make it past the security checkpoint. Normally I'd prefer to skip off into anonymity and grab an Uber, but the chance I'd be recognized and mobbed waiting for my ride near the gate was too big a risk.

Finally, the blacked-out Lincoln pulled through the security gate that separated the private area for performing acts from the chaotic masses, and I was already grabbing for the door handle before it came to a complete stop.

"To our hotel," I barked from the backseat, though he probably already knew that. "Please," I added as an afterthought.

My leg bounced, adrenaline pumping through my veins as the town car cruised smoothly toward my destination. When I saw the bright, welcoming lights of the hotel sign gleaming in the darkness settling over the city, I threw open the door and leaped for the asphalt before the car was in park.

I heard the driver yelling something after me as I stepped into the cool night air—a far cry from the intense heat of mid-day when this whole mess started—but I was already through the automatic doors and careening into the lobby without so much as a passing glance. Seconds later, I was jamming my pointer finger against the button for the elevator as though sheer force could will it to arrive faster.

The elevator doors opened and spilled me out onto the top floor, and I immediately stormed down the hallway to the left. Brilliant white door after brilliant white door streamed by in my peripheral vision, but I was laser-focused on the one room number I needed to reach.

647.

I still had it memorized, even though I'd avoided visiting it the night before.

When I reached the room, I pulled up short. Its front door looked like any other in this long hallway: bright white, a shining silver slot for a keycard resting just above the door handle. Yet unlike the others, this door mocked me. Reminded me of what I stood to lose.

Inhaling a steadying breath, I reached out a hand and hovered it just in front of the door. In my rush to get here, every word I prepared earlier in the day had vanished from my mind on a phantom wind.

I hesitated.

I chewed on the inside of my cheek for a long moment, the silence of the hotel closing in on me like a cage. A coffin.

Softer than I thought I was capable, I knocked three times on the door and waited.

No answer.

I knocked again, this time louder.

Nothing.

Unease gathering in my chest, I knocked again, this time loud enough to wake the dead.

Still no answer.

With a groan, I rested my forehead against the door, my hands bracing against the frame to keep me from collapsing to the blue carpeted floor altogether. There was no way she was asleep already, and even if she was, that knock should have woken her.

Did she see me through the peephole and decide to ignore me?

Could she have gone somewhere—stepped out for air?

With strength I didn't feel, I pushed myself back from the door and sprinted toward the elevators, boarding one and letting it carry me swiftly back to the lobby. In a few long strides, I reached the front desk, silently sending my thanks to the hotel gods that no one was in my way, checking in at such a late hour.

"Hi, I'm a guest in room 653 and I was trying to reach a friend of mine in room 647. Do you know if she's in?" I asked, willing my voice to come out even, patient, though I felt anything but.

The front desk clerk—a girl in her early twenties with chocolate brown hair that matched her eyes—looked me over, then turned her attention to the computer screen on the desk. "I don't typically take notice of all our guests' comings and goings or give out personal information," she started a bit tersely and I bit back my irritation, "but let me check to see if there's any notes on the room."

She tapped her fingers a few times against her keyboard, her long, painted fingernails *click-clacking* ominously in the otherwise quiet lobby, then paused. Her eyebrows knit together slowly, her small rosebud of a mouth twisting. "You're sure your friend is in room 647?"

I nodded. "Yeah, room 647. I'm sure."

Slowly, the hotel clerk raised her eyes to mine, a ghost of apology shining in them. "I'm afraid that guest checked out a few hours ago."

"Dude, what the hell is going on?"

I lifted my head from where I'd been cradling it in my hands for the last twenty minutes to find Peter storming into my hotel room.

Apparently, I had left the door ajar.

I let out a mournful groan and returned my head to its resting spot, the heel of my palms driving against my temples in slow, steady circles that usually calmed me down.

It wasn't working.

"Ezra. Look at me, man," Peter boomed, his heavy footfalls drawing nearer and nearer to where I sat on the edge of the bed.

I shook my head, left it in my hands.

I felt the springs in the bed compress as Peter's large frame settled in beside me. "You were a wreck out there, Ez. You're lucky most of the people in the audience were too buzzed or too damn happy to notice." There was an edge of barely concealed irritation in his tone, but his volume had softened significantly.

Slowly, I lifted my head to face him and dropped my hands into my lap. "I know, I'm sorry. I had... other things on my mind."

"I'm guessing it has something to do with why Andie was throwing a fit in the tour bus. And why Hannah was MIA today."

My eyes widened. "Have you seen her?"

"Andie?" Peter looked puzzled. "Yeah, duh. I'm the one who got rid of her today, remember?"

I waved my hands between us. "No, not Andie. Hannah."

Peter nodded slowly. "Sort of, yeah. I ran into her on my way to grab you for the autograph signing. She seemed upset. Said something weird, about me being right about..." His voice trailed off, mouth hanging open mid-sentence as his green eyes went wide.

"What? What did she say?" I demanded, sitting up straighter.

Peter zeroed in on me. His jaw feathered, nostrils flaring, and I recoiled from the quiet anger radiating from his every pore.

"You were hooking up with her," he breathed, his voice deadly quiet. It wasn't a question.

My face fell. I couldn't tell if he was angry about me sleeping with our account rep or that I hadn't told him. Either way, he wasn't happy.

I nodded once, though he didn't need the confirmation.

"We talked about this," Peter exploded, shooting to his feet with a grace no man that broad should ever possess. "It never ends well," he added, pacing back and forth in front of the bed. "She's not just some girl you can sleep with and then cut a clean break the next day, Ez. We have to work with her. And I *liked* her! A lot. She's smart and good at her job, and she understood what we're all about—"

"I know!" It was my turn to explode, my hands balling into fists at my sides as I shot up from the bed to stand in front of Peter and cease his endless pacing. Heat rose from deep within me, a simmering rage starting to boil toward a much-needed release. "You think I don't know that? Of course I do! Way more than even you, I might add. She's not just *some girl* I slept with. I care about Hannah, and I'm pretty sure she cares about me, too."

A beat of silence, then my hot, white anger began to fizzle just as quickly as it had flamed. My eyes dropped from Peter's in shame. "Or at least, I think she did. Before she showed up while Andie and I were…"

"What happened in there, anyway? What was Andie doing here?"

I sighed and dragged my fingers through my hair. "She showed up totally out of the blue, saying she wanted to surprise me before I came back to New York. She wanted to give us another chance. And before I could tell her I was not interested, she…"

Peter blinked and crossed his arms over his chest. He looked like some dickhead bouncer at a nightclub, posed like that in his signature black V-neck tee. Under any other circumstance, I might have laughed.

Instead, I just felt hollow.

"She kissed me. And of course that's when Hannah walked in and found us. Just a second before I could snap to reality and push Andie away."

Peter winced, his mouth stretching into a disgusted grimace.

"I know! I know. It's not good. As soon as Hannah took off, I knew I had to find her. To explain." I wrung my hands together in front of me. "By the time I could get out of Andie's grip and start looking for her though, she was gone. Lexi said she saw her heading for the exit not long after that. As soon as the show was over, I raced back here hoping she'd be in her room, but the front desk said she checked out."

"Shit, Ez."

I nodded, eyes cast at the floor. "She ignored all my calls and texts. I can't reach her."

Peter reached out and clapped a hand on my shoulder. "The way I see it, we've got one more day here, then it's back to New York. Which is probably where she is. You'll get your shot." He dropped his hand from my shoulder and took a seat on my bed once more, reclining so he was propped up on his hands. "I can't make any promises she'll want to date you though. She *is* smart, after all. Way too smart to fall for an idiot."

Against my will, one corner of my mouth turned up.

Chapter 24

HANNAH

It had been ages since I had woken up feeling completely rested. Clear headed.

It had also been ages since I had taken a weekend off work, I realized with a sinking feeling. And it hadn't even been a full weekend if you counted Saturday as a half day.

Which I did, if we were keeping score.

Saturday night, or more like Sunday morning if we got technical, my rest quickly turned fitful—disrupted by dreams of dark, shaggy hair tickling my cheeks and neck; chiseled cheekbones and a slightly crooked nose hovering just in front of mine; a flashing grin that turned into a harrowing grimace when its lips moved toward someone else; a ghostly figure who wasn't me.

I had shot up more than once, my breath heavy and stale in my lungs, sweat beading along my forehead.

I was still exhausted when I climbed out of bed at the crack of noon on Sunday. Like I promised Olivia the night before, I used the rest of the day to get some much-needed relaxation.

Sure, I had given myself just one teeny tiny hour to wrap up the project I started the night before—*morning? What was it considered when you started a project after midnight and didn't finish until almost five a.m.?*—but once that was all wrapped up, I shut everything down.

Laptop—off and unplugged for the day.

Phone, still occasionally vibrating with a new text from Ezra that I promptly ignored and pushed off to deal with another day—left on the charger.

And that night, I slept like the dead in a peaceful, dreamless slumber. A day to unplug was just what I needed before facing the music.

The soles of my Allbirds whispered against the floor, carrying me slowly down the hallway of cubes toward Annabelle's office. At a quarter past eight, it was considered early for the Rabbit's Foot office. Most of the desks I passed were still dark and vacant, but I had heard the telltale *clickety-clack* of Louboutins against linoleum about twenty minutes ago, signaling my boss's arrival.

As my feet drew nearer to her office, I paused and took a breath just before the threshold. One short moment to calm my nerves, remember the words I had practiced in my head on my commute. Then, I knocked and popped my head through her half-open door, mustering as bright a smile as I could. "Good morning, Annabelle."

"Hannah! I wasn't sure if I'd see you today," Annabelle replied with a start, sitting up straighter in her wing-backed chair. "How are you?"

Annabelle never once questioned my sudden request for time off over the weekend. Even now, her face was painted with genuine concern. I felt a small pang in my chest cavity at deceiving her.

"I'm doing, um, much better now. Thank you so much for your understanding on Saturday."

Annabelle waved one of her manicured hands casually through the air between us, her long fingernails still painted in the same fire engine red I was starting to interpret as her signature color.

In one motion, she leaned back more comfortably in her seat and adjusted the modest hemline of her pencil skirt to cross one leg over the other. "No problem at all. You've kept everything running for Olympus like a well-oiled machine these past few months, Hannah. And your results—" she shifted slightly to point one long, red fingernail at her computer screen where I assumed my latest report was open. "They speak for themselves."

My cheeks heated under the weight of her praise, a ghost of a smile curving my lips. I rarely received recognition at my last agency gig. To hear such positive feedback after so little time on the job was like being offered a carafe of ice water after weeks trapped in a barren desert. I dipped my head in thanks.

"So, what brings you by this morning?"

"Right, actually I was hoping to run an idea by you. Something I've been working on in my free time the last couple of weeks—" Another lie, but I couldn't very well let on that I had been up all night Saturday drafting this proposal when I was supposed to be dealing with a personal emergency, *off*-duty.

Annabelle arched her well-groomed blonde eyebrows at me, her gaze shifting down to the stack of stapled papers in my hands, fresh off the printer. I shifted my arms to extend one packet toward her, keeping its twin for myself. Then I dropped to sit comfortably in one of the chairs in front of her desk.

As my boss began thumbing through the deck cradled in her hands, I launched right into my slightly rehearsed pitch, following along in my packet. "As you can see, we've accrued significant costs sending a dedicated digital marketer for the full duration of Olympus's tour—" Annabelle nodded almost imperceptibly, pressing me forwards, eyes darting back and forth over the sums on the current page of the deck. "—plus content curators on-site for several shows.

"If we were to only send content curators to about half the tour dates on their second leg as I am proposing, I estimate we could save thousands of dollars with no significant impact to ROI."

Annabelle leaned in closely to examine the figures on the last page of my deck. It displayed a side-by-side comparison of reporting figures on my content versus the content I posted after receiving it from the curators in Chicago. Her mouth twisted slightly when she noticed the slight decrease in engagement on the professionally shot videos.

"Of course," I swiftly cut in at the downturn of her lips, "We probably need to do some sort of training with the curators in advance, figure out a process for keeping the content consistent and timely. I would be more than happy to work with the team assigned to this account to ensure that transition is as smooth as possible."

Annabelle nodded again and continued scanning through the proposal on her own. Silence stretched as she studied each page thoughtfully. My heart hammered in my chest, anxiety climbing with each tick of the metal wall clock hanging beside her desk.

After what felt like an eternity, Annabelle dropped the packet to her desk and leaned back, steepling her fingers together as her elbows braced against the armrests of her chair. Her cool gray eyes met mine. "It's hard to argue with hard data. And you know Dominic, he loves the words 'save money' more than the air in his lungs."

I did not know Dominic or his penchant for saving a buck, but I nodded enthusiastically.

"If you feel one hundred percent confident we can keep engagement up… then I'm open to giving this a try."

A satisfied smile tugged the corners of my lips up. "Of course! I will make absolutely sure the content team has everything they need well before the first tour date in January."

"And if we need to send you out to one or two shows, I suppose we could easily do that," Annabelle mused quietly, leaning over to jiggle her mouse and wake up her computer. I could see the gears whirring in her head, her brain already on to the next to-do on her list.

My throat bobbed as I swallowed and it took force to offer a noncommittal, "Sure."

"This is great work, Hannah. I know we threw you to the wolves your first few months here, so to speak, but you've really risen to the challenge. That hasn't gone unnoticed."

My smile widened into a grin, my nerves vanishing as pride swelled in my chest. I nodded my thanks, unable to find the right words to convey how much her acknowledgment meant to me.

Annabelle met my smile with her own and continued, "Now that we'll have you around more often, I've got another client that could benefit from your skillset." She paused at the sight of my arched eyebrows and quickly added, "No tour this time—at least, not for a while. I promise."

I released a small, breathless laugh and moved to stand.

Annabelle's expression turned thoughtful again, serious, and I tensed behind the chair I'd just vacated. "Before you head back to your desk though, I do want to stress how highly I value work-life balance on our team. Now that you won't be on tour anymore, I'm hoping to see your emails come through during regular business hours." She cocked her head at me, though her eyes danced playfully in the shadows cast by her desk lamp.

I almost had to laugh, my muscles unclenching. "You got it. No more midnight emails, I promise." As the words left my lips, I realized I meant them.

·❤·❤·❤·❤·❤·

I was back at my desk, bent over a cluttered inbox filled with dozens of emails I had archived from the road when I felt a prickle at the back of my neck. Cautiously, I turned my head to one side and found a pair of dark brown eyes peering down at me from the top of my cube wall. I nearly jumped out of my seat.

"You're back," my coworker Mei said in that flat way of hers as she stepped around the barrier separating us. The fabric of her beige, wide-legged, cotton pants swished with each step.

I forced a smile and willed my heart rate to return to normal. "I'm back."

I swiveled around in my desk chair as Mei took a seat at the empty desk across from me. She took her time, casually reclining and crossing one ankle over the other, making herself comfortable in the ergonomic chair. She reminded me of a cat, not afraid to stretch out, take up space.

"So, how was it?" Mei folded her arms loosely over her brown tank top. The deep color of it almost matched her eyes.

I watched her for a moment, eyes narrowing slightly. Her nearly black hair was knotted in two space buns at the top of her head, the same style she wore the first day I met her. Reflecting on that week reminded me I still didn't know where we stood, she and I. Her warning about Ezra that first week had turned out to be false—at least partially, anyway. Did she know that, though?

Emboldened by my last few weeks of freedom and the high praise from Annabelle still ringing in my ears, I decided to find out.

"It was good. Really good, actually. The guys were all so welcoming, they made my job easy. And getting to see free concerts two or three times a week was a nice bonus."

Mei nodded, picking at an invisible piece of lint on her pants.

"I also ran into Camila at the festival this past weekend," I added coyly.

A flicker of surprise on Mei's face as she met my gaze, then it vanished. "Really? That's... how did she seem?"

"Good. Great, even. She got a new job in California, with some help from Annabelle. She's living out there now with her girlfriend."

Mei's plucked eyebrows arched further. "Her... girlfriend?"

"Yep," I answered a bit smugly. "Turns out she was never involved with Ezra at all, but one of his best friends."

I tried not to give away too many details—at the end of the day, it wasn't my story to tell. There was a reason Camila hadn't confided in Mei or anyone else on the team.

Genuine surprise bloomed across Mei's angular features. Either she was putting on an Oscar-worthy performance or she really didn't know the full story at all. Something that looked like hurt shadowed her face.

I instantly felt guilty for gloating. "She seems happy," I added hastily. "But I got the impression she missed it here. Missed everyone here." A tiny white lie, but for a noble cause.

The corners of Mei's rosebud mouth quirked up in the ghost of a smile.

"Did I miss anything interesting while I was gone?"

A dismissive wave that turned into an excuse to check her manicure. "Pfft, nothing interesting ever happens around here."

After some coaxing, I got her to reveal some of the office gossip to me. Although she was right, it wasn't nearly as interesting as the hurricane that had weathered down upon me the last few nights of the tour.

"What about you? I read online that Ezra ended things with his girlfriend Andie pretty recently," Mei mused after she'd finished a story about someone getting embarrassingly drunk at the last team happy hour. One corner of her mouth lifted. "Anything interesting happen on the road?"

I remembered the look on her face, those kicks under the table, the day we met with Olympus for the first time. She had seen right through me. In spite of myself, my heart ached at the sound of his name. And Andie's. In the same sentence.

I wonder how the tabloids got wind of it, I thought to myself at first. Then, *wait a second, they* ended *things? That didn't make any sense.*

I shook my head, half in answer to Mei's question and half to push away the thoughts creeping back in. "Nope, nothing."

"Ah, well. Probably for the best anyway." She stood up to lazily stretch her arms overhead. *Definite cat vibes.* Then added, "Good to have you back."

I'd never seen Mei grin broadly. Her smile was usually subdued, a tiny quirk of the lips you might miss if you weren't careful. But the look she gave me as she turned back in my direction at the exit to my cubicle had to be the next best thing.

"Good to be back," I said. And for the second time that day, I had the feeling I meant it.

Mei took another step to leave, then stopped short just outside my cube. "Oh! Some guy called for you while you were out last week. I think he was a writer or something? I told him to email you. I don't like giving out people's personal numbers without permission." She rapped her knuckles twice on my wall and then she was gone before I could ask for more details.

I turned back to my laptop with a look of confusion. There were still a little over thirty unread emails I hadn't gotten to yet. I started skimming.

Junk.

More junk.

A flagged email chain from Annabelle about the Q&A results from last week.

Aha!

Subject line: Tried to reach you at the office...

Hannah!

Thought you might still be on tour, but figured I'd give your office line a try anyway. I'm going to be at Nowhere Fest on assignment this coming weekend and saw Olympus was performing. I thought we could

CATCH UP IF YOU HAVE SOME DOWNTIME IN THE EVENING. MAYBE GRAB A DRINK OR SOMETHING?

GIVE ME A CALL WHEN YOU GET THIS AND WE CAN SET SOMETHING UP. LOOKING FORWARD TO SEEING YOU AGAIN.

BEST,

TOM WESLEY

Crap.

I had forgotten about Tom after I ran into him Friday afternoon. Not only had I ignored his email—in all fairness, I hadn't seen it until now—but I completely blew him off when he asked to meet up.

I hurriedly clicked reply and tapped out a response, giving him an excuse similar to the one I had fed Annabelle on Saturday. I was about to press send when something made me pause. A memory of running into Tom at the brewery that time with Olivia.

He's hot, she had said. *And he's definitely into you.*

Getting involved with yet another guy I work with, albeit in the loosest sense of the word, was a bad idea. I wasn't sure if I was even interested in Tom. I had never really given him a chance. Both of the times I saw him, though... he had that tall, dark, and handsome thing going on. The one romance novelists wrote about for a reason.

What would Olivia do?

Before I could think twice about it, I added a vague note to the end of the email about meeting up for drinks in the city. I added my personal phone number just below it and pressed send.

Not ten minutes later, my phone buzzed against my desk and a smile bloomed on my lips as I read the incoming text.

Chapter 25

HANNAH

"Who are you and what have you done with my best friend?" Olivia asked from the doorway of our apartment, her athletic frame paused with one foot suspended midair just over the threshold.

I shot her a sidelong glance from my position on the couch. It was Friday and my feet were propped up on the coffee table, my laptop balanced against the tops of my thighs. Annabelle was out of the office most of the day taking client meetings, so I decided to hole up in our apartment after lunch, finally taking advantage of Rabbit's Foot's hybrid work policy.

After being on the road, I found myself distracted at the office. I'd get up every so often to amble around the winding cube hallways or drop by Mei's desk to see what she was up to, to the point that she—the veritable *queen* of slacking off—had even told me to bug off.

I forced myself to hang in there until five the past four days before slinking out. When I got Annabelle's message today saying she wouldn't be back, I figured it was time to give this remote work thing a try.

I was pleasantly surprised at how productive I'd been at home the last four hours, getting more done today than I probably had all week. Maybe those people on LinkedIn sharing articles daily about the benefits of working remotely were actually on to something.

"Hannah Maxwell. At home before four-thirty? Impossible. Inconceivable. Unthinkable."

I rolled my eyes good-naturedly, a smile tugging at my lips as I shut my laptop. "It's called work-life balance, Liv. Look it up."

"Oh, *I* know what it's called. I always thought that was a foreign phrase to you, though. Pardon me if I'm a little shocked," she chided, setting her work bag on the table by the front door before crossing the refinished hardwood floor to join me on the sofa. "What's the occasion? Got a hot date tonight you had to be home early for?"

I winced and leaned forward to set my computer on the coffee table. "Actually..."

I could feel Olivia's eyes widen, her jaw fall open, before I turned to face her. "Who?!"

I hesitated, biting down on my bottom lip, then decided it was best to plow through. "Do you remember that guy we ran into at the brewery before I left?" It was finally starting to get easier to talk about the band—about Ezra. "I think I may have told you I ran into him at the music festival, too. Before everything... happened."

Olivia nodded.

"Well, he reached out again and suggested we get dinner." I half shrugged. "And I figured, why not?"

Olivia's gaping mouth rearranged itself into a feline grin that could rival the Cheshire cat himself. "Look at you, getting back out there." Then, her grin twisted into more of a grimace. "Okay, so don't be mad, but—"

My eyebrows were already knitted together when a loud knock on our apartment door drew my attention. I glanced between the door and Olivia, who was still frozen on the couch beside me.

"Don't be mad," she repeated slowly as she stood to make her way to the door. "He texted me the other day and just wanted to talk. I told him he could stop by today because I didn't think you had plans."

My heart stopped beating, the world slowing down around me until all I could hear was the blood rushing in my ears.

It couldn't be. She wouldn't do that. Olivia was impulsive but never cruel.

Olivia reached the door and swung it partially open to whisper something I couldn't make out to whoever loomed in the hallway.

A second later, a broad, towering frame filled the doorway, clad in a tight-fitting black V-neck T-shirt and dark-wash jeans. I let out a sharp puff of air and reclined back on the couch.

"Hey, Han," Peter said a bit shyly from the doorway, one of his massive palms lifted in a tentative wave. "Can we talk for a minute?"

"What, are you two *friends* now?" My voice thundered louder than I had intended before I could stop myself.

Olivia visibly cringed at the harsh edge in my voice, but I didn't care. Peter stepped fully into the apartment, gently easing the door closed behind him, but didn't come any closer.

"Not friends, per se, but we've texted here and there since we hung out in Chicago," Olivia said gently, taking up a place beside

Peter. At least two yards still separated us, like I was a wounded animal that might lash out and bite them any moment.

Good.

I folded my arms over my chest and cocked my head. My mouth was a thin line. Olivia sighed and moved toward me, returning to her seat beside me on the couch. One of her hands reached out tentatively, like she wanted to touch my arm, then pulled back as she thought better of it. "Sorry, I didn't mean to spring this on you. I just figured if I asked, you'd say no—"

I cut her off with a dirty look, as if to say, *duh, of course I'd say no. This is a stupid idea.*

To Olivia's credit, she only hesitated for half a second before continuing. "I figured you'd say no, *but* you'd regret not listening to what he had to say. So just... hear him out. Please."

The earnestness in her eyes, in her face, melted some of my steel. Enough that I turned somewhat softer eyes on Peter and inclined my head subtly, giving him permission to speak.

It didn't go unnoticed the way his emerald eyes darted to Olivia first, before the tension in his shoulders relaxed and he took five steps forward, closing most of the distance between us.

When he realized there most definitely was not enough room on the sofa for three, especially not a six-foot-five could-be linebacker, Peter glanced around the room for another place to sit. Finding none, he smoothly picked up and carried over one of our dining room chairs in one hand, like it weighed nothing at all. He set it down on the other side of the coffee table and sat, turning his attention to me.

"Sorry for just showing up, but I wasn't sure what else to do," he began, wringing his hands together in his lap. It was the first time I had ever seen Peter nervous. Under better circumstances, the sight of it may have been funny. "I couldn't find you back in Atlantic City, and I realized I never got your number while we were on tour. You know, since you were always just a few steps away and all. And I just... I needed to talk to you."

"You could've emailed."

A wince. "I know, but it felt weird to write it down."

"So you came to say *I told you so* in person?" The joke fell flat. Peter's eyes widened in an expression of what could only be described as horror.

"Hannah, I would never... is that what you meant, when you passed by me at Nowhere Fest?"

I nodded and looked down at my lap, fingers picking at the string on my lounge pants.

Peter leaned forward in his seat, elbows resting against his knees. "I wasn't right, Hannah. That's why I'm here, actually. To explain and, uh, apologize for what I said back in Jones Beach."

Slowly, I lifted my eyes to his and almost withered under the force of his gaze. The sincerity in his green eyes. Even from across the table I could see a thin ring of gold surrounding his pupil that seemed to glow with earnest concern.

"He's been a mess since you left."

I bit the inside of my cheek and looked away.

"I know it looked bad back there with Andie, but he promised me it was a misunderstanding. That he'd been trying, not firmly enough, to get her to leave. To explain that he wasn't interested."

"I take it he told you about... us?" The words were barely audible.

Color rose to Peter's cheeks and it was his turn to look away. "Not everything, but yeah." Peter flashed his eyes back to me and cocked his head. "And I know everyone around here thinks I'm just a pretty face, but I'm not stupid. I could tell something was going on, even if I wasn't sure what it was."

A ghost of a smile curved my lips as I held in a laugh. Of course he noticed. The more I thought about it since returning to New York, the more I was sure they all had. Hard to keep secrets when you're living on top of one another.

Pulling myself back together, I asked, "If that's true, and it was just a misunderstanding, why isn't he here telling me this?"

"Well, when you ignored his five billion texts—and phone calls—I think he figured you'd call the cops or throw a chair at his head if he showed up at your door."

This time I did laugh. "So you're the guinea pig?"

"Something like that." Peter flashed me a grin and winked. His boyish charm dissolved what was left of my defenses.

"Great timing on your part," I drawled, glancing sidelong at Olivia as she grimaced.

"Ugh, I know. Sorry, I had no idea today was... not good for a reunion."

"What, you got a hot date or something?" Peter echoed Olivia's joke from earlier. For two people who could not be more different, sometimes they were eerily similar-minded.

I blinked back at him and his smile faltered.

Peter cursed under his breath and looked pensively out our front window.

Eventually, Peter broke the awkward silence. His voice echoed loudly in our apartment as he said, "Look, I'm not going to sit here and tell you what to do. If you want to go on a date, then go on a date. If you want to ignore everything I've said here today and move on with your life like the last six weeks never happened, then do that, if it's what's best for you. *But.* If you were asking my opinion, as your friend, I'd say you should at least talk to Ezra. Hear him out and say what you need to say, too."

"You're saying this as *my* friend, not Ezra's?" I asked, tilting my head.

Peter grinned. "One hundred percent."

I nodded, my thoughts beginning to wander.

Peter had a point. I probably did owe Ezra the opportunity to explain, to tell me his side of the story. If what Peter said was true, then I probably should have heard him out days ago.

And I owed it to myself to tell him how I felt.

But what would I say?

After the past week, after everything, I wasn't sure where my heart was anymore. I had been walking back to the tour bus that day to tell Ezra I wanted a relationship with him. A real relationship, not some hidden, dirty little secret.

Did I still want that?

I couldn't blow off Tom again, either. Whether this was a real date, a rebound fling, or just two industry acquaintances meeting up to talk shop, I owed it to him to go.

I nodded again to Peter and smiled softly as I said, "Let me think about it. I'll reach out to him when I'm ready."

Peter dipped his head, satisfied enough. Slapping his large palms against the tops of his thighs, he stood, his six-foot-five frame once again filling up our living room. "Thank you—" He looked from me to Olivia, then paused when their eyes met. "Both of you."

I arched an eyebrow at the meaningful glance that passed between them, but neither seemed to notice. Before the intimate moment could draw out any longer, I cut in. "Next time you two want to ambush me, give me a little notice, why don't you?"

"Wouldn't be much of an ambush then, would it?" Olivia winked and smiled sweetly at me, reaching out to squeeze my shoulder gently before she walked Peter to the door.

Chapter 26

HANNAH

The sound of my heels tapping against the uneven pavement below pounded a soothing rhythm in my ears as I hustled down another city block toward The Exchange, a funky little bistro not far from the apartment I shared with Olivia. I had only been there once before, but I knew they had an amazing wine selection and the best fried Brussels sprouts on the planet.

Tom suggested it during our text conversation after I vaguely mentioned I lived out this way.

Of course, I hadn't been stupid enough to give him my address. Or to accept his offer to pick me up for our date—or whatever it was—even if he was renowned in his field and ridiculously charming.

And hot.

Over the years, both living at home with my mom and away at college, I had watched enough true crime documentaries on Netflix to keep me wary. There would be no ending up in the bottom of a ditch for me. My pocket taser and matching mini pepper spray were stowed safely in my clutch, like they always were.

I thanked my lucky stars that, as I cruised through an intersection just before the WALK signal stopped flashing, the weather was still mild for an early October evening. When we had first made our plans official, I thought to myself that the five-block trek to the restaurant would give me time and space to clear my head.

And it would have. If I hadn't decided at the last minute to wear my favorite pair of nude strappy heels. They paired so perfectly with my sleek black cropped jeans and flouncy beige blouse that I couldn't resist. Unfortunately, they made run-walking five city blocks more than a little difficult.

Although, if I remembered correctly, Tom was pretty tall. These heels might help even the playing field a bit.

I rounded the final corner and slowed my pace, trying to catch my breath for the last few yards. I silently prayed my face hadn't turned tomato red during my journey.

Peter's surprise appearance earlier that afternoon had thrown me even more off my game than usual. Not to mention it made me late. I was so distracted I had to redo my winged eyeliner twice, eventually flying out of the apartment like a bat out of hell fifteen minutes later than I planned.

My head still buzzed from that conversation. Despite the soothing night air, I strained to pull breath into my lungs at a steady pace. I tried my best to shove those thoughts away though, pack them down. No time for that.

I was already awkward enough on first dates. I didn't need to be distracted on top of it.

As I neared the front entrance to The Exchange, I paused just outside the bistro and squared my shoulders, exhaling one final cleansing breath before pulling on the handle of the heavy glass-plated door.

Normally, my game plan would be to get here early, arrive first, giving me somewhat of an upper hand. Tonight though, I just barely made it on time. I stopped inside the vestibule of the restaurant, thankful the hostess was already speaking to another group of four about their reservation, and reached down to pull my phone from my clutch to see if Tom had texted me on my way here.

"Hannah!" a faint voice called from somewhere inside the dining area, and my fingers released my phone as my eyes lifted to scan the dimly lit interior, soon landing on—

Wow.

I had somehow forgotten just how strikingly handsome Tom was. In that moment, when the full force of his winning smile zeroed in on me like a laser, like the sun through one of those funky little eclipse-watching glasses, my breath caught in my throat. I swore time slowed to a crawl as he stood up from the intimate table for two in the corner and made his way to me.

"It's great to see you," Tom said when he reached me, easily sliding one of his muscled arms around my waist to rest his palm against the small of my back. He leaned his tall frame down—even with my heels, the guy still had a good four inches on me—and pressed the softest kiss to my cheek in greeting. My cheeks flushed, and it had nothing to do with my hustle to get here.

Words jumbled incoherently in my brain, so I smiled warmly up at him and nodded a greeting of my own. I allowed him to lead me toward our table, completely conscious of his hand still on my back the entire way.

Please don't let me be sweaty.

Tom pulled out my chair with one hand and guided me to sit with the other in one smooth motion. Then he circled around to the other side to find his seat.

The table was set with a white tablecloth and a matching assortment of flatware and plates arranged elegantly at each setting. A small candle set squarely in the center of the table cast the two of us in a golden glow.

"I hope you like wine," Tom said with a disarming smile, gesturing one of his slender hands toward a bottle resting at room temperature near the edge of our table. I could tell it was a red, but couldn't immediately recognize the variety from my vantage point. The label looked expensive.

"It's a Malbec, one of my favorites," Tom supplied, reading my thoughts.

"I love wine," I answered with a smile of my own, meeting his gaze across the table. I wasn't usually much of a red wine drinker, but I happened to like Malbec, too.

As if he'd been waiting in the wings, a waiter stepped up to our table and expertly uncorked the bottle, offering a taste to both of us first and, *yep*, it was probably the best wine I ever had. Better even than the rich and aromatic varieties they had served at Olivia's firm party last year.

I heard Tom emit a muffled chuckle at what I could only imagine was the look of pure ecstasy on my face. The waiter took that as his cue to fill both our glasses. I drank a healthy gulp of my own, then hesitated. This wine was delicious, but I needed to keep my wits about me. Best to take it easy.

"I was surprised to hear from you." Tom's voice broke my mental tennis match and I lifted my eyebrows at him as I set my glass carefully back down on the table. "In a good way. You're a tough woman to get a hold of."

I waved a hand dismissively in the air between us then rested it in my lap. "I swear, I'm not typically so all over the place. I'm not sure if Annabelle said anything, but I just started at Rabbit's Foot a few weeks before the tour, so it's been a whirlwind two months. I was at an agency before that. We had some clients in the entertainment industry, but I didn't work directly with musicians in this way."

Tom arched two perfectly groomed eyebrows the color of maple syrup and sipped casually from his glass of wine. "Wow, no, she hadn't mentioned it. Talk about trial by fire."

I laughed and nodded, feeling my body relax slightly as a warm hug from the Malbec settled over my bones.

"So that was your first big tour then? How was it?" Tom asked after setting his wine glass on the table.

I bit down on my bottom lip, taking a moment to think. "Good. Great! It was crazy, I can't lie. There was a huge learning curve there in the beginning. But this has always been my dream, so it was truly epic to be able to live it."

Tom nodded in understanding, one corner of his lips turning up as his sapphire eyes danced in the candlelight. "Quite accomplished, Miss Maxwell. Living out your dreams at such a young age."

I snorted, unable to stop the sound before it escaped, and quickly lifted a panicked hand to my face as if I could shove it back in. Tom merely chuckled in answer, his rich tenor echoing around us, and picked up his menu.

I followed suit, though the words seemed to blur in front of my vision, and tried to change the subject. "Speaking of accomplished, I must be one lucky lady to be at dinner with one of the *most renowned music journalists of today*."

Tom cringed across the table but I caught the ghost of a smile on his lips as I quoted the line from the Forbes 30 Under 30 list he'd been included in last year. "I think my mom has that article hanging up on her fridge," he joked.

I lifted my eyes to observe him while his attention was still focused on his menu. Most of his face was cast in shadow from the flickering candle between us, but somehow it only brought out the rich tan of his skin and accentuated his sharp jawline.

He looked even more handsome than before. *Ugh.*

"Has your mom always been supportive of your career?"

"Oh, no. Absolutely not."

My eyes widened in surprise and Tom looked up to meet my gaze as though he could sense it.

"I mean, she is *now*. But when I was just a rowdy teenager with a passion for writing and rock music, I was probably every mother's nightmare," he paused dramatically, wiggling his eyebrows, "my own especially."

I couldn't stop my laugh, trying to picture the well-put-together man in front of me as a teenage rebel.

"Once I'd been in the journalism program at NYU for a couple of years and started making somewhat of a name for myself in their independent paper and at a few unpaid local internships, she started to change her tune. But only just barely."

Tom sipped from his glass of wine and my eyes caught on his throat, the way his muscles worked as he swallowed. I quickly tore my eyes away before he noticed my stare, once again trying to decide on an entree.

I think I read the description for the salmon five times without understanding any of it.

"It wasn't until I landed my first story in *Billboard* as a freelancer that she was willing to admit there was something here. Don't get me wrong, she's always believed in me, in my talent. But she grew up in a generation, in a family, that doesn't think the arts make for a viable career."

I nodded, understanding more than he probably realized. My mom was always my biggest supporter. Growing up, with just the two of us trying to find our way in the world, the emphasis had always been on college; building a stable career that only I could make or break. Maintaining my independence.

I understood why. And in the end, it worked out well for me. I loved marketing. I loved my job at Rabbit's Foot. I loved being able to afford an apartment with my best friend, even if it was just barely.

I smiled widely at Tom and lifted my glass in a mildly mocking toast. "To making it on the fridge."

Tom lifted his glass, a bemused smile curving his full lips. "To following your dreams."

As both of us drained another sip—a very small one for me—our waiter appeared to take our order, and I had to scramble to figure out what I wanted. Fortunately, whatever Tom asked for sounded delicious, so I decided to follow his lead.

And he ordered the fried Brussels sprouts appetizer. *A man after my own heart.*

A comfortable quiet fell over our table when the waiter left, my mind still hung up on something about that toast.

About following your dreams.

Rabbit's Foot *was* my dream. Had been for quite some time. But at the end of the day, it was just a job.

What else? What about the rest of me?

I thought about Olivia's joke earlier, about me waiting until now to discover the *life* part of work-life balance. Then my thoughts drifted to Peter and our conversation that afternoon.

He's been a mess since you left.

And what Olivia said just days earlier.

Are you avoiding him because you actually think he played you, or is this an excuse to walk away before you're vulnerable?

I gently shook my head to clear the thoughts, vaguely aware that Tom was speaking to me. At the same moment, my eyes snagged on a head of tousled, dark hair at the back of the restaurant. The lean, almost willowy shoulders looked so familiar. The lithe frame, noticeably tall even while seated, tugged at something in my chest.

Ezra.

As my heart rate started to climb and my cheeks began to flush, the shaggy head turned to the side to give me a view of his side profile and...

It wasn't him.

A breath whooshed out from between my lips in relief at the same time something else hung heavy in my chest.

"Is everything okay?"

I slid my eyes back to Tom, willing the surprise—and small amount of guilt—not to show on my face.

"You seem a bit—"

"Out of practice?" I cut in quickly, trying to smooth things over. "Sorry, this has been my first date in what I'm embarrassed to admit has been several years."

"I was going to say distracted." Tom cocked his head thoughtfully to one side, his blue eyes narrowed in my direction. There was still a faint smile curving his lips, but I could see the question in his eyes.

My cheeks flushed.

This was a terrible idea.

Now I had two problems on my hands.

One: why was I still thinking about Ezra when I was on a date with an amazing, successful, hot guy who had been going out of his way to talk to me for weeks?

And two: we hadn't officially had *the talk* about whether this was a date or not. It felt like a date. All signs pointed to date. But I could've just completely put my foot in my mouth.

"Ugh, sorry. I didn't mean to assume this was a date. You probably weren't even thinking that—"

Tom's smile widened as he cut off my rambling to say, "Oh no, I definitely thought this was a date. At least, I would like it to be a date."

His sapphire eyes held mine and the depth of that stare had me biting on my lower lip and fidgeting in my seat.

"Oh," was all I could manage to say.

♥ · ♥ · ♥ · ♥ · ♥

After a small stretch of awkward silence, our conversation picked up where it had left off, the night somehow salvaged.

My thoughts still occasionally strayed to that head of dark hair in the back of the restaurant, who I later discovered looked nothing like Ezra when he walked past us toward the exit, and the bombshell Peter dropped on me earlier that day.

But Tom usually pulled me back to the present. A happy side effect of his job interviewing flaky artists, I assumed.

He was charismatic and easy to talk to. He asked thoughtful questions about me, my life, my family and friends. He made insightful observations about what I revealed, finding common threads between our two very different upbringings.

Tom grew up in a wealthy borough in Connecticut with his mom, dad, and two brothers, one older and one younger. On the outside, the perfect nuclear family I had always envied. On the inside, though, Tom revealed things weren't always as golden as they seemed.

I found myself grateful for my simple life in Pennsylvania, for everything my mom had sacrificed for and offered me.

"Thank you, for tonight," I said softly as Tom guided me to the exit of The Exchange with the light touch of his palm on the small of my back.

"I meant what I said earlier. I'm really glad you reached out."

I felt Tom pause behind me on the sidewalk just outside of the restaurant, so I spun around to face him. My cheeks felt warm and rosy despite the slight chill in the air, the flush due only partially to the two glasses of Malbec I'd downed with dinner.

Tom took one step forward to close the distance between us and I felt myself lean back the slightest bit in response. I told myself it was to incline my head, to be able to look up at his towering frame, but in my heart I knew it was more.

"I had a nice time." My voice was quieter than I intended as I tried to sort through my muddled thoughts.

"But..." Tom winced. He tried to smile but it didn't quite reach his eyes. "I'm sensing a but coming."

"No, no buts. I just..." What was I doing? Here was a perfect guy. Literally everything I was looking for in a partner. And I was hesitating.

"It's okay, Hannah. I'm not easily dissuaded. I'm willing to wait until you're ready." Tom reached out a tentative hand to gently grasp one of mine, his palm dwarfing my own as he held it between us.

I let out a sigh of relief and looked down at our hands. It was a gesture of kindness, and also a goodbye.

"I won't try to persuade you to let me walk you home, but please text me to let me know you got there safely," he added, giving my hand a small squeeze before releasing it.

I smiled gratefully at him—for his kindness, for his understanding, and his company—and nodded.

Even if things didn't work out between us whenever I figured out what I was doing with my life, I hoped we could at least be friends. He seemed like someone you'd want in your corner.

What am I doing with my life?

"What am I doing with my life?" I groaned as I leaned down to rest my face in my hands, elbows braced against the tops of my thighs for support.

"To be honest, I've been wondering that myself the last few days…"

I lifted my head just long enough to toss a cutting glare at Olivia, then returned to my huddle. "If you're trying to make me feel better, you suck at it."

"You didn't let me finish," she retorted sweetly, stepping around our Ikea coffee table to join me on the sofa. "Sure, things seem a little chaotic right now, but I also haven't seen you grab life by the balls this much in, I don't know, years! Well before graduation, at least. Possibly ever, if we're getting technical.

"Hannah Maxwell. Juggling two guys? No, *men*! Two hot, famous men." She laid a gentle hand on my upper back, sweeping slow, comforting circles. "Sure, maybe things seem like a mess now. But you're putting yourself out there. Trying things. Crawling out from beneath that rock you've been hiding under since senior year. The one made up of an excessive workload and impostor syndrome. I like this Hannah. I've missed her."

Slowly, I lifted my head again to look fully at my best friend, a watery smile on my lips. "You think this is a good thing?"

"I think anything that gets you exploring your feelings, thinking about something other than work, is a good thing. If being caught in the midst of a love triangle between two hot, successful, celebrity men is what it takes, then so be it."

I swatted a hand at her. "I'm not caught in a love triangle. I just don't know what I want to do. I don't know what I want, period."

I huffed and leaned back against the couch, reclining my neck to stare up at the ceiling. "I need a break. From all of this. Just one night where I don't have to think about Ezra or Tom or Peter or work or anything. A night where I can relax, maybe even have a little fun—"

I tilted my head to look sidelong at Olivia, one corner of my mouth tilting up. "I need karaoke."

Olivia groaned and grimaced indulgently. "Oh no, not karaoke. Anything but that," she deadpanned.

Anytime we had a hard time at Syracuse—with projects, tests, boys, you name it—karaoke at the local dive bar was our solution. Whether we'd been cheered or booed off the stage, it always had us doubled over in laughter by the end of the night. It made us realize whatever we were going through was a blip on the radar, and we'd get through it.

It also taught me that, despite my passion for the music industry, I could never, *never* make it as a singer.

It wasn't that I was bad. Not to toot my own horn, but I'd been complimented for my voice on more than a few occasions. It was performing for a crowd that skeeved me out. A dive bar with about twenty-five odd people in it, most of them drunk off cheap light beer and shots of well whiskey, was my limit.

"Come on, it'll be just like old times," I crooned, reaching out to clasp Olivia's hand in mine and give it a squeeze.

Olivia pouted her rosebud lips and cocked her head, pretending to weigh her options. Like I didn't know she'd cave. Like I didn't know she probably wanted to go just as much as I did.

"Fine, anything for you my little trainwreck." Olivia leaned over to wrap her long arms around me and squeeze tightly, pressing a hard kiss to the top of my head.

I rolled my eyes from within her grasp but tightened my arms around her just the same.

Chapter 27

HANNAH

"Wow, packed crowd tonight," Olivia said, letting out a low whistle as her beautifully shadowed and lined eyes scanned the bar. She somehow looked both elegant and casual in a black, seamless square neck tank tucked into a pair of black, distressed mom jeans that hugged her small waist.

I followed her sweeping gaze around the full bar, eyes widening at the press of bodies in the room.

The Dripping Tap was pretty full for a Sunday night, especially during football season when most people preferred the sports bar down the street, with its walls lined with television after television playing every game from every angle.

It gave me a headache just thinking about it, although they had the best hot wings in town.

"We better put our names on the list early if we want to get a slot," I said, taking a mental headcount.

Too many was my final verdict.

Olivia reached back to grasp my hand and tugged me toward the tables near the front of the bar, the complete opposite direction of the side stage where tonight's emcee maintained the karaoke list. "I think we need to grab a table before they all fill up. Most of these people probably aren't singing anyway, just here to watch."

"Fine," I huffed quietly, smoothing a hand over my white paper bag shorts and the black polka-dotted sheer leggings I had on underneath. I let her lead me through the throng of people, my favorite pair of black Chelsea boots thudding softly against worn hardwood as we dodged people queuing up at the bar to order drinks or chat with friends.

Taking up space was more like it, I thought.

"This is good, I need some time to think of a song," I said, changing my tune as we reached the last available two-top table. It was in the second row back from the stage, but right in the center of the room.

A great viewing spot.

I only realized after we arrived at the bar tonight that I typically sang something from Olympus when I wanted to let loose and still sound pretty decent. Unfortunately, singing "Need You Here" would only dredge up memories of the recent past. Memories I was trying to escape tonight.

"Perfect, hold down the fort while I go get us drinks," Olivia said, slinging her crossbody bag over the back of her chair, not even bothering to sit down. "You want your usual?"

I nodded and flashed her a wide grin in thanks and pulled out my phone as I slid into my seat. Atop our table was a stocky table tent with QR codes for the drink menu, food menu, and karaoke song list.

Convenient.

I scanned the code for karaoke and settled in, scrolling slowly through the list of songs the live band could perform to back up all of the eager amateur performers in the audience.

Olivia Rodrigo—that could be fun.

I do not have the pipes for Adele.

Oooh, they have Fall Out Boy. I could get into that.

Olivia joined me once again at our table, two drinks in her hands, right as the lights in the bar dimmed and a spotlight lit up the stage. I took a small sip from my craft beer as the emcee started in on her welcome spiel.

"Did you decide on a song yet?" Olivia leaned over to whisper in my ear over the dull roar of the crowd surrounding us, her eyes still trained on the stage.

I shook my head. "Not yet, I'm going to simmer on it for a bit while we watch some others go."

Olivia nodded absentmindedly and pulled out her phone. She quickly skimmed over an incoming text, then fired off her responding message.

"Don't tell me Bruce is already bothering you about work tomorrow," I joked, taking another sip from my beer.

"Hmm?" Olivia glanced up at me distractedly, then slid her eyes back down to her phone—another text—before hurriedly shoving it away in her crossbody bag. "Oh, no. That wasn't Bruce."

I lifted a brow at her, willing her to go on. But she didn't, her eyes once again trained on the stage. I shrugged my shoulders and followed her gaze to find the emcee still rambling on about something.

"Before we get started, we've got a special surprise guest who asked for first dibs on the karaoke mic tonight," she was saying, a knowing smirk tugging at the corners of her lips.

My eyes flickered to Olivia, eyebrows knitted high on my forehead, but she merely answered with a shrug. "No idea. Probably a local singer trying to build buzz with the bar crowd before a show."

I inclined my head and faced the stage once more as the roaring sound of applause filled my ears. Encouragement for our surprise guest.

Leaning back in my chair with one hand cradled lightly around the bottom of my pint glass, I basked in the contentment I felt. The joy of being anonymous, just one of many in a crowd full of people who didn't know me or expect anything from me.

After the emcee walked off the stage and resumed her post at the small booth beside it where she would camp out for the rest of the night, a tall figure stepped up behind her. I could tell he was male and taller than six feet, but the lights were too dim to make out anything else. A tall, lean shadow.

As he made his way slowly up the two steps to the small stage, the emcee crowed through her wireless microphone, "Please welcome to the stage, frontman to the multi-platinum band Olympus, Ezra Bell!"

I stiffened in my seat as the crowd behind me roared. It was a bit like watching a car crash. I wanted to get up and run, but I was completely immobile, unable to tear my eyes away as he glided across the stage, then grabbed for the microphone with shaky hands.

That was unusual. I had seen him play in front of a crowd of twenty-thousand people without batting an eye but... Ezra Bell looked nervous to be here.

He brought the microphone to his lips, a shy smile curving them, and waved tentatively with his free hand. His eyes scanned the audience, then stopped when they found home, his dark irises glowing molten amber when they met mine.

"Thanks for letting me interrupt your karaoke night for a bit," he was saying, but my heart pounded so loudly in my ears that I could barely make out his words. "I have something really important to get off my chest, and I thought this would be a good place to do it."

Regaining some of my mobility, I craned my neck painfully slowly to look at Olivia, quiet outrage flashing across my face. She grimaced back, exposing her palms to me, and mouthed the word, "Sorry."

The sound of the band counting him in drew my attention back to the stage, where I found Ezra's eyes still glued to me. My cheeks heated under the weight of that stare, anxiety replacing some of the rage I had just directed at Olivia.

His perfect tenor fit the opening notes of the song like a glove. It wasn't an Olympus song, I could tell that straight away. But then... my jaw fell open as I realized which one he'd chosen to perform. I could just barely make out Ezra's flushed cheeks under the bright spotlight.

A few beats later, Olivia asked from beside me, "Wait, isn't this—"

I cut her off with an emphatic nod, biting back the smile that threatened to spread across my lips. The song—my *favorite* song—from the series finale of my favorite show. Although Olivia had never watched the series herself, she'd been around me enough times in our college apartment to recognize it.

The show I had watched a million times over the years. The song I had confessed to him always made me cry. My heart skipped in my chest as the rich rasp in Ezra's voice added a pleasant edge to the chorus of 'Take on the World' by You Me At Six, arguably my favorite part of the song.

My hands shook where they rested against the table, silver lining my eyes as I watched him belt those lyrics, each word piercing straight through me.

I could see it for what it was. An apology. An invitation. A promise.

For a few brief moments, the rest of the room fell away and it was just Ezra and I in that dimly lit bar, his heart exposed on his sleeve. When he reached the second verse, I felt a warm presence at my back that drew my eyes from Ezra for the first time since he had begun. I turned to look behind me and found Peter at my back, Zach and Angel flanking him on either side, tender smiles on all their faces. A tear rolled slowly down my cheek as Peter laid a light touch on my shoulder, giving it the smallest squeeze of encouragement.

I turned back to face Ezra again as his voice lifted in the final chorus of the song, my heart pounding a steady rhythm to match the drumbeat backing him up.

When the song came to a close, the people around me erupted into a roar of applause and cheers. The air filled with shouts of "Encore!" and "Do 'Need You Here' next!" and I had to physically shake myself to regain consciousness, force myself to clap, to breathe normally.

Olivia extended a hand to squeeze my shoulder closest to her and suddenly I remembered there was an entire cast of characters surrounding me who had all been *in on this* without telling me.

"So how long have you been planning this little ambush?" I asked Olivia, willing my face into a deadly calm that was only partially given away by the upward tilt of my lips.

"We pulled it together fairly quickly," Peter interrupted, grabbing a spare chair from the table next to us and pulling it over to sit down on my right side. "After I heard about your date Friday night, I knew we had to act fast. Do it up big." He threw out his arms to emphasize his point.

My wide eyes blinked slowly between Olivia and Peter.

"Don't be mad. The guy wanted a chance—just one chance! So, I caved and told them I'd help," she shrugged. "You know I'm a sucker for big romantic gestures."

I couldn't help but laugh. "So this is what all the incessant texting was about?"

Olivia smiled and nodded, her shoulders hunching as though she was finally letting go of some tension. She lifted her beer to her lips and took a long swig, draining nearly a quarter of the glass in one go.

It took Ezra what felt like an eternity to claw his way through the crowd. Everyone who recognized him wanted the chance to pat him on the back or snap a quick photo. When he did reach our little table in the second row, I was full-on smiling, laughing with the group of friends around me. Peter, Zach, and Angel were taking turns telling us about their lives since they returned home from the tour. I had to meet Angel's fiancé. She sounded amazing.

It had only been a little over a week since I saw them last, but it felt like a lifetime after being cooped up on the road with them for so long.

"Hello," Ezra said timidly. What was the appropriate way to greet the group of people you plotted a top-secret karaoke ambush with *and* the girl you just surprised with said ambush? I doubted they had a handbook for that.

"Sounded great, my man. Might have to cover that one on the road," Angel answered brightly, throwing an arm around Ezra's shoulders for a quick side hug.

Ezra's eyes traveled from one face to the next: Olivia offered him a polite nod and a wave, Peter and Zach both shot him finger guns, and then he landed on me. His jaw flexed as I held his stare, feeling uncharacteristically relaxed despite what I knew was coming.

I could feel everyone's eyes on me, waiting for my reaction, my next move. Electricity snapped in the air like a live wire.

I leaned back in my chair once more, entwining my hands loosely in my lap, and said, "I think you're going to have a hard time getting out of here tonight without doing an Olympus song."

Peter howled, his head thrown back with relief. The lines knitting Ezra's forehead melted away, his restrained smile widening until the corners of his eyes wrinkled. My favorite of his smiles. The electric buzz in the air died off and the rest of our group resumed the conversation without me.

"Could we talk?" Ezra shoved his hands in his pockets, something I noticed he often did when he was feeling nervous or introspective. Or both.

I nodded my response and stood from my chair, offering it to Zach as I stepped around him.

Time to face the music.

·❤·❤·❤·❤·❤·

I trailed Ezra through the rest of the crowded bar, watching him receive pats on the back, gentle grasps on the shoulder, and shouts from those we passed. Then their eyes moved from Ezra to me, standing so close behind him as we zigzagged toward the doors. Some of them shot me a thumbs up, the ones who had caught Ezra's focus on me during his song. Others shot me daggers, their elevator eyes looking me up and down as though I didn't deserve his attention at all.

Once, I probably would've cringed inwardly at the weight of that attention. But it reminded me a lot of that night at the pizza shop in Boston, only amplified by a thousand. Reminded me of what Ezra had confided in me afterward. What it meant to him to be able to give even the smallest bit of love and appreciation back to his fans that he felt from them every single day he was alive and getting paid to live his dreams.

I lifted my chin, held my head high through all the stares, even meeting some of them in the eyes with a shy smile, until we reached the exit. The only place we'd get even an inkling of privacy and quiet was outside.

The door clanged shut behind us and I was slightly surprised to find the area outside mostly clear. It was occupied only by the bouncer checking the IDs of eager revelers trying to get in and a few people farther down the exterior wall sharing a cigarette.

Ezra continued walking in the opposite direction of the smokers, and I followed. He was close enough for me to reach out and touch his hand as it dangled at his side if I wanted to. We headed along the side of the building, stopping when we reached an empty alcove just under a vintage-looking lamp jutting from the wall that helped light the sidewalk leading to the bar's entrance.

I pulled up short beside him when he rounded to face me, a gnawing earnestness in his eyes I hadn't seen since the night we first kissed. Even with the slight heel on my Chelsea boots, I had to incline my head to see his face.

Ezra looked slightly windswept, like he had spent the last hour striding across a sandy beach, watching the sunset. Not pouring his heart out on a tiny stage in the heart of Brooklyn. His scent whispered around me, citrus and sandalwood carried on the October evening breeze. I let myself breathe it in.

"Hannah," he rasped, his voice strained. Then he paused again.

I lifted my eyebrows. "I think this is the first time I've ever seen you speechless," I said drily, a wry smile tugging at the corners of my mouth.

He chuckled, the sound more of an exhale than anything, and glanced down at his feet. "You seem to have that effect on me."

A shiver ran down my spine and, without thinking, I reached out to tuck my fingertips under his chin, tugging his face back up. "Tell me what you came here to say," I whispered with more confidence than I felt.

He reached one of his slender hands up, curling it around mine. His fingers were warm as he folded my hand into his large palm and held it suspended in the air between us.

"Hannah, I am so sorry. I tried to call you, and text you, to explain. But what you saw..." he trailed off and looked to one side, into the darkness surrounding us, searching for the right words. "There is nothing between Andie and me. She just showed up, completely unannounced. It caught me off guard."

I bit down on my bottom lip and nodded to myself, my own eyes turning distant. "I know," I said finally. Finally admitting to myself, really, that I believed him. That I believed what Peter told me the other day.

Ezra's head jerked back to face mine, his eyebrows lifted above wide eyes. "You know?"

"I mean, I do now," I clarified, fighting the urge to look away, to hide. "I didn't at the time. I thought…"

Ezra gave my hand a squeeze and I sighed. Then swallowed.

"I thought it was my fault." I held up my free hand to silence Ezra when I saw his lips part to cut in. "I pushed us to keep things under wraps, to avoid telling anyone what we were doing. I forced you to keep secrets from your best friends, and, unfortunately for both of us, your ex, too.

"And I did it because… because I was scared. Terrified. Terrified that when the tour ended, and the magic bubble burst, and the pot of gold at the end of the rainbow turned out to be fake pirate treasure from one of those tacky roadside attractions, that you'd find out there was nothing special about me in the first place. Certainly not enough to keep you around. I shoved you away that day in Ohio, made you agree we could be nothing more than friends. I had no right to be upset if you took that at face value."

Olivia had been right, I knew that now. That I had made myself think whatever I had with Ezra couldn't be real, because it was easier than trying. Trying and possibly failing.

Ezra's frown deepened, his pupils dilating until his eyes looked almost black with cold, seething rage. Not anger at me, but anger at whatever it was in my life, in my brain, making me think that way.

He shook his head to clear the dark thoughts and turned his eyes on me. "You *are* special. Special isn't even the right word for all that you are. You're smart, you're kind, you're generous with your time—probably too generous. Sure, you're crazy. Absolutely insane, actually, for not seeing what I see. What everyone else around you sees. And you're stubborn, even when you're wrong. But you always choose to see the best in everyone around you. And now... all I see is you. Hannah, I... you're the most beautiful person I've ever met."

My eyes widened, my mouth falling open. I felt a telltale prickle at the back of my eyes.

He gave my hand a tight little squeeze. "None of this was your fault. As far as I was concerned, we already *were* more than just friends. So much more than that. I know what you said that day in Ohio, and I understand why you said it. Yeah, it sucked at the time. It really sucked. I didn't want to be some secret, and it hurt to be called a distraction—" I winced but he soldiered on, "—but I was willing to wait. To bide my time and be whatever you needed me to be, in the hope that one day you'd come around." One corner of his mouth lifted. "One day *soon*, ideally."

My heart caught in my throat and I swallowed it back down, fighting a smile.

"I wasn't lying in Chicago when I said I felt something here, something between us," he continued. "I came out here tonight to tell you that. To sweep you off your feet with a big romantic gesture and ask you for another chance. To see what this is. What it could be."

"Did you learn the words to that song just for me?"

Ezra laughed and reached for my other hand. "I swear on Peter's bass guitar I never even heard it before now. I practiced for hours. It was a lot of work, and you know me, I *hate* work."

I didn't want to laugh, but my body wasn't listening to my brain. Ezra saw it and his answering grin lit his amber eyes.

"I'd do anything for you, though," he said in a quiet voice, his rumbling tenor igniting something deep in my core like a matchstick struck against powdered glass. "You deserve happiness, Hannah. And if that means I leave here tonight and never get to see you, or touch you, or kiss you again, then I'll go. But I'm really, really hoping it doesn't mean that."

I bit down on my bottom lip to hide my satisfaction at his confession and murmured, "All this because I went on one date. I didn't peg you for the jealous type."

Ezra's gaze turned feral and he took a step forward, closing whatever distance was left between us. "Speaking of, I still need to have a little chat with our friend Tom."

I rolled my eyes playfully, but heat bloomed in my lower belly at Ezra's closeness, at that look in his eyes I knew now was reserved solely for me.

Without needing to think more about it, I knew my decision was made. Had been made, even before Ezra showed up here tonight with his so-called *big romantic gesture*.

I liked Tom. He was a great guy, easy to make conversation with. Ungodly handsome. But what I felt between us at dinner the other night was more like a blossoming friendship than anything more intimate. A twinge of guilt pained my heart as I realized it was probably that date with Tom more than anything else that helped me to understand I still had deep feelings for Ezra. Feelings I still wanted to explore.

I didn't know if I loved Ezra yet. I wasn't sure if I had ever been in love. What I did know was that I couldn't picture any type of future that didn't involve this man.

"Tell me what you're thinking," Ezra whispered, echoing his quiet words spoken in the hotel bed our first night together. The memory brought color to my cheeks.

I looked down at our hands, still tightly clasped together, as I considered his words for a moment, the offer he extended.

I could picture our life together so clearly in my head. Traveling around the world with him whenever work could spare me; screaming the lyrics to every one of his songs from just behind the curtain on the side of the stage; spending the night in his bed with no fear of who might notice us leaving together in the morning.

It wouldn't be easy.

He would be away for the better part of the next year, between the second half of this tour and any upcoming promotion for their new album. It would mean long weeks on my own in New York, waiting until he could fly home or I could fly to him. Eventually the tabloids would find out and I would need to deal with a whole new level of attention.

But I'd never been a co-dependent type of girl. Or one to shy away from a challenge.

My half-smile widened into something far more devious. "I'm thinking I would have to be an idiot to ignore such a sweeping romantic gesture."

Ezra threw his head back, howling with laughter. The sound of it made my chest squeeze.

I reached up to swipe at a tear brimming in the corner of my eye, my face softening. "I'm thinking I'm still a little afraid because the future isn't a given. I don't know what comes next and the control freak within me is basically having a mental breakdown about it. The difference is, now I want to find out. To take that giant leap of faith into the unknown... with you."

Ezra grinned and the way his beautiful face lit up as I said those words was nearly enough to knock me backwards. "Hannah Maxwell, are you saying you're in?"

I gave his hands a small squeeze and leaned up on my toes, closing any distance left between us to softly press my lips to his in answer. Ezra didn't hesitate for a moment, his strong arms snaking around my waist to tug me closer as he deepened our kiss.

His lips were just as soft, just as inviting, as I remembered and I couldn't suppress my quiet moan at the feel of him. The memories it stirred.

Right as Ezra's tongue darted out to slide smoothly along my lower lip, cheers erupted from somewhere in the distance. The surprise forced us apart.

Our eyes followed the noise to a side exit of the bar, probably something for smokers to sneak in and out of, where we spied Peter and Olivia standing in the half-open door. They were both clapping their hands together and whooping in our direction, their faces lit with delighted grins. A moment later, I noticed Zach cowering behind them, exposing his palms to us defensively as he mouthed the words, "I told them not to."

I stared daggers at every one of them for eavesdropping and interrupting our first kiss as an official couple. Well, I tried to. But the sight of their unabated joy, genuine joy for their best friends, had me smiling back at them like a madman. Tearing my eyes from them, I glanced sidelong at Ezra and found a similar expression glowing on his face.

Slowly, he slid his arm from around my waist and reached down to gently clasp my fingers in his, giving me a small tug. I answered it with a squeeze of my own, letting the unspoken words hang between us as we made our way to the door, back to our friends.

Yeah, I'm so in.

Acknowledgements

There are so many people to thank for bringing this book to life, it's hard to decide where to begin! Publishing a novel has been a long-time secret dream of mine, one I very rarely (if ever) spoke aloud to anyone over the years. Until I started this book. And then, I wouldn't shut up about it.

To Kelly, thank you for listening to me babble on about plot ideas and editing strife, when I know most of it was probably incoherent. Thank you for never asking questions when I disappeared into my office (also, thank you for building me said office!) to work on this project and the countless others still left unfinished in my drafts folder. Thank you for keeping our beautiful daughter busy while I "did research" (AKA read as many wonderful books by uber talented authors I could to improve my craft) on the couch, in the car, and everywhere else I could manage. Most of all, thank you for believing I could do this when I was unsure.

To my amazing, intelligent, phenomenal and wonderfully kind (but radically candid) best friends and alpha readers Bonnie and

Breland: this book literally would not exist without you. You both are all the best parts of Hannah and Olivia and so much more. Thank you for supporting my writing journey and for being the first people to volunteer to read my work when I was too scared to let it see the light of day. And while we're at it, thank you to all my beta readers for giving me incredible feedback that made this a much better book than the first draft.

Shoutout to all of the talented creators on BookTok who opened my eyes to the world of indie publishing and showed me this was a thing I could do. You all inspire and motivate me everyday (not to mention, crack me up).

Most importantly, thank you to my readers, be there many or few of you out there. Thank you for taking a chance on a debut author and giving *Are You In?* a spin. If you enjoyed reading it half as much as I enjoyed making it, I'll consider that a win.

About the Author

Rachel Pluck is an author and marketing strategist living in southeastern Pennsylvania. This is her debut novel and she is beyond excited to share it with the world (finally!). When she's not obsessively reading, writing, or streaming old CW dramas (hello fellow TVD fans!) she can be found at home with her husband, wrangling their willful four-year-old daughter and three rescue pups.